The hair on the back of her neck stood up.

She walked faster, shifting the grocery bag and grappling for her keys in the front zip pocket of her pack.

Footsteps. Even with the rush of wind in her ears, Anna was positive she could hear footsteps. Quiet. Like rubber-soled boots. Gaining on her. She started running toward her building, ripping the keys from her bag, dropping them, then retrieving them. She kept running.

Footsteps behind her. Louder. Insistent.

She was at her door, too terrified to turn. She jabbed the key at the lock and missed, swearing, panic bubbling up into her throat, gagging her.

And then suddenly, just as she managed to insert the key and twist it, the footsteps stopped. He was right behind her, so close she was positive he could reach out and touch her.

Then he spoke. "Don't you know I'm always with you?" It came out in that whisper, that breathless, horrible voice.

Also available from MIRA Books and
LYNN ERICKSON
ASPEN

Watch for LYNN ERICKSON'S
next book

Spring 1998

LYNN ERICKSON

NIGHT WHISPERS

MIRA BOOKS

ISBN 1-55166-178-0

NIGHT WHISPERS

Copyright © 1997 by Carla Peltonen and Molly Swanton.

Printed in U.S.A.

NIGHT WHISPERS

ONE

The Hunter waited with infinite patience. He blended into the shadows of the dim, cavernous parking garage, unmoving behind a concrete pillar. He could wait like this for hours if he had to; he'd trained himself over the years, honed his mind and skills and physical abilities until he was, truly, the perfect predator.

It was cold in the garage, the dark, car-oil-scented cold that made normal people shiver and hurry. But not the Hunter. He was at his best in the cold, and it was still only September in Denver. His powers were merely gathering until real winter set in.

He waited, watching her car. She'd have to return soon, because it was almost eight o'clock, and the Tabor Center, the shopping center above the garage, would be closing. He'd been here for over two hours, watching and waiting with the absolute faith of a predator: soon the prey would appear—it was fated.

Her car. His light blue eyes switched to it. He knew it well, a metallic, pearl gray Toyota Camry. He'd seen it so many times, followed it so many times before this evening. It was as familiar to him as her face: the scratch on the passenger door, the Thule ski and bike rack, the Denver Zoo sticker on the rear window.

He loved the way she drove—sure and quick, impatient, always in a hurry. A busy lady. He let himself recall her face and felt the skin tighten around his head as it always did when he pictured her. His heart beat faster, and he felt himself grow hard at the thought of her, just the thought.

Her name was Anna Dunning. Anna. Dunning. A sweet name. An ugly name, too. His ambivalence toward her made him uneasy. Women were sluts and cruel, capricious piranhas. He hated women. He liked to hurt them, to make them scream and cry and beg forgiveness before their ultimate—and just—punishment. But this one was somehow different.

The first time he'd seen her, she'd barely noticed him. It had been almost six months ago. She was polite. She'd smiled, a careless, distracted smile, then walked past, chatting, her tan legs in shorts, scissoring in the summer sun.

And the Hunter had fallen in love. Like the flash of a match struck in utter blackness.

It was a bizarre feeling for him. It threw him off-balance, made his usually methodical mind roil with fantasies, with a compulsion to see her, to hear her voice, to—he dared hope after all these months— touch her.

It wasn't that she was so beautiful, although other men might consider her so. It was the way she moved, her blithe self-confidence, the athletic way she held herself, the pitch of her head, some indefinable challenge in her look. There was courage in her. Worthy prey. Yes, Anna Dunning was the perfect prey for the perfect predator.

Of course, he hated her, too. She was a woman, after all. Deceitful, vicious, treacherous, existing only to hurt men, to strip them of their manhood.

You had to be strong, the Hunter thought as he stood in the shadows. You couldn't let them get hold of you, lead you around by the...well, your *thing*. And Anna had said something once that had set him off. Oh, yes, she had a bossy manner about her. She'd spoken in that offhand way, carelessly. "I'd move that pile of debris, if I were you. Someone's going to trip over it."

It had been a dagger to the heart, her unheeding order. And then she'd given him a meaningless smile. He'd seen red.

She deserved punishment, and she would get it. He wanted to possess her; he wanted to be able to punish her at will. At his will. She had to be his, the same way he had to own his guns and his hunting knives, his spotting scope and snowmobile and the cabin. They were his, that was all. He loved them.

The Hunter heard the elevator clinking in its shaft. Approaching. *Anna*. The scratched yellow doors slid open and she stepped out. He blinked. *No*. It was a man, hurrying toward his car, shoulders hunched under a jacket, footsteps echoing loudly on the stained concrete. So loud the Hunter almost missed the other elevator.

His heart shot up into his throat, his stomach clenched. It was her. She was carrying two big shopping bags. Casual Corner. Brooks Brothers.

He shrank back farther. So easy in her smooth skin, so powerful in her femininity. She was striding briskly toward him, toward her car. He could hear her footsteps, and the distant, muffled roar of the man's car as it drove out, the shrill squeak of tires on concrete. Then it was quiet again, except for Anna's light, quick steps, closer and closer.

Beads of sweat collected on the Hunter's upper lip. He leaned forward a fraction of an inch to see her.

She was digging in the pocket of her brown suede jacket; he knew it well, knew every item of clothing she owned. She was fumbling, hands full, for her keys as she walked.

A metallic clatter. She'd dropped her keys. A muttered "Damn." The timbre of her voice sent a quiver through him, an arrow of pain and pleasure. He closed his eyes for a moment.

A moment later he opened them and watched as she stooped, one hand clutching a big bag swinging down toward the keys. He could see the way her hair fell forward over her face like a dark veil, the way her thigh flexed as she reached for the keys. Her ass was round, stretching her jeans tight across her hips. He drew in a quick, hot breath as she straightened, keys in hand, pushing her hair back.

She was at her car now. He heard the beep as she unlocked the door with the remote control. He'd seen her use the device often. She was careful about her car.

She'd be driving away in a moment. He heard the sound of her bags being tossed onto the seat, her foot scraping against the parking-garage floor. He felt ineffable grief.

He couldn't let her go.

Unable to control himself, he stepped out from behind the pillar, and moved toward her. Twenty yards, no more than that. He advanced as silently as a wraith on rubber soles. And there was no one else, not a soul in the deserted, dim, primordial cave that was the Hunter's lair.

She turned her head swiftly. Alert, yes, aware, poised for flight. She reminded him of a doe; he could imagine the skin of her flanks tremble under her clothes. Her eyes were wide. The Hunter felt himself swell with power at that unaccustomed glint in her eye, the same one he saw in a deer's eye when he had it in his cross hairs.

Her gaze touched him then moved on, turned away. No eye contact. She had her back to him now, getting ready to slide into her car, but he was behind her, right behind her, no longer a casual passerby on his way to his own vehicle. He was committed. He could smell her, he was so near. Her scent, oh, God, expensive suede, shampoo, a subtle perfume, light and heady all at once. And her hair, all those lush curls, bangs lying on her forehead, dark gold, swinging around her neck, the curve of her cheek. An ear. A pale, curved ear. His heart was ready to explode.

She whirled suddenly, and he could see her muscles gather, could almost see the adrenaline course through her veins. He took a step forward.

The sound came out of his mouth, a whisper torn from his throat. It surprised him.

"Anna," he said.

Her eyes were wide, truly scared now, her back against her car, the door wide open. He breathed in her scent.

"Get away from me!" she yelled.

Brave, a heart of courage. Worthy. The bitch.

He was going to do it then, right then, but his predator's senses registered the clunk of the elevator. He still had the control to be cautious.

"Help!" she was yelling, pulling the car door between them. "Help! Somebody help!"

And then the elevator doors were swishing open, and the Hunter was backing off, pulling his baseball cap lower over his eyes. He walked rapidly, disappearing into the darkness around a corner, escaping into the recesses of his cave.

Behind him he heard excited voices, followed by a car's throaty roar—her car—and the squeal of her tires as she backed out. He stopped where he was hidden in a black corner and watched as her glittering gray car flashed past headed for the exit ramp, too fast, way too fast.

The Hunter stepped out into the middle of the driving lane and raised his face to catch the last whiff of her car's exhaust as she careened out of the garage. He drew it in and possessed it.

Next time.

TWO

Mark Righter was in between opportunities. Everyone in Denver knew it. Even Barry, the guy who sold him bagels and espresso in a coffee shop on East Colfax every morning, knew it. Mark was a local celebrity. Of sorts.

"How're the job prospects going?" Barry asked.

Mark took the white paper sack from the bagel-shop owner and shrugged. "Same old story. Unless, of course, I want to sit in some warehouse all night playing rent-a-cop."

"There're worse things."

"Yeah, well," Mark said, "not for me."

Outside he bought a copy of the daily paper. He was planning to check the help wanted ads, as he did every morning. Maybe he'd have to take a security guard job for a while—at least until he was back on his feet. And there was still the unemployment line, although Mark cringed at the idea. It wasn't just the notion that he'd be one step away from welfare. It was more that everyone down at division would hear about it. He couldn't take the humiliation.

Ah, hell, he thought, something would turn up. It had to. His sense of humor, that well-trained cop's sense of humor, which separated a man—or woman—from bad news, was beginning to wear thin.

He strode along the vintage strip mall toward the tattoo parlor and spotted Lil Martinelli, the proprietor—and his landlady—out front sweeping the sidewalk. Right on time.

"Ready?" Mark held up the white sack.

"Sure," she said. "Go on back. I'll be there in a sec."

It had become a morning ritual. Ever since Mark had quit the police force four months before, he and Lil had sat behind her shop in the sun, sharing bagels and strong European coffee. Soon the mornings would be too cool to sit out and then, Mark guessed, they'd move the ritual inside her tattoo parlor. Or, he thought wryly, maybe he'd be employed by then.

Lil finished sweeping and came out onto the back patio through the shop. "Did you tell that Barry to dilute this mud for me?" she asked, sitting on a plastic chair and pulling a section from the paper.

"I told him. Whether or not he did . . ." Mark lifted an indifferent shoulder and noted Lil's getup, head-to-toe black leather. In the warmer months, she'd worn tight little black cotton items, but now that September was upon them, it was back to leather: vest, miniskirt, high boots. Everything was silver-studded, too, even the deep V in her vest. He couldn't help noticing that her cleavage, which was amply displayed, was going to seed, freckled and badly wrinkled from too many years of California sun before she'd moved to Denver. He also couldn't help noticing the tattoo on her chest, a colorful Pueblo Indian corn goddess, which she'd had copied from a museum display. She was very proud of it. Mark thought it was, well, a bit much. Lil still had a decent figure, though, small-boned and trim. But now that she was pushing fifty, her face had grown rounder, her makeup seemed too heavy and years of perms and black dye had all but destroyed her shoulder-length hair.

All that aside, Lil had become a good friend, she'd even taken him in when he and his wife had split up almost a year ago. He still lived upstairs and probably would for some time. The rent was right. Cheap.

"Your phone rang just after you went for coffee," Lil said as she chewed on her bagel.

Mark glanced up from the help wanted ads. "Probably my ex," he said dryly. "Her wedding's in a few weeks. Maybe she wants me to chip in for the reception."

"Hmm," Lil said, shaking her head at him. "Or maybe it's a job offer. You're a real popular guy, Righter."

"Sure," he said.

Lil's first customer arrived at ten sharp. She rose, dusted off her hands and winked at Mark. "Dude wants a dragon on his right cheek," she said.

"A dragon on his face?" Mark asked.

"No, stupid, his *cheek*." Lil turned around and patted her bottom, then caught the amused look on Mark's face.

"You always catch me," he said without rancor.

"You're an easy mark."

When Lil had disappeared inside, he tossed the empty coffee containers and white bag into the Dumpster just outside the broken fence. Then, paper in hand, he ambled upstairs, using the steps that ran up the back of the brick building. Halfway up, he turned and looked out over the city to the west where the mountains rose. The foothills were still snow-free. But beyond them, deep in the heart of the Rocky Mountains, the fourteen-thousand-foot peaks were gleaming white in the morning sun. Deer and elk season was just around the corner, and Mark wondered if he would be able to afford the annual hunting trip. It was going to be tight, at best. He shrugged, tapped the rolled-up paper on the railing and headed up the steps, telling himself to quit worrying.

When he entered his tiny one-bedroom apartment, he saw the red light blinking on his answering machine, and once again figured it was either his ex-wife or his ex-partner, Hoagie, touching base. They had both been doing that ever since Mark had quit the force in a rage. They probably thought he was going to stick a .45 in his mouth and end the suspense. Cops did that.

He stood over the machine for a minute and whispered a prayer. Let this be a break.

A man's voice came on; it was not Hoagie's. "This is Scott Dunning. I'd very much appreciate it if you'd return this call. It's a rather urgent matter, Mr. Righter." And he left a number.

Dunning, Mark thought. Scott Dunning. He knew the name. Some sort of a builder. Skyscrapers. And wasn't Dunning married to that defense lawyer? The one who'd neatly stayed in the background at the trial?

Mark searched his memory. Right. The woman was fortyish. Short and on the plump side. Small features and a mop of curly blond hair. Big round glasses. *Lydia* Dunning. He was sure of it. Now what in hell did her husband want with him?

Despite himself, despite the bitterness Mark felt toward the woman who'd helped destroy his career, he was curious.

He called Scott Dunning's number. He was showered and dressed and set to drive over to the exclusive Cherry Creek address an hour later.

It was habit for Mark to mentally file away peculiarities. As he drove toward Cherry Creek he couldn't help wondering once more why Dunning wanted to see him—the man had only repeated that it was an urgent matter—and, more curiously, why at his home and not his office? Something else was nagging him—this meeting had to have something to do with the Orchid Rapist trial. But what? It was over and done with, the rapist behind bars in Canyon City. Luckily, the jury had seen past the defense team's ploy, the finger pointing in Mark's direction, the insinuation that Mark had planted the woman's underwear in the rapist's apartment.

Okay, he thought, so the jury had looked at all the evidence and, despite the panty thing, found the creep guilty. But that hadn't helped Mark. The press had had a heyday. They still hounded him. And when his very own captain hadn't stood behind him, well, Mark knew he'd done the only thing he could—he'd quit. Fourteen years with the Denver Police Department and now zip. Thirty-six years old and going nowhere.

Mark turned south on University and drove past the upscale Cherry Creek Mall, looking for Dunning's street. He tried to swallow his bitterness, but lately it was hard, too hard.

He turned left on Belcaro, expertly maneuvering the green '76 Jaguar around the corner. He enjoyed driving the sports car—the Jag was his one true toy, his only luxury. He'd had it since before his marriage. He'd kept it when his two kids were born and they really could have used some extra cash. A man was allowed one little joy in life, wasn't he?

He turned left on Virginia and into the Polo Grounds, a rich man's subdivision, full of tract mansions.

The Dunning house was on Polo Club Circle. A better description for the place was estate-slash-mansion, Mark decided. As he turned onto the driveway, passing two impressive iron gates that stood open, he was instantly struck by the beauty of the grounds. There had to be at least an acre of lawn. Lining the curving driveway were beautiful spreading oak trees, their leaves fading, ready to turn to autumn gold. Several gardeners moved about, raking and pruning, their trucks barely visible behind the main house. Wouldn't want the workmen too noticeable, Mark thought wryly. As he parked, one of the men leaned on a rake, lifted a hand and waved. Mark returned the greeting.

The house itself was as impressive as the surroundings. It was English Tudor style, probably built in the late fifties, not atypical for this area of Denver—the city's first real suburb. Once, Cherry Creek had seemed a long way from the downtown core. There had been only a golf course and a few fine homes. Now the suburbs stretched almost all the way to Colorado Springs, and Cherry Creek was practically in the heart of the city.

Mark eyed the behemoth of dark wood and plaster. Yeah, Dunning had done all right for himself.

A maid ushered him through the main house into a greenhouse. She addressed him in Spanish, and Mark spoke to her in his scanty street version of the language.

Scott Dunning awaited him in the greenhouse. After introducing himself, he offered Mark something to drink. Mark asked for coffee.

"Do you garden, Mr. Righter?" the man asked after he handed Mark a cup of coffee from a tray on a side table.

Mark shrugged beneath his best sport coat. "I used to, a little. Had a house out in Aurora. Divorced now."

"I see," Dunning said. "I'm afraid I spend too much time in here. I should save it for retirement."

Dunning was a tall man, around six foot one, perhaps an inch shorter than Mark. But whereas Mark would be described as big and solid, Scott Dunning was lean and quite trim. His hair was silvering, razorcut, his tan impeccable. A nice-looking guy who carried himself well.

"Is that your skyscraper going up downtown?" Mark asked. "The one on the corner of Larimer and Twenty-third?"

"That's mine." Dunning nodded toward two wrought-iron chairs and they both sat. "It won't be completed till '99."

Mark took a drink of coffee. "Impressive-looking structure," he said.

"Uh-huh," Dunning replied, then smiled. "Well, you have to be wondering why I asked you here, Mr. Righter."

"That's true. And you can call me Mark."

"Okay, Mark it is. I'm Scott, by the way. And I'm sure you've realized by now that my wife, Lydia, was on that rapist's defense team."

Mark nodded and smiled thinly, curiosity pricking at him again. What did this big-shot builder want from him? Dunning was reportedly quite the philanthropist, gave to all the right charities, museums, the whole nine yards. Jeez, maybe Dunning wanted to set up an assistance fund for him, assuage his guilt over his wife's role in Mark's current unemployed state.

"Let me just get to the bottom line," Dunning said. "I like to be direct."

"Suits me."

"Okay," he said, "here's the deal. My sister, my younger sister, is being stalked. When she first got a couple of pretty lewd phone calls, she was ticked, but she wrote it off to a sick prankster. Then she got a couple of letters—horrible stuff, sexually explicit descriptions of what the creep planned to do to her. She took them to the police, but the cops couldn't do much. The notes were typed on common paper, a standard keyboard. There were no fingerprints, zip."

Mark nodded. He'd heard all this before. Too many times.

"She changed her telephone number, got an unlisted one and started taking precautions."

"Such as?"

"Well, she tries never to be out alone at night, things like that. She locks her car, even when she's driving. And at work . . ."

"Where does she work?"

"She's self-employed, runs a decorating business. Actually, she does a lot of restorations on old Victorians around town. She's getting a fine reputation."

"Uh-huh," Mark said. "So she's in contact with a lot of workmen."

"All the time."

"Does she have any suspects in mind? An old boyfriend, a fired employee?"

Dunning shook his head. "That's the hitch. Anna, my sister, doesn't have a clue. The thing is, she never really dates anyone seriously. She's never been married—nearly was once but he was killed. She's real gun-shy in that area. Doesn't know it, but she is."

"Uh-huh," Mark said.

"Here's the thing," Dunning went on, "the other night she was shopping late at the Tabor Center and a man approached her in the parking garage. She didn't get a good look at him, only had an impression of someone young. It was dark and he had on a hat, his collar was pulled up. She thought he was in his early thirties. A regular Joe. Could be one of a million guys. She told the police everything she could, but without a description . . ."

"And she really doesn't have the slightest idea who this man is?"

"Like I said, no idea whatsoever. The only thing the police can suggest is to hire a bodyguard."

Mark was beginning to understand.

"I talked it over with my wife," Dunning continued, "and she suggested you."

Mark's head snapped up.

"Believe it or not, my wife thinks you're the tops. You could serve as both a protector and maybe even uncover this guy's identity. If it ever came to a showdown, we both believe you can handle yourself."

"Yeah, well," Mark said, "that was in my prime. I'm a real mellow guy, lately."

"Of course you are," Dunning said with a smile.

Mark contemplated the proposal for a minute, then asked, "Why am I talking to you and not your sister?"

"To be honest," Dunning replied, "Anna is in what Lydia calls denial."

"It can happen," Mark said. Great, he thought to himself.

"She even said that maybe she'd misunderstood the situation in the garage. Plus," Dunning said, "she's in a bit of a financial bind right now. She and her business partner are just beginning to see daylight with their debts. Anna's afraid she'll never be able to afford a bodyguard. We settled that issue, however. If you'll take the job, if Anna agrees to this arrangement, I'll be writing your checks until she can pay me back."

"This is all fine and dandy," Mark said, "but it sounds as if she's not convinced."

"She isn't. She's the kind of girl who, well, she likes to think of herself as tough and independent. You know, a modern woman," he paused for a moment then said, "thing is, she hates like hell to admit she's scared. That's why I was hoping you could meet with her, talk to her, maybe explain a few things. I'm afraid Lydia is right—Anna's trying to escape from this whole thing by downplaying it. Call it denial, whatever. But she certainly needs to talk to someone with the knowledge and experience that you have."

Mark thought it over. This deal sounded like a royal pain.

"Anna can meet with you this evening," Dunning said. "At her place in Lower Downtown, you know, LoDo. She lives in a loft there."

"Look—" Mark began, ready to back out, remembering that it was Lydia Dunning who, in part, had put him in this spot.

"Say yes," Dunning urged. "Meet with her, feel things out. And I insist on writing you a check for your time, no matter how the meeting turns out."

Mark almost said to forget it, that he'd at least talk to Anna without expecting compensation, but Dunning had already risen and walked into an adjacent office to write out a check. Mark knew then that he'd take the money. He couldn't afford to be too proud at this juncture. He followed Dunning into the office.

"I hope this is enough," the man said, tearing the check out of a book.

Mark looked at it. Five hundred dollars. It was more than enough. He took the check. "It's fine."

"We can talk your salary over if Anna—*when* Anna—decides she's ready to face reality. All right?"

"Sure," Mark said.

Dunning wrote her address and telephone number on a piece of paper and handed it to Mark. "About eight this evening?"

"That will work for me," Mark said. As he left, he wondered if Lydia Dunning was home, avoiding him. Well, he thought, she damn well should. Another one of life's little ironies—the woman goes for his jugular then turns around and recommends him for the very traits she claimed to abhor.

The September day was warming up nicely, and before Mark headed out, he put the top down on the Jag. He could hear a dog barking somewhere and the buzzing of a chainsaw, neighborhood noises that were kind of pleasant. He got in the car, backed out, and he saw one of the gardeners again. He'd remember the guy later, but at the time all Mark noticed was that the man was pruning rosebushes, a long, impressive row of them, their leaves brown from the recent frost.

Must be nice to have money, Mark mused, money to have it all. And then he wondered as he gunned the Jag a little—where had his own life gone so sour?

Lydia Dunning dropped the curtain and turned to her husband. "Well, what do you think?" she asked.

"He's everything you said. Real hard-core. Wouldn't want to come up against him in a dark alley."

"Exactly," Lydia said.

"The question is, what's my sister going to think? Righter may intimidate her more than that creep who's hounding her."

"All we can do is wait and see," Lydia said.

Scott thought for a moment. "Did you really believe Righter planted that evidence?"

Lydia pushed her big round glasses up her nose. "All I can say is that he's capable of having done it."

"But everyone knew the cops had the right man," Scott said. "I wonder if it really matters if someone, say Righter, tried to make goddamn good and sure the guy couldn't slip through a legal loophole. Isn't it better the rapist is behind bars?"

"You're asking if the means justify the ends."

"Sure, why not? What if it had been our daughter? What if she'd been next on the Orchid Rapist's list?"

"Oh, God," Lydia said. "Don't ask me a thing like that."

"I *am* asking. You're the lawyer, but you're also the mother of a teenage daughter."

Lydia sighed. "Okay, then," she said. "I might have planted that evidence myself. Is that what you wanted to hear?"

"I don't know," Scott said. "I like that cop, *ex*-cop, Righter. I guess I'd like to believe he did a good thing."

"So would everyone, Scott, so would everyone."

THREE

The house was spooky. Anna stopped her car in front of it and checked the address: 3601 Osage Street. Yes, this was it. She sat there and looked at it for a minute, assessing the feel of the place, the impression she got from it. Every house had a personality, and Anna felt her job was to bring out that personality, to strip away wrongness and pretense, to help the structure's inner beauty shine through.

"A house psychologist," Scott had dubbed her, laughing.

"Yes," she'd answered seriously. "Why not?"

She cocked her head and studied the facade of the turn-of-the-century home. Dark stone in horizontal swaths with brick in between. A curved stone entranceway on the porch with a decorated keystone. Tall rectangular windows like empty eyes. Gables and spires reaching up from the turrets. Gingerbread coiling under the eaves. A wrought-iron fence around the whole thing, big trees shadowing it. Gargoyles sticking their tongues out at her from under the gables.

Spooky.

Perfection. She knew she could take this one and do a great job with it. She only hoped the Fenders, the couple who'd just bought the place, had enough money for the project. They wanted to make the house into a bed and breakfast, replete with ghost stories and creaky stairs and maybe even murder-mystery games offered on special weekends.

Sounded like fun, but what it took was money. And her talent.

Anna was one of those people who knew herself thoroughly, her good points and her bad. And she knew she had talent. Life had been easy for her, a pleasant affair that reflected her high spirits and her sense of being grounded. She took life as it came but was a tiger when it came to work, to her vision of how things should be done.

Until the tragedy ten years before. After that, Anna had backed off and turned inward, her ebullience banked, her trust in life tarnished. She'd come a long way from her first despair, but she still felt life lacked something—that one subtle spice that would make it delectable again.

Sometimes she thought that maybe she was just lonely. But she always rejected the notion, too uncomfortable to accept it.

Loneliness was not on her mind right now, though. Work was. And the Fenders. Where were they, anyway? Anna glanced at her watch: five-ten.

She got out of her car with her sketch pad and started up the walk, passing between the round-topped stone posts that flanked the gate. She turned as she reached the porch and looked up and down the street, studying the neighborhood.

This area of Denver was now called the West Side. It used to be solidly Italian—blue-collar, respectable, with well-built Victorian homes, bungalows and stately churches, lots of green parks. Now it was verging on trendy, with an eclectic mix of homes and businesses, mostly Hispanic. Old homes were being renovated at an increasing rate, and Anna was very pleased to be getting her foot in the door.

A dusty Land Cruiser drove up and parked behind her Camry, and a couple got out.

He was thin and fair and balding, with glasses; she was heavyset, with long brown hair and Birkenstocks. The Fenders. Sort of hippie types, Anna decided.

"Sorry we're late," Bonnie Fender called out, hurrying up the walk.

Just then Monica Brinson drove up and hopped out of her car, her long blond hair swinging. "Sorry I'm late," she said. "Traffic."

Introductions were made, and they all stood there in the coolness of the September afternoon, studying the house.

"Hideous, isn't it?" Bonnie said fondly. "I adore it. We're going to call it Fender's Folly."

"Let's get inside," Anna said. "I'm dying to see it."

They trooped toward the front door, Monica with her estimate sheets, Anna carrying her sketch pad, her backpack slung over one shoulder.

"Like I told you on the phone," Ted Fender was saying, "we've run into some problems with the contractor. He originally said he could do the job, but, well, it hasn't come along like we thought."

"Contractors," Monica muttered.

"A necessary evil," Anna put in.

While Ted fiddled with a large ring of keys, apologizing, Monica took a quick spin around the yard, jotting notes on her pad. Anna stayed on the porch, sketching the entranceway.

"We really can't afford to fire the contractor," Bonnie told Anna. "The trouble is, as you're about to see, he's in over his head as far as the restoration is concerned. I wish we'd known about you two in the beginning."

"Where did you hear about us?" Anna asked.

"From Evelyn Carter. You did a restoration for her in the Capitol Hill area."

"Just last winter," Anna said.

"Ah," Ted said, "here it is. We've had these locks changed twice now."

He opened the front door just as Monica returned from her reconnaissance of the house's exterior. They all filed in. Monica, with her usual tact, let out a couple of oaths when she saw the entranceway and vestibule.

"*Monica*," Anna said.

"Oops, sorry."

The truth was, the place was a mess. It was immediately apparent that the contractor, one Ed Michaels, had tackled the entire job at once rather than in stages. Greeting Anna and her partner was chaos: torn-up walls and ceilings, wiring hanging out, new and antique plumbing fixtures sitting half unpacked in the middle of rooms, floors partially refinished. Even the gorgeous curving oak staircase leading upstairs was sagging off the wall.

Anna rolled her eyes at Monica as Bonnie said, "It's awful, I know. We don't know where to turn. We told

Ed Michaels to shut the job down until we spoke to you."

"I'll bet he loved *that*," Monica said under her breath.

"What do you think?" Bonnie asked hopefully, still standing between the vestibule and the entrance.

"Oh, nothing's impossible," Anna said. "But Monica and I need to check the whole place out before I can tell you much."

"We still have a lot of work, don't we?" Bonnie said ruefully.

"It may seem insurmountable now, but eventually it will all fall together," Anna said reassuringly.

The Fenders stayed in the front of the house, going over Michaels's bills and invoices, and Anna and Monica went to work. Anna sketched the rooms while her partner measured and listed the time and materials needed. They moved from room to room. The light was getting dim, and only a few rooms had workman's lights, so they both switched on flashlights.

"It's a mess," Monica said as she stepped over a pile of wall plaster in the dining room, writing all the time.

"Yes," Anna agreed, "but look at this." She shone her flashlight on the fireplace. "Dutch tiles. It's beautiful. And good old contractor Michaels didn't tear it up, either."

Monica trained the beam of her flashlight on the wall. "Yeah, but his men made mincemeat out of the wainscoting."

"It can be fixed."

"Uh-huh," Monica said as they stepped into the kitchen at the back of the house.

They worked well together. In college, Monica had been a business major, with a good head for figures and balance sheets, while Anna, her roommate, was strictly artistic, just scraping by on her required courses while excelling in the arts. When they'd been seniors at the University of Colorado, they'd rented a house off campus. Anna had gone to the landlord and struck a deal: she and Monica would paint the house, inside and out, if he'd take off two months' rent. He'd been so pleased with the outcome that he'd recommended them to a friend, and that had been the birth of their business, Local Color.

That was ten years ago. Together they'd been through a lot, the death of Anna's fiancé, the premature death of Monica's mother. They'd had a rollercoaster ride in business, too. On one of their early projects they'd badly miscalculated the costs and gone into debt. It had taken two years to get their heads above water.

They'd survived, however. Now their reputation was spreading quickly, and there was more work than they could feasibly handle.

They made their way to the servants' quarters off the kitchen. These rooms had also been torn up; there were piles of rubble everywhere, layers of old wallpaper dripping from walls, molding missing, toilets and washstands dragged out of bathrooms and left standing, ancient plaster dust thick on the air.

Anna followed Monica's tall, reed-thin frame up the back stairs, their flashlight beams bobbing and jumping erratically.

The second story had four bedrooms and three baths—all in sad shape. Working their way through each room, they measured and figured and sketched.

They proceeded to the third floor, the old oak stairs creaking, their beams of light leading the way through the clutter. On this floor there were also four bedrooms, all with sloping ceilings, and two marvelous round sitting areas in the old turrets.

"It's going to be beautiful," Anna said, stepping over broken cardboard boxes. "I can feel it."

"What *I* feel," Monica said, "is one big expensive project for the Fenders. They may not be able to afford what it'll take to do the job right."

While Monica explored the bedrooms, Anna spent extra time sketching the detail of the turret areas. She didn't like being alone, especially in the gathering dark, and the rooms suddenly seemed awfully cold. Branches scratched against dusty windowpanes, grating on her nerves. She listened for Monica, wishing she'd come back, then dressed herself down for being so jumpy. She couldn't let this stalker thing get the best of her.

It was almost seven by the time Anna and Monica made their way down the precarious front staircase and rejoined the Fenders. Monica explained to the couple that it was going to take a few days to put together some realistic figures.

"Do you think we'll be able to still use Ed Michaels to complete the work?" Ted asked.

Anna shrugged. "Sure, with a little direction. There's no reason why we can't all work together on this."

"Oh, Lord," Bonnie said. "I certainly hope so."

The Fenders drove away while Anna and Monica stood under a streetlight by Anna's car and talked over the next day's work schedule. Anna checked her watch again, remembering that when she'd spoken to Scott that afternoon, he'd asked her to please not be late for the meeting with Mark Righter. Well, if she didn't get a move on, she'd miss him. And she still had to stop by the Safeway, grab something—anything—for dinner.

"Call me later," Monica was saying. "I want a blow-by-blow description of this meeting. And if you want my two cents'..."

"I don't," Anna said, unlocking her car.

"...I'd hire him. You've got to get rid of the creep who's hounding you. And from what I've read in the papers, this Righter character sounds like a man who can do the job."

"I don't want to talk about it."

"Yeah, well," Monica said, "who would? But that's not going to make it all go away."

Anna thought about that as she whipped through the supermarket. Maybe if she quit thinking about the maniac who was stalking her, she'd break his power over her. Maybe that was the key: ignore it and it would go away. But even as she returned to her car, a shiver crawled along her spine—was he out there? Watching her at this very moment? She got in her car, locked the door and felt a rush of terror wash over her before she fought it down. She couldn't let him take control of her life. She *wouldn't*. This jerk was not going to win.

She pulled into the alley behind her building on Blake Street in Lower Downtown Denver. These days, it was "trendy LoDo" or "historic LoDo." Anna got a kick out of that. What had only a few years before been the derelict neighborhood around Union Station, was now the site of Coors Field—home of the Rockies baseball team—hot night spots, Elitches amusement park, tons of sports bars and brewpubs and art galleries and restaurants. And lofts. Lots of lofts on the top floors of old, once-prestigious brick warehouses for those who wanted the new urban atmosphere. This renaissance was an exciting thing for Denverites, a new high in the city's boom-and-bust cycle.

Anna had bought her loft three years before, when it had been cheap. Scott had been against it, but she'd been right. He'd even admitted it once. To her face.

She grabbed her backpack, which she carried instead of a purse, her sketch pad and her grocery bag, locked her car and started down the alley toward the front of her building.

It was dark, and her breath froze in white puffs in the chilly air. She strode quickly, not liking the shadows. She'd never noticed them before, but it suddenly seemed dark and threatening in the alley, and she stepped quickly past piles of empty boxes and garbage cans. Ashamed of her nerves, she was nonetheless glad to be out on the street.

The building that housed Anna's loft ran from the corner of Blake and Eighteenth Streets halfway down the block. A landmark building, with an official plaque from the Denver Landmark Preservation Committee, it was two stories high, with shops on the street level, red brick with horizontal white sandstone moldings between the stories. The stone flowerpots on the street level held only dead petunias now, but they'd been pretty all summer.

She let herself in the front door; she felt safe being inside the building. Relief washed over her, followed by an intense irritation that this had to happen to *her.*

Anna opened her mailbox, dumped the mail into her Safeway bag and trudged up the stairs to her loft. Home. After closing her door, she flipped on the lights

with the one free finger she had left, then set her armful on the kitchen counter and sighed.

God, it was seven-thirty already. She had half an
hour. She kicked off her shoes, moving toward her
bedroom and dropping her leather jacket on the
couch—practically her only furniture. It was done in
a Southwestern pattern of green, gold, rust and black,
and was positioned in the center of the warm maple
floor, surrounded by stark white brick walls, exposed
pipes and white columns. A few good photographs and
brightly colored prints hung on the walls. The ceiling
was twenty feet high, pierced by skylights, and there
were two huge windows, from which Anna could see
the lights of Coors Field.

Her bedroom and bath were at the opposite end
from her kitchen. As she entered it, she stripped and
threw everything on the bed, then showered.

In jeans and a blue denim work shirt, and with her
hair wrapped in a towel, she padded barefoot to the
kitchen and put the pizza she'd bought into the oven.
She grabbed her shoes and jacket and tossed them into
her bedroom, then flipped through her mail quickly
and dropped it on top of the piles of papers on her
large, built-in worktable.

Some housekeeper, Anna thought. Shove it under
the rug. Except there were no rugs on the original maple floorboards Anna had painstakingly refinished.

Carefully, deliberately, she refrained from looking
toward her answering machine. She'd come to detest
that horrid little blinking red light. *He* left messages on
it.

She shuddered. She *had* to check her messages—
some could be work-related. Later, she'd do it later.
Maybe when that cop, Mark Righter, was here.

She shouldn't have to depend on anyone, though, to listen to her damn messages! And she'd gotten a new, unlisted phone number, so she hadn't had any calls from *him* in a couple of weeks.

Oh, God. Maybe that's why he'd accosted her in the parking garage the other night. Maybe it would be better if he just called.

Anna went to one of the big windows that provided her a wonderful view of the city. Coors Field was dark—no game tonight but it was the end of the baseball season, anyway. For a while there, it had looked as if the Rockies might make the World Series, but not any longer. Baseball, football, hockey, skiing. You name it. Denver was a big sports town.

Mountain climbing, too. But that was something she wouldn't think about. She never did anymore.

Abruptly it occurred to Anna that *he* might be watching. She stepped back as if pushed. Damn him!

Pulling the towel off her hair, she went into the bathroom to brush it out. It was still wet. Oh, well. She wouldn't even bother with makeup. Was she trying to impress this Righter character? No way. She'd meet with him, listen politely. But a man in her beloved loft? In her life? A bodyguard?

She stepped out of the bathroom and looked toward the answering machine. "Okay, okay," she muttered. "Sticks and stones can hurt my bones, but names . . ." She walked over and pressed the message button, standing arms crossed, bare foot tapping, while she listened to the tinny voices.

Two possible jobs. A message from Scott about tonight. A reminder from the head of the homeowners' association of the building about a meeting. Then, more electronic whirring and clicking, and . . . she stiffened as if someone had come up behind her.

"*Anna,*" came the whisper. "*I saw you again today. In that car. But I liked you better in the summer when you wore shorts and things. I could see more of your skin, tan, nice skin. Legs, arms. Do you shave your legs every day, Anna? Are they smooth? I'd like to feel them, to . . . lick them. Run my tongue up your skin, over your knee, thigh . . . all the way up. Oh, Anna, I'm going to enjoy you so much. And I'm always . . .*"

She didn't hear the rest. She went into her bedroom and shut the door. She hummed to herself, creating noise until the message was over. She paced in front of her dresser, back and forth, back and forth, feeling tears burning in her eyes. She wouldn't cry, she wouldn't. He couldn't make her cry.

Her mouth was dry and her hands shaking when she finally left her room, and even though the police had told her to keep all the tapes, she stabbed the erase button on her answering machine. She stood there gulping lungfuls of air, as if she'd just run a race.

He had her new number, her unlisted number. But how?

The smell finally hit the back of her throat and she looked up. "Shoot!" she muttered. The pizza was burning.

It was black, and the smoke pouring from the oven set off her fire alarm. It took her a while to hear the knocking at her door.

"Damn." She left the pizza on top of the stove, sizzling and smoking, and pulled open the door, realizing too late she hadn't buzzed him into the downstairs door.

"Sorry," she said all in a rush. "My pizza burned and the smoke alarm went off and . . ."

The man who stood there was big. Broad, dark-haired, with a dark mustache. Her immediate impression was that of an ex-boxer or football player, a little beat-up but still vital. Anna shut her mouth and took an inadvertent step backward.

"Anna Dunning?" he asked.

"And you're...uh..." The horrible thought flashed through her mind that this was *him*, that she'd thrown open her door to the stalker.

"Mark Righter," he said.

Her fear collapsed like a popped balloon. Of course, his build wasn't anything like that of the man in the garage. She managed a shaky smile. "Come in, Mr. Righter."

But he stood there looking at her, not moving.

"Aren't you going to . . . ?"

"Lady, first a neighbor buzzes me in," he said in a harsh voice, "and then you open your door to a perfect stranger without keeping the chain on. You haven't asked me for ID. I could be anybody."

Anna stood in her door and returned his cool gaze with one of her own. "Okay," she said smoothly. "May I see some identification?"

She watched as he flipped his sport coat back and reached into his pocket, producing a wallet. He opened it and pulled out a business card, handing it to her. It read, "Detective Mark Righter, Homicide." She eyed it, then palmed it and said nothing about his now being an *ex*-homicide detective.

"Now you can come in," she said.

He followed her inside, filling her loft with his unaccustomed size. He stood there and looked around her place, clearly assessing it. He wore a tweed sport coat over an open-necked white shirt and jeans. She noticed, too, that his eyes were a surprising blue under those black eyebrows, and that he had a look about him that was at once dangerous and competent. He wasn't one to mess with. He turned his gaze on her, the full weight of his intimidating blue gaze, and his lip twitched at the corner under the mustache. "You sure as hell did a job on the pizza," he said dryly.

Then, without asking her permission, he strode across the living room, his boot heels thumping on the hardwood floor. Going directly to the window, he twisted the wand to close the slats of the blinds. He turned back to her and said, "From now on, these stay closed."

FOUR

Earl always tried to mind his own business. He was a loner and liked being anonymous, just another face in the crowd. As a boy, he'd obeyed his teachers and his mother, staying to himself and never causing trouble. As a man, he was neither liked nor disliked. Friends were unimportant. If a fellow worker were to be asked about him, the reply would be, "Oh, what's-his-name. Yeah, he's okay. Hard worker." Earl appreciated his ordinary status.

He liked routine. It was safe. And that's why, when the lady in the big Cadillac rear-ended his truck out on the Sixth Avenue Freeway, his first reaction was gut-wrenching fear—the cops would ask for his name, his address, his phone number, the truck's registration. And that was unacceptable, entirely unacceptable. He felt a band squeeze his head, as if someone were ratcheting it tighter and tighter. Danger, his mind screamed. He couldn't let it happen.

He pulled over to the side of the freeway, followed by the woman who'd rear-ended his truck. As they got out of their vehicles, she launched into her apologies.

"I'm so sorry. Are you hurt? Oh, I hope I didn't damage your truck."

"I'm all right," Earl said. "Don't worry about the truck. It's old. It can't be damaged any more than it already is."

But she wouldn't let it go. "Maybe I can just pay for your damage outright. I don't want my insurance company to find out. You understand. I'll just tell my husband someone backed into the car at the shopping center. Oh, I hope the police don't make me file for insurance."

But the police weren't there. Not yet. And Earl knew if he could shut her up and get out of there, before a cop car happened by, nothing would come of it. She could tell her husband whatever she wanted; it was no skin off his teeth.

"Maybe we better take down each other's information," she said after a few minutes. "Should we call the police?"

Earl's mind was racing. If he just hopped into his truck and drove off, the woman might become suspicious of something, take down his license-plate number and give it to the cops. They'd check on the plates and find out they were stolen, and that just couldn't happen. But maybe, if he gave her his name and address, told her he'd get an estimate, or whatever, on the damage to his truck and mail it to her, they could both get in their vehicles and drive off.

He scanned the freeway as far as his vision would allow. No cops. *Yet.* "Look," he said. "I don't want any insurance company involved, either. Let's go ahead and exchange information and I'll let you know how much you owe me. Can't be more than a couple hundred dollars, lady." She had to go for it.

"Well," she said, "if you're sure. I mean, I was totally in the wrong."

"It's all right." Hurry up, lady, do it .

They exchanged information as fast as he could push her. Still no cops. Good. She took down his name—that *other* name—off his driver's license and called him by it. For an instant, he was swept by confusion and his heart knocked hard in his chest.

He wanted to say, No, lady, I'm Earl, the pleasant-looking young gardener, the nobody. But he couldn't tell her that, could he? So she called him by that other name again, the one on his social security card and on his driver's license, and he ignored it. I'm Earl, you stupid lady, that other guy's been gone a long time. The Hunter killed him.

He drove off as soon as he could, trying not to exceed the speed limit and draw attention to himself, realizing that he was sweating despite the cool September evening. There was something on his mind, too, something he was supposed to be doing. The trouble was, he couldn't quite get a handle on it. He was supposed to be going somewhere. But where?

Earl's apartment was nondescript. He had a tiny kitchenette, a comfortable chair, a bed, table and televison set. Next to the TV, neatly set against the wall, was his most valuable possession, a Soloflex machine. In his closet were some work and weekend clothes and a few of Kate's things. Yes, he thought, his mind feeling sluggish as he unlocked his door and went in, Kate did keep things here. For a split second, he wondered why that was and where she was but, uncomfortable, he decided not to think about her.

He was hungry. That incident on the freeway had thrown him off schedule. Earl heated up a can of soup and made himself a sandwich. He turned on the TV and sat down to eat, that sense of needing to be somewhere else still crouching darkly in a corner of his brain.

Soon the food sated him and he rose, put his bowl and plate in the sink and went into the bathroom. He turned on the shower, stripped and stepped into the stall, washing off the grime from a hard day's labor.

After his shower he padded naked to a foot locker, which sat against the wall near his bed. He opened it and took out a pair of combat boots, camouflage pants, an olive-drab T-shirt, a heavy brown-canvas field jacket and an olive-drab baseball cap.

He dressed, his movements automatic, his brain in neutral. When he was done, he walked into the bathroom and wiped away the remaining steam from the mirror. He stared at himself. Aloud, he said, "Good to see you," and the Hunter smiled back.

Seldom was Mark Righter impressed with a woman. He'd known all sorts in his thirty-six years: hookers, debutantes, athletes, even a movie star. His ex-wife was kind of a girl-next-door type, born and raised to be a good wife and mother while holding down a ladylike job.

Looks did not affect him. One of the most beautiful women he'd ever met had turned out to be a cold-blooded murderer. Brains in a woman were fine, but not a must. Sometimes the smartest ones had their heads in the clouds, and Mark considered himself an unbending realist.

But this Anna Dunning had something that stirred him. This surprised him because he'd been off women for a while now, and it was an unfamiliar sensation.

He stood next to her kitchen counter while she disposed of the burned pizza and couldn't help watching her, noticing pleasing little things about her—like the way her mouth curved up at the corners and the oversize watch she wore on her wrist. She talked to herself as she brushed blackened pizza crumbs into the sink, then pushed her bangs out of her eyes with her wrist.

"Yuck," she said. "I'm never going to be a cook."

Yeah, Mark suddenly understood why some crazy out there was so obsessed with her.

She turned to him and cocked her head. "I'm starved," she said, "and there isn't anything edible in my kitchen. Have you eaten?"

"A late lunch," he said. It was a lie. All he'd had was a Quarter Pounder around noon.

She shrugged her shoulders. "Let's go out then, okay? I'm really about to pass out from hunger."

Sure, what the hell, Mark thought. He had a few bucks; he'd already deposited Scott Dunning's check in the bank.

She grabbed a leather jacket from her bedroom, slung a much-used backpack over her shoulder, stepped into loafers, and she was ready.

On the way out, he couldn't help saying, "No police lock on your door?"

"I've been meaning to do that," she said. "Really, I have."

He shut his mouth. But as they got to the bottom of the stairs, he asked about the outside door. "Do you buzz strangers in?"

She looked at him and sighed. "I guess I have."

"What about the other tenants in your building? Do they routinely buzz friends in? Would you, for instance, let someone else's friends in if they buzzed your loft?"

"Oh, God," she said. "I can't stand this. I have no life anymore. Can't you see, he's trying to take it away from me."

"Yeah, sure, I see. That's why your brother sent me."

Anna stopped just outside the building and raised her face to him. Her eyes were dark. "Don't you understand, I can't let him control me. If I let him, he wins."

"This isn't a game," Mark said.

She bit her lower lip and glanced down. "He left a message on my machine today. He got my new unlisted number."

"Hmm. We'll listen to it after we eat. I'd like to get a handle on this guy."

"I erased the message," she mumbled.

"What?"

"I erased it."

"Jesus Christ. Didn't the police tell you to save your tapes?"

"Yes," she whispered, avoiding his eyes, "but I couldn't stand it. I wanted him gone, just gone."

"Listen, Anna, this is serious stuff," Mark said. "From now on, you save his voice, his notes, everything."

She nodded, albeit grudgingly. Then she turned and started walking down Eighteenth Street. He followed. The stalker had her unlisted number, he thought. Not good. That meant he probably had access to other information about Anna.

"So, you have no idea who the stalker is?" he asked.

"I have no idea. I've said that a million times. I guess it doesn't fit the usual MO, but I can't help that. It seems like no one believes me."

Mark grunted noncommittally. It *was* hard to believe.

"Do you believe me?" she asked plaintively.

"Uh-huh. But when we get this dude, it'll likely be someone you know or have seen, maybe just casually. Someone you don't remember."

"And how did he get my new number?" Anna asked in a worried tone.

"Who'd you give it to?" he asked.

"My business partner, Monica, Scott, my clients, some of my subcontractors, but only the ones I know. I mean . . ."

"There you go," he said. "And each of them might have given out the number to someone."

"But that's not very many people at all."

"He's close to you. He has access. That's obvious."

She made a chopping notion with her free hand. "Why doesn't he come out in the open and face me? He's a coward, a rotten coward!"

"True enough," he said. "Stalkers are always very insecure people. They have to be one hundred percent in control when they show themselves."

They walked a block in silence, then came out on Wynkoop across from Union Station, a heavy granite edifice with tall windows.

"Is the ChopHouse okay with you?" Anna asked as they crossed the street.

"The what?"

"Right over there." She pointed. "The Denver ChopHouse. The food's good, and it won't be too crowded on a weeknight."

"Fine with me. They're not too, uh, L-I-T-E at this place, are they?"

She laughed, and the sound reached down inside him. "No, they've got red meat and greasy French fries, don't worry."

"Hey, I eat salad. I just eat other things, too."

"I like this place. It's got atmosphere. They did a great job renovating it," she said. "You know it was the Union Pacific depot originally?"

"I take it you didn't do the work on it."

"How do you know what I do?" she asked, then, "Oh, Scott told you."

Mark nodded.

"What else did Scott tell you?"

He pushed open the door for her, warmth and a barrage of mouth-watering aromas hitting him. The tinkly piano sound of "Ain't Misbehavin'" filtered through the restaurant.

She turned to him, seemingly oblivious to the smells that were making his stomach growl. "Well, what else?"

"Not a whole lot. Mostly about the stalker. The deal at the Tabor Center garage the other night. That you really don't want a bodyguard."

"I don't," she said flatly. When Mark said nothing, she started to say something else, but the hostess came up just then to seat them.

They walked by potted palms and partitions of dark vertical wainscoting. Fans revolved lazily on the open ceiling and the tables were covered with white butcher paper over linen. Cute, Mark thought.

When they were seated, she started in as if there'd been no interruption in their conversation. "Look, it's not *personal*. It's not *you*. I just have to think this through. You can understand that. I'm busy, I have a busy schedule, I run around like a madwoman some days. I go jogging or hiking on weekends. I bicycle, I ski. I work hard." She paused and brushed her bangs up with a hand. A couple of strands stuck out, making her look very young. She didn't wear fake nails or polish—he could see this woman worked with those capable hands. "I date. I mean, I *do* have a social life," she finally said.

"But no serious boyfriend."

She rolled her eyes. "Scott told you, right?"

"Well, that would be a natural question. The stalker could be someone you were dating. The police must have asked you."

"They did."

"They weren't prying. They need to know stuff like that."

"I hate it, all this, all these questions," she said.

"Yeah, I know."

The menu was designed to be delectably sophisticated: pancetta-wrapped shrimp, apricot chicken salad, lobster potpie from the authentic wood oven, Thai chicken pizza, hazelnut chicken, teriyaki top sirloin, and beer brewed right in the restaurant. The waiters and waitresses were all young and terribly enthusiastic. They made Mark feel old and jaded.

Anna ordered the lobster potpie. Mark decided on the Iowa pork chops. When the waitress left to get their beers, he leaned forward, elbows on the table, and tried to explain some things to her. After all, this was what he was being paid to do.

"I was a homicide cop for fourteen years," he said. "I've seen it all—drugs, murders, rapes, knives, guns, gangs, the whole shot. I've seen the results of a few stalkers. 'Course, we got to them too late."

"Spare me," she said under her breath.

"You have to be realistic, Anna. You may think this dude is harmless, but statistics say otherwise. There are two hundred thousand stalkers in this country, we figure. Ninety percent of them have mental disorders. They think they love the object of their stalking, but it's a pathological love. The trouble is, and the guys down at precinct probably told you this, the law can only help so much. The law is in the business of catching criminals, not stopping a crime before it's committed. That's why they suggest a bodyguard."

She was staring off to the side, not meeting his eyes. Her mouth was set in a hard line.

"The stalker is your problem," he said. "I know it's not fair, but that's the way it is. You gotta deal with it."

"Why me?" she asked in a choked voice, still not looking at him.

"God knows. This person is irrational—they all are. Sick. Dangerous, though."

"Won't he stop eventually, get tired of it?"

"Probably not. They only get worse, more obsessive. You're dealing with an aberrant guy here, not people like you and me."

"What happens then? How long does it go on? Do they ever get caught?" She was looking at him now, her eyes dark and intense. She had slim dark eyebrows that were drawn together in a frown, her bangs just brushing their curves.

"Every story is different. I could tell . . . well, you don't want to hear old war stories."

"Go ahead, tell me."

"This might not be a good time," he said carefully.

"I have a strong stomach."

"Well, the food's here," he said, noticing their waitress approaching with plates. "We'll talk more about it later, okay?"

She ate steadily, not saying much. She had a healthy appetite—she wasn't one of those scrawny anorexic women who seemed to be so popular on TV and in the movies. She had substance to her. Her hair was kind of a shiny nutmeg color, dark reddish gold, and her eyes were dark pools you could fall into, fringed with impossibly long lashes.

Mark cut his pork chop and ate it with relish. Potatoes, applesauce from fresh apples. Zucchini with some kind of Italian spices. Warm rolls and butter. Really good food. Damn it, he hadn't been to a decent restaurant or eaten decent food like this in a long time.

Nor had he sat across from a woman he barely knew, an attractive woman, in an even longer time.

Suddenly Anna said, "Those people over there keep staring at you." He never would have noticed, but then he was pretty used to people staring at him lately.

"Uh-huh," he said.

"No, really. Is it from the newspaper stuff? Your picture and all being in the paper so much?"

"I guess," he said.

"And it doesn't bother you?"

Mark shrugged.

"Come on," she said. "It has to drive you nuts."

But all he said was, "It'll die down eventually."

Anna plucked a morsel of lobster off her fork and chewed. "So, where do you live?" she asked. Obviously trying to be polite.

"On Colfax. A small place. I'm not there much."

"You, ah, you have a family," she ventured.

He winced. It had all been in the papers—his divorce, everything. "Yeah, an ex-wife and two kids, if that's what you call a family," he said ruefully.

"The kids are certainly family," she replied. "Tell me about them."

Was she really interested? He shrugged again, ill-at-ease. "They're just kids. Kelly's twelve. She's real smart in school, plays soccer. Mark Jr. is ten. He wants to be a cop like his old man. I've been trying to discourage him."

"Why?"

"It's a thankless job, Anna. I'm living proof."

She sat back in her chair and wiped her mouth with her napkin. "You don't like to talk about yourself, do you?"

"What d'you mean?"

"You changed when I started asking you personal questions. I mean, your manner changed. As if you're embarrassed. I guess you're used to asking all the questions."

"Hey, that's not fair."

"Sure it is. You like knowing about me, but you're not so keen on me knowing about you." She leaned forward, a little smile playing on her lips. "How on earth could you live with me twenty-four hours a day? Do you know how many questions I'd ask you?"

He looked at her.

"See? Maybe we both better think this over. You're a police detective, not a bodyguard."

"I'm not a police detective anymore," he said tightly. "And if you don't like me I can probably recommend someone else."

"I just need time to think." She tapped her fingers on the tabletop. "Like I said, it's not you personally. I'm sure you're a really nice person."

"There're some criminals who might disagree with you," he said.

"Bragging, Mr. Righter?"

"Mark, call me Mark."

"You didn't answer my question. Mark."

"No, I'm not bragging," he told her. "I had a tough job to do, and I did it the best way I knew how. Okay, Anna, you're probably right on the money. I probably am a better homicide detective than I am a bodyguard. So go hire Kevin Costner."

She smiled, a secret woman's kind of smile. She'd gotten to him, and she knew it. Women.

It occurred to him to ask her something really personal, to push *her* buttons. He thought of one thing Scott Dunning had mentioned briefly, in passing. She'd had a fiancé who'd been killed right before they were going to be married. What if he blurted that out— Anna, how'd your fiancé die? How would she react to that? But no, he couldn't do that.

He finished his pork chops, wiped the last of the applesauce up with a piece of roll. He sat back, replete, and glanced up to see her studying him. It made his skin tingle in a funny way. He wiped his mustache with his knuckle in case there was food on it.

"Was your dinner good?" she asked.

"Sure was."

"Better than frozen pizza, even if it hadn't been burned." She gave a little laugh. "I'm not a cook. Don't have time. Not like Lydia. Now, she's a great cook. I don't know how she has time."

"Lydia?"

"Scott's wife."

"Right. The lawyer lady."

"Yes, *that* Lydia. We're very close. She's a great person."

He drank his beer in silence.

"I know she was on that rapist's defense team, Mark, but that was work. Her firm took him on. She had no choice."

"Right." He eyed her over the homemade brew. "Aren't you going to ask me if I planted that evidence? Isn't that the next question?"

She looked down. "No, I don't know you well enough to ask you that. I wouldn't be able to tell if you were lying or not."

He grunted. It was a good answer, better than most. And, somehow, he couldn't take umbrage at her truthfulness; she was simply stating a fact.

"Every woman in Denver owes you one for busting that crud," she said.

"Yeah, I'm a real hero," he said sarcastically.

She cocked her head and studied him for a time without speaking. Finally, she said simply, "I'm sorry about you losing your job."

He shrugged.

The bill came, and she reached for it. He put his hand on top of hers to stop her. Her skin was warm; it seemed to tingle under his fingers.

"I'll get it," he said gruffly.

"You don't have to. The burned pizza was my fault," she protested. "Really."

"I'll get it, Anna."

"How about Dutch treat?"

He was looking at the bill, mentally adding on the tip. It wasn't an expensive place, but it wasn't cheap, either.

"I said, how about—"

"Goddamn it, Anna, I've got it."

"Okay, fine." She smiled. "You're old-fashioned. I'm not used to that."

"I think you just insulted me," he said, pulling bills out of his pocket.

"No, I didn't. Honestly. It's just that, you know, you get caught up in aggressive feminism, and you can't let a man get one up on you. Especially if you deal with them on a business basis like I do."

"Uh-huh."

They left the restaurant and headed toward Anna's loft. The night was chilly, close to freezing, and all the stars were out, pinpoints of light in the black velvet sky. It was hard to believe that it had been so warm during the day that Mark had been driving around with the Jag's top down.

It was a great scenario: pretty lady, good meal, lights and good cheer spilling from places they passed. There was only one problem—he was supposed to be convincing this woman to hire him as her bodyguard, and that didn't seem to be going so well.

He cleared his throat. "You said back at the restaurant that you wanted to hear some of the war stories."

"I still do. I know I should learn all I can about this creep and how he operates."

"Okay," Mark said, "there are a few that stick in my mind."

"Go on."

"There was a woman, I can't remember her name offhand, but she lived in Wisconsin," he said. "She left her husband in 1992. She told a friend, 'He's going to kill me—just remember when I'm dead, I told you this.' Her friend remembered, all right."

"Oh, God."

"Yeah, he killed her. There was no antistalking law in Wisconsin, and they couldn't put him in jail."

"Do you have to—" Anna started.

"You told me you had a strong stomach." He went on relentlessly, "Then there was Sarah Auerbach in New York. She was killed by her ex-boyfriend in 1994, who then shot himself. In Boston, in 1992, there was a guy named Michael Cartier who killed his ex-girlfriend, Kristin Lardner. Then there was that nut case who stabbed Monica Seles in front of a huge crowd. She didn't know him, had never seen him before."

Anna was silent, her face averted. He couldn't tell what she was feeling.

"There are others," he continued. "Those just came off the top of my head. I'm not trying to be gruesome, I'm just trying to let you know this stalker of yours has to be taken seriously."

"Did Scott put you up to this?" she asked finally.

"What, to tell you these stories? No, that was my idea."

"You got your point across."

"Did I?"

They walked on. Behind them, the door to a brewpub opened, people and noise and loud jazz poured out, then were abruptly cut off as the door shut again. A dog barked somewhere in the distance. Cars rolled by on the streets of LoDo.

Mark couldn't think of anything else to say. Hell, he couldn't force Anna into hiring him. She was a grown woman with a mind of her own. He'd done what he could.

"You're quite an effective spokesman," she said.

He put his hands in his jeans pockets and shrugged his shoulders. "That wasn't the point."

"I know."

"Look, Anna, it's no secret. I could use the work. But no one can force you to hire me. It's your decision."

They were at the door of her building now, and she let the backpack slide down her arm so she could dig in it for her keys.

"I'm sorry for all your trouble," she said, her head bent over the pack. "Really. Thanks. I'm not saying no, honestly. I just need a day or two to think this out. And don't say I'm running from the problem. I'm not. I'm scared to death over this whole thing. I need a day or two to get my thoughts straight. That's all." She found her keys and opened the door. "Thanks for dinner. I enjoyed it."

"I'll see you upstairs," he said.

"You don't have to. I'll be fine. I mean, we're right here."

"Don't argue."

She shook her head and started up the stairs ahead of him. He hated to leave her here alone—anything could happen. That creep could be hiding somewhere right now, watching, waiting.

At her apartment door he gave it one last shot. "Listen, Anna, whether or not you hire me, there are some things you need to do."

"Mark..."

"Just listen. I can't make you do them, but I'll tell you anyway, okay?"

She nodded, her eyes fixed on him like a dark beacon.

"Okay, you've notified the police already. Good. Save all the tapes on your answering machine, report his calls. Get another new number. Get a good security system put in. I recommend Westec. Vary your routine." He gestured with his head. "I see your mailbox is down in the lobby. It'd be better to rent a box from a private service. And tell your friends and family never to give anyone information about you."

"That's all?" she asked.

"For now."

"I'll . . . I'll think about it."

"You damn well better do more than think."

"I hate this," she said.

"You already told me that. Now tell me you'll implement these precautions."

"I will. Of course, I will. And I'll decide about hiring you, really."

Sure, he thought. By morning she'd convince herself everything was all right. Like Lydia Dunning had said, Anna was in denial, and it could get her into big trouble.

She unlocked her door. "I'm safe now. Your job's done."

"Go on in, lock up. I'll wait."

She turned and held out her hand to him. "Thanks, really. Sorry if I'm difficult, but I do appreciate your effort."

Awkwardly, they shook hands. "You take care, Anna," he said soberly. "And if you make up your mind, you know where to reach me."

"Yes, sure."

"Okay, go in now. Lock up," he repeated.

She gave him a sad little smile and disappeared into her loft, closing the door behind her. He heard the bolts click into place. He stood there for a long time, just watching her door, as if she'd open it again any minute and tell him she wanted him to stay, to keep her safe, to find the maniac who was ruining her life.

Then he turned and walked down the stairs and out into the clear, cold September night.

The Hunter pulled his collar up against the cold and watched the light come on in her loft. He'd been waiting a long time and, although the cold didn't really bother him, Anna's change of routine bothered him a lot.

She'd been out.

He'd missed seeing her leave, but she'd just come back, and she'd been with a strange man. A big man, a tall broad man with a mustache who stood over her in a protective manner that grated on the Hunter's nerves.

They'd stood there on the street and talked—oh, how he wished he'd heard what they were saying— then gone into her building.

It hurt him that she could be so deceitful, but it was typical. All women were lying sluts. There was a terrible pressure in his chest and around his head, like a band that was tightening every second.

The man was up there with her, up there in her place, talking to her, touching, kissing...

His head hurt and he couldn't think, but the Hunter knew she was doing something unspeakable up there. He couldn't see in her window; the blinds were closed. He could only see the light leaking out around the edges. Once, though, she'd left them open, and he'd seen her in her underwear. Oh, God. He squeezed his eyes shut, remembering.

He'd actually touched her skin. Well, Kate had, jostling up close to her in a deli near her building. So close their arms had brushed. "Excuse me," Kate had said. A smile, polite, but too close, face to face. The thrill had almost made Kate pass out.

Pain brought the Hunter back to the present. Raw pain in his head. The man up there with her. With *his* possession. It was the worst sort of violation, filthy hands all over what was meant for *him*.

The door of Anna's building suddenly opened, and the man emerged. The Hunter almost collapsed with relief. He drew in a deep, cold breath and felt the pain in his head dissolve.

She hadn't let him stay.

The Hunter grinned to himself. She knew better, the slut. Good thing.

He watched the big man walk down the street, marking him in his head. He watched him stop at a green sports car, bend low to get in, start the engine and drive off down Blake Street. If he ever saw the man again, well, he'd have to do something drastic. He didn't like the way the man moved. Something dangerous about him, some competence in his physical being that angered the Hunter.

He stared after the Jag for a long time, thinking, trying to get a handle on what it was about the man that bothered him so much. Then he had it. The son of a bitch had that stride, that carriage. He was a goddamn cop.

FIVE

It was 11:00 p.m. by the time Mark got home to his empty apartment over Lil's Tattoo Parlor. He took off his jacket, discarding it haphazardly, and switched on the television, tuning in the national news on CNN. It was only then that he noticed the light blinking on his answering machine. Reluctantly, one eye on the TV, he punched the message button. It would be nice if someone had called with some good news for a change.

But it was only his ex-wife's voice. "Mark, it's Jennifer. Just called to remind you about the weekend after next. Little Mark and Kelly are really looking forward to that hockey game, so please don't disappoint them. Oh, and by the way, Jim and I really do want you to be at the wedding. Let me know."

Great, he thought, he'd be the perfect guest—lonely, unemployed, a sick smile plastered on his face. And he still wasn't sure how he felt about her remarriage. Jim was okay—at least he had a steady job—but Mark still had feelings for Jenn. It was, after all, *she* who had asked *him* to leave. Typical cop-style divorce. He'd been married more to his job than his wife.

He stretched out on his couch and half listened to a headline story on renewed terrorism in the Middle East. But his mind wandered, back to that evening and Anna. Suddenly he saw her as clearly as if someone had stuck her photo under his nose—the classic features, the bangs touching slim, arched eyebrows, the way she carried herself, the look of defiant determination that had gathered in her eyes when he'd been trying to explain the danger she was in.

But the job probably wasn't going to pan out, and it was likely he'd never see her again. Unless, Mark thought darkly, he woke up one day and saw her face in the obituaries.

Ah, hell, Mark thought, it was her choice. He'd given her some good advice. If the lady chose to ignore it, so what? He'd been on the streets too long to get mushy about another innocent becoming a victim.

Despite Mark's assessment of the situation, though, he made a mental note to call her tomorrow, to again urge her to take the precautions he'd laid out tonight.

After watching the news, he showered, then threw on a sweat suit, deciding that as long as he wasn't sleepy he could straighten up the place. It really was a mess. And if little Mark and Kelly spent the night after that hockey game, at least they wouldn't get a disease or something.

His heart wasn't in the task, though, and partway through gathering his laundry, he gave up and stretched out again on the couch, one arm flung over his head as he stared at the chipped paint on the ceiling. It was Anna Dunning again. Instinct told him she'd find a reason to put off hiring a bodyguard, and he couldn't help thinking about how her life was going to erode, how isolated she was going to feel as the days and weeks passed with some maniac out there stalking her. Soon, every time she walked outside her building, she'd wonder if *he* was there, watching, waiting. The creep would eventually leave her feeling helpless and terrified, waking and sleeping, and then he would have won.

Of course, most stalkers who weren't stopped only grew bolder and more powerful. And someday in the not-too-distant future, the man was going to act on his fantasies. Rape her. Or, the statistics said, the son of a bitch was going to kill her.

Mark realized later he must have finally dozed off, because suddenly he was leaping up, flailing his arms at an unseen enemy, his sweatshirt soaked. He'd had the dream again. Not about stalkers, but about the Orchid Rapist, real name Jarrett Colby, the rich twenty-three-year-old kid who'd raped at least nine women, brutally cutting them up and leaving an orchid behind each time. Two of his victims had bled to death before help had arrived. In Mark's dream, the sicko had escaped from prison and was in a store, buying a knife. It was never the dream, which made him wake with a cold, slick adrenaline rush, that bothered Mark. But rather, it was the persistent sense of being unable to stop the man. Mark was no longer a cop.

He finally stood and stripped off his wet clothes. He padded into the bedroom in his underwear, falling onto the mattress and pulling the sheet and blanket up to his chin, trying to force sleep. He was a lousy sleeper and always had been. It used to drive Jennifer nuts.

He tossed and turned, and at 5:00 a.m. he finally gave up and rose to make coffee. As he waited for it to brew, he pulled aside the dusty lace curtain to stare down onto East Colfax. A lone car drove by, heading west, the displaced air from its passing blowing an old paper into the gutter beneath the orange streetlight. Down the block a bum was staggering into an alley, probably going to check out the Dumpsters. Mark could hear the familiar wail of a police siren close by, and he wondered idly if it would wake Lil downstairs in her bedroom behind the shop. It sure would be nice to have someone to talk to at this cold, early hour.

Lydia Dunning's morning was normal—frantic. First she had to get her two teenage children up and fed and off to school. Then she had to leave directions for the maid and the cook and the gardeners. She couldn't forget to tell them to tidy up the greenhouse, prune dead leaves and fertilize—Scott had no time this week. She barely had a chance to kiss her husband goodbye and arrange to meet him for lunch before he left for his downtown building project. Then she had to rush to the store and the printer's shop to pick up the invitations for the Colorado Symphony fund-raising gala planned in mid-November.

She raced through her errands, munching on white-sugar doughnuts sitting open in a box on the passenger seat of her Mercedes. Bad, Lydia thought. She was blowing yet another diet—her four-hundredth.

After depositing three bags of groceries on the kitchen counter where the cook would find them to put everything away, she took thirty seconds to refresh her makeup in the powder room, then hurried out again, heading to her law office in downtown Denver.

Lydia steered along the gentle curves of Speer Boulevard, which followed Cherry Creek, and planned the rest of her day. She had a deposition to take at ten-thirty and a client coming in at eleven-thirty to discuss an upcoming trial. Lydia would not be in the courtroom during this client's testimony; her job as a criminal defense attorney was to prepare the clients of Whittaker, Goldman and Goldman to give testimony in court. It was a hard job; she not only had to cover every possible question the prosecution could ask, but also deal with frantic, depressed, miserable defendants.

But Lydia was calmness personified; she handled them all, day in and day out. It gave her a kind of mental rush to be able to control all these people.

As well as prepping clients for court, she knew she had the reputation for being the best junior partner at the firm when it came to research. It had been Lydia's research, ultimately, that had pointed a finger at Mark Righter for planting evidence against Jarrett Colby, the so-called Orchid Rapist.

She'd studied the photographs of the crime scene for so long—the pictures of the sprawled body, the bedroom, the twisted sheets on the bed—and, maybe because she was a woman, she'd been the only one to notice the minuscule blot of white sticking out from under the bed. She'd had the photos blown up, and was sure the white was a pair of lace-edged women's panties.

There was, however, no listing of panties in the evidence log, no panties tagged in a plastic bag, no panties in the police evidence room.

And yet, a pair of panties was found in Jarrett Colby's apartment, and they proved to contain the victim's DNA. Although there was other evidence linking Colby to the rape, the D.A. based his case on the underwear.

Lydia had become obsessed with those panties—she was sure they'd been removed from under the victim's bed and planted in Colby's place. She knew it.

She'd pored over the police log that recorded who was at the crime scene. Dozens and dozens of people. But Mark Righter was the only one who'd been there alone for a few minutes, and she'd had to conclude that it was he who'd taken those panties from under the bed and dropped them in Colby's apartment.

When she'd brought this theory up with the lead lawyer of Colby's defense team, he'd decided to go all the way with it—evidence tampering, attempting to frame a suspect, police wrongdoing, the usual stuff. Frankly, the lead lawyer had said, it was about all they had to defend their client.

The news hit the media like a tornado, of course, and Mark Righter was the one in the camera's eye. And then Righter's captain did an unconvincing job of standing by his man. In the end, the jury had looked past all this and found Colby guilty of murder in the first. But Mark Righter had been left twisting in the wind and had quit the police force.

Lydia pulled into the parking garage on Seventeenth and Welton and couldn't stop thinking about the case. She'd thought Righter was a real trooper during the trial, never cracking under cross-examination, a man of enormous pride and a peculiar kind of street dignity. The papers and TV stations had portrayed him as a hero, but a cop-gone-bad nonetheless. There were still stories running about him. At times, Lydia wished she'd never seen the discrepancy in the photos.

But she had. And it was water under the bridge. When she'd suggested to Scott that he try to hire Righter to protect Anna, Lydia guessed she felt guilty for being the catalyst that had ruined the homicide detective's career. The trouble was, Scott had called Anna this morning and found out that Anna was still hedging about hiring Righter. Too bad.

Lydia couldn't get Righter off her mind all morning. She wished Anna had hired him on the spot—something had to be done to protect her. But it was really the trial and Righter that were haunting her. She knew the evidence tampering had never stopped bothering her; she'd been profoundly sensitive to her effect on witnesses ever since the case in which that poor girl had killed herself.

At noon she was digging through storage boxes in the basement of Whittaker, Goldman and Goldman, looking for the transcripts of the Orchid Rapist's trial. When she found them, she lugged them to her car, went back into the office and signed them out. Maybe she didn't have time during the day to review the transcripts, but there was always the night.

She met Scott at the construction site on Larimer Street. She put on the required hard hat as she took the temporary elevator up to the thirty-eighth floor where her husband was reportedly going over some blueprints with one of his foremen. She loved to visit Scott at work—there was something terribly exciting about standing on top of an unfinished skyscraper, the city sprawling at her feet, the strong wind buffeting her. She loved Scott's buildings; to her, each one was a monument to their passion.

"Lydia," Scott called when the cage stopped at thirty-eight. "Over here."

He introduced her to the foreman, an attractive, quiet man somewhere in his late twenties or early thirties. Rod Miller. Scott turned to finish his discussion with the man while Lydia looked around the area.

"Be right with you," Scott called over to where she was standing by the edge of an elevator shaft.

"Take your time," Lydia called back.

"Hey," she heard, and she turned. It was the foreman, Rod. "Lady, you can't stand that close to the shaft. It's dangerous."

Lydia smiled. "Don't worry," she said. "Scott knows I'm careful." But the instant the words were out, she saw a look sweep across the man's pleasant features. Uh-oh, she thought, it was always wrong to point out that she was the boss's wife and could do as she pleased.

On the way down in the construction elevator with Scott, she mentioned the silly incident. "I think he was pretty ticked, you know, the boss's wife pulling rank and all that."

"Rod's okay," Scott said. "But you know how the guys are about women on the job." He shrugged apologetically.

Lydia brushed it aside. After all, if anyone knew how hard it was for a woman to compete in a man's world, she did.

It was after lunch, when she was driving Scott back to the job site, that he noticed the two big file boxes in the rear seat of her Mercedes.

"Bringing work home tonight?" he asked.

Lydia sighed. "It's kind of extra work."

"Such as?"

"Oh, well," she said, steering carefully through the midday traffic. "I may as well tell you. The boxes contain the transcripts from the Orchid Rapist trial."

Scott lifted an eyebrow.

"It's that Righter business. I want to reread his testimony. His and his partner's."

"Why in God's name are you doing this?" Scott asked.

"Because there was always something... Something about those panties."

"Of course there was," Scott said. "They were probably planted at Colby's place. For heaven's sake, Lydia, you were the one who discovered that."

"I know, I know," she said. "But Righter was so damn adamant about his innocence. Something never quite rang true."

"Like what?"

"I don't know. Something. Call it instinct, but I've got a feeling, like an itch I can't scratch."

Scott sighed. "I can't believe that as busy as you are, you're going to waste your time on this thing. It's history, Lydia. And it sure as hell isn't your fault that my stubborn little sister wouldn't give Mark Righter that job."

Lydia said nothing.

"Well," Scott said, "will you please give this up?"

She pulled up in front of the construction site and stopped. "No," she said. "I won't and I can't. If there's something there to find, I intend to find it."

SIX

"I swear to God you look better," Monica said.

Anna held the end of the tape measure to the top of the curtain rod. "I feel better."

"So the jerk really hasn't called or anything in three days?"

"Three whole glorious days and nights." Anna shifted her weight carefully on the stepladder. "But I'm still going to have Westec put in some sort of security system."

"Like that cop told you to do," Monica commented as she wrote down the curtain measurements on a notepad. "Good idea. Better safe than sorry. I suppose, though, that you've aced out hiring the guy for protection now."

"Well," Anna said, "not a hundred percent. It's just that it seems so extravagant when nothing's happening anymore."

They were finishing a job on Capitol Hill. The owner of the newly remodeled Victorian mansion was in oil, and he and his wife were in Houston, at one of their other homes. They wouldn't be back in Denver till

Thanksgiving, and the wife had given Anna and Monica free rein with the draperies and upholstery throughout the elegant sixteen-room house. This was the first time anyone had trusted them enough to allow them to select the materials with absolutely no input. But then again, Mrs. Wainwright couldn't have cared less about decorating. She was far too busy, a social butterfly who owned not only the Denver and Houston houses, but also a ranch in Hawaii and a condo in Carmel.

Anna climbed down the ladder and dusted off her hands on her old gray college sweatshirt. Despite the sudden cold front that had swept down out of the mountains, ushering in October, she was sweating. She pulled a barrette out of her jeans pocket and fastened her hair up off her neck.

"Cute," Monica said sarcastically. "Did you know you've got a stain from the banister on your cheek?"

Anna shrugged, folded the aluminum ladder and carried it to the next window.

"The worst part about this whole thing," Anna said, "is that he's done this before."

"Who's done what?"

"The stalker. He's laid off for up to a week before. I start feeling really relieved and then suddenly there's his voice on my machine. Or a letter in my mailbox."

"Has the phone company changed your number again?"

"It's supposed to be done by tomorrow afternoon."

"What else did that cop tell you to do?"

Anna started up the ladder again. "Lots of stuff. Like changing my routines, never being out alone at night. Renting a post-office box somewhere. That kind of thing."

"And you've done it all?"

"Everything's in the works."

Monica measured the windowsill. "Jesus, this one's almost an inch shorter than the other."

"I guess Close Enough Construction must have built the original house," Anna quipped.

They worked together till three in the afternoon before Monica had to rush home and clean up. "Brad's taking me to Boulder tonight, to a play or something. He said to dress."

"So go on," Anna said. "You know it takes you hours to get decent."

"Very funny."

"Go on," Anna repeated. "I can finish up in a couple of hours."

"You're sure? You don't mind being alone?"

"Of course not," Anna said emphatically. "Besides, it's still broad daylight."

"If you're sure . . ."

"I'm positive."

"Then I'll meet you here tomorrow. Early."

"Perfect. How's the estimate going on the Fender place, anyway?"

"Just about done."

Monica helped her lug some heavy catalogs of upholstery swatches in from her car, then took off. In truth, Anna was glad for the peace and quiet, a rare commodity these days. She hauled the upholstery samples into the living room, pulled the dust sheets off the furniture that was stacked in the center of the room, then carefully pushed pieces across the newly stained floor into the spots that seemed fitting to her.

It *was* a beautiful home, one of the most elegant Victorians of its era. It had been remodeled in the mid-seventies, but the Wainwrights wanted a lighter, updated appearance. Anna had chosen fawn for the gingerbread and latticework and a chocolate brown for the wrought-iron fencing and window trim. She'd had the gazebo in the backyard completely redone, adding cushioned benches and a small fountain with two stone frogs spewing water built near the brick walk. The inside of the house had been garishly decorated— too much velvet on the walls and the furniture. For a subtler, warmer look, Anna had removed a lot of the wallpaper, replacing it with earth-tone paint. The master bedroom and the baths were still papered, but quietly, with smaller, unobtrusive prints. The drapes in the downstairs would be less formal. For the bedroom windows, Anna was thinking of sticking to off-white Belgium lace.

The biggest decision now was the upholstery for the living-room sofas and the seats of the twelve heavy dining-room chairs. The Victorian rooms demanded some color and pattern. But which? And how much?

Sitting cross-legged on the floor, she flipped through book after book of expensive fabrics, eyeing the entire room. Outside it was getting grayer, the golden leaves from the tall oaks whipping by the windows. The house creaked and protested a little as the temperature fell. It was getting so dark in the front of the house that Anna had to switch on the lights.

She worked till five, her mind totally absorbed with the job. Finally it was time to pack up and head home. She lugged the heavy sample books to her car, then went back inside, going up to the second and third floors to check windows and lights. On the third floor a workman had left a window open a crack in a bathroom. The new screens weren't installed yet, and leaves and dust had blown in. Anna stooped and picked up as much as she could, carrying the crushed leaves in her hand—there was no wastebasket in the room yet. She checked the rest of the rooms then headed down to the second story, suddenly not comfortable in the gathering darkness. She laughed at herself, though, telling herself that she was being silly. She'd been alone in rambling old Victorians dozens of times, and it had never bothered her. She refused to let her circumstances start getting to her now. *Especially* now, Anna thought, when she hadn't heard from the creep in days.

She went down to the first floor thinking about him, wondering if he'd been killed in a car accident or something—hoping he had. It was amazing to her how someone could manipulate your life, your movements, your very thoughts. Uninvited, any nut could enter your life and turn it upside down.

"Not fair," she mumbled to herself. But who ever said life had to be fair?

It came at her out of the blue. Suddenly, without any warning, it flew right toward her screeching and squawking, its big black wings flapping.

Anna hit the floor, her heart crashing against her ribs. "Oh, my God!" she breathed, terrified. A magpie, her brain tried to tell her, somehow a magpie had gotten inside. But it was a full minute before she could shake off her fear and deal with the situation.

The bird flew over her head again, still squawking furiously. "Stupid bird," she said, her hand pressed to her heart as she got to her feet. It took at least ten minutes to coax it outside through a tall dining-room window. She closed the window, locked it and then remembered Monica mentioning a weird scratching sound in one of the chimneys. They'd both chalked it up to leaves. Wait till she told Monica. A stupid magpie.

Finally, she checked the back door in the kitchen, then went out through the front of the house, feeling as if the walls were watching her. It was *him*, of course. He'd done this to her. And for an instant before she locked up, she almost wished he'd show himself again—so at least she'd know where he was.

In spite of her darkening mood, Anna hummed to herself on the drive home. The wind was still whipping out of the mountains, making it difficult to drive. In a few short weeks, she realized, it would be ski season in the mountains.

Monica and Brad would invite Anna to go along on ski weekends. She'd take them up on it a few times but, really, three could be a crowd. Brad might try to fix her up for a little weekend tryst in Vail—and she might just go for it if the guy was in it for fun. But nothing serious. Anna wasn't ready for all that—not again. Not yet.

She drove toward LoDo thinking she should stop at the store on her way home. But then she changed her mind. She'd park in her spot behind her building and walk to the grocery store, the small independent one near the Oxford Hotel. It was dark out, but the streets were well-lit and besides, hadn't Mark Righter told her to vary her routine? Plus, the stalker hadn't bugged her for a while. Maybe he was gone for good.

She parked and found herself still humming a tune that wouldn't leave her head. She felt okay, freer than she had in weeks. Safer. She'd almost forgotten how good she could feel. And to think she used to take it for granted.

The walk through the alley to the street still bothered her, but she supposed it would be a long time before she fully got over her fears. She fell in behind a nicely dressed couple walking down the same street, their heads ducked against the cold wind, and she thought again about Mark Righter. Righter had street smarts but he didn't know everything. He'd tried to make her believe that the stalker was never going to leave her alone. But he'd obviously been wrong. She thought that maybe in a fews days she'd give him a call, thank him for his advice—for checking up on her the way he had—and tell him that everything was all right now. What a blessed relief. She needed to touch base with Lydia, too. Her sister-in-law had been really worried about her.

At the grocery store, Anna bought some fresh vegetables and packaged rice. She'd throw it all together and put her feet up, maybe catch the news and go to bed at a reasonable hour. She got to the checkout and put her groceries on the counter.

The clerk, a fresh-faced young college type, stared at her, then pointed at her face. "You've, ah, got something on your cheek."

Anna's fingers automatically went to her cheek. "Oh," she said, breaking into a smile. "It's stain. I forgot."

The young man smiled back. "I always tell people, you know. If I have something on my face, I'd want someone to tell me. You know."

"Sure," Anna said, pulling out her money. She realized what a fright she must be: stained, dusty, hair sticking out every which way. Real cute.

She left the store and, bowing her head to the wind, she walked home, thinking about a hot bath. Food was going to have to wait.

She could see her building just ahead. Great, she thought, then suddenly heard a shuffling noise behind her.

The hair on the back of her neck stood up.

She walked faster, shifting the grocery bag and grappling for her keys in the front zip pocket of her backpack.

Footsteps. Even with the rush of wind in her ears, Anna was positive she could hear footsteps. Quiet. Like rubber-soled boots. Gaining on her.

Oh, God.

She started running toward her building, ripping the keys from her bag, dropping them, then retrieving them. She kept running.

Footsteps behind her. Louder. Insistent.

She was at her door, too terrified to turn. She jabbed the key at the lock and missed, swearing, panic bubbling up into her throat, gagging her.

And then suddenly, just as she managed to insert the key and twist it, the footsteps stopped. He was right behind her, so close she was positive he could reach out and touch her.

Then he spoke. "Don't you know I'm always with you?" It came out in that whisper, that breathless, horrible voice.

Anna was held paralyzed by fear. The figure stepped around, right next to her, and she could smell him—heat and sweat and something he'd eaten, spicy. She had a vague impression of him; it was the same man, in the same clothes, from the parking garage. And that voice.

She shrank against the building, her breath shut tight in her chest.

Suddenly, three people appeared from around the corner—three men, maybe college students, talking and laughing, walking obliviously into the circle of light by Anna's door. Her heart leaped, her mouth opened, and she was alone—*he* was gone, disappeared into the darkness.

She never quite remembered how she got the door open or how she got upstairs. She only remembered slamming her door and locking it, leaning against the smooth wood. And then the tears came.

Hoagie Billings looked down at his plate of meat loaf, homemade mashed potatoes, gravy and string beans. He sighed in delight. "Goddamn, Mark, I love this shit. It's gonna kill me, but you gotta die somehow. Am I right?"

Mark grinned. "You know," he said, "the older you get, the cruder you get." He glanced at his own blue-plate special: hot roast beef on white bread, and a huge mound of mashed potatoes dripping with butter and dark brown gravy. "But you're right," he had to concede. "Maybe we better change restaurants before we do die."

"Not a chance," his ex-partner said. "This dump's fine by me."

Wednesday-night dinner down the street from Mark's apartment had become a ritual. Hoagie, who was on his third wife, wouldn't miss it. The story he gave Teresa was that Wednesday was his night at the department to catch up on paperwork. Teresa, like Sally Ann and Margo before her, bought it. Cops, after all, kept weird hours.

"How's the marriage going?" Mark asked as he dug into his dinner.

"Okay." Hoagie shrugged. "They're all the same, though, you know? Sexy as hell, angels until after the wedding and then all they wanna do is change you. I'll never figure it out."

"Why do you keep getting married, then?"

"The old cliché. Can't live with them, can't live without them. And what about you? It's been what? A year? When are you going to find yourself a lady?"

Mark frowned. "Just not in the mood yet, I guess. I'm sort of off women."

"You off jobs, too?" Hoagie's sagging face split into a grin.

"That's a cheap shot, partner. I'm trying."

"You ought to come back to homicide. You know you miss it."

"Not a chance," Mark said.

"Never say never," Hoagie remarked. "You'll forget about all the publicity, and then you'll wish you were back."

"No way."

"Ah, your feelings are just hurt."

Mark grunted. "I got thrown to the wolves, Hoagie."

"Nothing new there. Hey, the media looks at it like any other entertainment. It's all a soap opera to them. You just happened to be the star for a while."

Mark shoved his plate aside and took a drink of hot coffee. "They still won't let it die. Hell, you'd think I was the only story in Denver. Haven't they got something else to write about?"

"It's still good copy," Hoagie said. "It was the trial of the decade here. And besides, no matter what people believe about the evidence-tampering thing, you're a hero."

"Some hero," Mark grumbled under his breath. "I can't even get a decent job. I'll be damned if I'm going into security."

"Hey," Hoagie said, "something'll turn up. You could always move, you know. Try some mountain town or something. Not everyone's heard of you."

"In Colorado they have. Besides," Mark said, "my kids are here. They're all I really have of value."

"You've got the Jag," Hoagie said with a straight face.

They ate in quiet companionship for a time. Mark couldn't help thinking about what Hoagie had said, that he could go back to the police department. And as much as he hated admitting it to himself, he missed the hell out of police work. Whereas Hoagie was a wizard on the computer, Mark had a nose for the street end of his job. He'd always been able to get the feel of a homicide case; just a whiff had sent him off on a track. He ran a good network of informants, too— pimps and hookers and junkies and gamblers, petty thieves, the street people. They trusted him. And he'd always treated them right.

Yeah, he guessed he missed it more than he'd admit even to his best friend, Hoagie. For Mark, walking onto the scene of a homicide had always been a little like coming home.

They ordered apple pie à la mode for dessert. Dinner, coffee and dessert for two came to $9.76. It was the best deal in town. It was also the funkiest, grungiest restaurant on East Colfax. They both loved it.

After dinner, Hoagie hitched his trousers up over his pot belly, and they walked through the cold wind back to Mark's place, just two blocks away. They talked about the upcoming hunting season and made their annual plans. Mark didn't have it in his heart to tell Hoagie that it might be off this year. Money. He'd wait and see.

They walked up the steps to his apartment, Mark fishing for his keys in his jeans pocket. "Damn, it's getting cold out," he said.

"Hey, it's none of my business, you know, but what about you and Lil downstairs? You banging her yet?"

Mark swore and opened the door to his place. "You really are crude."

"That's not an answer."

"And you're not going to get one."

"Jeez," Hoagie said. "I only asked. She's still a good-looking gal. And that tattoo. Turns me on."

Mark went to the refrigerator door and took out two cans of beer, tossing one to Hoagie. "Lil's almost old enough to be my mother, for God's sake."

Hoagie lifted his narrow, sagging shoulders. "Well, she's not old enough to be *my* mother. Maybe when Teresa and I split up . . ."

They both settled on either end of the couch, feet up. Mark turned on the TV and started surfing channels with the remote. It was Hoagie who noticed the light blinking on Mark's machine. "You gonna listen to your messages, pal? Might be important."

Mark sighed, reached over and pressed the message button. He hit the mute on the television remote. The first message was from Jennifer, reminding him again about that October weekend with the kids. The second message was from a reporter at the *Denver Post* who wanted to do a follow-up story on the rapist trial.

"Over my dead body," Mark said between clenched teeth.

"Merciless sons of bitches," Hoagie muttered.

Then he heard the familiar voice of Scott Dunning. Mark's ears perked up. "...if you could call me as soon as possible," Dunning's voice was saying. "It's urgent." He left his home phone number.

Mark made the call. When he hung up, Hoagie asked, "Is that the Dunning character who builds those skyscrapers?" he asked.

Mark nodded.

"So? What gives?"

"He's got a sister, a younger sister. She's being stalked. I saw her the other day."

"And?"

"And her brother wanted to hire me as a bodyguard, and obviously to do some detective work, but she wasn't ready."

"And?"

"*And* her stalker friend confronted her tonight, I guess. Dunning said she's over at his place right now and pretty shook up."

"So she'll hire you now?"

"Looks like."

"And you want the job?"

"Sure," Mark said. "The trouble is, I think she's going to be a problem."

"I can imagine," Hoagie said. Then his face lit up. "Hey, is she a looker?"

Mark shook his head. "A real dog."

"Too bad," Hoagie said, still grinning. "So I take it you're heading over there."

"Yeah, right now." Mark went into the bedroom and returned with his .45 and shoulder rig, slipping it on.

"You got a license for that?" Hoagie asked as if he really cared.

"Of course." Mark put his coat jacket back on, feeling the reassuring weight of the pistol against his side. It had been a while. He buttoned his jacket, then unbuttoned it, as if rehearsing.

Hoagie finished his beer, crushed the can and stood up. "I better take off."

"Yeah, I have to go."

"I suppose you'll be calling on me soon."

Mark frowned apologetically. "I could probably use some computer help, if you don't mind."

"Sure," Hoagie said. "I'd be hurt if you didn't ask." He walked over to Mark and patted the bulge under his jacket. "Try not to shoot anyone, old pal," he said.

"Wouldn't dream of it," Mark replied, a smile tugging at his lips.

SEVEN

Lydia placed a mug of hot chocolate on the kitchen counter in front of Anna. "Drink this, it'll warm you up."

Anna sat on a stool, hugging herself. She was clenching her teeth to stop from shivering. "I'm not cold," she said.

"Okay, you're having a reaction. Drink it, anyway," Lydia said.

Tears sprang to Anna's eyes. "I feel so . . . so . . ."

"Violated," Lydia finished for her. She took the stool next to Anna's and patted her sister-in-law on the arm.

"Violated. Yes, that's it."

Lydia sighed. "I hate to say we told you so, honey, but if you'd . . ."

"Then don't say it. Okay, you were right, I give in, I give up. He's won, damn him. He's won and I hate it!"

"It's just temporary. Sooner or later the stalker *will* get caught. Look, Anna, I've seen the kind of investigative work Mark Righter does. I've seen it up close, and I can tell you he's good."

"He'll tell me where I can go and what I can do, like I'm a kid. I'm not a kid, damn it, Lydia, I'm a grown woman."

"I know. It'll be inconvenient, but I'm sure you and Mark will be able to work things out."

Anna put both hands around the mug and felt its warmth penetrate her icy fingers. "Lydia, you've seen him. Mark Righter's a big, tough macho guy, and he'll be sleeping in my living room!"

Lydia smiled. "I can think of worse things to have in your living room."

Anna shot her a look. "Careful, my sense of humor is down to zero."

"I'm trying to lighten the atmosphere."

"I don't want him in my living room," Anna cried. "I don't want *anybody* in my living room. I want my independence."

"You're going to have to deal with it. You could be a lot worse off."

"That's what *he* said," Anna mumbled.

"Well, Mark's right."

Anna made a face. "Oh, God, I thought it was over. I thought the creep was gone."

"I know, honey, I know. Now drink your hot chocolate."

Anna looked at the mug she was holding and took a sip.

"See? Food cures all the ills of the world," Lydia said lightly.

They both heard the doorbell chime and looked at each other.

"He's here," Anna said miserably.

"Be nice now," Lydia warned.

"He's already seen me in my hell-bitch mode. It's too late."

"This is business, honey. Mark Righter is a professional—he'll be able to handle things, don't worry. You're a client, nothing more."

"Sleeping in my living room," Anna muttered under her breath.

Mark Righter followed Scott into the big country kitchen. Anna hunched over her mug and refused to look up. She was embarrassed, scared and angry, but most of all, right there in the safe, warm kitchen, she felt utterly defeated.

Lydia rose and held out her hand. "Good to see you again, Mr. Righter. Scott and I thank you for coming over on such short notice."

He hesitated a split second, then shook her hand. "Mrs. Dunning," he said, nodding.

"Please, call me Lydia."

"Anna?" Scott prompted. She finally had to acknowledge Righter's presence.

Slowly she stood up, aware that she looked like a mess: hair uncombed, dirt on her sweatshirt, sawdust on the knees of her jeans, stain smudges on her face. She felt slightly nauseated, like a schoolkid in front of the principal.

"Hello." She couldn't meet his eyes. "Uh…I…well, thanks for coming." Oh, God, this is awful, she thought.

"Like I told you, I could use the work," Mark said in a neutral voice.

Scott spoke then, breaking the tension between them. "We've already called the police and reported the incident. Of course, there isn't a thing they can do. And Anna's going to stay here tonight, Mark. It's too late for her to go home now. But you two can talk, decide how you're going to handle things."

Lydia went to Anna and put an arm around her. "You gonna be okay?"

"Yes, sure, I'll be fine."

"Good. Scott and I are going to hit the sack now. We've both got to get up early. You're in the downstairs guest room, Anna, okay? And you know how to lock up after Mr. Righter leaves."

"Okay." But Anna felt sudden acute anxiety at the thought of being left alone with the ex-cop.

"Good night, Mr. Righter," Lydia said, "and thanks again for coming."

Scott shook his hand. "We can discuss the money angle tomorrow, if that suits you," he said in a quiet voice. "Call me."

But Anna heard him. "I'm in on this, too, boys," she said.

"All right," Scott said, "fine. We'll settle everything tomorrow." He nodded at Mark and followed Lydia to bed.

They stood for a moment in the warm, wood-toned kitchen with its hanging copper pots and chintz curtains and butcher-block island. Outside, the wind picked up, flinging rain against the windows like handfuls of pebbles.

"You okay?" was the first thing Mark asked, standing there, arms crossed, his jaw shadowed with heavy stubble.

"Pretty much. Not really."

"He didn't touch you?"

"No."

"Did you get a good look at him?"

She shook her head. "It was dark, and I was trying to unlock the door. He had on a baseball cap and his collar pulled up, like last time."

"Any impressions? Details, anything?"

She thought. "He had on strange clothes, you know, like army things. His pants were that camouflage splotchy stuff."

Mark grunted.

She put a hand to her head. "I didn't even know I noticed that."

"Okay, well, that's a start. We'll talk more tomorrow. I'll have a lot of questions. A lot."

She nodded, swallowing.

He went on, soberly, with a kind of steely precision. "You're going to have to listen to me, Anna. I'll lay out the ground rules, we'll discuss them. But if you don't follow them, this won't work. I can't take responsibility for you if you don't stick to the rules."

She nodded miserably.

"I'll try to be as unobtrusive as possible. When you're in a situation where there are people around and I feel it's safe, I'll leave you alone."

She finally found the courage to meet his gaze. "Oh, hell," she said, "he's won, hasn't he?"

"Not yet, he hasn't."

"He's ruined my life. He's won."

"We'll get him, Anna," he said, and something in his tone, a sense of strength and confidence, came through. He was standing over her, big and tough and knowledgeable, and for the first time in hours, Anna felt a faint hope rise in her. Suddenly she believed it might be—it could be—all right again.

They sat in Lydia's cozy breakfast nook, with a mug of hot chocolate each, and talked.

Mark made it easier than Anna had thought it would be—he was, as Lydia had said, very professional.

"Did you get your phone number changed yet?" he asked.

"No, they're supposed to come tomorrow."

"Okay, good. Cancel it. We'll keep your old number and put a trace on your phone. I'll take care of it."

"A trace on my phone?"

"We can trace a call instantly. If he's calling from his home, or any regular spot, we'll have him in no time."

"The police can do that?"

"With the phone company. It's your basic crime-fighting technology. Nothing to it. Of course, if he's smart enough to use pay phones, we're out of luck."

"Why didn't the police suggest this when I first went to them?"

"Well, they can't do it for every crank call. It's got to be a serious matter. Law enforcement can't tromp on anyone's civil rights these days. They've gotta be real careful."

Silently, she looked down at the dregs of chocolate left in the bottom of her mug.

"You won't go out alone at night, not anywhere, and nowhere during the day where there aren't people around."

She continued to study her empty mug with fierce concentration. Outside, the wind still swept down from the mountains, sighing through the big oaks. She suddenly looked up sharply, "Oh, God," she said. "Are you going to have a gun? In my place?"

He hesitated, then nodded.

"You're wearing one now, aren't you?"

"Yes."

"I don't want to see it. Please."

"No problem," he said. Then he went on, as if her fears about his gun were of no account. "I'll be spending a lot of time checking out people you know, men you've come in contact with. Everyone from the mailman to the bagger at the grocery store. All I'll need is one piece of information, like the vehicle he drives, where he works, an acquaintance, fingerprints. If our stalker's ever worked, has a social security number, pays taxes, owns a house, a vehicle, anything like that—if I get a line on it and he's in the computer, we've got his ass."

Anna said nothing.

"It'll be okay. We'll get him. He's crazy, remember? His obsession will be his downfall—he'll slip up. He can't help it. They always do. Criminals are basically crazy or stupid and can't make it in the real world."

"I wonder." Anna looked up, her eyebrows drawn in a frown. "Do you think he's done this to other women?"

Mark was sitting at an angle with his legs straight and crossed at the ankles. He smoothed his mustache thoughtfully with a knuckle. "Maybe. If he's got a prior and he's in the computer, anywhere in the country, the FBI has him. The trouble is, we have to narrow him down—statistics say there are two hundred thousand stalkers in the country. That's why I need more facts—his MO, prints, something. But I'll put an order in for a printout on stalkers in this area in the recent past, then we'll widen the search. I'll use the list to cross-check people you've had contact with."

"Put an order in?"

"With Hoagie, my ex-partner down at headquarters. He's one of those computer geniuses. He loves that stuff." Mark shrugged. "Me, I liked the street scene better. We made a good team, though."

"And he'll do it for you even though you don't work there anymore?"

"Sure will. He lives for his computer searches."

Anna cocked her head. "You'll really try to get this guy."

Mark nodded soberly. "To tell you the truth, I'm fairly sure the average bodyguard would never go this far. What I am is a detective. I guess you might say you're getting both for the price of one."

Mark put down his mug and stood, tugging at the waist of his pants. "Hey, it's late," he said. "You need some sleep."

"Don't you need any?"

He gave her a lopsided grin. "Sure I do. I'm a bad sleeper, though. Don't need much."

He stretched, as if he'd been sitting too long. "Okay, so what time do I show up tomorrow?"

She thought a minute. "I'll have to go home and change, and I've got to be at the Wainwright house by about ten. I'll call Monica in the morning . . . Can you be here at, say, nine-thirty?"

"Yeah, no problem."

"God, I feel ridiculous."

"Don't."

"I'll try not to."

"I'll be here at nine-thirty."

They walked to the front door and Anna held it open. "Thanks again," she said.

"You don't have to thank me. I'm working for you."

"It's not quite a regular job."

"No, not quite."

Anna bit her lower lip. She took a breath. "I should have hired you the other night. I'm sorry. I just…I just thought that maybe it would all go away somehow."

"I understand."

"Well, good night, Mark."

"Good night, Anna. Lock the door behind me."

She watched him go down the flagstone walk to the driveway. The wind plucked at his hair and pressed his jacket against his body. He slid into a low-slung sports car, which seemed to fit around him like a glove. It roared to life and rolled forward on the circular driveway, its lights knifing through the wet night.

Anna watched until the car was gone. Then she closed the door and locked it.

The next morning dawned bright and clear, but there was a distinct wintry chill in the air, and frost lay on the grass in a glittering shroud.

When Anna awoke, Scott and Lydia were long gone. The kids were running out of the house as she came into the kitchen wearing the same clothes she'd worn the day before.

"Bye, Aunt Anna," they chorused, jamming toast into their mouths. Francie had just turned sixteen, so she drove her younger brother David to school in the used Volvo Scott had bought for her. "Very safe," he'd told Anna solemnly.

Mark drove up at nine-thirty sharp. Anna was ready, feeling that maybe she'd exaggerated the danger in her own mind. Maybe the man who had approached her last night hadn't really been the stalker. Maybe she shouldn't have let Scott call Mark.

"'Morning," he said. He was wearing gray flannel slacks and the same sport coat with a trench coat over it. The outfit made him look like a cop. She thought about the gun she knew he had.

"Hi," she said.

"Nice day. Cold, though."

"Um, definitely fall."

"So, where to?"

"I've got to go home to change my clothes and pick up a few things. Then to the house we're working on. It's on Capitol Hill."

"I'll follow you."

"Okay. That's quite a car you've got, by the way."

He smiled, a genuine smile that changed his face entirely and made him look like a boy.

"Yeah, it's my baby," he said fondly. "Had it since college. I tinker with it all the time."

"Not very practical in the winter."

"You sound like my ex-wife," he said with humor.

"Oh, sorry, I didn't mean to do *that*. It's none of my business." She laughed.

She didn't think much about the night before as Mark followed her to her place. But as they stood in front of the door to her building, it all came back to her like a bad dream. It was dark, windy and cold, and his footsteps were behind her. She could feel him breathing down her neck, smell him . . . She shook her head. Today was different—bright daylight, people on the street, Mark there, right behind her.

"What's the matter?" he asked.

"Nothing," she lied.

He waited while she opened the door, then said, "I'll need a key, both for this door and your loft."

"Sure, I've got a spare set."

She was very aware of Mark behind her as they climbed the stairs, his size filling the narrow space. She felt more comfortable once they were inside her apartment.

He waited while she changed into clean clothes, and as she came out of her bedroom, she saw him studying her collection of books.

"Interesting stuff," he said, gesturing to her bookcase.

"It's mostly for work. Victorian stuff, pictures, antiques, you know. And art books from college."

"Where'd you go to school?"

"University of Colorado," she said. "Boulder."

"Me, too."

"I graduated in 1985," Anna said.

He cleared his throat. "I was out and married by then, with a kid on the way."

"You're not so old," she said lightly.

"Depends on what kind of a day I'm having."

Anna started gathering some papers from her desk. "I hate to bring this up, but it's been bothering me. Food. I mean, who shops, who cooks dinner? I told you, I'm a lousy cook, I hardly ever have anything in the house. And, anyway, I don't have the time to do it for you."

"I'm no gourmet chef, myself, but I guess we'll share duties."

"And grocery bills?"

He shrugged. "Sure."

"Okay, good."

She looked at him, papers in her hand. "I need to get my messages. The light's blinking." Her voice was careful as she tried to hide the dread she felt.

"I'll do it. You don't ever have to listen if you don't want."

"I want to listen," she said simply.

He went over to the machine and pressed the play button. Anna felt her breath come in hot, shallow puffs. First it was Monica calling to say that the Fender estimate was ready. Then a client, and Mrs. Wainwright from Texas. When she heard a man's voice, she stopped breathing entirely. Mark shot her a glance from under black eyebrows, but it was only her friend Taylor Forman asking her to call him. He said he wanted to see her, go out to dinner one night soon.

That was it. No sibilant, chilling voice. Anna started to breathe again.

"This . . . uh . . . Forman," Mark said awkwardly.

"A friend who's a stockbroker. I've dated him casually." She looked up, startled. "You don't think . . . ? Oh, Lord, not Taylor. Besides, he's dark and skinny and real tall, nothing like the guy I saw."

"Okay. Just checking. I can't take anything for granted."

"You've got a suspicious mind."

"It comes with the job," he replied matter-of-factly.

He tailed her to the Wainwright house, then parked behind her car and followed her into the house. He made the tour, checking out the rooms, the back kitchen door, the French doors leading out to the grounds.

Anna found Monica in the dining room, papers laid out in front of her on the new twelve-place mahogany table, which was covered with a dust cloth.

"I'm only marking up the paint and wallpaper ten percent," she said, looking up from her hand-held calculator. "But the upholstery and drapes go twenty. Okay?"

"Fine," Anna said over the sound of the plumber banging on a pipe upstairs.

"I think they do that just for fun," Monica said. "Serves no purpose whatsoever."

Mark appeared in the doorway. "What's that?" he asked Anna.

"The plumber."

"More to the point," Monica said coolly, "who're *you?*"

"Oh, sorry," Anna said. "He's my..."

"Ah, the bodyguard." Monica came around the table, her long, pale blond hair swinging, her hand held out, her eyes devouring Mark.

"Mark Righter, Monica Brinson," Anna said, feeling small and colorless next to these two tall people, one fair, one dark.

"Nice to meet you, Miss Brinson," Mark said in a formal voice.

"Oh, please, call me Monica. I guess we'll be seeing a lot of each other, won't we?"

"Could be," he said.

"And you're going to take real good care of my little friend Anna?"

"I plan to."

"Are you sleeping with her?"

"*Monica!*"

"Sorry, I meant that you're staying at her place," Monica said calmly.

"I am staying at her loft," Mark replied without inflection, but a hint of a smile played around his mouth.

"Good, good," Monica said with mock gravity.

"You're embarrassing yourself, Monica," Anna said.

"Am I? I hadn't noticed."

Mark excused himself gracefully. "I'm going to talk to the plumber, ladies. I'm sure you have lots to do without me interrupting."

When he was gone, Monica turned to Anna, her eyebrows raised above her big blue eyes. "Holy shit, Anna, he's a hunk! You sure he's your bodyguard and not some guy you picked up in a bar?"

"I'm sure."

"I wonder what Brad would say if I hired a bodyguard who looks like that?"

"Something choice, I'm sure."

"So that's Mark Righter. Ooh, he looks tough. I love 'em like that."

"Calm down, Monica. He's not the least bit interested in me—or you—or any woman, as far as I can tell. He's got an ex-wife and two kids. He's unemployed..."

"Not anymore," Monica said meaningfully.

"Oh, shut up. We have work to do."

When Mark reappeared at about 11:00 a.m., Anna looked up questioningly from her notes and measurements.

"I'm going to need a list of all the men who've worked on this house," he said, "and the last few houses—let's say for the past six months."

"*All* of them?"

"Every last one."

Anna sighed. "I guess Monica can get them off the subcontractor billings. There'll be dozens."

"Names, phone numbers, addresses," he said. "And all your friends."

"Does that mean you're going to check out Monica?" she asked sarcastically.

"Your *men* friends."

Anna put a hand to her forehead. "Are you going to go around confronting every guy I've had dinner with?"

"No, I'm gonna run them for priors. Cross-check them with a printout of stalkers. If anyone looks suspicious, I'll check him out in detail."

"I can't believe this."

"You knew I'd have to do this, Anna."

"I didn't realize . . . Oh, I don't know, it seems so . . . sordid, so intrusive. They're all innocent, and you're running their names through the police computer."

"They're all innocent but one man, Anna."

"You think the plumber is the guy?" Sarcasm tinged her voice again.

Mark held her gaze with his hard blue eyes. "He's sixty-five and out of shape. I don't think so."

She rubbed her eyes with one hand. "Sorry."

"If you fight me, it'll be harder," Mark said in a surprisingly gentle voice. "Now, I'm going to go see Hoagie with what I've got. You're safe here for now. I understand a painting crew is showing up after lunch. I'll be back then. Don't go anywhere alone."

Mark returned as Anna and Monica were finishing their sandwiches and laughing over a joke Monica had told.

"There's an extra sandwich," Monica said, "if you're hungry." The way she lingered on the word *hungry* made Anna roll her eyes.

"No, thanks, I grabbed something earlier." Pausing, he asked, "Did Anna tell you what I need?"

"A list of workmen." Monica nodded. "I'll run it tonight. But there may be a few missing, some guys not on a contractor's payroll." She was all-business now.

"Okay, whatever you've got."

"You're gonna find this guy, aren't you?" Monica asked.

"Sooner or later, you can count on it."

Not long after that, Monica left. The plumber banged on some more pipes, drilled some holes, then he left, too. At two-thirty the painters showed up late and began unloading ladders and drop cloths, cans of paint, rollers and brushes.

Anna was aware of Mark watching them, and it struck her that his patient wariness was very much like that of an animal—a wolf, maybe. Unobtrusive, but very alert, with a frightening power beneath the stillness. She couldn't help imagining him in her loft, sleeping on her couch. She'd never lived with a man; ever since Kurt's death, she'd told herself that she liked being single, that she didn't want all those complications in her life again. And now here she was about to let a man move into her place—a stranger, really. She almost wished he was an ugly little guy with thick glasses or something. That would be easier. But Mark Righter . . .

She was wondering about why he made her so nervous, when he came up behind her, making her jump.

"Sorry," he said.

"Oh," she said distractedly. "It wasn't you."

Shortly after that, Anna decided to return home and do a lot of the ordering by phone.

They stopped at a grocery store on the way and wheeled a cart up and down the aisles together. Anna was interested in the stuff Mark pulled off the shelves— pretzels, cookies, pop and beer, Mexican TV-dinners and jars of pasta sauce. And he in turn scrutinized her choices. He picked up one item and read the label. "Alfalfa sprouts. Hmm. What do you do with them?"

They split the total at the checkout counter, then pushed the cartful of bags out to her car.

"I never buy this much at once," Anna said, putting the bags in her trunk.

"Neither do I."

"It's a good habit to get into," she said. "It saves money to buy in bulk, they say, more than if you shop every day."

He grunted.

Mark parked his car beside hers in the alley behind her building. When he got out, he had an overnight bag in his hand.

It struck Anna again—he really was moving in. He was going to be living in her loft, sleeping on her pullout couch, getting up, eating, brushing his teeth. Like a live-in lover or a husband. She snatched her eyes away and opened her trunk. She wouldn't think about it.

He helped her carry the bags up the stairs. How domestic, Anna thought. She wondered if he'd done this for his ex-wife.

When they were inside the apartment, Anna noticed the light on her answering machine was blinking.

"Ugh," she said, "the damn machine. I hate that thing."

Mark set the grocery bags on the kitchen counter. "I'll do it."

She busied herself putting groceries away, her back to Mark. Relief battled her hate of dependency. She'd been dependent on a man once, and it had gotten her nothing but heartache and bitter emptiness. Well, she'd have to get used to this man doing certain things for her. She'd just think of him as a subcontractor. Sure, she could paint and plaster and all that stuff, but there were experts for all that, and she could hire them to do it. So, she'd just think of Mark as a subcontractor, a specialist.

"What should I keep out for you to eat?" she asked, but Mark held up a silencing hand. Then she heard it— *his* voice, the awful rasping whisper. A bubble of fear rose in her throat as the voice droned on and on, the vile, sick workings of the stalker's mind spilling into the air of her home, dirtying it. He'd grown bolder, his revolting fantasies taking new, more disgusting turns— there was no part of her anatomy that he didn't fantasize about: her breasts, her stomach, her thighs, her most intimate places. He had plans for her, *all* of her.

Sick, sick, sick, she silently screamed.

She clapped her hands over her ears and moaned, sinking onto the kitchen floor, her back hard against the cupboard doors. She cowered there for a long time, knowing a strange man was standing in her living room listening to the filthy sexual fantasy spewed out by another strange man. *No no no no,* she repeated in her head. Then she felt a hand on her knee—Mark's hand, big and warm and solid—and she opened her eyes, blinking at him.

"It's okay," he said. "It's over." Gently he pried her hands away from her ears. "It's all over." He was down on one knee, looking right into her eyes, and she saw in the midnight blue depths that he cared, that he was concerned about her.

He still held her hands, dwarfed in his. "Come on," he said. "Get up."

She rose, holding on to him. She had the irrational notion that he was her anchor, her lifeline, and that he'd keep her safe. As she stood, she felt dizzy and she swayed against him.

"Easy does it," he said.

She leaned into him for a minute, head bowed, until the vertigo passed. Even when she straightened, she could still feel the imprint of his arm on her back, as if it had burned a brand into her skin.

"Sorry," she said.

"It's okay." He let go of her hands.

She shook her head sadly. "No, it's not. It won't be okay until you find him and stop him."

EIGHT

Mark pulled the Jag into a parking spot in front of Mary Ellen's City Bail Bonds and killed the engine. He got out, crossed Cherokee Street and looked up at the modern police administration building. Right up there, on the third floor, by that window, was where his desk had been. His and eleven other homicide detectives'. The place looked so familiar, so welcoming, that he felt a twinge in his belly.

He crossed the courtyard, which separated the Pre-Arraignment Detention Facility—the politically correct term for the jail—and the central administration building, and went into administration. Greeting him was the desk sergeant and the familiar sign: No Picture ID, No Entry. Mark looked at the sign, then the sergeant, and shrugged apologetically as he walked past and headed to the elevators. Even when he'd been official, no one had paid much attention to the sign.

He got off on the third floor and walked down the corridor to Crimes Against Persons, where Homicide was located. He passed the interrogation rooms and the tiny holding cell, and strode into Homicide, his chest beginning to ache. It was all so familiar: the smell of stale cigarette smoke, of adrenaline and sweat and paper, of electronics hard at work, of leather and metal and gun oil.

The office was empty on Saturday, which was precisely why Hoagie had told him to bring in the list then. And Mark's former captain, Franklin, didn't work on weekends, barring emergencies that made him look good on television. He was probably off at one of his requisite golf games, Mark thought bitterly.

Mark walked through the rabbit warren of empty desks, recognizing where each detective sat, as if they were his brothers. Buddy Sevilla's stained coffee cup shaped like a woman's ass, the precise neatness of Charley Heatherton, Sam Danzig's old *Sports Illustrated* swimsuit calendar, the human skull that sat on the windowsill behind George Stanley's desk.

Everything was the same. He felt at home here; it was as comfortable as an old slipper.

Hoagie was waiting at his desk, his computer terminal booted up.

"Hurry up, Teresa's got me for lunch," he said, reaching a hand out for the list. "This is it? Only, what, thirty-five lousy names?"

"That's it. All the subcontractors she's worked with for the last year. And their workers—the legal ones, anyway."

"Awright," Hoagie said, hovering over his keyboard like a race-car driver at the wheel. "I'm gonna run 'em for priors—anything—then we'll narrow it down, throw out unrelated stuff and descriptions that don't fit this fruitcake."

"She never got much of a look at him," Mark said.

"We'll do it rough. You know his size, right? And he ain't black or Hispanic or Oriental."

"Right."

Hoagie started typing in the names, his hairy fingers fast and accurate, as always, impressing the hell out of Mark. Hoagie's hangdog face was set with concentration, his jowls quivering in time with his fingers, his pouchy eyes gleaming with the thrill of the chase. The equipment he was using was state-of-the-art: he was hooked into the main national computer, which linked him to the Colorado Bureau of Investigation and, ultimately—if you knew the right log-in code—into the FBI records department in Virginia. Not many of the guys were effective at digging through the system. Hoagie, however, was not only adept, but a damn good computer hacker.

It took him maybe fifteen minutes, then he called up the printout and sat back to wait for it.

"So what's this broad really like?" he asked, his hands clasped over his belly.

"I told you," Mark said.

"Yeah, but you lie. I'll bet she's a real dish."

"A dish. Hoagie, no one's called anyone a dish since the thirties. Where do you get this stuff?"

Hoagie grunted. "So she's a knockout, right?"

"She's a nice lady."

"Nice. Uh-huh. That means she really is a dog."

"Yeah, well," Mark said, "she does have some good qualities. She's real independent and busy, you know the type. She hates having me around."

"You cramping her style?"

"Nah, it's not that. She doesn't seem to go in for men so much, not interested. One of those modern women."

"Aw, Christ, Righter."

Mark lifted his shoulder. "It's a job. Her brother's paying me good money, over a grand a week, and she really needs protection."

"You watch your ass, my boy. You know how nuts those stalkers can be."

Mark laid his hand gently on the bulge under his coat. "Don't worry about me, partner."

Hoagie stood and went to retrieve the printout, bringing it back to his desk and laying out the pages. He adjusted his reading glasses and started down the list, Mark reading over his shoulder.

On the first run-through, they crossed out three-quarters of the names, either because they had no prior arrests, or because their arrests were for unrelated crimes—mostly small stuff, like DUI's or minor bar fights.

"You know," Hoagie said, "your perp may not have a record at all."

"I know," Mark replied soberly. "Just keep searching, though, will you?"

"Till I draw my last breath, partner."

They went through and eliminated all the men whose height, weight or race didn't match the stalker's. Five names were left, four of whom had either relocated to another state or were otherwise unlikely suspects.

There was one left.

"James Daniel Moran," Hoagie said. "Five-ten, blond, blue eyes, thirty-seven. Arrested last year for knocking his girlfriend around. On probation for a year."

Mark checked Monica's list for the name. "He was an electrician on some house they did near Washington Park. He's about the right size."

"Present address in Lakewood. Think he's worth checking out?"

"Sure. Like you always said, Hoagie, you gotta start somewhere."

"It's a long shot."

"Isn't it always?"

Hoagie looked at him over his glasses. "The stalker's probably some guy who saw her once in a store, a gas station maybe, went home, had a wet dream and wants to repeat the thrill. Probably no connection at all between them."

"This guy got her unlisted number. He has access. He's someone who works or lives near her. He knows her. There's some connection."

"He could work for the phone company. Remember that weirdo back in '90? Called ladies from work, said some nasty things. It's like that movie all those years ago, *The President's Analyst*. The phone company controlled the world."

"Sure, Hoagie, I'll bet that's it," Mark said with heavy sarcasm. "Why do I bother with any of this sleuthing business when I only have to ask you?"

"Or the mailman. Those guys can open anybody's mail, pull out checks, get phone numbers, anything."

"Can we get on with this? There's a connection here, and I have to find it."

"Yeah, sure, but sometimes it's only in the stalker's mind. Pretty hard for normal folk like us to pick up on."

"He'll make a mistake sooner or later," Mark said. "They always do. He'll get too bold. You know the progression. I'll get him one way or another."

"Sure you will. You always get your man, don't you?" Hoagie said, smiling. "You're a relentless son of a bitch, Righter."

"I *was*, Hoagie, I was."

"And the leopard changes his spots and gets all pretty in pink," Hoagie replied. "Damn, Righter, you belong back here and you know it."

"Lay off."

"You're not a bodyguard, you're a detective. A homicide detective with the best street nose I've ever seen."

Mark thought about that. It was true. He should be working the case a hundred percent, ferreting out the stalker. The hours he spent with Anna were wasted. Hell, she could hire a brainless gorilla to protect her. Still, he needed the job and the money. He'd just have to steal whatever time he could to smoke the guy out. After all, that's what he did best.

Mark took James Moran's address and stuck it in his pocket. Hoagie was ready to leave, but Mark stayed behind to use the phone. He sat down at his old desk, which now belonged to some rookie named Bernard Wu, and leaned back in the chair, closing his eyes in a kind of sad, futile pleasure, like illicit sex. It felt good, and he hated that, and he resented this Wu character, whoever the hell he was. He opened his eyes and picked up the phone, dialing the number of the cellular phone he'd given Anna to carry.

Her voice came on, panting, and he could hear background noises. He knew where she was—he'd heard her make careful plans that morning before he left to meet Hoagie. She was jogging in Cheesman Park with Monica.

"Anna?"

"Yes, Mark? I'm here. It's hard to talk when I'm running."

He could picture her running on this warm day, her strong tanned legs, the shorts, red shorts, bright against the bare skin of her thighs. She'd worn a tank top; he could picture her slim arms with the tiny blond hairs. She had skin so smooth it looked like molten silk. His fingers had known what it would feel like from the first without even touching her. He shut that thought down—he was off women, especially *this* woman.

"I'll make it quick," he said. "I'm going to check up on a guy named James Moran who did some work on a house for you. Electrician. Does the name ring a bell?"

He could hear her breath rasping in and out, then she must have asked Monica about Moran, because her voice became muffled. She came back on in a moment. "Haven't a clue, neither of us."

"Okay, I'm going to try to locate him. So I won't be meeting you for lunch. You'll be with Monica, right?"

"Yes, we're going back to the loft to shower, then lunch at the Wynkoop Deli."

"Stay with her until I get back this afternoon. It won't be late."

"All right. See you later."

He hung up and rose, turning away from his old desk. The room was empty, very quiet. Down the corridor in Fugitive Recovery a phone rang and someone answered. Familiar, comforting sounds.

But it wasn't his life anymore. Slowly, Mark glanced around, drawing in the look, the scent, the feel of the place. Then he straightened his shoulders and walked out.

Howard "Hoagie" Billings was an unlikely combination: irreverent and foulmouthed but charming, softhearted and tough-minded, realistic but romantic, all wrapped up in a homely package—hangdog face, narrow shoulders, skinny legs, potbelly. Women loved him because he loved women. He saw something beautiful in all of them, and they saw something in him. His two ex-wives remained friends, which he felt proved his point.

He left the department that Saturday, got into his old Buick and pulled out of the parking garage. He drove automatically, his mind on his ex-partner. It damn near killed him to see Mark sneaking into the office on a weekend, having to ask Hoagie for help. Baby-sitting some poor little rich girl, for God's sake! He often wondered if Mark regretted quitting the force—not that the stubborn bastard would ever admit it. Man, but he could be thickheaded. Pride, too much pride. One of the deadly sins, that was for goddamn sure.

Everybody in Homicide despised Franklin. Big deal. You did your work, you tried to ignore the jerk, you made jokes behind his back.

You didn't *quit.*

The car radio was tuned to an oldies-but-goodies station, and Hoagie tapped his fingers on the steering wheel in time to the tune. Hoagie remembered the day Mark quit. It had upset the whole department. Suddenly, every detective on duty had become real silent, finding excuses to leave, checking on a snitch, anything to get out of the office. The mood had been one of stunned disbelief, and the word had spread like wildfire throughout the building: Righter quit, Righter turned in his badge.

Hoagie had tried to stop him. He'd seen Mark come in and he'd recognized the signs—they'd been accumulating for weeks, ever since Franklin had been forced to distance himself from Mark over the evidence-tampering thing.

"Hold it there, old buddy," Hoagie had said, putting a hand on Mark's arm. It was quivering—Mark was shaking all over with rage and indignation.

"Goddamn it, Hoagie," he said, flicking the newspaper in his hand with his finger, "you see this? Did you see this new crap?"

"Ignore it."

"They just about came out and said I did it!" Mark snarled.

"Forget it, Righter. They're just . . ."

"I can't forget it. I can't goddamn ignore this. They're saying I'm a bad cop, Hoagie."

"Take the day off. Go home, Mark. Cool down. It'll pass."

"No, not this time. I've had it. I can't work under this pressure anymore."

"Cool it, old buddy."

But Mark didn't cool it. He took the newspaper and marched into Franklin's office, and everyone in Homicide could hear the raised voices.

Hoagie had sat at his desk, head in hands. Righter was burning his bridges, he thought, the fool, the sorry fool. Didn't he realize that he was a cop, pure and simple? A good cop, a *great* cop, and that nothing else on earth was ever going to satisfy him?

Hoagie would never forget that day; he'd never forget the sense of loss he felt, the sadness. He'd never forget what Mark looked like, stalking out of Franklin's office—murderous, pale, his eyes straight ahead, not looking at anyone. He'd marched past his desk, not even stopping, not even acknowledging Hoagie, his partner and his best friend.

Big and furious and mean as hell.

Hoagie drove toward his house, which was in an older, middle-class neighborhood: small, cozy houses, well-kept lawns, a nice park nearby. Convenient. He liked the house, which was actually Teresa's house, left to her when her husband died. He liked Teresa, too—broad across the beam, big knockers and not *too* pretty, but so lighthearted and warm and full of all sorts of passions—for food and friends and sex and her two grown children, and for Hoagie. Teresa restored his faith in human nature every day when he went home to her. So he had to put up with a little nagging—par for the course. Maybe he and Teresa would stick.

Poor Mark. Not that the big dope would want pity, and not that Hoagie would ever dare *show* him pity. No wife, no home, no job. It was a goddamn crime.

Well, he had this job now. Hoagie supposed it was better than nothing. Some dough, anyway. Maybe things were looking up for Righter, he thought. Baby-sitting a debutante. God.

He turned off University onto Yale, his Buick rocking on its soft shocks. There was his house. And there was Teresa, familiar and comfortable, with her pretty dark hair, her too-tight jeans and an oversize turquoise sweatshirt, raking leaves on the front lawn. Which he was supposed to have done.

He pulled into his driveway and rolled down the window. "I'll do that, honey."

Teresa leaned on the rake and ignored his offer. "How was Mark?"

"Okay."

"Really okay?"

"No," Hoagie said, "but he's hanging in there."

"Poor Mark," Teresa said.

Hoagie got out of the car. "Don't let him hear you say that."

"You think I'm crazy?"

"Only sometimes," Hoagie said, and he grinned at her. Yeah, Teresa was real nice to come home to.

NINE

Earl had woken that morning with an elusive wisp of memory that slipped from his mind like a darting fish. Something he had to do. It wasn't work, because it was the weekend. He'd lain there wondering about it, then he'd gotten up and shaved very carefully, the way he always did. He was blond, and his beard was fair and sparse, but he liked a real close shave.

He drank instant coffee, putting the mug in the sink of his kitchenette, and turned on the tube, channel-surfing. News, Saturday-morning cartoons, weather. He'd stopped for a time on the shopping channel to watch ladies model sweaters. Sluts, all of them, he thought, sticking their tits out like that.

He'd finally found what really interested him. A workout program, with a man and two women in leotards, doing exercises. They were strong women—tough, muscular and sweating. The guy had bulges like a Mr. Universe. Earl had watched and appreciated the workout, but the women, he thought, flaunted themselves disgustingly.

He'd then worked out on his Soloflex in cutoff sweatpants and a Gold's Gym tank top, his weight belt tight around his narrow waist. Still watching TV, he did his leg routine, squats, lunges, hamstring curls and toe raises. He alternated days: first his upper body then legs for six days, then he took a day off. Like God, he often thought.

Finished, he'd flung himself on his bed and lain there sweating for a time, recovering. When he got up, he ate breakfast—cold cereal with milk—and washed the dishes, stacking them neatly, just as his mother had taught him.

What was it he had to do? It was so frustrating that he couldn't remember. He pressed the remote control, running through the channels again, and stopped short at the CNN anchor lady, a pretty brunette with bangs. She reminded him of somebody. Yes, she looked familiar, but who?

Earl took a long shower, soaping himself carefully and washing his short, bristly hair. He liked to be clean and smooth. He shaved his underarms and his legs, letting the hot water beat down on his back.

Kate hated dark, hairy men.

When he got out of the shower, he opened the bathroom door to let the steam escape, then cleared a spot in the mirror with a towel. He smiled at the misty reflection in it. It was Kate—pretty, sweet Kate—and he sure was glad to see her.

"Hello," Kate said brightly. "You naughty boy, you forgot to tell me what I had to do today, didn't you? It's that lady, that Anna. I have to find her. You wanted me to find her today and get close to her, remember?"

Kate dried herself and rubbed lotion into her skin. She sprayed on perfume, then started on her makeup, standing nude in the bathroom. She got the wig out of its special box and adjusted it, then checked the mirror: pretty, golden curls that went well with the pale blue eyes and long lashes darkened with mascara, and the pink lipstick.

She dressed in tight jeans and a long-tailed, embroidered blue denim shirt, which she left hanging out. She had a narrow-hipped, boyish figure that she was proud of, but she definitely needed the help of a padded bra. She checked herself in the mirror. Very nice: not flashy, perfect for sporty Denver on a nice, seventy-degree fall day.

Kate drove Earl's old truck to LoDo and parked in one of the big, new parking garages. She'd like a more ladylike vehicle, she thought, and then a momentary haze of confusion encased her. Earl liked his truck. So did the Hunter. She'd better not say anything to either of them about her desires—they'd just laugh at her, anyway. No, she'd keep some things secret from those two boys.

The haze cleared and she felt better. She got out of the truck, humming to herself, swinging her bag over her shoulder as she walked along Blake Street. Men noticed her, and she smiled back at them. Not in a sexy way, just friendly.

The sidewalk cafés were full as Denverites sat, enjoying the last of the good weather. It was lunchtime, and there were customers in all the restaurants, too. But Kate didn't stop; she had something to do.

She halted across the street from Anna's building and looked up at the windows. The blinds were drawn, but then they were always drawn lately. Kate never got to see inside anymore. She continued around the building to the alley and walked down it, but Anna's

Camry wasn't there. Neither was that man's green Jaguar. Kate felt dizzy at the thought of the man who'd been in the loft with Anna for days now.

It came to her with utter clarity. That's why the Hunter had sent her here today. Of course. The Hunter couldn't get near Anna with that man around. But Kate could. *That* man. The big, dark, hairy one, the kind Kate despised. She shuddered, and felt the Hunter's terrible anger well up in her. She pushed it down. But she couldn't get out of her head the thought of Anna and that man together, all night long, every night. God knew what kind of perverted things they were doing up there. She felt betrayed by Anna.

She'd wait for a while. Maybe Anna would come home. Maybe the dark man was gone and he wouldn't come back. Kate found a coffee bar diagonally across the street from Anna's building and sat sipping cappuccino and reading a *Denver Post* someone had left on a table. She was very patient.

Her luck held. Twenty minutes later, the silver Camry sped down Blake, turned the corner into the alley, and shortly after, Anna and her tall, skinny blond friend came around to the front door. They were dressed in shorts and T-shirts and running shoes, their hair up.

They'd been out jogging.

Kate ordered a sweet roll and sat there, reading about another drunk-driving accident on the mountain highway to Black Hawk, where gambling was legalized. A real problem, Kate mused, those gamblers who drank too much then set out to drive home. She read on: Aspen had raised its lift ticket prices again. The Denver Avalanche, the hockey team, was set to open its season soon, and the Denver Broncos were playing Kansas City at Mile High Stadium tomorrow.

When Kate saw Anna and her friend emerge from the building, she put down her paper. They'd obviously showered and changed, and they started walking down Eighteenth Street toward Union Station.

Kate got up calmly and left enough money on the table to cover the bill and a small tip. She swung her bag over her shoulder and walked out of the coffee shop, sauntering down the street, keeping the two women in sight. The tall blonde made it easy.

The Wynkoop Deli. So, she thought, they were going to eat lunch. Kate followed them in and saw that they were sitting at a small round table near the back of the restaurant.

Kate sat down at a table next to them; luckily, the place wasn't very busy and she had her choice. She pretended to read her menu, but she was really watching the two women and trying to listen to their conversation.

"Brad wants me to," the blonde was saying, "but I . . ." Kate couldn't hear the rest over the other voices in the restaurant. Their heads were close together, and they were talking quite animatedly. When their waitress appeared, they ordered, and Kate had to follow suit when the waitress turned to her. She chose chicken soup and a roll.

"He tries to stay out of the way," she could hear Anna say, "and he's really considerate, but it's driving me nuts, Monica." Then something Kate couldn't hear.

Kate watched them for a long time, spooning up soup, tearing the roll into tiny pieces. They kept talking, on and on. Nothing important. Just gossip, girl talk. Kate felt a kind of self-pity that *she* didn't have a girlfriend like that to talk to. Sure, she had Earl, but he didn't talk much. There was the Hunter, but he was scary, although she liked to do things for him, to please him.

Kate had no other friends. She'd had her mother, once, but something bad had happened to her. The Hunter always said her mother had deserved it. It made Kate very frightened to think about that.

She suddenly noticed the blond girl, Monica, was getting up, and Anna was laying some money on the table. "I'll get it," Anna was saying, "because you had to come. You had no choice."

"Oh, for goodness' sake," the blonde said.

They'd be gone in a moment, Kate realized. She stood up and took a step toward Anna's table. "Is this yours?" she asked, modulating her voice in that nice, ladylike way. She held out a dollar bill to Anna and smiled her friendly smile.

"Oh," Anna said, "is that mine?"

"You must have dropped it," Kate said.

"Thanks. Gosh, guess I didn't notice, just throwing money around," Anna said lightly.

"You're welcome," Kate said, and she watched the two women walk out of the deli, her heart pounding with her own cleverness and temerity. She could still feel where Anna's fingers had touched hers when she took the dollar bill.

Mark drove out to James Moran's Lakewood address, sensing in that cop's way that this trip was a waste of time. First of all, Moran was not on probation for stalking. Second, nothing in life came this easy—not in Mark's life, anyway.

He found the address, parked and eyed the apartment building. It was brick and substantial-looking, probably built in the seventies when the Denver suburb was taking shape. A nice neighborhood, relatively safe. There was a kid's tricycle overturned on a patch of lawn in front of an apartment, a barbecue in front of another.

He found 603 and knocked, wondering if he'd find this character home on a Saturday. A woman answered and she asked Mark to wait while she got her husband. He wondered if this was the woman Moran had abused.

He spoke to Moran in the hall, introducing himself as a private investigator working a theft on the Washington Park house Moran had wired last year. Mark could have told the truth but, hell, he wasn't a cop anymore, and it was better to come at a potential perp in a roundabout way and catch him off guard.

"Oh, man," Moran said, running a hand through his dark blond hair. "I haven't been near that place in months. What's the deal?"

Mark leaned against the wall and crossed his arms. "I'm just checking everyone who worked there this past year. You did do an electrical job for Local Color?"

"Yeah, sure, those two chicks, the remodelers."

"That's right."

"They gave you my name?"

"Yours and some others."

"Great," the guy said. "Well, I don't care whether you believe me or not, but I wasn't involved in any theft. No way. I stay as far away from anything to do with the cops as possible." Moran was shaking his head, agitated, when he looked up sharply. "Say, when did this robbery happen, anyway?"

"A few nights ago."

"Well, shit," Moran said, "me and Betty were up at her folks' in Nebraska all week. Her dad's real sick. Hey, I can prove I wasn't even in the state."

For the sake of thoroughness, Mark took a look at Moran's gas receipts, and on the night Anna was accosted in front of her building, it did seem that James Moran had been in Nebraska.

"Satisfied?" Moran asked at his door.

"Sure," Mark said, "and thanks. Sorry for the trouble."

"Uh-huh," Moran said, then closed his door firmly.

Mark drove back toward downtown feeling low and somewhat frustrated. And he was pretty sure his mood was only going to get worse before something broke. It usually did. Hell. It *always* did.

It was Saturday night. Francie Dunning had gone out with friends to a movie at the Cherry Creek Mall, and David was spending the night at a friend's house. The elder Dunnings were home alone.

"Very sexy," Scott said, coming out of the bathroom in pajama bottoms and a T-shirt, his favorite sleeping attire.

Lydia looked up, her concentration broken. "Who, me?"

"No, the other lady in my bed."

Lydia pulled her glasses off and pinched the bridge of her nose. She sat propped against the headboard of their king-size bed, in a ratty flannel robe, her knees up, reading the Orchid Rapist trial transcripts. She'd been reading them for hours while Scott watched the news on the TV at the foot of the bed. "Sorry," she said, "but this is really bugging me."

"Finding anything?"

"Not really. I can't tell who's lying."

"You hardly ever can."

"Well, someone lied. The underwear was planted in Jarrett Colby's place, and as far as I can tell, Mark Righter was the only detective alone there, even if only for a short time."

"Maybe someone else was there before him."

"Scott, he was also alone at the victim's home. They record the name of every person entering or leaving a murder scene, as well as the times."

"Maybe they missed somebody. Or got confused, just didn't notice."

"Who? Even if there was someone else, no cop'll ever rat on another. Maybe Righter didn't do it, but he still might know who did."

"It's too late now, Lydia, and you can't do a thing to change it one way or the other. The guilty party's in jail, and that's good."

"Scott, I have to be comfortable in my own mind. All right, so I came up with the evidence tampering, but I wasn't positive who did it. Then Whittaker grabbed it and ran with it. I warned him, but he didn't have much else to go on."

"Every defendant is considered innocent until proven guilty, and is entitled to a fair trial and competent representation, right? Isn't that what you keep telling me, Lydia?"

"Yes."

"Well, then . . ."

She put her glasses back on and looked at her husband. "It's just that this thing with Anna has brought it all back. Did you see the way he looked at me that night?"

"Who?"

"Righter. Like I was something slimy from under a rock."

"You imagined that."

"No, I didn't. He didn't even want to shake my hand."

"Cops generally don't like defense lawyers, Lydia. Even ex-cops."

"This was more—it was personal." She set aside the papers she was reading. "I ruined his life."

"Well, you did your good deed. He's got a job now." Scott sat down on the side of the bed and put his hand on her knee.

Lydia bit her lip. "Baby-sitting," she said. "That's what he's doing as far as he's concerned, Scott."

"He's doing a good job. Even Anna has to admit that."

"Uh-huh."

"What's the matter, you don't trust him?" Scott asked.

"I do, I do trust him. That's what's bothering me so much."

"You're too softhearted, Lydia. You should have been a social worker or something."

"I'm a good lawyer," she said indignantly.

"I know, sweetie. You're brilliant. You just let yourself get too emotionally involved." Scott rubbed her bare knee where the robe had fallen back.

"I can't help it. Ever since . . ." She looked at her husband, and he nodded. He knew what she meant.

"I'm going to take a shower," Lydia announced, changing the subject abruptly.

She stood under the hot water for a long time, as if it would wash away the stuff she'd been reading: entry wounds and bodily fluids and bloody clothes and vaginal tearing. Maybe, too, it would wash away what Lydia thought of as her sins—those times when she'd worked on the defense of a guilty person who'd been found not guilty because of Lydia and the defense team's clever legal maneuvering.

Of course, she had to keep reminding herself of the many truly innocent people she'd helped to exonerate. It was the system, the imperfect American legal system, but it was all there was. Consider the alternative, senior partner Leland Goldman liked to say. He was right.

But there was one case that still stuck in her craw, one besides the Orchid Rapist case. The hot water pelted her heat-pinkened skin as she remembered it, unable to head off the feelings that recurred periodically.

A man had been arrested for a liquor-store holdup in which a clerk had been shot. The man had sworn he was innocent, and Lydia had believed him, but he fit the description of the shooter, owned a gun of the correct caliber and had been arrested previously for a traffic offense in which he'd threatened someone. The cops were sure he was the perp, and he didn't have an alibi.

The man had no money, but Lydia's firm did a little pro bono work, and the case fell to Lydia. She'd dug and dug and harassed her client, until he'd admitted he *did* have an alibi, but he didn't want to get the person involved. He'd promised not to.

Lydia found out who the alibi was, went to her and begged her to go to the police. There was a hitch, though, and Lydia finally got it out of her.

The alibi witness was her client's girlfriend, and he'd taken her to Salt Lake City the day of the shooting to get an abortion. She was pregnant and he had no money to marry her yet, and her family was staunch, hard-line Catholic. Her uncle was a bishop in Denver, she told Lydia, and her father would kill her. He couldn't find out. Lydia would never forget the young girl's tears.

Despite it all, she convinced the girl to go to the police to save her boyfriend. The cops promised to keep the testimony quiet and drop the charges, but there was a leak. The press grabbed it, and there were headlines and names and dates until the story was milked dry.

The suspect got off, and Lydia got a raise. The girl committed suicide a week later.

Lydia turned the water off and stepped out of the shower. She wrapped her hair in one thick rose-colored towel, her body in another. She'd never forget the girl's face, and she'd never forget how she'd felt when the newly freed suspect had called her. "You killed her, you dirty bitch. I told you not to but you did it anyway, and now she's dead! You ruined her life! You ruined mine!"

You didn't get over something like that very easily, Lydia knew, unless you were hard. And Lydia wasn't hard. Competent and practical, but not hard.

She came out of the bathroom and sat on the side of the bed. Scott was watching an old black-and-white movie—ladies in heels and hats and gloves and men in suits and hats. Lots of cigarettes and clever repartee and familiar, now-dead movie stars. Surprising herself, Lydia burst into tears.

"Aw, sweetie," Scott said, sliding over next to her, arm around her bare, wet shoulders. "What's the matter?"

"That poor girl," Lydia said, weeping, "that poor kid. Not much older than Francie. And I did it. It was all my fault."

"No, it wasn't, Lydia. It was not your fault. You were only doing your job. Hush now."

She turned her tearstained face up to Scott's. "I did it again—I ruined someone else's life."

"No, you didn't. Lydia, stop it. You're a fine lawyer and you do great work. You've saved lives and kept innocent people out of jail."

She wiped her eyes with the corner of the pink towel and took a deep breath. Scott kissed the side of her neck by her ear.

"Stop punishing yourself," he said.

"I know. I try. I tell myself . . ."

"You're wonderful and smart and a good mother. A great cook, too."

She tried to smile. "You're too easy on me."

He put his arms around her and kissed her nose. "You're hard enough on yourself for both of us, sweetie."

"Hold me, Scott."

"I am, I am."

"It'll all come out all right, won't it?"

"Sure it will. You'll make it come out all right."

She kissed him and hugged him fiercely. "I like it when everyone lives happily ever after."

"They will, Lydia. You'll see to it."

Lydia could never be that close to Scott for very long before the warmth kindled in her belly. She loved his body with a passion that had surprised her from the first. Chubby Lydia, with her big glasses, pretty enough if she'd only lose some weight. A wallflower. She'd been shy and self-conscious as a teenager, and a brain in school, which was almost the worst thing you could be. No one asked her out. She took her pimply cousin to her senior prom.

College had been better, a new start where her intelligence hadn't been a drawback. But it wasn't until she'd met Scott Dunning, one of her law firm's clients, that her life had been transformed.

She'd been shocked by the strength of her physical response to him, then she'd given in and accepted it, even gloried in it. And it gave her an everlasting thrill that by day she still looked like chubby Lydia—sexless and ordinary—while at night she turned into a wanton female. It was her and Scott's secret, their shared joke on the whole world.

She felt Scott's arms on her, and she moved her lips to meet his. She sighed and kissed him deeply, their tongues mingling. He pulled at the corner of her towel, and it fell away, and his hands slipped over her, to her back, her shoulders, her breasts.

The TV movie played on, the people yattering away, the blue electronic light pulsing into the room. Lydia pulled Scott's T-shirt over his head and slipped her hand down the waistband of his pajamas. "Ah," she said, feeling him.

"Mmm," he replied.

They fell back together on the bed. The kids weren't home; they could leave the lights on, make as much noise as they liked.

He was so slim and hard, and she was so soft, like an eiderdown comforter, Scott had once told her. They fit together with perfection.

He played on her flesh, rubbing, stroking, tickling. He knew exactly where to touch her, how to time himself, and his control was extraordinary.

Scott pulled her on top of him, entered her, and she supported herself over him, sliding up and down, her insides screaming with fierce delight. Faster and faster, her breath coming in panting gasps, Scott's face transported, his eyes closed, gripping her hips.

Afterward, sweaty and drowsy, they cuddled together.

"Superwoman," Scott whispered.

"Uh-huh." Lydia smiled into the darkness. "Go to sleep, you sex slave."

"Okay, sweetie, you're the boss."

TEN

The evenings were the worst. Days Anna could handle—she was busy and preoccupied, and she could pretend that she didn't notice Mark's presence. Then again, he left her for hours sometimes while he worked on her case. But after six, when night started falling, he stuck to her like glue.

He never did anything to disturb her routine, exactly. He was just always there. An awkward male presence in her life. Although he was careful to clean up, she'd find shaving cream residue in the sink and a few dark whiskers. There were a dozen similar constant reminders of him. Some she could tolerate; others, like the gun he wore in a shoulder holster, made her cringe. As promised, he kept the thing out of her sight, but once he'd taken off his jacket and forgotten about it. She'd glared at him. He'd said, "Sorry," then taken it off and hidden it beneath his jacket.

At night, he mostly read the daily papers or watched sports on TV, keeping the volume low. Sometimes they ate dinner together; sometimes he skipped the meal. But in the morning, she'd notice a pot and a bowl or plate in the dishwasher that hadn't been there when she'd gone to bed. He kept weird hours, obviously a poor sleeper, as he'd mentioned.

She lay in bed at night, her bedroom door safely shut, and thought about him in her living room. She strained to hear him moving about, but the thick old walls of her loft muted sound and it was hard to hear him. She'd lie there and try to imagine what was going through his mind. Why was he such a bad sleeper? What demons assailed him in the dark? What had his ex-wife done when he couldn't sleep? She pictured him on her pull-out couch, tangled in the blankets, a leg, an arm, a bare chest, all covered with dark hair. She wondered how his face would feel with the dark stubble that was there in the morning before he shaved. Both rough and smooth, warm. His mustache, the way he smoothed it with his knuckle—how did it feel? The hair on his chest, black, tangled.

She'd noticed the way his wrists broadened abruptly into his hands—so male, so different from her own hands.

She couldn't stop the images that piled like an ice dam in a spring thaw, one fragment pushed by the melted water upon the other, shifting and grinding, swept under only to have another take its place—then another.

Stop it, she'd tell herself. Sure, her mind would whisper back. He was just beyond her bedroom wall.

Anna stacked her dinner plate in the dishwasher and dried her hands, glancing into the living room where Mark sat on the couch, his back to her, reading the paper.

"You sure I can't heat you up something to eat?" she asked.

He finished the sentence he was reading, then turned. "No, thanks," was all he said.

He was always like that—quiet and totally self-contained. She couldn't tell if he was merely trying to let her have her privacy, or if he truly was the silent, pensive type. The truth was, Anna had no idea what he was really like. Even yesterday, when she'd asked him about that Moran character he'd gone to check out, he'd only said something like, "Not the guy. His alibi was airtight."

Anna looked at him sitting in her living room and wondered how long she could stand this. "Well," she finally said, "I guess I'll turn in. Early call tomorrow."

He folded the paper, put it on the coffee table and stood up. "I know you're getting a little tired of this," he said, "but I've got a few questions. It'll only take a couple of minutes."

Anna sighed. "Okay," she said, "but you're right. I'm real tired of this whole thing. For all we know, he isn't even around anymore. It's been days . . ."

"He's around, Anna," Mark said in a quiet voice, "he's around. And I'll guarantee he knows I'm here. If he's got any sense at all, he's probably figured I've got a trace on your phone, too. Oh, believe me, our pal is just biding his time. Now, about those questions."

"Sure," she said. "Sure."

He asked her at least a dozen things he'd asked before, as if she might suddenly recall something of profound importance. Of course, she didn't, and she found herself snapping at him.

"Are you sure there isn't someone you're forgetting, someone you just went to dinner or a movie with? Someone Monica fixed you up with? Maybe you went skiing last spring and—"

"No," Anna interrupted sharply. "I've told you everything. My God, I've practically given you a blow-by-blow description of every minute of my life." She glared at him, her nerves raw. "I'm surprised you haven't asked who I've slept with in the last year."

Mark returned her stare coolly. "Who you had sex with is irrelevant."

"Really?" she asked, surprised.

"Really. A man can become obsessed without sex. Sometimes even more so. Stalkers are often impotent."

She made an annoyed gesture. "What about you?" she said. "You sit here night after night and grill me about *my* life. Let's talk about you."

He folded his arms and stared at her. "I'm not the one being stalked. You don't need to know anything about me."

"You pulled this before. This time I'm not accepting that excuse."

He looked cornered and grumbled something under his breath.

"Come on," she said, "I warned you I'd ask a thousand questions. At least tell me where you're from."

"I'm a native. Born and raised in Denver. I have a married brother and sister. They moved away because of jobs. My folks retired to the desert. We all try to see each other at Christmas."

"And you've just been married the one time?" she said.

"That's right."

"Pay child support and all that?"

"Sure."

Anna looked at her lap, then up again, scanning his face. "Did you run around on her? Is that why you got a divorce?"

"Whoa," he said. "Now you really are getting personal."

"I take it that's a yes," she said smartly.

But he shook his head. "Actually, I never ran around on Jenn. The divorce was typical for a cop—I wasn't home enough to be the husband and father she expected."

"That's . . . sad," she said.

"Yeah, I suppose it is."

"So is there anyone now?"

"No."

"But you must know women—you know, from your job."

"Oh, I know plenty of women," he said. "Hookers, junkies, barflies." He shrugged and, infuriatingly, she could see the hint of a smile on his lips.

"Some life," she said.

"Yes, isn't it."

Again, Anna looked at her lap. "Will you tell me the truth about something?" she asked.

"Maybe."

"Did you . . . I mean . . ."

"Plant that evidence?" he finished for her.

"Yes." She looked up.

"What do *you* think?"

"That you're capable of it. You're . . . a hard man, Mark Righter. You're cynical. Sure, I think you could have done it."

"And how do you feel about that?" he asked in a neutral tone.

"I don't know," Anna said slowly. "I guess if you did what had to be done to put that horrible man behind bars, well, I honestly can't argue with it. No woman in Denver could. Even Monica thinks you're some sort of hero. So do most women."

"And you?" he asked.

She shrugged, trying to look disinterested. The truth was, she, too, believed he was a hero. A dark hero, perhaps, but someone a woman could count on. And beneath that exterior, she could sometimes see the shadow of someone in a lot of pain and need. But she could never get close enough to find out what it was before the shadow disappeared. It was frustrating.

She looked at him and felt a warmth spread up her neck and into her cheeks. He was waiting for an answer, studying her. "Do I think you're a hero?" she finally said. "Actually, I don't know who you are. I think you do an excellent job of covering up who you are and what you really feel."

"You got me there, Anna," he said and turned back to the couch and his paper.

Anna looked at him, then went into her bedroom and closed the door. She later heard him use the bathroom and make a couple of phone calls. His voice was low, but as she switched off her bedside lamp, she could hear part of his end of the conversation.

"I know, Jennifer, but it's a job. Yeah. And at least I won't be late with the payments for the kids." There was a pause. "Okay, all right, let's not argue. The fact is, unless I finish this job, I can't keep the kids overnight after the game." Another pause. "I'm sorry, Jenn. It's been a rough couple of months." Anna couldn't hear what he was saying for a time, but she did catch his last words. "No," Mark said, "there's not a chance in hell I'm coming to the wedding. I don't care what the kids think. Tell them whatever you want. I'm not made of steel."

Oh, yes, you are, Anna thought, but she caught herself. He might be the toughest guy she'd ever been around, but there was something under that hard-edged surface. There had to be; he couldn't sleep at night.

She closed her eyes and could just barely hear him moving around the kitchen. In the background, the television was on low. He ran some water in the sink. Shut it off. As she started to drift into sleep, she had one last waking thought: Despite how much he irritated her, when Mark was close like this, just a few feet away, there was nothing in the world she had to fear.

Mark was awakened early the following morning by the front-door buzzer. He got up, disoriented, tugged on a pair of sweats over his underwear and padded groggily to the door. He pressed the button to find out who it was. Monica's voice came over the intercom. "Somebody let me in, will you?"

He buzzed her in, then ran a hand through his hair and tried to shake off the cobwebs as he became aware of water running in the bathroom—Anna in the shower. The smell of freshly brewed coffee emanated from the kitchen. Coffee. God, he needed a fix.

But first he let Monica in.

"Oh, my, look at you," Anna's partner said as she swept in, her arms full of books of wallpaper samples. She dumped them on Anna's worktable and turned. "Alarm isn't working?"

"Anna didn't say how early 'early' was. I think I just got to sleep." He headed to the kitchen and found the coffee mugs. He held up the pot. "Want a cup?"

"No, I've already filled up today."

He poured himself a cup and took a big drink, eyeing her over the rim. A real good-looking woman, he thought again. Long limbs and plenty of spunk.

He put the mug down. "You two have been together a while," he remarked offhandedly.

"Sure have," she said. "Ever since the guy she was ready to marry went off and killed himself rock climbing."

"Really," Mark said.

Monica walked toward the kitchen. "Maybe I will have just a touch more caffeine."

He poured.

"We were roomies up at C.U., so I've known Anna since long before the wedding thing."

"Tell me about it," Mark said.

"Cop's curiosity?"

"Sure," he allowed.

Monica shrugged. "We were all up in Aspen. It was June and we'd just graduated. Anyway, everyone was there. A zillion Dunnings, all of Kurt's family..."

"Kurt?"

"His name was Kurt Hillman. The big event was two days away, and we were all partying like mad. You know, lunches, dinners, everyone running around with last-minute arrangements. Then Kurt decides to go rock climbing with his best man, Bill something-or-other. Anyway, Bill came back and Kurt didn't."

"What happened?"

Monica grew serious. "They were on some mountain up Independence Pass—New York Peak, I think.

A boulder slipped. Bill was above, Kurt below. He was killed instantly. Crushed."

Mark was quiet for a moment. Then he said, "And Anna?"

"You mean you haven't figured it out? A big, smart cop like you?"

"Why don't you put it into perspective for me." He heard the shower turning off and the plastic curtain rings being slid aside. Inadvertently, he glanced toward the bathroom.

Monica looked at him carefully. "She's scared shitless of relationships."

"That's blunt."

"In a nutshell, it's true. She dates, sure, and men love her. I mean, she's not exactly unattractive." Monica smiled. "But you've probably noticed."

He let it slide.

"Anyway, she's afraid of being hurt. She was broken up over Kurt for a long time.

"Sounds like she still is."

"Oh, it's not about him—it hasn't been for years. But no one wants that kind of pain, not if they can avoid it. So she avoids it."

"You make it sound easy."

"Oh, far from it. It takes all her effort to keep relationships real simple. I'll bet you guys are having a ball cooped up like this."

"Tons of fun," he said. Then the bathroom door opened, steam poured out and Anna appeared, one towel wrapped around her body, another around her head.

"Oh, hi, Monica," she said, walking toward her bedroom. "Just give me a couple of minutes." As she disappeared, Mark was left with the impression of long, shapely legs, still tanned from the summer, and smooth golden shoulders.

He felt Monica's gaze. "So," he said easily, "what about you? Never married? Scared of men?"

"*Moi?*" she asked, a slim finger pointing at her chest. "I adore men. Women scare me, but never men."

"That I can believe," he said and got up, heading toward the bathroom.

When Mark had showered and dressed, he followed them over to a job they were just beginning on the West Side for a couple named Fender. There were plenty of people around, including a hotheaded general contractor named Michaels. But the women seemed to handle him okay, so Mark took off, making Anna promise to stay there until he got back.

"Sure," she said, distracted.

"I mean it," he said, his car keys in hand. "I'll be back around lunch."

"Fine," she said, but he could hear it in her voice— she was getting fed up and slipping back into denial. People did that. Especially when their tormentors left them alone for a few days. It was all a part of the game.

He drove across a viaduct into downtown and crossed up into the Capitol Hill area. The day was cool and brisk, the humidity low. The sun was out, but a bank of clouds lay on the foothills of the Rockies. Snow, he thought. It was coming. He'd never been a winter sort of guy. There was something about the short days, the lack of light. Nature became a monochrome and his spirit tended to reach toward the spring.

He parked in front of an address he'd gotten off Monica's list. Carter, read the mailbox in front of the stately Victorian. This was it, then. Monica had jotted down the name and address, underlining the name with a note next to it—"weird son." Whatever that meant. It was a lead, though, however small. And thus far, Hoagie's computer search hadn't been much help.

He felt good to be on the hunt, doing some real detecting for a change. It was hard as hell playing bodyguard twenty-four hours a day. Frustrating. He needed to be on the move. Like now. He hadn't let himself remember over the last couple of months, but now he couldn't evade the truth—he loved being on the chase. It made him come alive, bursting with satisfaction. Yeah, it was a shoe that fit.

He walked up the porch steps and rang the bell, noticing the fresh look to the place. Nice job. There were pretty trees in the yard, which were quickly losing their leaves now that full autumn had gotten a grip.

The door opened a crack to reveal a maid. "*Sí?*" she said.

In his best street Spanish, Mark asked to see the lady of the house. He flipped open his wallet so fast that the poor girl wouldn't have known what she saw. He said, "*policía,*" in an official manner. They didn't need to know the sorry details of his life.

A few moments later, an older, very well-dressed woman came to the door. "I'm Evelyn Carter," she said briskly. "What's the trouble, Officer?"

"Detective," Mark corrected. "Detective Righter." But he made it sound like Rider in case she'd read about him in the papers.

"Go on," she said in a curt voice.

But Mark wanted to get inside. "Listen," he said, "I'd rather not talk out here. I'm undercover."

She eyed him, then opened the door wide, ushering him into the entrance hall. "Well?" she said.

"I'm afraid there have been some robberies in the area, ma'am," he began. No lie there. Her house sat around the corner from the governor's mansion. There were always robberies in Capitol Hill.

"And?" she said.

"I was wondering if you or any of your family have noticed anything strange in the neighborhood. Someone loitering, a car . . ."

"Young man," she said, "I would have called the police if I'd seen anything out of the ordinary."

"I see," he said. "I'm glad to hear it. Now, I wonder if any other member of your family is here?" He looked around and saw a photo of a young man in a silver frame on a desk near the front of the stairs. Along with half a million other men, this one fit the description of Anna's bad boy.

Mark couldn't help pushing a little. He nodded toward the photo. "Nice-looking. Your son?"

She followed Mark's gaze. "Yes, that's Kenneth."

"Is he home?"

"Kenneth is busy, Detective. I'm afraid I am, too. If you don't mind?"

Mark agreed to leave, but not before catching the barest impression of someone standing in the shadows near the upstairs railing. Kenneth, the weird son?

East Colfax Avenue was only three blocks north, and Mark drove out to the strip mall where he lived. He walked into Lil's shop and nodded at the phone. "Can I make a quick call?"

Lil was just finishing with a customer. "Where on earth have you been?" she asked, putting down the needle and dabbing at the tattoo on the man's shoulder with some cotton.

"I'm still on that job. The stalker." He went to the phone and dialed Hoagie's line at the department.

"Work," he heard Lil mutter. "Thank God."

"Ah, Hoagie," Mark said when he heard his ex-partner on the line. He turned his back to Lil. "Got a sec of computer time?"

"What's the name?" Hoagie asked.

"Carter, Kenneth."

"No middle initial?"

"Not that I know of."

"I'm searching, pal. Hold on."

Mark could hear Hoagie tapping his computer keys. "Anything yet?" he asked.

"Hold your water, partner. Nothing in this database. This guy a local yokel?"

"Yes."

"Let's try another database." A few moments later, Hoagie said, "Ah-ha."

"Yeah?"

"There's a Kenneth Carter, Capitol Hill address . . ."

"That's him."

"A little trouble as a teenager. Seems your boy has a prior as a petty thief. Broke into a neighbor's house, judging by the address. Stole some lady's stuff."

"Such as?"

"It doesn't say. All it says is ladies' articles."

"Interesting," Mark said.

"Yeah, well, it could have been some teenage girl he had a crush on, you know, and he ripped off a bra or something. Happens every day when their little dicks start twitching."

"Crude, Hoagie."

"So you've said."

"Well, thanks, I'll tuck his name away. Anything else new?"

"Nothing of interest. Oh," Hoagie said, "I take it our dinner is off."

"'Fraid so."

"Next week, when you've nailed that creep?"

"Sure," Mark said.

"Say, how's that dog of a lady doing, anyway?"

"She's starting to bark at me," Mark said and he hung up.

He spent a couple of minutes chatting with Lil. He'd missed their morning coffee klatches and could tell that she had, too.

"So it must be weird," Lil said, "sleeping in some strange woman's living room. I mean, I got that right, don't I? You *are* in her living room and not in the poor girl's bedroom?"

"Lil," Mark said, sitting casually on a corner of her cluttered reception desk, "you know how I feel about the ladies. I'm taking a real sabbatical in that area."

Lil stared at him.

"Really," he said. "Scout's honor."

"Okay, I guess I believe you," she said. "But remember, I get first crack at you, Righter—when you're ready, of course."

It was a joke between them. "I remember," Mark said lightly.

It wasn't yet noon, and Mark had to make one more stop before joining Anna. He drove directly into downtown Denver along East Colfax, cut onto Larimer and headed over to Scott Dunning's new building. He found the man near the chain-link fence surrounding the huge project. Dunning wore a hard hat and was bent over blueprints with four men.

He looked up as Mark strode over. "Good news?" he asked hopefully.

But Mark shook his head. "I'm on my way back to Anna's job. I only stopped to see if I could get a print-out on your crew. I take it they've all seen her around. I'll keep it confidential."

"You don't suspect . . . ?"

"No, no. But I'm not leaving anything to chance."

"I'll have my accountant prepare a list this afternoon," Dunning assured him. "Good luck," he added.

"By the way," Mark said before leaving, "I'm trying to figure out how this guy got Anna's unlisted number. I know you have it, but did you give it out to anyone, or did your wife?"

Dunning paused before answering. "No, I didn't give it to a soul. And I'm sure Lydia wouldn't."

"Ask her, okay?"

"You bet. I'll let you know."

"Anyone else who works for you have it? In your office, your maid? Your kids' friends?"

"No, absolutely not."

Mark thanked him and left, registering that at least two of the workmen sitting on steel girders and eating their lunches fit the description of Anna's stalker.

He got back to the West Side and the Fender house shortly after twelve. The first thing he noticed was that Monica's car was out front, but there was no Camry. He gripped the steering wheel of the Jag as he parked.

"She *what?*" he shouted at Monica inside the torn-up building.

"Take it easy," Monica said, backing up a step. "She only went to that Italian sub shop a couple of blocks away. She said she had to get out for a minute. You know. Alone. It's daytime and . . ."

Mark swore. Then he ran a hand through his dark hair and let out a breath. "Sorry. I'm not mad at you."

"Could have fooled me." They both heard a car pulling up outside. "Go easy on her," Monica said. "This has been rougher on her than you can imagine."

"Then she damn well should realize I'm trying to help her," he said grimly.

He tried to keep his cool when Anna walked in carrying a white sack. He honestly did. But then she smiled casually at him and swept past.

"I got three sandwiches," she announced. "Where do you want to sit?"

He could feel something inside him break. Normally, for weeks and months on end, Mark kept his bad temper in check. But every so often . . .

"What the hell do you think you're doing?" he bellowed.

She turned to him, looking confused.

Monica carefully slipped away.

"You heard me," he said in a tight voice.

"I went out. I went out and got sandwiches. What's the big—"

"Don't you give a damn? Don't you have any idea of the danger you're in?"

"Look, Mark," she began, "I only wanted a little time to—"

"These creeps kill, Anna, they goddamn kill!" he interrupted. "This is no game we're playing. If you can't follow orders—"

Her back went rigid. "Orders? *Orders!* Who the hell do you think you are to give me—"

"If you don't like it," he said between clenched teeth, "then, lady—"

"You're fired," she said in a cold voice. "Leave. Get out of here. I can take care of myself."

But Mark only grinned. "Sorry," he said, "but you aren't writing the checks. Your brother is."

She glared at him, then sputtered something and threw the bag of sandwiches at him. "I can't take any more of this," she cried. "I just can't. I want my life back. I can't go on like this." She strode away, her shoulders shaking.

Mark realized she was crying, but there wasn't a thing he could do about it. Damn it, he thought, *she'd* done this. He had every right to chew her out. Didn't she know he was only trying to save her life?

The day did not improve. If anything, it got worse. Monica tried to pacify both Anna and Mark but finally threw her hands in the air in frustration and quit for the day, saying, "I've never seen two more unreasonable people in my life."

Dutifully, Mark followed Anna back to LoDo at five. He was batting back and forth between anger at her and understanding—hell, he couldn't imagine being in her shoes, afraid and helpless. And when he thought that, he was overwhelmed by a fierce need to keep her safe. Damn, but this woman was driving him nuts.

They parked in the alley and walked around to the front of the building in stony silence. Anna was still so angry that she fumbled her key in the lock.

He tried to help. But she'd have none of it, shoving his hand aside.

Upstairs in her loft, the light was blinking on her machine. "Oh, God," she breathed, "not this. Not *him*. I can't take it. I just can't *do* this anymore."

He almost went to her to comfort her—just a pat or a touch. But he couldn't. He wouldn't allow it. *She* wouldn't allow it. And besides, sympathy wasn't what she wanted. He was bad at giving it, anyway.

She went into her room and closed the door, calling, "You take the messages. Please, I can't."

He stared at her door for a long moment, then turned to the blinking red light. Don't be there tonight, he thought, give the lady a break.

There were five messages. One from her sister-in-law, Lydia, reminding her about an annual autumn festival next weekend in Cherry Creek. Another from Bonnie Fender. One from Mrs. Wainwright. There was a wrong number then a man's voice—Taylor Forman, the stockbroker, Mark recalled—asking if she'd go to dinner. Tonight. The guy knew it was short notice and all, blah, blah, blah. He wanted Anna to call him and left his number in Boulder.

Mark pressed the save button then tapped on Anna's door. "Go away," she said.

He opened it slowly, certain she was going to heave something at him. But she was lying on her bed, one arm flung over her eyes.

He couldn't help noticing that her breasts pressed up against the shirt she wore and that her belly was more than flat, it was hollowed. Her hair spread out on her quilt like a fan. He was going to say something, but it stuck in his throat.

"I really want to be alone," she said in a quiet voice.

"I wanted to tell you it was all right. You might want to listen to your messages."

She finally got up and wiped her eyes, looking angry and a bit embarrassed. "Okay," she said. "Okay."

She listened to the messages, then sat down on a small wooden stool next to the phone stand and dialed the Boulder number. Mark went into the kitchen and took a beer from the refrigerator, popping the can open with his thumb. It was impossible not to hear her end of the conversation.

"Sure," she said, shifting the phone to her other ear, "I'd love to. I haven't been dressed up and out on the town for ages." A pause. "Oh, I'll fill you in. It's pretty gruesome." Another pause. "Me, too. I've missed you. See you soon." She hung up.

"Anna—"

"I'm going out," she cut him off. "Period. I'm going to shower and get decked out and have a normal evening. You can't stop me." She stood up and her eyes met his. "I'll be fine. Taylor Forman the *Third*," she said with a laugh, "is perfectly capable of handling anything that might come up."

"Of course he is," Mark said levelly.

She disappeared to dress, and he found himself wandering around her loft aimlessly, troubled. Taylor Forman. Uh-huh. Maybe the guy had a black belt and carried a gun. Maybe he could protect Anna in a pinch. Yeah, right.

Mark found himself studying a photo on the wall over Anna's desk. Anna and Monica, in ski outfits, smiling and red-cheeked. The jagged Rockies as a backdrop.

He stared at the picture for a long time, then he straightened, switching his eyes away and putting his mind back on the business at hand. The stalker.

Almost an hour later, Anna emerged from her bedroom a transformed woman. No more sweatshirt and jeans and hastily swept-up hair. Anna Dunning, decorator, victim of a nut case, was now a lady about to go on a real date.

Despite himself, Mark gave her a thorough assessment. She looked beautiful and a little funky in a calf-length print skirt and a long black sweater. She wore soft black leather boots and gold loop earrings that glinted when she turned her head. Her bangs lay feathered on her forehead and the rest of her hair fell in a shimmering dark curtain.

An irresistible urge grasped Mark—he wanted to run a thumb down her white neck, beneath her hair and feel the smoothness. He wanted to lean close and breathe in her scent, taste her skin with the tip of his tongue. He loved the way the skirt swirled around her legs and the sleeves of the sweater hung over her hands. Oh, God, he was going nuts.

"You look nice," came out of his mouth, and he was surprised at how normal he sounded.

"I feel great," she said, digging in her closet and coming up with an oversize, long black wool coat and a long red wool scarf. "I'd forgotten how good it feels to be human."

Mark was sitting on the couch, the newspaper spread out on the coffee table. He'd had an hour to think about trying to dissuade her from going out, but he could see there was no way that was going to fly.

"You aren't still mad, are you?" she asked, and she smiled at him. A whole new woman—perhaps the woman she used to be before her stalker came along.

Mark raised his eyes to hers. "I'm not angry. I'm concerned."

"Don't be. I'll be perfectly fine. Really. And I *am* sorry about today."

"It's okay."

"Listen," she said. "When Taylor rings, I'm going to meet him downstairs. I . . . well, it might be awkward, you know."

"Sure," Mark said.

"And I'll be fine. Really." The buzzer rang. "Oh, it's him." She smiled again. "I'll, ah, be back soon. Just a few hours."

"Fine." Mark returned to his paper.

She closed the door behind her and he was on his feet in a moment, grabbing his jacket. There wasn't a chance in hell he was going to let her go out alone with some stockbroker from Boulder who probably couldn't fight his way out of a paper sack. He felt like an ass as he went down the steps, out the back door and into the alley but, damn it, if anything happened to her . . .

He followed Forman's car, a white, 500 series BMW, as it crossed town then took an entrance ramp onto Interstate 25. Where were they going to dinner, Mark wondered, Colorado Springs?

But the BMW's right blinker went on just before Hampden, and Mark immediately guessed their destination: the Denver Seafood House. Nice spot. Jennifer had always liked it.

He was right. The BMW pulled into the shopping center near the interstate exit and parked. The restaurant was at the far end of the parking lot, busy as always.

Mark was careful to park his Jag in a darkened area several rows away from the BMW. He still felt like an idiot, stalking Anna himself. But he wasn't willing to risk her being accosted by her tormentor. The jerk had always approached her after dark. It was too dangerous a situation to leave in the hands of Taylor Forman.

He watched Anna and Forman cross the asphalt to the entrance of the seafood restaurant. Forman had a hand at the small of her back. They disappeared inside. Mark got out of the car, stretched and eyed the parking lot. There were a lot of people coming and going at this hour. There was a big Super Savings grocery store in the shopping center and plenty of folks were pulling in and out of parking spaces.

He tried to study them all, especially anyone entering the restaurant. Mostly, there were couples and families, but every so often a guy would go in alone. No one particularly fit the description of Anna's stalker, though. Mark hadn't really expected anyone to follow her here, especially when she was on a date, but you never knew. Once in a while these crazies went berserk and stormed a crowded place, gun in hand. You couldn't predict what was going to push their buttons.

Anna and Forman were inside for almost two hours. It was cold outside and Mark was hungry. He thought about darting into the grocery store and getting some chips or something, but he didn't want to risk missing them leave.

When they did finally come out, they both looked happy. Forman held the passenger door for Anna and leaned close to her ear before she got in, saying something. She laughed, the bright overhead light near their car shining in her hair as it swung.

He followed them back toward downtown Denver and LoDo, keeping his distance, his stomach growling.

Despite his weary agitation, Mark was on alert as he watched Forman and Anna walk to her door. No one was on the street, except those two, at least no one that Mark could see. He stood by the far corner of her building, studying the parked cars and the dark windows of the building across from hers. He could be out here. He probably was. And there was the happy, oblivious couple. Mark glanced at them. Jesus, Forman was putting a move on her, so obvious it was laughable. Anna had to know it; maybe she'd even invited it. They kissed, and Forman's hand went to the back of her neck, their bodies pressed together.

Cute, Mark thought, looking away.

He wondered what the stalker thought about it from his hidden spot. Mark could almost sense his rage, his helplessness. Dumb, Anna, he thought, the creep could go over the edge any moment.

Nothing happened, though, and in a minute or two Anna apparently said good-night and let herself into her building. Forman stood there for a couple of seconds, then he went back to his car. Mark waited outside, watching. From his place in the shadows, he scanned the street again, straining his eyes to catch any movement, a black shadow gathering against the darkness. He strained his ears, listening, but there were only the normal traffic sounds and faint music from somewhere.

But the stalker was out there, close. Every fiber of Mark knew it, felt it. The hair on his arms was raised. He had a sense, a sixth sense, that he often laughed at in broad daylight, but at night on the city streets, he *knew.*

What are you thinking? he silently asked the stalker. Who are you? His breath froze on the cold air as he waited, but there was no answer. I'll get you, he promised. You crazy sucker, I'll get you.

He stepped around the corner of the building and used his key to open the outside door. He could feel eyes on his back, as if he were in a hunter's cross hairs, and it made him tense up. Oh, yes, he was out there.

Upstairs, looking bewildered, Anna was standing in the middle of her loft, her coat dangling from one hand.

"Where *were* you?" she demanded. "I thought, well, I thought something had happened. I didn't know what to think."

"Good of you to be concerned," he said, tossing his jacket on the couch. "Were you worried about me or worried about yourself?"

"I—"

But he cut her off cold. "You realize," he said tightly, "that your stalker pal's outside right now. He caught that act out front."

"Act?"

"The kiss, Anna."

She looked at him blankly for a long moment, then her expression darkened.

"If you set him off," Mark continued, "if he loses his cool, he'll be ten times more dangerous than either of us can imagine."

She let out a ragged breath.

"My God," she said, "you followed us."

He stared at her, then shrugged.

"You son of a bitch," she said. She turned on her heels and walked to her bedroom, slamming the door.

For a minute, he stared after her. Finally, he turned away, saying under his breath, "Good night to you, too, Anna," and went to the kitchen, opened the door to the fridge and began searching.

The Hunter couldn't get his breath. He felt as if a hand was squeezing his chest as he stood across the street from her building and stared at the blinds drawn over her windows.

He had an erection, a rare experience for him. Normally, only the pleading of a woman in fear could arouse him. But Anna had this effect on him, ever since the first moment he'd laid eyes on her.

The scene of her kissing that man played like a broken record over and over in his head. Then she'd gone up to her loft and *he* had followed, that big, dark cop. She was screwing him right now, the Hunter knew, her tanned legs wrapped around his thighs. Two men in one night. The whore.

The hand squeezed his chest more tightly and his erection grew steel-hard. He'd make that cop pay. Hurt him so bad he'd want to crawl in a hole and die. Then it would be Anna's turn. He'd keep her alive for a very long time. Some of them could live with the pain and fear for weeks. Anna would be the prize. He'd bet she'd make it for months if he were careful.

He stared at the window, the images of her betrayal with those men beating in his head. Soon, he thought. Real soon the snow was going to fall and work would shut down. Soon. And then the Hunter would be at his best, his strongest. Come quickly, winter, he thought, come quickly.

ELEVEN

A noise woke Anna up. It had taken her a long time
to fall asleep, to let the anger bleed out of her veins
until she could relax. And now she was wide-awake,
her bedside clock reading 3:52 a.m. She lay there for
a moment, wondering what had woken her up. Had
she really heard something? Her skin prickled and her
heart bumped against her breastbone.

It came again, a low groan, full of frustration and
pain. Anna slipped out of bed and tiptoed across her
bedroom. She could see a bar of light under her door.
Oh, my God, she thought, someone was out there.
Mark? Where was Mark?

She fought the urge to hide in her room, to cover her
eyes and wait. She couldn't do that. Putting her hand
on the doorknob, she twisted it very, very slowly, letting the door swing back toward her until the light
spilled in, making her blink.

She peered into the living room, cold with dread.
Her line of vision showed nothing but the far wall and
the windows. She stepped into the room a little farther.

Mark was sitting in the middle of the sleeper sofa, sheet twisted around his waist, dark, tousled head bowed in his hands. The lamp next to the couch was on, shining in a pale circle on the bed, the floor, the back of the couch, Mark's bare torso.

Anna closed her eyes in abject relief and drew in a breath. He must have heard her, because he pulled his head from his hands and swiveled to face her.

"I . . . I heard something," she said.

"Go back to bed, Anna."

"Are you all right? I heard something and I thought . . . I was scared to death."

"I'm fine. Get some sleep."

"Was that you?" she asked. "The sound?"

"Yeah. Sorry I woke you."

"Did you have a nightmare or something?"

"A dream, just a dream."

She stepped into the circle of light. "I thought it was . . ."

"It wasn't."

"Do you have these dreams often? I mean, should I plan on getting used to them?"

"Go to bed, Anna," he said tiredly. "It's four o'clock in the morning."

"Do you want to talk about it?" she asked.

He shot her a scathing look.

"Oh, I forgot," she said, "you're the man of steel. Next time I hear a ghastly moan, I'll ignore it."

He ran a hand through his already mussed hair until it stood on end. "I said I was sorry. It won't happen again."

"Fine," she said. She went back into her room, closing the door with elaborate care.

It was hard for her to fall asleep again. Leftover fear and irritation and a kind of reluctant curiosity vied with one another in her head. The last image she saw before finally drifting off was of Mark sitting there in the half light, his face dark with a five-o'clock shadow, his eyes deep pools of blackness, his strong arms folded across his torso, smooth and brown with a mat of black hair on his chest. A vivid image.

The next morning, breakfast was a disaster. Mark was prickly and defensive, and he looked as if he hadn't slept at all. Anna was filled with an unreasoning, unfocused annoyance.

"Maybe even the stalker's in a better mood," she said pointedly.

Mark shot her a look from under his eyebrows.

Standing at her kitchen counter, she finished her toast, drank the last of her coffee and felt her claws unsheathing. It was unlike her, but Mark brought out the worst in her. She put her dishes in the sink, then turned to him very deliberately, rehearsing the words in her mind.

"If you ever," she said in a deadly monotone, "if you *ever* follow me again when I don't know it . . ."

He looked straight at her. "You'll what?"

"Just don't do it."

"Listen, Anna, I was hired to do a job, and I'm going to do it. If you think you're safe just because you're out with a guy who has some Roman numerals after his name, you're as crazy as your stalker."

"What makes *you* so special?" she asked angrily.

"Training. Experience." He shrugged. "The deal was, I told you right off, there've gotta be rules here. It's my judgment, my call. You cooperate or I'll quit."

"Fine. Quit."

He just grunted.

Still furious, she drove to the Wainwright house with Mark following. The electricians were there hanging the enormous crystal chandeliers and finishing the wiring. Mark hung around for a while, then left, telling her not to go anywhere. Those were the only words either of them spoke.

Anna waited till his Jag had driven away, then she phoned Monica, who was home doing the quarterly taxes. She spilled her guts to her partner.

"I can't stand it. I'm telling you, he's in my *face*, Monica. It's like I'm a kid. He followed Taylor and me last night, *followed* us!"

"He was jealous," Monica suggested.

"Come on! He's a pain. He doesn't even like me, for God's sake."

"Uh-huh."

"I tell you, I can't stand it anymore."

"Stand it, Anna."

"No, damn it, I'm going to get rid of him."

"Where is he now?"

"Somewhere. I don't know. And I can't leave here till he gets back."

"I'll bring you lunch, okay? And a big chocolate bar for those endorphins you're so obviously lacking today."

"*Monica.*"

"I'll be over soon. Bye."

Anna then dialed Scott's number, impatient and angry. She reached him at his office.

"Will you fire Mark Righter?" she blurted out. "It seems I can't."

"Fire him?"

"He's rude and crude and a terrible person. I can't stand him another second."

"What's he done, Anna?"

"I'll tell you what he did. He followed me on a date last night. Secretly. Followed me."

There was a moment of silence. "He must have had a reason."

"Sure, my date couldn't protect me. Only big, tough Mark Righter can do that. Scott, I'm telling you . . ."

"That's all?"

"Yes, isn't it enough?"

"And you've had no more run-ins with the stalker, no more letters or phone calls?"

"No," she said sullenly.

"And you don't think he's effective? Anna, you're sounding like a spoiled brat, and you're not normally like that."

"Don't preach to me, Scott. I want Mark Righter fired. Find a replacement for him. Ask Lydia."

"I'll do no such thing. Listen, Anna, we're not playing games here. It's not like he's a hairdresser you can change if you don't like the cut you got. This man is the best, and you'll have to make it work. You better not aggravate him, either."

"Scott," she said, "please don't make me put up with him anymore."

"Then leave Denver. Go somewhere else for a while. It's an option."

"You know I have to work. I can't do that."

"Then you're stuck with Righter."

"Oh, God." Anna hung up, seething. She was still seething, unable to concentrate on the job, when Monica arrived.

"Lunch break," Monica said, dangling a greasy bag that smelled of garlicky Chinese food.

Through mouthfuls of Kung Pao chicken and shredded pork, Anna ranted about Mark. Monica ate calmly, nodding occasionally, the perfect sounding board.

"He's rude," Anna said. "He watches sports all the time. He eats unhealthy stuff. He won't let me go anywhere. I can't bear him another minute."

Monica studied her over a forkful of food. "Methinks the lady protesteth too damn much," she said calmly.

Anna ate some chicken and peanuts, chewing angrily. "You're all against me," she said.

Monica pulled a big chocolate bar out of her purse. "Here, have some. It'll make you feel better. And by the way, you're wrong about that. We're all *for* you. We're trying to save your life. Even Mark, believe it or not."

That sobered Anna a little, and she tried to get a handle on why she was so upset. It was, she guessed, the business about Mark following her and Taylor last night. Okay, she decided, she just wouldn't accept a date again until this was over. Then he couldn't skulk around in the shadows. She thought of kissing Taylor last night, and tried to dredge up a feeling of pleasure or excitement, but she couldn't. She kept seeing Mark instead, bare skin, black curling hairs, muscles moving under his skin. Pain on his face.

Mark drove out to Aurora, taking the familiar route to his house—Jennifer's house. He wasn't looking forward to seeing Jenn, but he was hoping to catch the kids after school and there was some mail he had to pick up. He doubted Jim would be there. *He* had a job—a good job, in fact, an engineer in one of those new high-tech companies. A safe job with good pay and regular hours. Jenn must love the guy for that alone.

Every once in a while, a scene of Jenn and Jim in bed together would pop into Mark's mind, and he'd feel a jab in his gut. But he knew it was inevitable and he had to let it go.

He pulled into the familiar driveway behind her car. Good, he thought, she was home.

It always felt strange, knocking on his own door, but he forced himself to do it. He knocked, then tried the knob. Finding it open, he went in.

"Jenn? It's me, Mark. You busy?" he called, going into the living room.

She answered from the kitchen. "Hi, come on in. I'm cooking."

"Smells good," he said, entering the room.

She patted a piecrust into a pan. "Thanks. Hey, I was going to call you. I could use a little help this afternoon. Mark's got his orthodontist appointment, and I have to meet Jim at the lawyer's office, some legal stuff before the wedding. Do you think you could pick up the kids and get Mark to his appointment? And I promised to get Kelly a sweater she saw, it's in the Joslins right next to the orthodontist . . ."

"What time is his appointment?"

"Three-thirty. He's got a note to get out early. So does Kelly."

Mark hesitated, then agreed, realizing he could easily fit it in before he had to meet Anna at the Wainrights. "Okay."

"And Kelly's sweater? You can use my charge, she's got the card. Would you mind? She wants to wear it to a party this weekend."

"Yeah, I can do that."

"Great, thanks. You've lost weight, Mark. Do you ever eat meals? You want lunch?"

"Hey, you don't have to."

"I'm eating, too. No problem." She poured something into the piecrust and put it in the oven. "There. Tuna sandwich okay?"

"Sure, fine."

After lunch, he got his mail and used the phone to call Hoagie to see what info his ex-partner had dug up on the Carter boy.

"God, I hate that stuff," Jenn said, frowning, when he hung up. "That police stuff, prying into people's lives."

"I know how you feel," he said. "This isn't police business, though. It's the Dunning thing, the stalker."

"Same thing."

He could feel the familiar anger ignite inside him. She'd never understood. She took the fact of her safety for granted, but she never understood there were people putting their butts on the line every day so she could be safe.

He ran some errands then drove to the kids' middle school at three-fifteen. He always waited for them with anticipation and trepidation, as if he was afraid they'd forget him between meetings, although he saw them as much, perhaps more, now that he was unemployed. But it wasn't the same.

His son came first, running, jacket flapping, grinning when he saw the Jag. "Hi, Dad, I thought Mom would be here."

"She's busy this afternoon."

"I got an A in spelling, and Jeff Donahue didn't, and he even told me he studied harder."

"Good work," Mark replied, "I don't think I ever got an A in spelling."

He saw Kelly emerge from the door of the school and glance at the Jag with surprise.

"Where's Mom?" she asked, sliding in, jostling her brother to find their usual positions in the cramped two-seater.

"Busy."

"But she promised to get me that sweater," Kelly began.

"I know, sweetheart. We'll get it."

"Okay."

"Mom told us you have a new job," Kelly said.

"Yeah, a temporary one."

"What is it?" Mark Jr. asked.

"I guess you'd call me a guard," Mark said. He didn't like to discuss his job with the kids. Jenn didn't like it, either.

He steered through the familiar streets to the orthodontist's office, and pulled into the parking lot. "Should I come in with you?" he asked.

"No, you don't have to," Mark Jr. said. "Mom usually goes on some errand and picks me up."

"Hey, does somebody have to pay for this visit?"

"Geez, Dad," his son said, "Mom just gets a bill."

"Oh, sure." Christ, he didn't know how anything worked anymore.

Mark Jr. got out and slammed the car door.

"Okay, Dad," Kelly said, "Joslins."

The big department store was bewildering to Mark, but his daughter led him right to the sweater she wanted. She lifted it from the shelf lovingly and shook it out.

"Isn't it beautiful, Dad?"

It was blue with some kind of pattern. He couldn't see that it was any different from a million other sweaters, but Kelly liked it, so he guessed it was beautiful. "Yeah, sweetheart, it's real pretty."

"Should I try it on?"

Mark glanced at his watch. "Um, well, we've got to get your brother, and I . . ."

"It's okay. I already tried it on," she said, and Mark could tell she was a little disappointed. He'd failed her again, he realized. He loved his kids, but it seemed that he couldn't show it. No matter how hard he tried, something always went wrong. But it was getting late, and he had to get back to Anna before the workmen left for the day.

He wouldn't let Kelly put the sweater on Jennifer's charge card, though. He paid for it himself. It was the least he could do.

"Thanks, Dad," Kelly said, carrying the bag close to her chest.

Mark Jr. was waiting in front of the orthodontist's office when the Jag pulled up. When he got in, he sat on Kelly's Joslins bag.

"Careful, dummy," she said.

"Well, move over then."

"Kids," Mark warned.

"Will you go fast around that corner, Dad?" his son asked. "And hit the speed bump?"

"Only if there're no cops around."

"*You're* a cop." His son giggled.

"Was, son, *was*," Mark said.

He dropped them off at home and saw them into the house. Jennifer would be home by five, she'd said. He waved goodbye from his car and they waved back, then he backed out of the driveway and sped down the street. It was almost four-thirty, and he had a fair drive through rush-hour traffic to get to Capitol Hill. Maybe he should stop and phone Anna, tell her he'd be there soon, but after this morning . . . No, better not. She'd be snippy, and he'd get pissed off. He pressed the accelerator and the Jag shot ahead. He'd just show up, and she'd have to put up with him.

When Mark came back late that afternoon, he looked very tired. Anna decided to be civil—cool and distant, but civil. The way you'd act with a roommate you were stuck with in a college dorm, she thought, one you didn't like.

Monica had left by then, and the electricians were nearly done. The house was looking better—some of the paint was finished, and some of the wallpaper was up.

"Where did you go?" she asked out of courtesy.

"To see my kids."

"Oh." She walked around the living room, holding the upholstery sample up against the newly painted walls. "Um, were they okay?"

"Fine. I picked them up at school and drove them home. Jennifer hates them to drive in the Jag with no seat belts, but they love it."

She busied herself packing away swatches and paint chips to take home. Jennifer—his ex-wife. He had a family. She forgot that sometimes.

"I also did some other things." He ran a hand over his face tiredly. "Checked on that Carter guy. Mrs. Carter, her son. He's got a record."

"Evelyn Carter's son?"

"Yeah."

"I never saw him."

"But maybe *he* saw *you*." Mark sat on a sheet-covered chair. "And your brother's giving me a list of all his construction workers."

"Oh, how strange. Why?"

"They've seen you, right? Who knows, one of them could be a crazy."

"That's a pretty farfetched scenario."

"Yeah, sure, but the stalker's out in left field, so I have to try everything."

"Maybe he's gone. Maybe he gave up. It's been a few days..."

Mark looked up at her. "He's still there, Anna. Don't kid yourself. He's waiting. Maybe I set him back a little, but he's not dumb. He's just thinking, figuring things out."

"How do you know that?"

"Trust me, I know. I can feel him. He's out there."

"My God," she said. "You're as weird as he is."

"Yeah, that's right. What do you think makes a good cop, a good detective? We're the flip side of the criminal."

She looked at him, shaking her head. Scary, she thought. It takes a thief to catch a thief. Does it then take a killer to catch a killer?

He followed her over to the Fender house later that evening. The couple had accepted Monica's estimate, and now Anna had to refigure the measurements for the Sheetrock in the turret rooms.

"I'll only be a few minutes," Anna told him on the sidewalk in front of the Fenders'. "You can wait out here if you want."

But, of course, he wouldn't. He collected the daily paper—the sports section, naturally—from the front seat of his car and followed her inside while she found the workmen's lights and plugged them in.

"There's a couple of chairs in the kitchen," she said in the hallway. "I think the light works, too. If you want to read in there . . ."

"I'll be fine," he told her. "Go on and do your measuring. Just call if you need anything."

"Oh, I'll manage," she said, heading up the first flight of stairs.

It was dark on the second floor, and she tripped over the end of a torn-up section of old carpet. "Damn," she muttered, and she heard Mark call out from somewhere to see if she was okay. "I'm fine," she called back, her voice echoing through the halls and down the stairs.

She made her way to the third floor, feeling along the wall. Two of the lights did work, faintly illuminating the long hallway. She could see enough to measure one of the turret rooms, and the other one was identical. This was only going to take a few minutes. She went to work, stretching out her metal tape, scratching figures on a pad of notepaper.

"Six feet two and a half inches, door to window," she said aloud. "Eight feet three inches, floor to ceiling. Um. Odd height." She hummed a little, pulling the tape across the window seat. An upholstered cushion with a delicate pattern was going to look super, she thought, maybe in a pale sea green . . .

She heard Mark on the stairs at the far end of the hall, the old wood protesting under his weight.

"I'll be done in a minute," she called out from her position on her hands and knees.

No answer.

She shrugged and went on working. Then another creaking sound. Floorboards under someone's foot.

She sat up on her knees, glanced down the dim hall. "Mark?"

There was no reply.

Her heart began a heavy rhythm in her chest. "Mark?" she said again, but her voice was so weak she knew he'd never hear her.

Another creak of boards and a scratching sound, the dry shuffle of a foot. Who was it? If not Mark...who?

She knelt in the dim room, the light casting her shadow in front of her like an elongated stain, and all around her the darkness receded into corners, hemming her in.

There was another creak in the hall, closer this time, and a sound like someone breathing. Or was that the wind outside? The image filled her head, her whole body: someone breathing and moving toward her along the dark hall. "Oh, God," she moaned. It was *him*. He'd gotten inside, past Mark, he'd killed Mark, he was coming for her . . .

She couldn't move. She crouched there, paralyzed, her heart leaping, her breath frozen in her chest. She was trapped in that room with no way out, and *he* was coming.

"Mark," she tried, but it came out as a dry click, another moan. Mark couldn't hear, if he was even . . .

The lights in the hall flickered, once, twice, and then there was only blackness. A terrible, breathless blackness.

She must have made some noise. She wasn't sure, but something inside her burst, and she bolted to her feet and ran, wildly and blindly, staggering down the black hall past all the empty rooms. Down the stairs, bouncing off the walls, nausea rising like a scream in her throat. Down to the second floor, still stumbling, feeling her way, blinded, thumping into a wall, and then down the staircase again.

She was on the first floor. It was pitch-black. Mark, she thought, groping for the front door, Mark! But no sound came.

And then she heard swearing. Mark's voice?

"Anna? Damn it, Anna, where are you?"

"Mark?" she got out in a huge gasp.

"I'm right here. Damn lights went out."

She careened off him in the darkness. "Mark," she gasped again, "were you, did you come upstairs? Did you ..."

"No," he said. "I was trying to find a breaker box. Why?"

A light came on, startling her. It was the weak beam of the flashlight she'd left on the table. Mark held it and swept the room, washing over her.

"I heard ... I swear, someone was upstairs," she panted.

The flashlight beam stopped and fixed her. "Did you *see* anyone?" he asked. *"Did you?"*

"I ... no, I didn't ... I ..."

"Anna, the door's locked from the inside, and I was here the whole time."

"I know," she breathed, "I know."

"Do you want me to go up there and look?"

"No. There couldn't have been anyone, I know that. It's just these old houses, they make noises."

"Yeah."

"I'm just, I guess I'm just a little . . . nervous."

He looked at her carefully. "You okay?"

"Sure," she said. "Sure I am. I got a little spooked, that's all." She even managed a small laugh. "Silly me."

"Uh-huh," he said. "Silly you."

They left Fender's Folly and walked down the sidewalk. Anna shuddered. She had a desperately strong urge to turn around and look back at the house, to search all the blankly staring windows. Because she knew, she just knew, there'd be a face staring out of one of them. Looking down, watching her.

She kept herself from doing it, though, and continued walking. She realized Mark was holding her arm above the elbow, his hand firm and warm. She looked down at his hand, then up at his face. He was studying her.

"You're sure you're okay? Can you drive?" he asked.

"I'm fine. I'm okay."

He let go of her arm, still watching her. She almost staggered when his support was gone, but she held herself rigid and fumbled for her car keys in her backpack.

Mark followed her home and parked next to her in the alley. Anna had tried to calm herself; she'd even grown angry with herself for being so stupid. There hadn't been anyone in the house.

She had to admit one thing, though. Thank God Mark had been there. Maybe it wasn't such a bad idea to have him around. Maybe she'd have to swallow her pride and independence—for a while.

She unlocked the front door to her building, Mark looming right behind her, and they went inside. She was reaching for her mailbox when she saw something that made her stop.

There was a white envelope wedged into the crack between her mailbox and her neighbor's.

"Mark," she said, her throat dry.

He stepped swiftly up to the bank of mailboxes and took the letter by the corner. "No stamp," he said. "It has your name on it."

"Oh, no," she said faintly.

"He got in here," Mark said grimly. "He got someone to buzz him in."

"No," she whispered, staring at the plain white envelope with her name typewritten on it. "I can't take anymore."

Mark eyed her, his expression unreadable. She looked in horror at the envelope in his hand, then her eyes lifted back to his face.

"Earlier today you wanted to fire me," he said. "Sure you don't want to reconsider?"

She looked at him, defeated, and said nothing.

"I think I'll stick around."

Anna barely remembered getting upstairs. She went into the bathroom and splashed her face with water, trying to calm down. He might have been inside the Fender house. He'd for sure been in this building, *in her building*. Right outside her door, with only a couple of inches of wood between her and him.

When she came out, Mark was opening the letter, very carefully prying up the flap, trying not to contaminate it. She waited, watching him from across the room, her heart squeezed with fear. It was as if her few days of respite had never existed.

He had it open and was pulling out a piece of folded white paper. Then he held it up to the light by a corner, his big hands remarkably steady. "No watermark, probably cheap copy paper or something."

She saw that there was typing on it. "What does it say?" she dared to ask, but he didn't answer. He had the note spread out on the counter, reading it. It took maybe thirty seconds, but it seemed like a very long time to Anna. She watched his eyes scan the lines and saw his face darken, a subtle change of expression. He was turning dangerous right there before her eyes, and she was suddenly afraid of him.

"Let me see it," she said.

"No."

"Yes, I want to see it."

"Do you really?"

"Yes," she whispered.

She approached slowly, and Mark stepped back.

"Don't touch it, don't touch anything," he warned. "I want the letter to go to the police clean."

She stood over the white page, and it blurred in front of her eyes for a moment before she focused. Typing, neat lines of typing. No greeting, no signature. She shuddered again and read.

You are indecent and you took that man into your home, Anna. What do you do with him? He's there with you right now, isn't he? And I know who he is. He's the cop that was in that trial. I even know his name. Is he touching you now, you whore? You're spoiled goods. I thought at first you were different, but you're just like all the rest, lying, cheating, disgusting. Now you deserve to die, Anna, because you betrayed me.

She could practically hear his voice screaming at her from the paper. Her eyes flew up to meet Mark's and she said, "Oh God, he'll do it, won't he? He'll really try to kill me."

Lil Martinelli checked her appointment book: Steven Hurst, 6:00 p.m. She had ten minutes. She went to the bathroom in the back of her shop, then washed her hands carefully and returned out front to wait for the client.

She was proud of her shop and her reputation. Lil's Tattoo Parlor. She'd opened it with the money her ex-husband had settled on her, which hadn't really been enough. Nevertheless, she'd bought the entire building on East Colfax. It wasn't a very good neighborhood, but it was perfect for a tattoo business.

She lived in a cozy room right off the shop. She didn't need much in the way of space or furniture because she spent most of her time in the shop anyway. Weekends, all sorts of late hours. People often wanted tattoos on the spur of the moment, and she was there for them.

A few years earlier, she'd had the upstairs remodeled and rented it out, most recently to Mark Righter. She liked having him close by. It wasn't just for protection, either. No, it was a whole lot more. And that made Lil sad. Mark was unattainable, at least for her. For starters, there was the age difference—thirteen years, at least—and that certainly would have factored in if he'd ever considered her as more than a friend, which he hadn't. But even taking that into account, Lil knew he'd never look at her *that* way. They were way too much alike: streetwise, cynical, realists to the core. Mark would always be attracted to an opposite, an innocent, like Jennifer had been. A woman who was raised "nicely," who knew how to behave at a PTA meeting and how to dress just so. Oh, she'd have to have something special about her, some moxie, to attract Mark, but she'd also have to need him real bad. Once, Lil had fit that role. But then her scars had healed over, and she'd grown even tougher, and she'd known that it was never going to happen between them. The knowledge hurt, a lot, but she'd never let him glimpse it, *ever*. It would kill her if he found out how she really felt. After all, she had her pride. And she did have a portion of Mark Righter. She had his friendship.

Lil straightened the small waiting area, restacking magazines and emptying the ashtray, and realized she missed Mark now that he was working. Jeez, she hadn't seen him for days. She missed the morning-coffee talk, the easy companionship. Even Barry of Barry's Bagels asked about Mark.

"He's working," Lil had told him. "Finally got a job."

"Doing what?" Barry asked.

"Bodyguard for some chick in LoDo."

"Huh," Barry said as he counted out her change.

If Lil acknowledged her downfalls—she'd married a loser, would never have kids, would never be a suburban housewife *and* she was in the throes of menopause—at least there was one area in which she knew she excelled. She considered herself a true artist. A damn good one. She adhered carefully to every rule of good health, too, using latex gloves, new needles for each and every client, always cleaning and disinfecting and sterilizing. And she did it all right in front of the clients, so they could see how careful she was. She had the usual tattoos to choose from: roses and hearts and dragons and all that stuff. She also had designs she'd dreamed up herself, and certain people, those of discriminating tastes, chose her originals.

Some were cartoons of her own creation, some were animals, flowers, still-life pictures. Some were even copies of famous paintings, or at least elements of famous paintings. Her personal favorites were Toulouse-Lautrec's women of Montmartre. Very strong stuff.

She'd done a rendering of one of the women—Jane Avril—on a man's ass once, and he'd liked it so much he'd come back for more. That had been a nice affair, for as long as it lasted.

The bell over the door finally jingled, and her six o'clock client came in. He was of medium height and a little heavy, not a physical type. He had brown hair and dark eyes set too close together. His clothes were good—khakis and a sweater and a tasteful leather jacket.

"You're Lil?" he said. "Lil Martinelli?"

"That's me. And you, I see, are Steven Hurst. Nice to meetcha, Steve."

"I'd like a tattoo."

"Well, I didn't think you were here for a root canal."

He cracked a smile. Nervous. But then, lots of guys were nervous the first time.

"Where do you want it?" Lil asked.

"Well, not too noticeable, you know. I thought on my shoulder, maybe."

"Okay, we'll be subtle. On the back of your shoulder or the biceps?"

"The back, I guess."

"Okay. Do you know what you want, what picture?"

"Uh, no, something small."

"Well, here, look through my collection. They're life-size. Colors can be changed."

It didn't take Steve long. He scanned the pictures on Lil's walls and pointed to one: a rattlesnake, coiled and raised, fangs showing. It was a small one, only an inch and a half high.

"Nice," Lil said. "You sure that's it?"

"I'm sure. How long will it take?"

"Hour or so. It'll cost around seventy-five, eighty bucks."

"That's fine."

"Okay, Steve, take your sweater off. You'll sit here. I can draw the curtain if you want." And she went into her routine, setting the customer at ease, preparing her equipment, putting her phone on the answering machine so she wouldn't be disturbed.

She sketched the snake on his shoulder and showed it to him in a mirror. Yes, that's where he wanted it. Then she started in on the real work.

For the first few minutes Steve was quiet. Then he started relaxing and talking, asking all sorts of things—how long she'd been here, what were the most popular tattoos, how many customers. He told her how his girlfriend wanted him to get the tattoo because they really turned her on.

Lil kept up her end of the conversation, remaining friendly. She perked up her ears when Steve said he'd read in the papers that she had a famous renter upstairs. He said it slyly, and she wondered if he'd chosen her because of that one fact.

"Mark Righter," he said, "the ex-cop, he lives up-stairs, I read somewhere."

"Yeah, he does."

"He got a bum rap, that guy, didn't he?"

"He sure did."

"You think he really planted that evidence?" Steve's voice was avid.

"Nope, he didn't." Lil would defend Mark till her dying breath; it wasn't because of her secret feelings, either. Hell, she owed Mark. Big time.

"That's what I always tell people," Steve said. "I mean, he didn't have to, did he? There was plenty of other incriminating evidence, right?"

"That's right, and even if there hadn't been, Mark Righter wouldn't have planted evidence. He's a stand-up guy."

"You know him real well?"

"Pretty well, pretty darn well." She started doing the rattles on the snake's tail. "Don't move now."

"Scary-looking guy," Steve said.

"Aw, he's a pussycat. Looks don't mean a thing."

"He is, really? He's a nice guy?"

"The best friend you could have. If Mark's your friend, he'd do anything for you."

"Really."

"Don't say it like that. It's true. I know."

"Pretty hard to believe that. He looks mean. Ouch!"

"Listen, Steve, Mark Righter did me a favor once that I'll never be able to pay him back for. He saved my life." She dabbed away blood from his skin.

"No shit."

Later, Lil would kick herself in the butt for talking so much, but at the time she was concentrating on her artistry, not the conversation. "It was two years ago, and I knew Mark kind of casually at the time," she said. "Met him when he came in here looking for information on some druggies. I sort of helped him out, you know what I mean? Hold still now. Anyhow, I got in some trouble with a biker. He was drunk and I was doing a tattoo on him, and he turned mean.

"He started slapping me around. A big guy, crazy as hell. I got to the phone, called 911, then he dragged me off. To make a long story short, Mark Righter was in the area and took the call. He came in here, charged in like a bull and beat the living crap out of the biker. Saved my butt."

"That's quite a story."

"Yeah, isn't it? And that's not all. He came to the hospital to visit me. I was in there for a week, and he came three times. Just to see how I was."

"So he really is a nice guy."

"Sure is. And it's a sin and a shame the way he's been treated. If it was up to me, he'd get every commendation there is, he'd be chief of police. And I'll tell you something else, too. He's a good father, worries about his kids. It kills him not to see them more. Hold still. I'm doing a real delicate part."

"What happened between him and his wife?"

"He doesn't talk much. I don't really know. Who knows what goes on between a man and woman? I think she was nuts to leave him."

"Was it other women?"

"Goddamn it. No, it wasn't. He loved her. Jennifer. But she didn't have the guts to stick it out with a cop, that's all."

"You sure do know him, Lil. Got any other interesting stories?"

Lil stopped short, holding the needle up. Behind Steve's back, her eyes narrowed. "What the hell is this, the third degree?"

"No, no, just interested. I told you, Mark Righter's my hero."

"And you just happened to want a tattoo, Steve, right? And you just happened to pick *my* place?"

"Yeah, sure." His voice had an edge to it, a quiver.

"You're so full of it, it's coming out these little holes I'm poking in your skin. I can smell it, Stevie-baby. Now tell me what you really want."

"Nothing. A tattoo, that's all. Can't a guy get a tattoo?"

"You lie like a rug." She came around and stood in front of him, and when she saw his shifty eyes, she knew. "You're a goddamn sneaking lying reporter," she said to his sweating face. "Aren't you? Fishing for a story. I swear to God, you guys are worse than sharks. Can't you leave him alone?"

"I'm not a reporter," Steve said, but his words lacked conviction.

"You taping this conversation? I'll stuff it in your mouth, you little prick."

"No, what do you mean?"

"You know what I mean!"

"I have no idea. Aren't you going to finish my snake?"

Lil took a deep breath. "Give me a minute till my hands stop shaking."

"Sure."

She went around to his shoulder and started working again, concentrating, as furious at herself as she was at him. Steve didn't say a thing. His fat back was slick with sweat, though.

"Now, don't think just 'cause you're a no-good reporter I'm going to mess up my work. I have a reputation. I'm an artist, Steve. So, you'll get a good tattoo—the best. Don't you worry."

She worked on, with utter precision. When the tattoo was done, she stepped back, looked at it and nodded. Very good. Excellent. She'd done him up proud.

"You want a mirror?" she asked.

"Uh, sure, I guess so."

She held her hand mirror up at just the right angle so he could see his new tattoo in the full-length mirror in front of him. She got great pleasure at the way his eyes bugged out and his voice strangled in his throat.

There it was, a gorgeous coiled rattlesnake, its head raised—but instead of the rattler's fat cheeks, forked tongue and fangs, there was the head of an erect penis.

"That'll be fifty bucks," she said. "I'm giving you a discount."

"You're crazy," Steve yelled, his face red as a beet. "You mutilated me!"

"Pay me, Stevie-baby."

He threw some bills at her, grabbed his sweater and jacket and rushed out into the October night. But before the door shut behind him, Lil snarled at his back, "A prick for a prick, you jerk."

TWELVE

Mark's day got off to a bad start. Waking him from another lousy night's sleep, Anna announced that he had a call.

She put the phone down next to him on the mattress. "It's your landlady," she said, and she padded off to the bathroom.

It was at least a minute before Mark could clear the cobwebs. He sat up, dragged a hand through his hair and picked up the receiver. "Lil? What in God's name...?"

It took at least five minutes for Lil to tell him the whole story.

"Um," Mark said.

"I have no idea who that jerk writes for, but I'll guarantee he's a reporter. I'm so stupid, Mark, how could I have fallen for it?"

He told her it wasn't her fault. "Some people are just born to snoop and write about it. I'm used to it, Lil, don't sweat it."

"Yeah, well," she said, "his mother should have had an abortion."

Mark laughed groggily. "That's nice, Lil. But anyway, not to worry. Maybe he won't even write it up."

Then she told him what else she'd done—the snake's head.

Mark whistled under his breath.

"I know," Lil said. "I probably made it way worse."

"Guess that guy won't forget *you* too soon," Mark said.

"Are you mad at me? God, Mark, I'm really sorry, me and my big mouth."

"Nah, don't worry, Lil. What can he say I haven't already read about myself?"

"I . . . um, I told him about the guy you beat up, and me in the hospital."

Mark didn't say anything.

"Mark? You mad? Hey, I didn't say anything bad about you."

"It's okay, Lil." She sounded so worried, so upset. And he knew she meant well. Ah, what the hell.

"I'm really sorry, Mark," she repeated.

"Forget it. No sweat."

"Still friends?" she asked anxiously.

Mark hung up, knowing what a liar he was. He wasn't mad at Lil, true, but the notion that he was going to be in the news again made a fist tighten in his gut.

It all came flooding back. He remembered the humiliation on the witness stand when that sick rapist's lawyers had insinuated that Mark had planted evidence. Under the rules of cross-examination, Mark had not been able to speak his mind or defend himself. And, of course, his own department had done a piss-poor job of defending Mark with the media. For two days, Mark had endured that cross-examination, sitting on the hard chair, rings of sweat on his shirt, his mouth dry. The guys at headquarters had patted him on the back. "Glad it ain't me, Righter," they'd all commiserated, and he'd laughed it off. "Ah, screw the newspapers," Mark had said. But the papers and TV had screwed *him*. They'd written up his whole life, as if there hadn't been any *real* news to write about. He'd become that hero-antihero in Denver.

His ex-wife had even called, sick of the whole thing. "Damn it, Mark, why do you always have to be in the limelight? My friends are driving me nuts, teasing me. It's hard on the kids at school, too. Everyone in Denver's talking about you."

Not once had Jenn sympathized. No one knew the torment he'd suffered. No one ever would. He sat in Anna's loft realizing Lil had just given a new story angle to a reporter and he felt like being sick. But who in hell could he talk to about it? Anna? Sure.

The morning did not improve. Anna was cranky, having barely slept herself. The wear and tear of this ordeal was beginning to take its toll on her, and no matter how upbeat Mark tried to be, he knew she was only going to deteriorate as the days crawled by. It was a pattern, and all the victims of stalkers followed it. He wished to God there was something he could say or do to help. But the only real solution was to stop that son of a bitch. Stop him cold. And then Anna could get on with her life.

He stayed out of her way while she finished in the bathroom and made a few phone calls. He took the opportunity to speak with her neighbors, asking each of them never to buzz anyone into the building again unless they knew exactly who it was. *Someone* had buzzed the stalker in yesterday, though no one admitted it.

Only one neighbor gave Mark any grief—a single man, one of those "me-first" types. Apparently, he thought he could take care of himself, and his fellow residents should be able to do the same.

"Don't come waking me up in the morning, buddy," the guy said at his door, "telling me what I can and can't do in my own building. I'll do what I want."

There was only one way to handle him. "Fine," Mark said, "but if anything happens to Miss Dunning, you'll answer to me. I guarantee, I'm a helluva lot meaner than you." Mark left, his point made.

Then he had to tell Anna about the next day.

"Look," he said, "I promised to take the kids to the hockey game tomorrow night. I was supposed to keep them overnight, but that's out."

"Because of me," Anna said defensively.

"Hey, Jenn's used to this kind of thing. She understands."

"I'll bet."

"So you can stay with your brother or Monica maybe, and after the game I'll pick you up." He hesitated a moment, cautious. "Or you could come with us. I bought four tickets."

She looked up, surprised. "Me? With you and your kids?"

"Why not?"

"I can think of a few reasons why not."

"It'd be different, get your mind off things."

"You don't really want me along," she said.

"I wouldn't have asked. Come on, Anna, you should know me well enough by now, I don't make politically correct gestures. You're welcome to come. I mean it."

She sighed. "Okay, anything's better than moping around Scott's, and Monica's busy with Brad."

"That's what I like about you, your enthusiasm," he said dryly.

The next hitch in an already flawed day came when Mark went to start up the Jag. Dead battery. Fortunately, Anna hadn't pulled out of her parking spot yet. He climbed into the passenger seat of her Camry and frowned.

"Damn cold weather. I'll have to pick up a new battery on the way home tonight," he said. "This one's seen its last."

"We can stop. No problem."

"And there's another errand. I don't know . . . oh, well," he said. "Maybe it won't hurt for you to see how the gears of my profession grind."

She had on sunglasses. She lifted them onto her forehead, stared at him and said, "What?"

"On your way to work, I want to drop off that letter with Hoagie. He can take it over to the lab and have it examined."

He thought Anna would protest the stop at the station. But, surprising him, she said she'd like to see where he worked. *Had* worked, she corrected.

"Why?" he asked as she pulled out of the alley.

"I don't know," she said. "I suppose it might tell me something about you."

Mark had no trouble getting them past security with visitors' passes clipped to their shirts. Everyone, of course, knew Mark, knew him and liked him. Everyone that was, but his captain.

Mark still got uptight whenever he thought about Franklin. The man could have—*should* have—stuck up for him. So Mark avoided him like the plague. It still hurt too damn much. It was only because of Anna that he was breaking his cardinal rule of not entering headquarters when Franklin was there. Yeah, she was right—his reaction to Franklin *might* tell her something about him.

Franklin spotted him the minute he entered the homicide division. "To what do we owe this honor, Righter?" Franklin asked as he strode up.

"Nice to see you, too," Mark said evenly. He introduced Anna, and he couldn't help pointing out that she was Scott Dunning's sister. "You know him," Mark said. "He's a real good friend of the mayor's."

Franklin became the perfect gentleman. Did Anna want a cup of coffee? Could he give her a tour? Mark said nothing.

Despite the circles beneath her eyes, Anna was certainly a breath of fresh air in this place. Even in jeans—which fit nice and snug—a T-shirt and a sweater draped over her shoulders, she had a certain carriage. He was very aware of the many stares in her direction. One of the detectives actually whistled. Anna took it well, smiling at him, and it was clear the young rookie fell instantly in love.

Luckily for Mark, Captain Franklin was polite and amiable. After all, Mark had Scott Dunning's sister in tow. Wouldn't want to tick off the mayor. Mark steered her over to Hoagie's desk.

"Hey," Mark said.

Hoagie dragged his eyes away from the computer screen. "Hey, yourself, partner," he began, then he saw Anna. He got to his feet. "Don't tell me."

"Anna Dunning," Mark said, "meet Howard—Hoagie—Billings."

"You son of a gun." Hoagie took her hand in his, but kept staring at Mark.

"What?" Anna asked, smiling in confusion.

"He told me you were a dog."

Anna looked at Mark and cocked her head.

Mark shrugged and gazed at his feet.

"Sit down," Hoagie said, pulling out a chair for her. She sat. "When you fire this creep," Hoagie said, "I'm next in line. I want you to promise."

Anna laughed. "Sure, okay. You want me to fire him today?"

"Now, on the spot," Hoagie said.

Mark cleared his throat. "If you two don't mind?"

He gave Hoagie the letter, which was now sealed in a clear plastic bag.

"It'll probably be clean," Hoagie said.

"I know, but it's worth a try."

"I'll take it right over to the lab myself."

"Thank you," Anna said. She stood. "And thanks for all the rest of your help. The computer searches and all that."

"Anna," he said, "I'd go to the ends of the earth for you. Just give me the word."

Again she laughed, and Mark realized he'd never really seen her laugh so openly before. Now, why didn't *he* have that effect on her?

Hoagie opened a desk drawer and produced a manila envelope with Mark's name on it. "Geez, partner, I almost forgot this. I was gonna call you today."

Mark took the envelope and lifted an eyebrow.

"It's that printout on the second list of names you gave me. And also the police shrink's report on the tapes and notes Anna gave us before you came online."

"Thanks," Mark said.

"Just don't let anyone see it," Hoagie said, grinning again at Anna. "You stop by anytime, anytime at all."

"I'll try," Anna said, smiling and shaking her head at him.

They left shortly thereafter. While Anna drove, Mark opened the envelope and took out two sheets of paper. One was the list Hoagie had printed out from Scott Dunning's work force. Hoagie had underlined three names, but only one stuck out, a guy named Rod Miller. It seemed Miller had a prior for disobeying a court restraining order on an ex-girlfriend. He'd been arrested for stalking her.

Of course, Mark thought, that had been a girlfriend. Plenty of guys just didn't know when it was over and got in trouble with the cops and courts. Still . . .

Mark recalled Anna mentioning some sort of autumn festival that would be taking place on Sunday in Cherry Creek. She'd said Scott and Lydia helped sponsor it and had invited everyone they knew, including Scott's crews. Would this Miller character be there? Mark sure hoped so, because if not, he was going to have to hunt the man down and have a chat with him.

He read the shrink's notes next. The psychiatrist hadn't had much to go on: two typed notes and one tape from Anna's answering machine. Her impression was that the stalker was highly insecure, positively despised female authority figures, like mother types, and lived as inconspicuously as possible. Probably worked manual labor. That, at least, was of interest to Mark. It fit in with the possibility that Anna's stalker was someone from a job site, hers or Scott's.

"That stuff's about the stalker, isn't it?" she asked.

"Yes," he said. "Just some notes from Hoagie. Wouldn't interest you," he lied. No point in stirring her up.

"I want to see them." Her voice held that tone he'd come to dread—dogged stubbornness.

"Anna . . ."

"I'm involved, wouldn't you say? I'm a grown-up, so stop trying to protect me from things that won't hurt me. That's not your job."

"It's really not interesting, but you can see it, sure. Not while you're driving, okay?"

"Okay," she said. Then, after a moment of silence, Mark saw her mouth curl in a smile.

"What?" he asked defensively.

"I like him," Anna said, giving Mark a sidelong glance.

"Who?"

"You know who."

"Oh, you mean Hoagie."

"Yes. Tell me about him."

So Mark did. Surprising him, she said, "I can see why he's been married three times."

"Anna, he's a dirty old man. Crude as they come."

"So? He's a very sexy old man."

"You gotta be kidding," Mark muttered.

Before they headed to Anna's job site, Mark had her drive by Evelyn Carter's house on Capitol Hill.

"What's this going to prove?" she asked.

"It might jog your memory," Mark said. "The man's name is Kenneth. The picture I saw of him fits the description of your stalker. You must have seen him at that house."

"I swear I never did. And besides, what would make you suspect him?"

Mark knew better than to try to be evasive. "His name came up on one of Hoagie's printouts."

"What did he do?"

"Petty teenage stuff. Stole some neighbor's personal things. A girl's stuff, you know."

"That's probably not uncommon, Mark. Boys will be boys."

"Yeah, well," he said, "maybe the kid brought some of his bad habits into adulthood. It's worth checking. You sure you never saw at least a picture of him?"

"I must have," she said, her brow furrowed as she pulled up to the curb in front of the Carter house. "Although I think Evelyn had everything pretty much put away or covered when we were there working."

"Think," Mark said.

Staring at the house, she said, "I am. I am thinking. I just don't remember a son. I don't . . . I don't always pay attention to people, Mark. I, well, sometimes I'm distracted or too busy, you know? It's a kind of self-ishness, I guess, or maybe it's from being a single woman living alone—you try not to make eye contact. I just don't *see* people."

Mark got out of the car and told Anna to keep an eye on the door—he was going to try to get Kenneth Carter to show his face. *If* he was even there.

Evelyn Carter came to the door. She was as rude as Mark remembered, a real sour old lady. Ignoring it, he launched into his cock-and-bull story about neighborhood robberies.

"I haven't heard of any robberies," she said coolly. "What was your name, young man?"

Young, he thought. "Rider, Detective Rider," he lied. "And the reason you haven't heard about them is that the insurance companies want it hushed up. No point advertising that this is a wealthy area."

"I see," she said.

"I wonder if your son's home," Mark ventured. "Maybe he's already at work? I'd like to check with him, too."

"Kenneth is home," she said, "but he's unavailable."

"It would just take a minute. He may have noticed something in the neighborhood. You understand."

"He didn't."

"If I could just—"

But she cut him off sharply. "Detective," she said, "my son has agoraphobia."

"Ag...?"

"Kenneth hasn't left this house in three years. He's barely left his room."

"I see," Mark said, digesting the information and realizing he'd reached a dead end on this one. He'd still check out her story, but somehow he knew this woman was telling the truth.

A few minutes later, he was back in the car. He told Anna what he'd learned.

"Wow," she said. "I *do* remember something... Right! Evelyn wouldn't let *anyone* near the third floor. She said she wasn't going to go to the expense of remodeling a bunch of rooms that were only good for storage." Anna nodded. "My God, I even recall Monica joking that the old lady probably kept dead bodies or something up there."

"Little did Monica know," Mark quipped.

Anna started up the car. "So much for the Carters," she said. "You're never going to find the stalker like this, are you? You can check these guys out till we're both blue in the face, but until he actually shows himself in broad daylight, you'll never nail him." He heard the weary, frightened edge return to her voice.

"The guy will slip up, Anna," he said. "They always do." But he was beginning to wonder. That too-familiar frustration fell around him like a shroud.

THIRTEEN

Lydia attacked the Orchid Rapist trial transcripts with her usual determination. It should have driven her family nuts, because she was studying every bit of police testimony at home. But Scott never complained. Nor did her children. Somehow she managed to juggle it all—marriage, children, career and social life. She knew that someday she'd burn out. Everyone did. She only hoped that day would wait till her kids were out of the nest.

Scott did not sound surprised when she telephoned him on his cell phone at work to cancel their lunch date. "I'm sorry, darling," she said, "but I've snagged Leland Goldman for lunch. There's something I have to run by him."

"Don't tell me," Scott said, "it's that Mark Righter thing."

"Uh-huh. But don't worry, I think I've about got it nailed."

"No kidding."

"I may have figured out just how those panties got into Jarrett Colby's apartment."

"And what are you going to do about it?" Scott asked.

Lydia sighed. "I'll cross that bridge when I come to it." Then she remembered. "Oh, and don't forget to invite the entire crew to the Octoberfest on Sunday."

"I already have."

"Oh, you are a dear," she said. "And tell them parking will be impossible anywhere near Cherry Creek. The city's blocking off a bunch of streets. I think we'll have a thousand people show up this year."

"If the weather holds."

"It'll hold. I'll make it hold," she said.

She and senior partner Leland Goldman went to lunch at the Ship's Tavern in the Brown Palace Hotel. The Tavern was not Lydia's kind of place. It was attractive in a dark, British men's club style, but it was too good-old-boy Denver for her. Lydia was not a rabid feminist, but she was still competing in a man's world, and there was just something about these stodgy men that rubbed her the wrong way.

Of course, when Leland had said, "How about the Ship's Tavern," she'd said fine.

She toted along a twenty-page section of the transcripts in her briefcase and set it on an empty chair at their table. She ordered soup and salad, trying to be a good girl; Leland ordered a roast beef sandwich and fries—big, delicious, greasy fries. Oh, well, Lydia thought, there would still be fries in the world tomorrow.

After the waitress left, Leland folded his hands on the table and smiled at her. "So," he said, his kind but shrewd blue eyes resting on her, "what on earth is so important that we couldn't do this at the office? Not that I mind having lunch with you, you know I very much enjoy it. But I must admit, I'm curious."

She started from the very beginning, reminding him of how the victim's panties had turned up at their client's apartment, how she'd seen them in a photo of the victim's place. And how, as far as the crime-scene logs were concerned, Detective Mark Righter had the opportunity to do the dirty work.

Lydia pulled the transcript pages from her brief-case. She pushed her big glasses up her nose and launched in. "I don't know if you're aware of this," she began, "but Scott has hired Mark Righter as a sort of bodyguard-detective for his sister, Anna." She went on to explain the situation.

"I didn't know," Leland said. "I'm sorry. The experience must be terrifying for your sister-in-law."

"Yes," Lydia said, "it's wearing her thin."

She continued by telling him about her suspicions, about how it had been almost too easy to point a finger in Righter's direction at the trial, and about how the knowledge that she may have overlooked something was still troubling her. "I suppose it's why I suggested to Scott that he hire Righter."

"Guilt."

"Absolutely," Lydia said.

"So you got the transcripts out."

"Yes. And I think I've found something. I want you to look at it, and then I need your advice."

Leland frowned. "Why do I think I'm not going to like this?"

Lydia smiled apologetically then stuck the pages under his nose. "I've highlighted the areas I need you to read."

Their lunch arrived and somehow, while Leland flipped through the pages, they both managed to eat. When the dishes were cleared and they were sipping coffee, he shuffled them back into a neat pile and handed them to Lydia.

"You think it was Franklin, don't you?" he said gravely.

"It could have been," she said. "As you've just read, that beat cop who was first on the murder scene couldn't remember if everyone had been logged in. He testified that he thought Captain Franklin had come by sometime only to look the scene over, because he had a press conference, but he wasn't officially on the case. No one logged him in. After all, he was the top honcho."

"True."

"Anyway, I find it a little too coincidental that Franklin also stopped by Jarrett Colby's place that same day. No security had been set up yet, and no one had really taken charge until Mark Righter and his partner got there."

"Yes," Leland said, "but the patrolmen couldn't recall anyone but Mark Righter being in Colby's apartment alone."

"That doesn't mean Franklin didn't go in. It only means that no one *noticed* him. He wasn't an investigating officer. And what was he doing there, anyway? Just looking at the building?"

"Oh, I read the pages you gave me the same as you did, Lydia. And I agree, it would appear that Franklin came and went as he pleased. Captains can do that. But why would he tamper with the evidence?"

"He, of everyone connected to the case, needed a conviction the most. He's a political animal, you know that, Leland, and he's a glutton for the press."

"Well," Leland said, "it wasn't good press when one of his detectives was accused of tampering with the evidence."

"It was a calculated risk, sure, but he guessed the rapist would be found guilty, anyway. His own record would stand—the tough-on-crime candidate. And he didn't care that he threw one of his best detectives to the wolves."

"You could have something there."

"Mark Righter always swore he was innocent. And Franklin never stood up for him. I always wondered about that. I just never considered Franklin might have done it himself."

"You know," Leland said, "this is all very interesting. But where's it leading? I mean, Lydia, you don't want to go public with this, do you? Let's face it, Jarrett Colby was guilty as hell."

"I know."

"You can't be thinking of requesting a retrial because new evidence has come to light?"

"No," Lydia said, taking off her glasses and rubbing her eyes. "Justice would certainly not be served if that man somehow got off in a new trial. My God, Leland, I have a daughter practically the same age as one of his victims."

"There you are."

"But it was wrong to hang Mark Righter out to dry."

"He quit his job on his own. My understanding is that no one forced him to leave."

"Pride."

"Yes, I'm sure."

"It would just be . . . fair if someone knew the truth. The mayor, the police commissioner, *someone*."

"No one can afford for this truth to come out, Lydia."

"I realize that. But maybe the score could be evened up just a little."

She thought about that all afternoon and into the evening. She knew she could go to either the mayor or the chief of police with her suspicions. And maybe someone would contact Righter and say, "Hey, you might have taken a bum rap, but life goes on. This is not a perfect world. Come back to work. In a year or two, no one will even remember your name in connection with Colby's trial."

She *could* start the ball rolling. On the other hand, hadn't she already interfered in his life enough?

Anna was beginning to think that maybe she should just go away for a while and hide, let the creep who was destroying her life find someone else to torment.

She approached Monica about it after work. "If this maniac isn't caught soon," she said, "I'm thinking I may go away for a time."

Monica looked aghast. "Never," she said harshly. "If you do that, if you even *think* that, he's won. You'll live in fear the rest of your life. Every time someone even says boo to you, you'll jump out of your skin."

"At least I'll be alive."

"You've got Mark. He *will* find out who this guy is."

"You can't know that."

"I do know it, though. I know it in my gut, Anna, he'll get him."

Anna locked the door to the Wainwright house and glanced at Mark, who was waiting for her by her car.

She turned back to Monica. "And what if you're both wrong? What if that creep gets me first?" she asked, so tired, so sick of the constant fear.

"It's going to work out," Monica said, "you'll see." She put her arm around Anna's shoulders and walked her down the path.

"I hope to God you're right."

She let Mark drive. Normally, she loved driving, darting in and out of traffic, pushing the limits. But this evening she felt only defeat. Defeat and that horrible, shaky, heavy feeling of not having had a real night's sleep in a very long time.

They stopped on the way home to pick up a new battery for Mark's Jag, and he groused about the price as he lifted it into the trunk of her car. He climbed back into the driver's seat and started the Camry. He put it in Reverse and looked at her. "How about dinner out tonight?" he asked. "On me."

Anna sighed. "I don't know. I'd like to go to bed early. But I'm afraid I'll lie there and my brain will start working on overtime. Oh, I don't know. I don't know anything anymore. I think I may lose my mind."

Mark pulled out of the lot, not saying anything. She was obviously driving him crazy, too. Maybe she should go to dinner, try to forget. But it was so hard. The letter last night, knowing how close *he* could get if he wanted. She felt a sick, oily fear writhe in her stomach. No, she thought, no food.

She waited outside her building while Mark changed batteries in his car. He worked like all men seemed to— cussing, scraping his knuckles, losing his tools, but in the end smiling. "There," he said. "Good as new."

Mark suggested they go for a drive in the convertible. Anna protested. "It'll be too cold with the top down. Put it back up, please?"

He ignored her, opened the trunk and produced a big, heavy wool coat that had seen better days. "Put the collar up around your ears," he said, helping her into it. "You'll be fine." Then he held the passenger door for her.

"I don't know, I'm really too tired," she said, but he insisted.

He drove straight onto Interstate 25, then navigated the infamous Mousetrap and headed west on Interstate 70. It *was* cold, dark and cold, the stars already bright over the mountains as they climbed into the foothills. But Anna was surprised how toasty she felt, except for her cheeks and nose. She leaned back in the seat, stretching her legs into the tunnel next to the warm, purring engine.

"Doing okay?" Mark asked over the roar of the wind.

"Um, fine," she said, staring at the black bowl of stars overhead.

He drove well, shifting the Jag in smooth, fluid movements, his big hands steady on the wheel as he put the car through its paces. It darted around corners, hugging the road. She relaxed and tried to just feel the wind in her hair.

"Maybe you'd let me drive your car sometime," she said.

"What? Can't hear you."

"I'd like to drive your car sometime," she repeated over the rush of the wind and the snarl of the engine.

He flashed her a look. "Yeah, sure, sometime."

She had to laugh. "I'm a good driver."

"Uh-huh."

"Did your wife ever drive it?" she asked.

"Once," he said.

They made the loop up through Evergreen at over eight thousand feet in altitude. It was really cold in the mountains, and Mark flipped the heater onto high. It felt good. Everything felt good—the icy wind, the heat on her legs and feet, the big wool coat. For the first time in weeks, Anna felt alive.

"I did this for days after I quit the force," Mark said. "Just drove and drove. Clearing my head."

"It must have been a bad time for you," she ventured.

"Still is."

She leaned back again, resting her head on the seat and closed her eyes, breathing in the piney smell. "Why'd you do it?"

"Do what?"

"Quit. Why'd you quit your job?"

He was silent for so long she thought he wasn't going to answer her. Finally, he cleared his throat and gave a short laugh. "I've been trying to figure that out myself. I felt like the department let me down, I guess. I have a bad temper at times. Makes me do things I wish I hadn't—afterward. But Franklin really got to me. He wouldn't stand up for me. You know, after all that rotten press in L.A., everyone assumes all cops are crooked. Most of us aren't, but there's always a few bad ones."

"And you're not one of them."

He hesitated. "I've done some stuff, nothing too terrible. Some shortcuts. Only when I was sure the perp deserved it."

She turned in her seat to face him. He was looking straight ahead. "Why are you telling me this?"

"Damned if I know," he said.

They took a two-lane route back down into Denver, stopping at an overlook. The city spread out below on the high prairie as far as the eye could see. A combination of diamond-bright strings of lights and big, gaping black spots of parks and reservoirs and open space.

Anna sat in the car and sighed, breathing in the cold air. "Is this where you used to bring all your women?"

"Anna," he said, "I was married, remember?"

"I mean before that."

He grunted. "I may have come up here once or twice."

"I'll bet," she said.

It gave Anna a funny feeling to think of Mark as a teenager, a college kid, coming up here and necking with girls. She wondered if he'd dated a lot. He must have been drop-dead handsome back then—not that he was so bad now. And he looked as if he'd played football or hockey, maybe. She wondered if she would have noticed him, say, on campus, and if they would have been attracted to each other.

She gave him a sidelong glance, admiring his profile, his hair ruffled by the wind, his strong square hands on the wheel. A shiver went through her.

They left the overlook and drove down the winding road into Denver. Mark stopped and bought a take-out pizza, and then they headed into LoDo. With each passing mile, Anna's mood began to degenerate. Home. She used to love her home. But now, all she could picture was that damn red blinking light on her machine.

Mark took the messages for her while she used the bathroom. Mercifully, there were none from *him*. Monica had telephoned, so had Lydia, reminding her about Octoberfest on Sunday. At least it was going to be a busy weekend. When she was occupied, it was better—for a few minutes here and there, she could actually forget.

They ate the pizza, or rather Mark did. "You know," he said, "you have to eat."

"I know that," she said. Still, she wrapped up most of her dinner and put it in the fridge. Then she took a hot shower and put on her old robe over a short cotton nightgown. She looked at herself in the mirror. She was pale and losing weight, with dark circles deepening beneath her eyes. Oh, God, she thought, how long could she keep going like this?

The phone rang at ten past ten, and Anna felt her stomach knot. She was in the kitchen, making a cup of tea, and she spilled it on the counter as the machine clicked on. Mark stood near it, listening and frowning, but his eyes were on Anna.

Then came the voice. "Anna? If you're there, pick up, it's Monica."

She walked around the kitchen island and picked up the receiver. It was Monica just wanting to touch base about an invoice. "I swear to God, that guy told me nine-fifty a yard. He invoiced us at eleven-twenty-five, the jerk. You remember the nine-fifty, don't you?"

"Sure," Anna said lethargically.

"Well, do you?"

"No. Not really."

There was a pause. "Hey, you okay?"

"Yeah, sure. Just real tired."

"So, get some sleep. We'll talk tomorrow."

"Sleep. Sure," Anna said.

She tried. But it seemed the more tired she was the harder it was to sleep. She tossed and twisted in her sheets, the digital click blinking the minutes by: 11:07, 11:42, 12:03. Every time she was ready to drift off, she'd hear that voice on her machine or envision the letter sticking out of her mailbox.

The worst, though, was the memory of him standing so close to her just outside her building, so close he could have killed her right there. And in the Fender house. *If* he'd even been there. But she knew he was waiting, as if engaging in some sort of sick foreplay, waiting for the climax, holding it off but mad with the anticipation of what was to come.

Anna rolled over again and punched her pillow. Nothing worked. She opened her eyes and saw the light spilling under her door. Mark was still up.

She closed her eyes, but it was no good; her limbs were trembling and her heart was beating as if she'd run a race. It was exhaustion, she knew, that and the constant fear, which lurked inside her like a beast about to pounce from a dark corner of her soul.

She sat up in the blackness and bit her lower lip, fighting tears. Then she looked again at the bar of light under the door.

She got up and went to the door, her hand hesitating on the knob. She didn't really know what she was doing or what she expected to happen when she finally twisted the knob and went out into the living room.

He was there, of course, sitting bare-chested on the pull-out couch. He'd been reading a magazine. He lowered it when he saw her.

"I ... I can't sleep," Anna whispered, pausing, uncertain.

He stared at her and nodded, and she went to him. He lifted an arm and she silently slid onto the couch, curling next to him. He drew her near but still said nothing. She lay her head on his chest, shut her eyes and listened to the strong beat of his heart.

FOURTEEN

"Turn left at the next corner," Mark instructed Anna, "and it's the third house on the left."

They'd taken her car to his old house in Aurora, because there was no way the two of them and his two kids were going to fit into the Jag. She drove. She was still tired and would have asked him to drive, but after last night and falling asleep next to him like that, she'd had enough of this dependence on a man—enough to last her a long time.

"Is that the house?" Anna asked, slowing.

"That's it," he said.

They were in a seemingly endless subdivision of nice tract homes on artificially curving streets. Aurora butted up against Denver on the east, now just about as big a city as Denver. It sprawled out on the prairie, flat and dry all the way to Kansas. "Saudi Aurora," Denverites called it. The people who lived there called it convenient and affordable.

Anna pulled into the driveway, turned off the engine and swiveled to face him.

"I'm nervous," she said. "I've never met your kids, you know."

Mark nodded. "All I can tell you is that they don't bite."

"There are other things, though," Anna said. "And I'm feeling far from my best."

"Hey," he said. "In case you don't realize it, your worst is about a hundred percent better than most people's best."

She looked at him, bewildered.

"You'll be fine with the kids," he said. "That's all I meant."

He got out of the car, and she sat there waiting, tapping her fingers on the steering wheel. It was a nice day, cool and sunny, but there were thick clouds building over the mountains to the west. Snow clouds.

It felt safe here in this suburban neighborhood—very ordinary and very innocuous. But still Anna watched everybody with suspicion. *He* could be here, following her. He could be anyone; that man mowing his lawn or that one getting in his car. He could be in one of these houses, or he could be driving by on the street. She hated that he'd already succeeded in twisting her mind.

The front door of the gray split-level house opened, and Mark came out. Hanging from each of his hands was a kid. Mark Jr. on one side, a gangly dark-haired boy with a mouthful of braces. And a girl on the other—Kelly, with light brown hair in a ponytail, wearing tights and a pink sweatshirt.

Mark's children. How odd he looked in the role of father. Did his kids see him as the big, brooding dangerous ex-detective, or was he just Dad to them?

He led them up to Anna's car, and she got out to meet them.

"Kids," he said, "this is Anna Dunning. This is Kelly and Mark."

Anna smiled, aware of Kelly studying her very closely. Mark Jr. put his hand out to shake hers, very manly, his blue eyes so like his father's it was uncanny.

"Nice to meet you," Anna said, feeling out of place.

Just then, a woman came down the walk. She had golden blond hair cut in a pageboy and dark eyes, and was very pretty, dressed casually in slacks and a white blouse. Jennifer.

"Wait, Mark," she said. "I forgot to show you this." She said it with a kind of smug satisfaction, and she held out a newspaper to him.

He turned to her, and Anna saw his face tighten. "I know about that, Jenn. Lil told me. The guy put one over on her."

"You should read it. *I* didn't even know some of this stuff."

"Uh, look, Jenn, we've got to go." Then, a little embarrassed, he said, "This is Anna Dunning. I told you about her. Anna, this is Jennifer."

Jennifer sized her up. "It's so nice to meet you. I hope everything turns out all right."

Anna wasn't sure precisely what the woman was alluding to, so she smiled and said, "Thanks." Then she held out her hand for the newspaper. "Do you mind if I read the article?"

Jennifer handed the paper to her. "Be my guest. It's not badly done. I've seen a lot worse written about Mark."

"Anna, for God's sake, do you really want to read that junk?" Mark asked.

Jennifer kissed both of her children on the cheek. "Be good, kids. Don't drive Dad nuts. Enjoy the game."

Anna walked around to the passenger side as Mark looked at her questioningly. "You drive," she said. "I *am* going to read."

Mark drove them out of the labyrinthine subdivision and back onto Mississippi, while Anna found Steven Hurst's article. She was aware of Mark's dark frown, and his kids were hanging over her shoulder from the back seat.

"Read it out loud," Mark Jr. said.

"No way," his father said.

"*Dad,*" Kelly said, sounding miffed.

"You guys have been through enough with this whole thing. Forget it," Mark said. And then, to Anna, "It was rough. For a while, I was in the papers every day."

"TV, too," Kelly chimed in. "It was neat. Dad got really ticked, but everyone said he was cool."

"My dad's a real hero," little Mark said.

"A hero," his father muttered.

Anna decided it was best to let it lie and say nothing. She wished now she'd just put the paper down and read the article later, but it was too late. And, besides, their mother wouldn't have given the article to Mark in front of the children if it was all that bad.

So she read on. But to herself.

"What's it say?" little Mark kept asking.

"Shh," his older sister said. "Let her read it first."

Mark drove silently, eyes on the road. But Anna could feel his tension.

When she finished reading, she refolded the paper, dropped it on the floor by her feet and said, "It's nothing bad. Your dad just helped this lady out once. He saved her life, really, and they're still friends."

Kelly sat back in the rear seat and shrugged. "Oh," she said, bored, "that was Lil. Everyone knows *that.*"

Mark only shook his head.

They drove toward town in silence, but Anna couldn't help thinking about the story, about how Lil Martinelli had been beaten, and Mark had saved her and gotten her to the hospital, visiting her several times. Now she was his landlady and his friend— maybe more.

She thought about that—Mark the savior of women in distress. He was so tough on the exterior, but Lil had told the reporter that inside Mark was just a pussycat. Anna had to wonder what her own relationship would be with Mark after this job was over. Would they really be friends? It seemed as if all they ever did was go for each other's throats. Last night had been an unforeseen interlude.

"Where are we going, Dad?" Kelly finally asked.

"I'm going to drop by my apartment and get some clothes, all right? Just for a minute. Then we'll get lunch. You want pizza?"

"Yes!"

"No!"

"Okay then, subs?"

"No!"

"Yes!"

Anna spoke up. "We can go to Pizza Run. You can get both."

Mark shot her a grateful look.

His apartment was funky—small, airless and relatively neat, the furniture and artwork probably from the Salvation Army.

Mark Jr. jumped on the bed, making it squeak. Kelly picked up a magazine from the coffee table. *"Playboy? Dad!"*

"Put that down, Kelly. Lil left it here. It's from her shop."

Anna watched Mark's daughter, a girl teetering on the edge of puberty. She would be very pretty one day. Tall like her father, features like her mother. She felt a muted hostility from Kelly, and she wondered about that.

Mark was rooting around in his closet. Anna could hear hangers rattling and dresser drawers opening. She moved around the apartment, noting that there was not one personal item in it, nothing to give a clue as to who Mark Righter was.

But the newspaper story had provided an interesting twist on him. She looked at his daughter, heard his son bouncing on the bed and talking to his father, heard Mark's replies. And she couldn't quite fit her mind around these contradictory facets of him. He was a man who danced with his own shadows.

"Are you my father's girlfriend?" Kelly asked her after a long silence.

Of course, she thought. That's what was bothering her. Anna smiled and sat down next to the girl. "No, I'm not, Kelly. Your dad is helping me out. There's a man who's, um, stalking me. Do you know what that is?"

"Uh-huh." Kelly looked at her. "I saw a movie on television."

"Well, your dad is kind of protecting me from this stalker until he gets arrested. So, well, we have to hang around together."

"He's like a bodyguard."

"Yes."

"Why is the man stalking you?"

"Oh, gosh, I wish I knew. I don't have any idea. He's not really sane, I guess."

"Sane," Kelly said, pondering that. "Oh, you mean he's like nuts, bananas."

"Exactly," Anna said as they both started laughing.

Before leaving, the kids insisted on seeing Lil, so they all trooped in the back door of her shop. She was with a client, but she left him for a minute to say hello and hug the kids.

"Sorry about the reporter," she said. "Me and my mouth."

"No big deal," Mark said. "This is Anna."

"Oh, hi," Lil said. She stripped off a latex glove and shook Anna's hand in a very friendly manner, saying all sorts of nice things about what a swell guy Mark was and how Anna was in the best of hands. Then they all said goodbye, and Anna saw the stealthy, longing glance Lil gave Mark, and she knew instantly and irrevocably that Lil Martinelli was hopelessly in love with him.

As they were all getting back in her car, Anna gave Mark one of her own surreptitious glances. He didn't know, she realized. The big, smart ex-cop hadn't a clue. And she'd bet her bottom dollar that Lil was never going to tell him, either.

They stopped for lunch, then took in the afternoon show at the Imax theater at the Denver Museum of Natural History. Anna dozed on and off throughout the movie on flying.

"You slept the whole time," little Mark said to her after the show.

"Well, not the *whole* time," Anna corrected. She thought about last night, about what little sleep she'd gotten, and she wondered what time she'd finally gone back to her bedroom. It had been late. She'd dozed against Mark's chest for quite some time.

As they were walking to her car, Mark checked his watch and said, "How about we stop by your place? We've got time before the hockey game, and I can drop off my stuff. We can relax a while. Maybe even order in some food."

"Where do you live?" Mark Jr. asked Anna.

"Down on Blake Street in LoDo," Anna told him.

"By Coors Field?" He beamed.

The kids liked Anna's loft. They both looked around, wide-eyed. "How come the pipes aren't in the walls?" Mark Jr. asked.

Kelly went to the window. "Can I open the blinds? Are we real near Coors Field?"

"Uh, Kelly, leave the blinds down," Mark said, and his daughter gave him a swift, knowing look.

Anna was shocked. Imagine, a kid that age coming up against a thing like this. Not even questioning it.

Mark Jr. had turned on her TV set and was playing with the remote, sitting cross-legged on the floor. "The Red Wings are on, Dad, against the Kings," he announced.

Hockey, Anna thought. Boy, they start young. She sat down on the couch, let her head fall back and closed her eyes. Maybe she could stay here and sleep while they all went to the game, she thought wistfully.

"Tired?" came Mark's voice.

She opened her eyes and rubbed them. "Uh-huh."

"Can you handle the game tonight?"

"Sure." She knew he'd never leave her here alone.

"I could take them home early, forget about the game."

She sat up. "God, no. They've been planning this for weeks. You told me that."

"Yeah, but . . ."

"Mark, you can't disappoint the kids like that."

"I was thinking about you."

"Never mind. I'll feel better in a crowd, anyway. Sitting around here gets on my nerves."

They stopped at a Burger King on the way to Mc-Nichols Arena, where the Avalanche played while waiting for their new Pepsi Center to be built. The Avalanche, née the Quebec Nordiques, was Denver's newest addition to its sport collection, the biggest thing to hit Denver since the expansion baseball team, the Rockies.

The traffic around McNichols was heavy, with cars and buses streaming in from the four corners of the state. People drove all day to watch the Rockies or the Broncos or the Nuggets or the Avalanche play. Mark parked the Camry in a ten-dollar parking lot across from the arena on Federal Boulevard, and they walked the rest of the way.

It was a festive atmosphere, with people milling around wearing team paraphernalia, people with season tickets carrying their Avalanche cushions to lie on the hard seats.

"Hang on, kids," Mark said. "Don't get lost in the crowd."

"I'm too old for holding hands," Kelly said.

"Well, I'm not," Anna replied. "Here, you hold mine."

"If you get lost, go to the first policeman you see," Mark said. "I'll give you each a ticket stub, so you'll know where our seats are."

Jostled by the crowd, Anna held on tightly to Kelly's small hand. She usually went to games with Scott and Lydia, always in private boxes. But this was pretty exciting.

Finally, they got seated, high above the ice. Vendors worked the crowd, hawking their wares. Music played, people yelled and banners fluttered from the raised ceiling.

Mark Jr. was excited, waving his Avalanche cap, while Kelly tried to look blasé. They were a lot like Scott and Lydia's kids had been at that age. Now Francie was a young lady with her driver's license, and David's voice was changing. Mark's kids would be there soon... Kids. Abruptly, Anna felt a weight press on her, and in the midst of the clamorous crowd, she felt a vast, black sadness. She had no kids; at this rate, she'd never have any.

"What's the matter?" Mark asked quietly.

"Oh, nothing, just tired."

The teams skated onto the ice, and the crowd screamed and stomped, drowning out the organ music. The game started. The players, huge in their pads like knights in colorful armor, shot the puck back and forth, streaking and stopping in the glitter of spraying ice, and checking one another with vicious abandon.

Anna watched, hearing the crowd roar and registering the action in front of her eyes, but she wasn't really there. The noise and turmoil were a convenient shield to hide behind, an easy out. Her mind whirled wearily, wondering where *he* was now. Waiting at her building? Here, in the crowd?

She felt Mark's hand on her arm and looked down, surprised, then raised her eyes to meet his impassive gaze. She blinked and realized his hand was gone, and he was telling his son something about the game. "If it crosses the red line, it's icing. See the ref blow his whistle?"

"Yeah, Dad, I see."

They bought popcorn and Coke. The kids had one spat, but Mark stopped it quickly. He was good with his kids, his gruff mannerism notwithstanding. They paid no attention to it, anyway.

The game came to an end with the Avalanche losing by one goal. Mark Jr. was dejected. He threw his hat on the ground and yelled, "Darn it!"

"Next time," Mark told him. "They played real well. It was a good game."

Kelly looked up at Anna. "Hockey's okay, I guess. But they sure are animals out there."

"Sure are," Anna agreed, catching Mark's look over his daughter's head.

They filed out, enclosed in the slow-moving throng. In the broad corridor beyond the seats, Kelly said she had to go to the bathroom.

"Can't you wait?" Mark asked.

"*Dad.*"

"All right. We'll stop at the first one we come to. We'll wait for you."

"I'll go in with her," Anna said as they arrived at the door marked Ladies. She pushed on the scratched steel door. "Come on, Kelly. Let's hurry up." The particular smell of public bathrooms assailed her as they went in.

The Hunter had wanted to come, but Kate wouldn't let him. She knew better. She'd been terribly clever, following Anna. She'd waited half the day until Anna had finally come home—with the dark man and two kids. His kids, she guessed.

She'd followed them in Earl's truck, carefully staying back, until she realized where they were headed. The opening hockey game. Oh, too bad Earl wasn't here, she thought. He enjoyed hockey.

Kate could take hockey or leave it, and she had to pay an exorbitant price to a scalper to get a ticket fast, so she wouldn't lose sight of them. It irritated her to no end. The Hunter would have to pay her back.

Kate positioned herself by a railing overlooking their seats. Anna seemed very subdued during the game, barely smiling. She looked worn-out, poor thing. That man must be running her ragged with all those things he did to her. Disgusting things. She'd bet the man, that big, dark ex-cop, even did things to Anna right in front of those kids. The thought made Kate wince. Children were so innocent, and adults were always hurting them. Awful, awful.

Kate followed them at a safe distance when they got up to file out with the rest of the fans. It made her nervous; if she lost them, the Hunter would be very angry. He could be frightening, with his cold rages and his weapons.

Her luck held once again. Oh, my, but Kate was a fortunate girl, she thought, watching Anna and the man's daughter go into the ladies' room, while the man and his son waited outside.

Kate walked right past him, right past the notorious Detective Righter. She was sure she even brushed his sleeve, and he never noticed her, never even looked up from whatever he was saying to his son. Her own courage astounded her. The Hunter was going to be proud.

Inside, the bathroom was very big and echoing, with soggy toilet paper strewn about the dirty white tile floor. A dozen gray metal stall doors faced a bank of sinks underneath spotted mirrors. Kate went to a sink and washed her hands, carefully watching in the mirror. Two women, who were also at the sinks, dried their hands and left.

A toilet flushed, then another. The young girl emerged from one stall, then Anna, right behind her. They both stepped up to the sinks and washed their hands.

"Let's hurry," Anna said. "Your dad's going to be impatient."

"Oh, his bark is worse than his bite," the young girl said.

Anna was right next to her, Kate thought. *Right next to her.*

Anna reached for a towel, her arm inches from Kate's face. "Excuse me," Anna said politely, and Kate had the nerve to turn toward her and give her a brief, impersonal smile, like only women in a smelly public bathroom would give one another. Then Kate finished drying her hands and walked out, back into the milling crowd. Her heart pounded in her chest like a wild thing.

Mark saw Kelly come out of the ladies' room first, followed by Anna. It struck him like a hammer that something had frightened Anna. She was white as a sheet.

"What is it?" he asked sharply.

"That . . . that woman," she said haltingly.

"What woman?"

"The one in the bathroom. The only other one in there. *The tall blond one.*"

"I didn't notice a woman."

"She walked out a minute ahead of us." Anna drew in a breath. "She was weird. She looked at me, and I know...I know I've seen her before. Somewhere." She put a hand to her forehead. "I can't remember, but she looked familiar."

"Yeah, Dad, a lady walked past us just before they came out," Mark Jr. said.

"So, she seemed familiar?" Mark said questioningly.

Anna looked at him, her eyebrows drawn together, her face as pale as dough. "Her hands, I mean, she was washing her hands. They were ... Oh, God, Mark, they were big—men's hands. And the eyes, scary. I think she had ... she'd shaved. It was blond, but you can tell. I think it was a man, Mark."

It only took Mark a second, then he swore out loud. It was *him*, the stalker; Mark knew it as surely as if the creep had tapped him on the shoulder and said, "Hey, look, dummy, it's me. I'm in drag." The bastard.

"There!" Anna was pointing. "That blond head. He's looking at us. Mark..."

"Come on," he said. "Fast." He dragged at Anna's hand and bustled the kids in front of him, walking then running down the nearly deserted corridor. Damn! A woman. He should have felt his presence, he should have known!

The blonde, with pretty golden curls, was tall for a woman. He tried desperately to keep her—him—in view. His only advantage was that the bastard didn't know Mark was on to him.

At the main door, in the light, with people milling about, he left them. "Stay here," he ordered. "Don't move. Wait for me." He took off, down the broad-tiered steps, across the pavement and into the hopelessly snarled parking lots along the sidewalk.

Up ahead, the blond head bobbed in the crowd. Adrenaline shot through Mark like an illegal drug. Suddenly, *he* turned and looked back across the people and the hoods of the cars, and their eyes met. Even across that distance, their eyes met like two coins clicking together in an open palm.

Mark ran, shouldering people aside, and the blond wig started running, too. The stalker knew he'd been made, and he was running for his life.

It was like one of those nightmares where you can't move, when you're underwater and something is holding you back. People, cars, kids, parking attendants—there was a thick, unmovable morass between him and the stalker.

Mark's breath was rasping in his throat as he dodged cars, families, fathers carrying tired toddlers. "Jeez, mister, what's yer hurry?" someone yelled at him.

He reached Federal Boulevard. Across the street, the stalker was running, no longer like a woman but rather full out like a man. The light turned red just as Mark got to the street, but he charged across, as behind him cars streamed, a solid, gleaming mass of lights and chrome and tires. He could still see the blond hair up ahead like a golden halo. Mark put his hand on the gun under his arm.

Suddenly, the head disappeared, and there was a moment of silence. Then Mark heard the sputter and cough and roar of an engine. Two beams of light cut the darkness as a vehicle shot out from the curb and sped away from him.

Mark stood there, chest heaving, and swore bitterly into the black night. Then he turned and started back to where Anna and the kids waited. They'd be worried, he registered somewhere in his brain. It wasn't fair to them.

But what was in the forefront on his mind was the vehicle—an old, dark, perhaps blue, pickup truck. Chevy or Dodge.

The license plate was from Wyoming—no one could mistake that black bucking bronco on the white background—and three of the numbers on it were 495.

A grin slowly spread across Mark's lips. "Gotcha, you sick bastard," he said.

FIFTEEN

Anna whipped eggs with a fork and listened intently to Mark's end of the phone conversation. He'd already spoken to Hoagie and, despite it being early Sunday morning, he'd given his ex-partner the partial Wyoming license-plate number. Hoagie, however, couldn't get a run on it till the next day at the very earliest.

But the conversation Mark was now engaged in was of far more interest. He'd telephoned the police psychiatrist at home. They knew each other from when Mark was a cop, and she had readily taken his call.

Mark's end was friendly. "So, you're telling me it all fits," he said. "The guy in the camouflage and the guy in drag, they could easily be the same person?" There was a pause. "Could this sicko have another personality?" he asked. Another pause. "Really. Amazing." Pause. "Wow. But you still think they're all passive except for the one who approached Miss Dunning?" Pause. "Uh-huh." Mark said nothing for awhile, just listened intently. Finally, he said, "Hey, thanks, Charlotte. You're a real pal."

"Tell me everything," Anna said as she used a wooden spoon to scoop the cooked eggs onto plates.

"Mmm," Mark said, dragging a stool up to the kitchen island. "Eggs look good."

"*Tell me*," Anna repeated.

He talked while he ate the eggs, using a piece of toast to shovel them up. He told her that they were correct in their assumption that the stalker had now appeared to her in the two personas: one male, a macho, military type; the other female, friendly, subdued and anxious to please.

"Charlotte gave me a lot of psychobabble. You know, like protective delusional scheme, feelings of inadequacy, unconscious homosexual conflict, all that stuff. Oh, one more—strong bonding of aggressive and sexual drives. I like that one because I understand it."

Anna frowned.

"He could have what's called multiple personality disorder. And Charlotte also thinks there's a need in him to strike out at women because of some problem with his mother. The other interesting thing is that she believes you had to have met the real man behind these other personas. Somehow, you pushed his buttons. Charlotte said it could have been something as minor as looking at him the wrong way."

"Oh, God," Anna said. "Well, if I met him, shouldn't I recognize him? I've seen him . . . what? Three, four times now? I saw the one in army clothes in the garage and in front of my building. And the woman, well, last night, and I know it was the same one who handed me a dollar at the deli. I *know* it. So if I've seen this weirdo so many times now, in all these different disguises, why can't I remember the first time?"

"Maybe he looked entirely different. It wouldn't take much. A change of clothes, glasses, the way he combs his hair." Mark shrugged. "It's probably somebody you don't usually notice, a gas-station attendant, a clerk in a store."

Anna mulled that over.

"Today," Mark said, "at this street party—"

"Octoberfest."

"Whatever. Today, we're going to scour every face there. You said your brother invites his entire crew?"

"Yes."

"Well, to be honest with you," Mark said, "there is one guy who stood out on the list I had Hoagie run. A guy named Rod Miller."

Anna's forehead knitted. "The name doesn't even sound vaguely familiar."

"Yeah, well, he fits the profile. And there's another thing. Charlotte's initial report, which was based on the notes he sent you and that original answering machine tape you gave the cops, says that he's most likely a blue-collar worker."

"What about Monica's list? The men I've worked with on the remodels?"

Mark frowned. "Nothing so far since Moran."

He put the breakfast dishes in the dishwasher. "You cooked," he said, taking a plate out of her hand. "I'll clean up."

He was trying very hard, she knew. And she appreciated his effort. She could barely recall her first impression of him as the big tough cop. Their relationship had shifted in some indefinable way. Maybe, Anna thought, they really *were* becoming friends.

She sat on a stool at the counter, reading the Sunday paper. There was a big ad for the Octoberfest;

Lydia had probably arranged it. She glanced up and idly watched Mark's back as he worked. He was so big he looked curious bent over her sink. He was wearing a plaid shirt, and it pulled across his back, so that she could see the muscles playing under the fabric.

Hmm, she thought. He doesn't look so tough right now. And it flew into her mind without a bridging thought: What kind of lover was Mark Righter? Aloof and selfish or slow and gentle?

Anna was grateful he didn't turn around then; she could feel herself flush. What a mind, she thought. She was getting to be like Monica.

Mark swore under his breath as he dropped the soapy sponge and splashed himself. She leaned into her elbow on the counter and smiled to herself. Tame the wild beast. Make him do the dishes.

When he finished wiping the sink and the counter around it, he turned to face her.

"Anna," he said, "listen."

She put the section of the paper down. "I'm all ears."

"He'll be there today. He'll have to be. He knows all about this street-party thing, and he knows you'll be there." Mark stood in her tiny kitchen, with his sleeves rolled up over muscular forearms and his big hands pink from being in hot water. "He may not be in his camo gear or the female disguise, but he'll be there."

"Then how will I know him?"

"The eyes. You look into his eyes. You'll know."

She shivered. "I can't just go up to every man and stare into his eyes."

"No, but you can stay sharp. He won't be able to resist being there. It's gotta be getting to him by now, not being able to get close to you. He's going to slip up again, worse than before."

"*When* is he going to do all this?" she asked.

"When his obsession gets the best of him. That's when he's most dangerous. It'll be soon."

"Mark," she said, "did the police psychiatrist say anything else? I mean, did she say whether the man would act on his threats?"

"Anna, no one can know that."

"You're lying," she said. "Tell me."

"Anna . . ."

"Don't treat me like a child."

"No one can tell you what a nut case is going to do. They don't know, themselves."

"Oh, God." She turned around and put her face in her hands.

"Anna." His voice was full of sympathy. He moved closer behind her and placed his hand on her shoulder. It felt good there, solid and comforting, and she didn't want him to move it. She put one of her hands over his and just sat there for a moment, her back to him, hardly breathing, afraid he'd snatch his hand away.

She knew that if she turned around, they'd be chest to chest, and maybe he'd take her in his arms and hold her, the way he had that other night. That was really the only time she felt safe—in Mark's arms, with his heart beating under her ear.

But she didn't turn around.

At noon, they both dressed warmly in jeans and sweaters and jackets. The forecast was calling for intermittent snow showers in the Metro Denver area. Winter was around the corner. They drove toward Cherry Creek, and Anna was sure that Mark said at

least three times, "I know I've seen that pickup truck
before. *Somewhere.* If I could just place it . . ." But the
memory continued to elude him.

Despite the chill in the air and the occasional gusts
of wind that carried the lonely snowflakes, hundreds
had turned out for the street festival. It was, after all,
the last hurrah before winter. Golden leaves swirled
down from the trees and lay gathered in the gutters and
at the corners of buildings. Yes, thought Anna, winter
was threatening.

Parking, as Lydia had warned them, was practically impossible. They'd taken Mark's Jaguar and had
to leave it on a residential street nine blocks from the
heart of Cherry Creek. On the walk toward the festiv-
ities, Mark scanned the street for any sight of an old
pickup.

Dozens of art displays, food booths and trinket
stands lined Second Street. In the park an upscale rock
band played. Restaurants, like Legends, Rodneys and
Chinooks, were selling beer and food along the side-
walks, and jugglers and balloon artists walked among
the crowd. Someone even showed up in a clown's outfit riding a unicycle. The children obviously loved it,
despite their having to be bundled up.

They found their hosts, Lydia and Scott, having
lunch at Duffy's Cherry Cricket with the mayor and
his entourage. Introductions were made. It was clear
the mayor knew exactly who Mark was, and even
Anna could feel the glacial chill in the air when he
shook Mark's hand. She watched as the mayor licked
his lips and glanced around to see if anyone in the
crowd had noticed him shaking hands with a crooked
cop.

Anna looked at Mark, and she saw with a pang that, he, too, had noticed. It isn't fair, she thought.

They left the group and walked the streets, both of them searching the crowds. Anna kept staring at men she passed, her brain automatically registering their coloring and size. She felt like an assembly-line worker who could sort the bad items from the good without conscious thought. They flashed in front of her eyes, and she wondered if she'd actually recognize him. She could be staring at him right now. He could be that man watching a juggler, hands in his pockets. The stance was similar, and there was something about his hair, the line of his jaw . . . No, it wasn't him.

She realized with a jolt that she was glad it wasn't.

She went on—fair men; skinny and medium-size men, men with thick features, fine features, long necks, short necks, close-set eyes, wide baby blue eyes. It was as if a cartoonist were sketching hundreds of faces and throwing the pages in front of her.

Maybe she'd already seen him, passed over him, eliminated him by mistake. Maybe he was behind her, following her. She moved closer to Mark.

"He may not even be here," she said to Mark.

"He's here," Mark said. "He's here, all right."

"You're so sure."

"*You're* here, aren't you?"

When they circled back past Scott and Lydia, Mark took the opportunity to speak to Scott in private. While the men talked, Lydia patted Anna's arm.

"Oh, honey," she said, "this has been a terrible strain on you, hasn't it?"

Anna nodded. "I look like a freak, all pale and drawn. I'm losing weight, too."

"Don't take this wrong," Lydia said, "but maybe that's what *I* need. A stalker."

Anna gave a weary laugh. "Best diet I've ever been on."

"How are you two getting along?" Lydia nodded toward Mark.

"Okay, I guess."

"It's not too awful having him in your loft?"

Anna cocked her head. "I may be done in, Lydia, but I can see where you're headed."

"He *is* attractive. Not your average handsome banker, but attractive in a sort of dangerous way. I always thought that. Some women, not me, of course, would be turned on by a big tough guy like Mr. Righter."

"Okay, Lydia," Anna said, "the answer is no. We are *not* sleeping together."

"Oh," Lydia said.

"Disappointed?"

"Certainly not."

Lydia told Anna about reading through the trial transcripts and her suspicions.

"I've met Captain Franklin," Anna said, surprised. "I mean, I just met him on Friday. And you think he actually planted the evidence and let Mark take the blame?"

"He had the opportunity."

"If Mark knew..." She looked at Lydia. "I don't know what he'd do. My God, Lydia, if he ever finds out..."

"Tell me, Anna," Lydia gave her a shrewd look, "you know him better than I do."

"I barely know him at all. He's not exactly open, you know."

"Tell me, anyway, if you were his wife, say. . ."

"Lydia."

"Let me finish. If you were his wife, would you want him to know that Franklin could have done it? Knowing, mind you, that you couldn't ever go public with the fact, because it might force a retrial?"

"Oh, boy, Lydia, that's a tough thing to ask, especially when I'm in such a blue funk."

"Think."

Anna looked over to where Mark was talking to Scott. She saw the way he carried himself, the size of him, so solid-looking, the bulge of the gun that she knew he carried. Her protector. A predator, stuck with her.

"Yes," she said. "I'd want him to know."

"Hmm," Lydia said.

"Are you going to tell him?"

"I don't know. I'll have to think about it. Don't breathe a word to him."

Anna nodded.

"Has he said anything about being innocent of the charges?" Lydia asked.

"He's never given me a straight answer," Anna said. "Then again, he's got that keep-it-all-inside routine down real pat."

"I'll just bet he does," Lydia said, and both women glanced in his direction.

When Mark and Scott finished talking, Mark rejoined Anna and they set off again into the throng. "Your brother says Miller is here, all right," Mark told her. "Thinks he's wearing a plaid wool jacket. Maybe red-and-black."

"Half the people here are wearing wool jackets, Mark."

"So we keep looking till we find him."

Mark was tireless on the hunt, like a bloodhound totally focused on the task. He made Anna jittery, almost as much as the thought that even now, as they moved through the crowds, that maniac could be right behind her. Her skin crawled.

"Mark," she said, stopping in front of a table laden with ceramics. "I really am exhausted. This is getting us no—"

But he put up a silencing hand.

"What?" she began.

"Over there," he said, his whole demeanor changed, alert and ready. "See him?"

"No," she said, craning her neck. "I . . ." And then she spotted him.

Earl thanked the lady who'd sold him the bottle of Coke and turned back to check on Anna's whereabouts. She was right there, almost looking directly at him. But he wasn't worried. She couldn't recognize him. She knew the Hunter, who'd sent him today, and she knew Kate. But she'd never noticed Earl before. She hadn't even noticed him when she'd smiled and ordered him to move that pile of debris before her brother got mad. Earl, of course, had not minded. But when the Hunter found out, *he'd* been furious and had wanted to hurt someone.

Earl saw them—the dark man and Anna—moving through the crowd in his direction. Then an odd thing happened. It was as if he could hear the Hunter speaking to him inside his head. But the Hunter wasn't there—he'd stayed home today with the truck because that silly female, Kate, had nearly blown it. The man had seen the truck.

The Hunter's voice droned on in Earl's brain. "You listen to me, Earl," the strong one said, "and listen real good. Don't let them get too near you. And for God's sake, no matter what happens, don't let that man see your driver's license or any ID. Run if you have to."

Then the weirdest thing of all happened. While Earl was standing there holding his Coke, it seemed as if the Hunter could see through his eyes. "She looks good, doesn't she, Earl?" the Hunter said in his brain. "Looks real good in that pretty red sweater and jacket. I'd take her hunting, if I could. Right now." The Hunter's voice went on, saying pretty disgusting things about what he'd do to Anna Dunning. Very weird stuff. It frightened Earl a lot.

He turned away from the man and Anna, moving off into the crowd, just like the Hunter told him to do.

"Miller, Rod Miller," Mark said. "Hey, man, hold up there a minute."

The man finally stopped at a street corner and turned around, facing Mark and Anna. He peered at Mark and cocked his head. He took a casual drink from his pop bottle then lowered it. "Do I know you?" he asked.

"Maybe," Mark said. Anna held back, standing behind him.

"What does 'maybe' mean?"

Anna stared at him fiercely, her nerves leaping under her skin. It *could* be him. With a camouflage jacket and hat. Or in a blond wig. The eyes, sharp and blue. The fair skin. It *had* to be him. Or did it?

"You work for Dunning, right?" Mark said.

"Yeah. So what?" He looked past Mark and stared straight at Anna. Her stomach dropped to her knees.

"You're Dunning's sister," he said. "I've seen you around."

"Never mind that," Mark answered for her, and Miller's gaze shifted back to him.

"What's this all about, anyway?" the foreman asked. "You know, buddy, you smell like a cop."

Anna could see a muscle working in Mark's jaw. "You know all about cops, don't you, Rod?" he said. "You got into a little trouble with them over a girl-friend."

"What the hell?" Miller said.

"Your girlfriend," Mark said. "You gave her some real trouble. Wouldn't leave her alone. Even when a judge ordered you to stay away, you just had to go back one last time. They arrested you, right?"

Miller glared at him. "What the hell has this got to do with you, man? And who the hell *are* you, any-way?"

"You've got it straight," Mark said. "I am a cop. And if I get a little cooperation here, I'll be out of your hair in a flash. If not, well, let's just say I can be a difficult guy."

Anna tried to catch her breath. Between Rod Mil-ler—who could well be the man who'd been torment-ing her—and Mark, a frightening stranger right now, she wanted to scream and run.

Mark turned to her and he nodded toward Miller. "Well?"

She swallowed. Her mouth was cotton-dry and suddenly she was terribly cold. "I . . . I don't know."

"What?" Miller was demanding.

"I just don't know, Mark," she repeated. She wanted to be away from there; she couldn't bear facing either of them.

"How'd you get here?" Mark asked. "To the Octoberfest?"

"In my truck." Miller was angry, his chest stuck out in an aggressive stance. "What's it to you?"

"What kind of truck?"

"What the hell *is* this?"

"What kind of truck? And you know I can check it in a second, so don't bullshit me, Miller," Mark said.

"A '94 Ford pickup, one ton," Miller snarled.

"Color?"

"Red, you asshole. Now, you gonna tell me what's got you in an uproar?"

"Any other vehicles?" Mark ignored his question.

"No, I can barely make the payments on one."

"I want your address, Miller," Mark said, taking out his notebook and a stub of pencil. "I'm checking you out, and you better be telling me the truth."

Anna watched the process, horrified yet fascinated. She forgot for a second that Rod Miller could be her stalker and watched Mark handle the situation like a cop—cold, cruel, fast, and efficient. He was like a surgeon, inflicting pain in order to cut out a cancer. This was *him*, it was what he did.

He let Miller go after taking the man's address and phone number.

"Do you think it's him?" Anna asked.

"Don't know."

"You don't have any of those feelings you talk about?"

He was staring after Miller, his brow furrowed. "I don't like the guy, I can tell you that."

"I . . . I'm sorry I couldn't identify him for you."

"That's okay. It's like a police lineup. Half the time the witness fingers the wrong guy, anyway. It's pretty common."

"Can we go home now?" she asked in a small, tired voice.

"Yeah," he said. He turned his blue gaze on her, and she watched it soften. "Anna, you've been real good about this. It's tough, I know."

"It's like fighting...oh, I don't know, fighting a shadow."

He touched her cheek with his big fingers, like a gentle brush of butterfly wings. "Hey, stick with me, kid. We'll get him. Now let's go back and say goodbye to Scott and Lydia."

They found them where they'd last seen them. As Mark and Anna approached, they both looked up.

"Did you find Rod Miller?" Scott asked in a concerned voice.

"Sure did."

"Well, what happened?"

Mark shrugged. "Nothing."

"So he's not the one," Scott said.

"I didn't say that. I won't know until I check him out. He says he has a red Ford pickup. That right?"

"Yes, he does. So, does that mean he's okay?"

"He could have another truck," Mark said. "Could be lying."

"I've got to tell you, I hope it isn't Miller. He's a damn good foreman. Now, what about the make on those plates? Is that what it's called, a make?"

"Yes," Lydia said. "That's what it's called, dear."

"I'm hoping I can get a run on it tomorrow," Mark said, "but the plates could be stolen. There's always that possibility. It could lead nowhere. I still want to confirm the information Miller gave me, dig a little more."

"I suppose you suspect everyone," Scott put in.

"At this point," Mark said, clearly frustrated, "I'd suspect my own brother."

They left Scott and Lydia and wandered along the streets, Mark keeping terribly quiet. It wasn't as crowded, because the temperature had dropped dramatically and snowflakes swirled in earnest out of a gunmetal gray sky. Anna suspected they'd awaken the next morning to a couple of inches on the ground. As much as she loved skiing, winter was long enough. And this cold, dreary weather was doing nothing to improve her mood.

They drove back to LoDo. Anna sat in the passenger seat of his Jag, feeling shaky and depressed. "Today was a flop," she said, staring out the window.

"Not entirely." She could sense his gaze shifting to her. "I intend to do some more checking on Miller. I didn't much like the guy. Too cocky for his own good."

"You don't *know*, though."

"No, I don't."

"And neither do I. I couldn't tell. I feel so stupid."

"You aren't stupid, Anna."

She looked over at him, studying his strong profile, and she wondered what he was going to do with the rest of his life. She couldn't see him as a security guard, in one of those official-looking uniforms. Mark Righter was a detective, through and through. Right now he was just a bit lost, searching for himself and questioning the direction his life was taking.

Lydia, Anna remembered. Lydia could exonerate him—at least privately or within the close brotherhood of policemen. Maybe that would help. She hoped so, and she was surprised at how much she cared. She'd definitely bring it up with her sister-in-law. She wouldn't let Lydia forget. Mark deserved that much.

They parked in the alley and went around to the front of the building. Anna walked with her eyes cast down, not wanting to look up and see another letter sticking out of her mailbox. She was acutely aware of Mark scanning the street as the snow began to drift out of the darkening sky at a steadier pace. She could feel the nearness of the stalker, too. She was getting quite good at it, she thought with bitterness. And it occurred to her that Mark was right, *he* was preparing himself to make a move.

By six, Anna was showered and in her robe, ready to try for a solid night's sleep. Just one night, she knew, and things would look brighter. Tomorrow, Hoagie would run that license plate and maybe, finally, the tide would turn.

The phone rang at 6:08. As always, Anna's heart knocked against her ribs. But it was Monica's voice on the answering machine.

Anna picked up the receiver and the machine shut off. They spoke for several minutes about their work schedule on Monday. The Wainwright job was almost finished, and it was time to devote their full energy to the Fenders. Anna said she'd stay in and work on the material lists. Monica told her she'd taken three other calls from prospective clients.

"It's time we think about setting up an office," Monica said. "A *real* office. What do you think?"

"Sure, fine," Anna said. "Whatever you want."

"Oh," Monica said, "right. We'll wait till your mind's a little clearer. Speaking of which, how is everything going with our cop friend?"

"Fine."

"That's all? I mean . . ."

"I know what you mean." Anna turned her back to Mark, who was spreading the Sunday paper out on the couch.

"Well, then," Monica said, "any leads on the creep?"

"A couple."

"Really. Great! You can tell me all about it tomorrow. Get some sleep now."

"I'll try."

"Do it. You're starting to look like Brad's mother, and that ain't good."

"Why, thank you."

"Any old time."

After the call, Anna fixed herself some hot tea and was saying good-night to Mark when the phone rang again.

"Let the machine take it," he said automatically.

"Sure," she said, holding her breath for those few seconds that it took for the message to start recording.

Then *his* voice sliced through the air. Every nerve in her body thrummed. Her eyes met Mark's.

" . . . today at the festival. I like your jacket, Anna," came his coarse whisper. "I like those jeans, too. I haven't seen them before. Nice and tight. I could see how they fit high up into your crotch, Anna, and it gave me some ideas."

On and on he went; fouler by the minute, bolder, sicker, stronger, threatening that her time was very near.

Anna could barely look at Mark. He'd risen and stood near the phone, his hands on his hips, his face dark with unfathomable emotion.

Oh, God, she thought, stop. *Shut up!* She'd never felt so humiliated, so guilty and dirty, and his voice just kept on and on, sawing through her brain, cutting into her soul.

She bit her lower lip until it was bleeding. "Mark," she whispered over that horrible voice. "Oh, Mark, please . . ."

For a long, awful moment, Mark's eyes met hers, then he exploded. He grabbed the receiver, shutting off the tape, and put it to his ear.

"You're dead," he said harshly, "you sick son of a bitch, *dead!*" He slammed down the receiver and hissed something under his breath, quickly dialing the police number to see if they'd traced it.

"A public phone at the Market Street bus station?" she heard him say, then, "Yeah, he's long gone by now. Goddamn it!" He slammed the phone down again and whirled, hitting a fist into his other hand.

Anna just stared at him, her heart in her throat. And for a moment, for a heartbeat of time, she didn't know who frightened her more, the stalker or Mark Righter.

SIXTEEN

On Monday morning, Hoagie called the Wyoming Department of Motor Vehicles in Cheyenne and asked them to run a sort routine on plates with the numbers 495.

"It's a murder investigation," he told the clerk, just so there'd be no foot dragging.

"You don't know the county?" the clerk asked.

"No, only those three numbers."

"It may run to thousands," the clerk said officiously.

"Fine, no problem, fax me whatever you got. I appreciate your help."

Next he called the main police headquarters in Cheyenne and asked for information on any stalking crimes documented in the state in the last five years. "Also any murders related to stalkers or even unexplained murders," he added for good measure. Maybe the fruitcake had already done someone in up there in Wyoming. 'Course, he realized, the creep could have traveled anywhere between the time he left Wyoming and reached Colorado and offed a few poor females in other states. But Wyoming was a start.

By eleven-thirty, Hoagie had the long computer list of license plates—thanks to Wyoming's small population. He ran down the list, his finger tracing the numbers. He crossed out the vehicles that were not pickups and the owners who were women or married couples.

He was left with several dozen license-plate numbers, one of which had been reported stolen in 1992 in Carbon County, Wyoming.

"Hello, hello," he muttered.

He waited on pins and needles till after lunch, when the printout of stalking crimes and unsolved murders came in from Cheyenne.

There weren't a lot of stalkings—Hoagie guessed cowboys had better things to do. But one item popped right off the page and smacked him in the eye. In 1992, a twenty-five-year-old woman had disappeared after receiving some threatening phone calls. Six months later, the state police had listed her as a probable murder victim, no body recovered. Her name was Valerie Duchesne. Address: 0391 County Road 102, Baggs, Wyoming. Disappeared on January 15, 1992. Carbon County.

Hoagie checked the printout on the license plates. The stolen one was also from Carbon County, but almost a year later, in December 1992.

This had to be it. But why had Valerie's murderer waited a year to steal the license plates? Maybe he hadn't left the area until the following winter, when he'd realized he needed to cover his tracks. There could be a lot of explanations, but he knew this perpetrator was the guy.

Hoagie called the police department in Baggs and talked to a guy there who was the town's clerk-treasurer as well as the daytime dispatcher. The one police officer was out checking on some cattle on the highway, and the dispatcher hadn't been there long enough to remember the 1992 disappearance of Valerie Duchesne.

"Is there anyone around who might remember?"

"There's Grant Denny, he might recall. He was mayor for years."

"Could you give me his number?"

Grant Denny remembered, all right. "The Duchesne kid. A real tragedy. Just up and disappeared. We all thought her boyfriend musta done it, but he didn't. He was broken up about it, too. Her family searched for years and never found hide nor hair."

"And the phone calls?" Hoagie pressed. "The report says she received threatening phone calls, mighta been a stalker."

"I don't know about that." Denny paused, and Hoagie heard the electronic whisper of ghost voices on the line. "It was a bad year. The worst we usually have in Baggs is a car wreck or a fool hunter shooting himself in the foot, but that year, well, that winter, we had a real murder."

Hoagie's ears perked up. "You don't say."

"Almost a year later, December, I guess, in one hell of a storm. Poor John Larkin found his mother, Margaret, killed, slashed to hell, all her money gone, her truck stolen. Some drifter."

Hoagie was writing down the names. "John Larkin, mother Margaret. December 1992, that correct?" The truck gone, he thought.

"I think so. Yeah, because my daughter Ellen had her baby that month, and she was all upset, said it brought on her labor prematurely."

Hoagie saw Franklin watching him from his office. "Well, Mr. Denny, you've been a great help."

"You think you have a lead on whoever killed the Duchesne girl—that is, if she's dead?"

"I can't really comment on that until I have some more information, but you've helped the investigation a lot."

"Well, I hope you come up with something. Frankly, I don't hold with unsolved crimes."

"I might have my partner call you, ask a few questions. That okay?"

"Sure."

"His name's Mark Righter," Hoagie said. "Detective Mark Righter."

Mark felt the familiar surge of elation. "John Larkin, Margaret Larkin, December '92. Valerie Duchesne, January '92. Okay, got it. Baggs. Got a number? And the plate, give me the whole thing. Yeah, stolen '92. 4, 3, 4, 9, 5, 1."

"What?" Anna asked behind him. He held his hand up to silence her.

"Yeah, I'll pick up the reports. Uh-huh. Good work, Hoagie. Thanks. Listen, one more thing. Can you check out Rod Miller, works for Scott Dunning. I need to know if he's got a red Ford pickup, '94. Also, if he's got any other vehicles registered to him."

"He's the one on the list, the one with the prior?" Hoagie asked.

"Yeah. I talked to him yesterday, and I want a follow-up on his truck." Then he remembered to ask,

"Hey, I know this is pushing my luck, but you wouldn't happen to have any info on that letter I left with you? The one that was stuck in Anna's mailbox?"

But Hoagie hadn't heard back from the lab.

"It would sure be nice to tie this Wyoming crime in with our stalker," Mark said.

"Sure would," Hoagie agreed.

"Anyway," Mark said, "don't be getting in trouble with Franklin over this stuff. I can pretty much run with the ball from here."

"Like Pussy Franklin really scares me," Hoagie said.

"Uh-huh," Mark said. He put the phone down and turned to Anna.

"Well?" she asked.

"A woman disappeared up in Wyoming, same place as that license plate was stolen from. Also, there was another murder, which may not be connected, but a truck was stolen."

"But *who's* the stalker?"

"I don't know that yet, but I do know where he came from. His hunting grounds."

"Where is it?"

"Carbon County, Wyoming. Baggs."

"Baggs, Wyoming. Isn't that a joke?"

"Nope. It's real."

"And Hoagie got all that from the three numbers you saw?"

"Clever guy, Hoagie."

Anna was pacing the floor, her arms crossed. She looked better today; she'd obviously gotten some sleep. At least a few hours, anyway. She'd been doing some work on the Fender job all day, drawing, looking in books, frowning, pacing, talking to Monica on the phone, sketching some more. It was interesting to watch her work, and Mark had been spying on her most of the day.

Until the phone rang, and Hoagie's voice had come on the answering machine.

"Now what?" Anna asked.

"I go to Baggs."

"But he's *here*," she protested.

"And we don't know how to find him. We don't even know his name. We're fairly sure he's disguising himself as several people. You've seen two of them. There could be others. You know what the psychiatrist said—I have to start at his beginnings. His past'll catch him, Anna."

"Baggs," she said.

"It's about, say, a six- or seven-hour drive. I'll leave in the morning, probably be back on Wednesday. You can stay at your brother's for a couple of days."

"Why do you have to go?" she asked. "Phone them. Hoagie found out lots over the phone. It's faster."

"I don't work that way, Anna. I'm the street cop. I need to go there, sniff the air a little, see people's faces. I get vibes." He shrugged. "It's how I do things."

She scanned his face. "I don't want to be left here alone," she said in a small voice.

"You won't be alone. You'll be at Scott's."

"I mean—" she bit her lip "—you won't be there, you know, with me."

Her words hit him like a soft blow, and he was at a loss for a moment. "Scott can get someone," he said finally. "A guard. If you don't feel safe. I mean, I'm sure he knows . . ."

"*You* make me feel safe," she said, not meeting his eyes.

"Anna . . ."

"Do you have to go?"

"Yeah, I do. I really do."

She walked to her desk and leaned on her work-table, elbows locked, head hanging. She was wearing sweatpants and a gray and blue C.U. sweatshirt, but he could see the shape of her rear and her legs under the fabric. He switched his eyes away.

"I'll go with you," she said.

"What?"

"I'll go with you."

"Uh, I don't think that'll work out so well. I'll be busy, running my butt off. Looking real official."

"It'll be good for me to get away. Everyone keeps telling me to leave town. Monica can cover for me." She turned around to face him.

"Goddamn it, Anna."

"I'm going."

He smoothed his mustache with a knuckle and tried to come up with a valid reason why she couldn't go.

"I'm not staying here without you," she said stubbornly.

She had a point, but he hated to admit it. He gave in with poor grace. "All right, all right. But you'll have to stay out of the way and keep your mouth shut."

"Fine." She nodded obediently.

"I'll be . . . uh—" damn, he hated to admit this "—telling those folks up there that I'm still on the force."

"Naturally."

"You'll have to be, oh, I don't know, some rookie in training, along for the ride."

"Okay, I'll just act dumb."

He peered at her closely, to see if she was making fun of him, but her face was expressionless. He frowned. "We'll leave early tomorrow. Eight, no later."

"I'll be ready." She paused. "Whose car, yours or mine?"

He thought for a minute then gave in to the inevitable. "I'll look more official in yours, I suppose."

"I agree. Besides, there aren't any seat belts in the Jaguar, and it'd be dangerous if we ran into an early storm."

"Damn, Anna, do you have to be so practical?"

"Someone has to be," she said, "Detective Righter."

The plan was simple: an early dinner, early to bed, an early wake-up, then off to Wyoming. But, like so many well-laid plans, fate intervened.

Anna got the call just before five that afternoon. She stopped what she was doing and listened to the voice come on her machine. It was, astoundingly, her mother. She picked up the receiver.

"Mom, what a nice surprise." She shot Mark a look. "Uh-huh," she said. "You are? You're at Scott's?"

My mother, she mouthed to Mark. "That'd be great. Sure. I'll meet you there."

"Oh, I'm fine, and the loft is coming along." Thank God, she thought, Scott hadn't said anything about the stalker.

"You want to come over here first?" She turned, stricken, to Mark. "Oh, wow, the place is a mess. Give me some time to straighten up."

They finished their conversation and she hung up and whirled to face Mark. "Oh, my God, my parents are in town. They'll be here in an hour. What am I going to do?"

"What's the problem?" Mark asked.

"They can't find out about the stalker. It would kill them. They can't find out about *you!*"

"You haven't told them about it?" Mark asked.

"No, certainly not. Would you tell your parents about something bad that was happening to you, if there wasn't a thing they could do about it?"

"I didn't even tell my folks about my divorce," he said ruefully. "Jennifer did."

"See?"

"Okay, so what are their plans?"

"They want to see my loft. Mom's curious. Then we're going to a Thai restaurant on Colorado Boulevard that they like." She started putting things away in the kitchen.

"Do they often show up like this, out of the blue?"

"Sometimes. They retired and moved to Santa Fe, but they have lots of friends here still, so they come back a lot. Look, Mark, go check the bathroom and hide anything of yours. Put your stuff in the linen closet."

She plumped the cushion on the couch, checking to see that none of the sheets or blankets Mark used showed anywhere. She'd have to shower, change her clothes . . .

Mark returned to the living room. "You can't go alone, you know."

"They'll come here, then we'll both drive our cars. I'll be with them all the time."

"What about Scott and Lydia?" he asked.

"They can't make it."

"And on the way home?" he asked.

"I'll have them follow me, okay?"

"I don't like it, Anna."

"Oh, for God's sake, Mark. It's a dinner with my parents. I won't be alone."

It was a hard sell, but in the end Anna held firm; she was going to dinner with her parents and that was that. She was going alone, too, although she swore she'd have them follow her home. "I'll tell them something . . . I'll tell them the Camry's been stalling and it would help if they follow me back to LoDo."

"I don't like this," Mark repeated, but Anna was unrelenting. The one thing she did agree to was carrying along the cellular phone.

"Okay, okay," she said, wiping a spot off the coffee table with the sleeve of her sweatshirt. "God, the place is a mess, and Mom's such a nitpicker."

"The place looks great," Mark said, but Anna just gave him a look.

She took a quick shower and dried her hair. She pulled on a pair of leggings, a long, bright blue sweater and boots. Pushing up the sleeves of the sweater, she could hear her mother asking why the sleeves were so long, couldn't Anna send it to the cleaners? She finished her outfit off with two silver bangles on her wrist and a whimsical pair of earrings—silver cowboy hats.

She pulled her bedspread straight, hurried into the living room and shook her head over the jumble on her worktable. Never mind.

"I'll introduce you when they get here," she said. "You'll be, oh, some subcontractor. We were talking about a job. Then you leave, and when you see us leave, you're safe to come back in, okay?" She looked at him in horror. "You wouldn't follow me, would you? I'd be a wreck. Mark, promise me, you won't follow me."

"If you promise not to go anywhere alone. No kidding, Anna."

"I swear. I'm a wreck, but I'm not crazy."

Her parents arrived on time. Anna always thought of them as an attractive couple: he was tall and slim, an older replica of Scott, while she was a little stout, but still pretty, with a gleaming cap of hair like Anna's, with only a streak of gray at each temple.

"You look great," Anna said after she let them in, feeling her smile too tight. "Mom, Dad, meet Mark Righter. He's a subcontractor on one of my houses."

They shook hands.

"Did we interrupt anything?" Ian Dunning asked.

"Oh, no, I was just leaving," Mark said, and Anna breathed a little easier. "Nice to meet you, have a nice evening." And he left.

"Attractive man," Barbara Dunning said when he was gone.

"Ah, yes," Anna allowed. Then she added, "He's married, Mom." And that was that.

Dinner was pleasant, with her parents chatting about Santa Fe and how much it had grown since they'd retired there. They caught up on family stuff, Barbara's weekly bridge game, Ian's golf trip to Costa Rica. Her parents were both busy and had lives of their own apart from their children's. Anna was endlessly glad Scott had said nothing about the stalker. The only difficult moment came when Ian mentioned that Anna looked tired.

"Oh," Anna said, "just work. Monica and I have been real busy."

"Making money?" Ian couldn't help asking.

"Lots, Dad."

The conversation shifted to Monica and her boy-friend, Brad. The Dunnings knew his parents. Then they talked about their upcoming trip to Egypt. "In about ten days," Barbara said.

"Sounds great." Again Anna was glad not to have to worry them over her troubles. Someday, when it was over, she'd tell them. *After* Egypt.

It was finally time to leave. Anna was ready to launch into her spiel about her car problem, when Ian spoke up. "Well, I'm glad Scott's house is close," he said, signing the credit card receipt. "These glasses of mine are god-awful at night. My new ones won't be ready for a few more days."

Anna swallowed. Her mother was night-blind, and now this.

But she'd *promised* Mark. Okay, she thought, so she'd get in her car right outside the restaurant; her parents would be there with her. She'd lock her doors and drive home; she'd even park in front of her building, not in the alley. She could, for that matter, phone Mark from the car so that he'd meet her on the street.

Nothing could happen, nothing.

She considered calling Mark and having him come and pick her up, escort her home, but it was too ludicrous. It was only a twenty-minute drive, with locked doors and a phone. And that was assuming the stalker had followed her tonight, which was probably a ridiculous assumption in the first place. Well, *maybe* it was ridiculous. He had followed her to the hockey game....

They stood outside in the parking lot, saying their goodbyes. "We'll do Thanksgiving at Scott's," Barbara said. "Your father can play all his videos of Egypt."

"Oh, great," Anna said, smiling.

They hugged and kissed and it was time to go. Ian and Barbara got in their car, and Anna got in hers. She made sure her doors were locked and felt in her purse on the seat next to her for the cellular phone; it was there. Silly, she kept thinking as she followed her parents' Grand Cherokee onto Colorado Boulevard, headed north. Keeping their taillights in sight, she drove extra carefully, looking around, checking her rearview mirror.

Her parents turned left onto Belcaro, and Anna continued another few blocks to Cherry Creek Drive, which would take her directly downtown. The minute she turned off the heavily traveled Colorado Boulevard onto Cherry Creek, which ran between the creek and a park, she felt herself grow nervous. It was dark, there was little traffic and nothing but grass and trees on her right, the river on her left. She pressed the accelerator and sped along, thinking she could call Mark at any time. He'd be waiting.

She suddenly noticed headlights behind her. Just headlights, she told herself. Don't be paranoid.

But the car didn't pass her; it stayed right behind her. So what? she thought. So he drives the same speed as I do. The lights crept closer. She could see them in her rearview mirror, filling it with their glare. Too close.

She sped up. The lights followed. Her heart began a slow, heavy drumming. No, she told herself, it's not him. It's some kids out joyriding. Drunk maybe.

She could call Mark. But what could he do now? Not a thing.

She was going too fast, streaking around the curves that followed the river. She almost laughed, wishing a traffic cop would appear and chase her, give her a ticket. For the first time in her life, she'd love to see the gumball on a police car and hear the siren. But there was nothing except a dark river on one side, a dark park on the other. Ahead, though, she knew was a shopping center, people, traffic, lights. Just a short distance.

It came so fast she had no time to do anything but react. The vehicle pulled up beside her, then steered sharply toward her, into her. She swerved to her right, slammed on the brakes and felt a tire sink into a soft shoulder. She fought the wheel, aware only of a scream building inside her head, but she had no time to think, to feel, to be afraid.

Her car came to a stop, listing badly, the headlight beams knifing through the dust of her skidding halt. She was aware of the bulk of a dark vehicle up ahead, a truck, then she saw a man coming toward her through the twin beams. Anna knew who it was—the walk, the cap, the jacket, the silhouette, coming toward her through the darkness.

There was no one else on the road, no cars in sight, and she couldn't wait. The phone. Could she stay locked in the car and call for help? Frantically, she watched him coming, and she saw he held something in his hand—a gun, knife? A tool of some sort. He'd smash her windows and get her.

Spasmodically, she grabbed her purse with the phone in it, slid across to the passenger seat, pushed open the door and sprang out. She ran, with everything she had, raced wildly across the crunchy, frost-silvered grass, her purse flapping, banging against her side, out to the street. A car would come— it had to. Any second, a car would come, and she'd wave it down.

In the middle of the street, there was nothing, no one, not a vehicle in sight. She caught a movement out of the corner of her eye—on the verge, cutting across the beams of light. She ran across the street and down the embankment to the bike path along the river—the pleasant bike path filled in the day with joggers and in-line skaters and cyclists.

Not now. Now it was filled only with shadows and her own monstrous fear. *Run.* It was cold and her breath made white puffs, her feet slapped on the pavement. He'd hear her. She dodged off the path, onto the grass. *Don't fall, don't trip.* Her chest hurt and her legs felt weak, watery with terror.

She knew he was behind her. He'd seen her cross the street. *Mark.* Oh, God, he'd be so furious. *Mark.* She ran. Up ahead, she saw an underpass, shrouded in black. Her footsteps echoed inside it. As she emerged, she noticed a bench and a stand of some kind of thick evergreen shrubbery. She raced across the grass and scrambled through the branches, feeling them catch, tug, rip. She fell to her knees and crawled down into the deepest, darkest part. She huddled there, panting, trying to be quiet, gasping, too loud. He'd hear her.

Footsteps on the path, running. *Him.* Then they stopped. She shut her eyes, held her breath. *He knows where I am.*

Then it came, the low rasp. "Anna." She could hear as if he spoke directly into her ear. "Anna."

Mark. Oh, God, she wished he was here. She should have listened to him. Never again would she disregard his warnings.

She lay there, heart pounding so loud she was afraid he'd heard it. She kept her mouth half-open, taking in air in tiny, quiet breaths, and she could hear him moving. So close.

The sound came to her ears as if in a dream—a police siren, the throbbing wail far-off but getting closer. Could she run up onto the street and wave down the cruiser? No, he'd get her first. There must be something . . . She ruled out the phone—he'd hear her talking.

"Anna," came the voice from a different direction. He was looking for her.

The siren was closer. Maybe the cop would notice her car sitting up there on the shoulder, engine running, slanted headlights still on. Or had *he* turned them off?

Closer and closer, the screaming wail vibrated inside her belly. It was right there. Then she realized with sick disappointment that it was racing past, noticing nothing, leaving her at the mercy of a maniac.

Shaking with cold and fear, she stayed crouched there for long minutes that went by like water dripping endlessly. She'd fight. She wouldn't go easily. She'd kick and scream and gouge.

Time passed in jerky, uneven intervals. Her knees ached, her nose dripped from the cold and her fingers were like claws. She listened, breathing shallowly.

Nothing.

She waited. Still nothing. Hope flared like a tiny ember. She dared to shift her position a bit. Had he gone? Had the siren scared him off? Or was he still out there, patient as a cat, waiting for the mouse to stick its nose out of its hole?

How long could she stay here? Indecision gnawed at her. She listened and heard only a car swishing by on the road. The creek made muted, winter sounds. An airplane droned by overhead.

Wouldn't he say something more if he was still there, wouldn't he taunt her with his terrible whispers? She was shivering now, her teeth clenched shut to keep from chattering.

Was he gone?

She started to move, crawling to an opening in the branches. She'd never been so aware in her life, her brain checking every sound, every smell, alert to the tiniest movement of air around her. Mark said he *felt* the stalker. Oh, God, she wished she could. But fear blocked that instinct.

Her eyes had grown accustomed to the dark, and she saw the night landscape in shades of silver and gray and black. There wasn't a sound, nor a shadow anywhere but the grass, the trees, the bench, the underpass. She tried to *feel* him.

He was gone, she thought.

But if he wasn't....

She could make a break for it, run up to the road, but her muscles were so stiff and cold, she wasn't sure she could outrun anybody.

Did she dare use the cell phone? If he was there, he'd hear her.

The moment came when she knew she had to move. Anger began slowly trickling into her veins, replacing fear. Goddamn him, making her cower like this in the dark!

Screw him, she thought, let him come and get her. She'd fight. She crawled out from under the thick branches, her clothes catching. She yanked her leg and heard fabric tear. She was aware of scratches on her hands and of one on her neck that stung. She came out of her dark hole and stood up, aware of every sound, ready to flee.

Nothing.

She took a deep, cleansing breath then stepped forward, once, twice, listening, poised to run. But there were only the sounds of night and the river and cars up on Cherry Creek Drive.

She walked swiftly up the embankment, nearly running, and reached the road. She could see the headlights of her car piercing the darkness a hundred yards away. The engine must still be running. There was no sign of the truck. Thank God.

She moved, hugging herself against the cold, walking faster and faster. She crossed the road to her car. The keys were still in the ignition. She thought it was crazy no one had stolen it, a car sitting like that, lights on, engine running. It felt as if hours had gone by since she'd abandoned it, but it couldn't have been that long. How time distorts when you're frightened, she thought, when your life is threatened.

She slid behind the wheel and locked her doors, feeling the warmth penetrate her. She rested her forehead on the steering wheel for a brief moment in total exhaustion. Then she shifted into first, spun the wheels for a moment in the soft shoulder and lurched forward. She shot out onto the street and drove, too fast, tears blurring her vision.

When she pulled up on Blake Street in front of her building, she was shaking again. She flung open the car door, slammed it behind her and ran to her building door, fumbling at the lock. She got it open, ran up the stairs, heart kicking in her chest, and reached for her own door.

It flew open in her face.

"Oh, Mark," she cried.

"What is it? What happened?" Mark pulled her inside. "What the hell happened?"

"Oh, God," she got out.

"I *knew* it!" he said in an anguished voice. "Jesus Christ, Anna!"

She stood there in front of him, shoulders slumped, hugging herself, trembling.

"Never again," he said viciously. "You'll never go anywhere without me again."

She shook her head dumbly. She felt his hands on her shoulders, and it seemed the most natural thing in the world to let him pull her close, enfold her in his arms and stroke her damp bangs back. She stayed there.

Just stayed there.

SEVENTEEN

The mood was very tense between them the next morning. Neither of them spoke much, and Anna felt as if all her emotions were dulled, as if she had simply used up all her stronger feelings.

Mark didn't even bother giving her the lecture she expected. He spent a long time on the phone to the police, making a report. He told them she'd be in when they got back from Wyoming to sign the statement.

She packed a small bag and tried to eat a muffin. Her eyes were puffy and red from last night, her hands scratched and there was a long, red line on her neck. But she was fine otherwise.

And she had Mark with her.

He hung up and picked up their overnight bags. "You all set?" he asked.

She nodded.

He gave her an assessing look, and she saw something in his blue eyes, a spark of something. Admiration perhaps. Then his eyebrows came together, and he said in a grave digger's voice, "I'll say it one time,

Anna. You won't be out of my sight again, not for a minute."

"I understand," she said solemnly.

"Okay, let's hit the road."

Sunday's lousy weather still had a grip on the Rockies as they drove up into the mountains. The roads were clear for the most part, though it became icy at the Eisenhower Tunnel and the Vail Pass. A semi had jackknifed at the summit, holding up traffic. But it was smooth sailing on to Vail and down through Glenwood Canyon.

They stopped for an early lunch at the Glenwood Springs exit, then got back on the interstate and continued west to Rifle. They headed due north along another valley to Meeker and Craig and into Wyoming.

They talked little. Mark was behind the wheel—she liked it when he drove her car, and that was surprising. But he handled it well, never pushing, always careful on the ice. He had a soft touch. It ran through her mind unbidden that he probably handled a woman much the same way as he did a car. Men were predictable that way. Then, on the heels of that notion, she wondered when he'd last been with a woman.

He interrupted her thoughts. "That pickup truck is driving me nuts. I've seen it somewhere. You didn't see the plates, you said."

"I barely saw anything." She shuddered, remembering. "All I can tell you is that it was big and dark-colored."

"It was the same truck," Mark said. "And I've seen it before. Damn it. I can't remember."

"There are a million trucks like that."

"I've seen it," he repeated.

She didn't want to think about it—her mind was tired. Mark would take care of it. She'd relinquish her pride and independence and she'd let him do all the worrying. She turned her head to look out the window and watched the scenery. She'd never been in this area of Colorado and Wyoming before. But then, unless you were an antelope or rabbit hunter, why would you be?

It was desolate. Huge and unending high prairie lands cut by deep, arid washes. She couldn't even see the mountains any longer. Just this unforgiving open range that stretched on and on. Few trees, if any, lots of sagebrush and tumbleweed.

"What do the animals eat out here?" Anna asked.

"God only knows," Mark replied.

They arrived in Baggs before three. It was a tiny place just across the Colorado state line, normally empty. But this was antelope season, Mark explained, and the town was full of hunters. It was still gray and chilly, with a wind scouring the dry river valley, blowing up dust devils and tumbleweed.

The town consisted of one street, two gas stations, a grocery store, a motel-restaurant, a Laundromat, a Mexican restaurant and a clinic. The only rooms left in town were in the Antlers Motel and the motel owner told them they were lucky to get them.

"We're going right to the police department," Mark said after they'd checked in, "before they close for the day. I'll do all the talking, okay?"

"No problem."

They walked to the police department through a cold, stinging wind, jacket collars up, past the few lonesome buildings. No one was around, but Anna

was sure the hunters would come into town later to
drink beer and yuk it up, away from their wives.

There was one man sitting at a desk when they entered the police station. His nameplate read Darrell
Kelly.

"Officer Kelly?" Mark said, and Anna could hear
something in his voice, an authority that was foreign
to her ear. "I'm Mark Righter, Denver, Homicide. My
partner, Detective Billings, spoke to you."

"Ah, that was Jamie Orr he spoke to yesterday. Jamie does dispatch duty when I'm not around. He told
me about you, though. I'll do whatever I can to help.
This is a murder investigation, I take it?" While he
spoke, Anna noticed him staring at her as if he'd never
seen a woman before—a woman cop. She smiled back,
one cop to another.

"This is Officer Dunning," Mark said. "It's her first
homicide investigation."

Darrell Kelly stood and shook hands with both of
them. He didn't ask to see their badges. He wouldn't
have dared, not with Mark Righter staring him in the
eye.

Mark pulled a small notebook from his pocket and
gave the facts to Kelly. "We think the guy in Denver
may be connected because I saw Wyoming plates on
his vehicle—almost caught the guy, too. It's a truck, a
blue '70 to '80 Chevy or Dodge pickup with the plates
stolen here, in Carbon County, back in '92."

"So you figure the guy stole the truck, then stole
plates and hightailed it to Colorado?"

"Could be. The truck could have belonged to Margaret Larkin, who was found murdered here about the
same time."

"Margaret Larkin, God, you mean John Larkin's mother?"

Mark looked at his notebook. "That's the one."

"Holy cow. Well, John's still here, took over the ranch. He's married now, and has two kids."

"Think he'd talk to me?"

"I can call him, sort of pave your way, you know."

Mark nodded and continued, "Then the young woman, Valerie Duchesne."

Kelly shook his head. "That was before my time. But I do know the Duchesnes moved to Severy."

"I'll want to talk to them, too," Mark said.

"Yeah, sure. You think the two are connected?"

"Could be," was all Mark said.

Anna watched as Darrell Kelly phoned the Larkins and the Duchesnes. He got John Larkin's wife, Tammy, on the line and handed the phone to Mark, who set up an appointment. The Duchesnes weren't home, and they didn't have an answering machine.

"I'll keep trying them," Kelly said.

"Okay, thanks. You've been a great help."

"You know," Kelly said, "you might want to phone Sheriff Doble up in Rawlins. There should be some records there. The sheriff has jurisdiction here outside of town."

"Good idea," Mark said. "Can you give me his number?"

On the way back down the street to the motel, Anna hugged herself and shivered. "Godforsaken place, isn't it?"

"It isn't LoDo."

"No." Then she went on, curious. "What will you ask the Larkins?"

"I'm not sure, I'll know what to ask when I talk to them." He stopped on the sidewalk and turned slowly, looking up and down the main street at the hunters' trucks and trailers, the dead antelope tied to the top of truck cabs, the dusty store windows and orange signs proclaiming, Wyoming Hunting Licenses available. Welcome Hunters. Beer $2.99 a six-pack.

"He was here," Mark said. "I can feel it. This is where he's from. That camouflage clothing he wore..."

She hugged herself more tightly, staring at Mark.

"It's like I know him," Mark said. "He was born here, probably handled guns and hunted all his life. He considers himself an expert outdoorsman. He killed that Duchesne girl, God knows where he hid her body. Then he waited a year and killed the Larkin woman, stole her truck and money, stole plates so the truck couldn't be traced."

"You know all this?" Anna whispered.

"Uh-huh. Like you know what color to paint a house or what furniture goes. But I have a problem with the year he waited. Why? Where was he that year? And why did he kill Valerie Duchesne without a trace, then kill Larkin's mother viciously, slashing her, and leaving her body in her house?"

"Oh, God, Mark," she said faintly.

"Sorry, I'm used to Hoagie. He's my sounding board. Anna, I didn't mean to ..."

"It's all right." She took deep breaths. She was cold standing there on the street in Baggs while the wind tugged at her and a clump of tumbleweed blew across the street. "I want you to find out who he is, you know that."

"Yeah, I know that. But it's hard on you. It's my job, not yours."

"No," she said, "but it's my life."

Mark called Sheriff Doble in Rawlins from the motel room and asked him to fax any related material to Hoagie. Doble didn't have much more information than Mark already knew.

"I don't need any more reports," he told Anna. "I want to talk to the people who were involved. Sometimes I learn things they don't know they've told me."

"Have you learned anything like that from me?" she asked.

He gave her a guarded look. "No, nothing," he said, and she knew he was lying.

The Larkins lived a few miles from Baggs at the end of a dirt road on a broken-down ranch littered with leaning, sun-bleached outbuildings, rusty coils of barbed wire and old farming implements in untidy heaps. Whoever lived in the house obviously tried, but it was a losing battle against the fierce sun and raging blizzards. A barn sagged behind the house, and sheep were scattered on the brown hillside beyond like dirty cotton balls, shadowy in the dust.

The mailbox read John T. Larkin, and there was a thin line of smoke rising from the metal stovepipe. A battered pickup sat parked in front of the wooden steps and a rangy tan mutt ran out to greet them.

John Larkin was about thirty, weather-beaten, fair and stocky. Pleasant-looking. His wife, Tammy, was lean and dark-haired and seemed suspicious of them.

"It was years ago, before we were even married," she said. She was holding a baby and had a toddler attached to her leg.

"Tammy, take it easy," John Larkin said. "Come on in. Sit down. Coffee?"

They sat on a lumpy couch that was covered with a hand-crocheted afghan and drank strong coffee while Tammy did something in the kitchen, well within earshot.

"My mother," John said, "was all alone out here. My father left years ago. She had to be . . . hard. She had to raise us by herself."

"Us?" Mark asked.

"My brother and me. Bob, my older brother. He moved away years ago."

"You know where he is?"

John looked a little uneasy. "No, gosh, we haven't kept in touch."

"But he still lived here when your mother was killed?"

"No, he'd been gone for a while by then."

"I see. And no one saw anybody strange in town, hanging around the day she was killed?"

He shook his head. "I was working in Baggs, trying to make a little cash. It was winter, just before Christmas. There was a bad storm, so I stayed in town that night."

"And the truck never turned up?"

"No, and I could have used it, too. I got a little insurance, though, bought the one outside."

"Your mother have any enemies?" Mark asked.

A slight hesitation. "No, but she was a hard woman, like I said." He shrugged apologetically.

"Did she have a boyfriend, someone she was seeing?"

Tammy stepped out of the kitchen, drying her hands on a towel. "Why don't you tell them the truth, Johnny?"

"Tammy . . ."

"John's mother was a dreadful person," Tammy said defiantly. "She was a terrible mother. It was a good thing she died. Whoever killed her did us all a favor, so help me God. And she hated men."

"Tammy," John started again.

"No, listen, she beat her sons, she was abusive," Tammy went on. "Scared them so bad. Threats, stuff like that. Johnny hated her. Didn't you, Johnny? Admit it."

"My mother and I didn't get along very well," John said carefully.

"And Johnny had an alibi," Tammy said pointedly. "Everyone in town saw him there that night. The storm was too bad for him to get home."

Mark looked up from under drawn eyebrows. "And your brother, Bob you said his name was, how did he get along with your mother?"

"Not very well," John admitted. "That's why he left. It was better that he left."

"But she had no specific enemies?"

"Only everyone in the county," Tammy said.

"Did you know Valerie Duchesne?" Mark asked.

"She was a little older than us, ahead in school," John said. "But we all know what happened, I mean that she disappeared."

"Did you know about the phone calls she'd received?"

They both looked blank.

"And your brother, Bob, was he still here when Valerie disappeared? That was in January 1992, the year your mother was killed."

"You think *Bob* had anything to do with it?" John asked warily.

"Just checking all possibilities."

"I don't know. I can't remember. Maybe he was here."

Tammy sat down next to her husband on the couch. "Tell them, Johnny."

"What?" he asked his wife.

"How strange Bob was. You told me."

"Strange, how?" Mark asked.

"My mother was harder on him than me, because he was older. It made him . . . weird. He'd go off by himself a lot. Play games. Pretend. It was his escape."

"Would you happen to have a picture of your brother?" Mark asked mildly, and Anna tried to hide her surprise.

"You know, he took them all when he left. I don't have one. Remember, Tammy, I looked? Not even from when we were kids."

"Well, thanks a lot. I appreciate your help," Mark said.

"So, do you think that whoever killed my mother is the one you're looking for?"

"I can't really say yet. The truck is similar, but it's a pretty common type. I'm just checking out all possible leads."

The wind blew harder in the dark, whipping dust against the car, flattening loose pieces of paper against fences. After they'd driven back onto the highway Anna finally asked the question that had been stewing in her head. "You think it's his brother?"

Mark drove with concentration, the twin beams cutting the dust-blown night. "Could be. The age is right. But he wasn't around, or so his brother said. And the mother. Sounds like an abusive mother to me. Abused children can get real twisted, grow up and try to get even with the world. Psychopaths."

"Stalkers?" Anna asked.

"Yeah," Mark said.

At the motel there was a message from Darrell Kelly: Call the Duchesnes. They'd be glad to talk to Mark and Anna. And he'd left a number.

Mark tapped the pink note on the counter of the motel office. "I know you're tired and hungry," he said to Anna. "We could go out to the Duchesnes' tomorrow morning."

Anna stared at him. "Yeah, right. Tell me you aren't dying to go this very second."

"Well," he said.

Mark was on the hunt and he could be a dangerous person to someone who'd broken the law. But there was another side to him, and she remembered the times he'd held her. She grew warm all over. The feel of him was still imprinted on her body, even though they'd avoided the subject. It was taboo to both of them.

He'd only held her to be nice, she told herself. She'd cornered him; what could he do? And yet, his arms around her hadn't been merely dutiful. His touch had meant more, it had been full of something she could not—or dared not—put a name to.

Mark Righter was a paradox. He could change from gentle to dangerous in the blink of an eye. Now he was in the role of a man on the trail of evil. He'd withdrawn from her in a way, living inside himself, gathering and processing information. She knew why he'd been such a good detective, and she knew he should be one again. It was a shame that he'd quit, and he was too stubborn ever to go back on his own.

But if he were asked? If the right person asked him, he might reconsider. Scott and Lydia knew all the right people. She wondered....

Mark got directions from the motel clerk, and they headed east out of town. "It's only a little before eight," she said. "It's not too late to be bothering the Duchesnes."

The Duchesnes' place was another ranch on the great barren prairie, this one in better condition—though the outbuildings still leaned drunkenly away from the prevailing winds.

Mr. and Mrs. Duchesne were sturdy ranching folk, both gray-haired and sun-faded beyond their years. They wanted to talk about Valerie, their oldest child.

"It just about destroyed us," Sally Duchesne said. "It was the not knowing. I kept her room ready for years. It's a terrible thing to lose a child."

"Valerie had been getting phone calls," Mark urged.

"Some wacko, I guess," Sid Duchesne said. "One of them guys can't take no for an answer. But Valerie never knew who it was. She didn't tell the police because it didn't seem important. And no one ever connected the calls to her disappearance. They coulda been made by whoever . . . took her. We just don't know."

"Do you know what the caller said?"

"She told me he said awful stuff," Sally said. "What he was going to do with her. Disgusting. But Valerie would just hang up and laugh it off."

"Guess we shoulda paid more attention," Sid said soberly.

"There was no way of knowing," Mark said. "Don't blame yourselves."

"That's what we've been telling each other for five years now," Sally said wearily.

"She was going to be married that June," Sid said. "To the nicest boy from up Rawlins way. For a time, the police suspected him, but it wasn't Bill. He loved Valerie."

"Do you have any pictures of Valerie and Bill?" Mark asked.

"We have lots," Sid replied. "Sent one out on those milk cartons. Girl missing. Didn't do no damn good."

Sally got up and went to an oak rolltop desk, from which she drew an album, a box of pictures and a high-school yearbook.

Anna looked at Mark. He appeared to be interested and concerned, his attention wholly on the Duchesnes.

They passed around pictures one at a time. Valerie in school, Valerie at 4-H shows, Valerie and her sisters and brother. Valerie with younger versions of her parents. Then Valerie and Bill, a Li'l Abner sort of fellow.

Then they looked at the yearbook—Little Snake River Valley School, class of 1985.

"See, there's Valerie," Sally said. "'Most fun,' that's what was under her name."

Mark looked at the picture and nodded, passing the book to Anna, who stared at the photograph of the pretty young girl, her smile so bright and hopeful. She had dark eyes and long lashes, a tipped-up nose and a wide mouth. Her hair was shiny brown. Anna felt her eyes fill with tears. She could be looking into her own eighteen-year-old eyes. Idly she turned the pages of the yearbook, scanning the faces of the class of '85, just a few years behind her own.

He was there, two pages past Valerie: young, fair, the pale blue eyes looking into the camera with ferocious intensity, the same long jaw and pointed nose. Anna stared at the picture. Her heart clutched in her chest, and her mouth went dry.

Finally, she switched her eyes to the name under the picture. Robert Larkin.

"Anna?" Mark was saying, but all she could see was the motto beneath his senior picture: "The heart is a lonely hunter."

EIGHTEEN

The Hunter peered through the gathering dusk and felt the band tighten around his head. He'd always been patient when stalking his quarry. Antelope, deer, elk...women. But this one. She made his insides twist with frustration and rage.

Where was she?

The darkness crawled out from the alley, collecting on the street and inching upward on her building. Lights came on as tenants returned from work. But no Anna. She was always home by now. Even with that cop whom she thought could protect her—she was never this late.

Suddenly light squeaked out from between the slats in her blinds and the Hunter knew—a timer. If she were home, he would have seen her. She'd put a light on a *timer*.

Terrible thoughts shifted through his mind: she'd gone away—she'd gone away with *him*. She might stay gone for days, weeks, *forever. He'd* taken her away. The cop had picked up the phone that night and threatened the Hunter, and then he'd taken Anna away.

The Hunter would never forget the man's words. He'd been thrilled and frightened at the same time, hearing the fury in the cop's voice. It was good to be able to bring someone to that pitch.

What the Hunter didn't like was knowing how the cop felt about Anna. It had been in his voice—possessiveness, desire, fear for her. The Hunter didn't like that at all.

As cold as the evening was, sweat oozed from the Hunter's pores, soaking his underclothes, his shirt, the hair beneath his cap. It was the anxiety of wondering where the cop had taken her. It was unthinkable that she might have left the city—not to see her again, not to smell her scent or imagine the feel of her skin.

That fool Kate. A sniveling, whining female. She'd blown it big time when she'd gotten too close in the bathroom. Stupid bitch. The Hunter had warned her, but she'd gone and done it anyway, and now Anna had fled.

Or had she?

Earl had seen her up close and personal at that street festival. He'd walked right behind her, close enough to see the snowflakes gather in her lovely dark gold hair. Gather and melt. There had been something terribly sensual about that. Earl had experienced a pain deep in his groin, and he'd been surprised.

"You ass," the Hunter had said. "You want to fuck her."

"No," Earl had protested, troubled and afraid.

But the Hunter knew. "Oh, yes, you do, you rotten liar. But I'm the one who's going to have her. I won't even let you watch."

The Hunter was powerful now, riding roughshod over those two pathetic creatures, Earl and Kate.

They'd be lucky if he ever let them see Anna again. He'd made the mistake of letting Kate get near Valerie Duchesne, and Kate had damn near let the bitch escape. No, this time Anna was going to be his alone, for weeks, months.

If she returned.

His eyes strained through the darkness to her windows. He felt the awful frustration eat at him. He'd wait all night, all day tomorrow if he had to—and again through the night. Night after night till she came home. He finally had the time. Earl had made enough money for the winter, so they were free now. He'd wait here outside Anna's building for as long as it took.

And when she got back, he'd be through waiting. The blood pressed against his skin from the inside, and he felt the pressure build until it ached, and he knew he was going to have to hurt someone soon. He couldn't wait long.

Mark and Anna had a late dinner at the café in their motel. The place was crammed with hunters and cowboy types, loud music and louder talk. It smelled of cigarette smoke and grilled onions, hamburger grease, sweat and gunpowder. Anna shook her head. But Mark liked it.

"It's got atmosphere," he said as he dipped a french fry into a pile of ketchup. "Hoagie and I hunt every year with these two guys from Robbery. There's this place right out of Pagosa Springs that's, well, a lot like this."

"Lovely," Anna said. "Male bonding at its best."

"Sure is," Mark said, grinning at her.

She took a fry off his plate and chewed on it, looking around. "You know," she said, "I'd honestly rather be here than home. At least right now."

Mark nodded.

"I keep wondering, though, what if he followed us? And this is his stomping grounds. I mean . . ."

"He didn't follow."

She looked at him questioningly.

"He didn't. I watched the whole way up here. No one followed." He grinned again and laughed a little to himself.

"What?"

"Oh, nothing."

"No, what?"

Mark looked at her, deciding to tell her. "I was only thinking that our boy's probably going ape-shit right about now."

Anna paused then nodded. "I hope he's going crazy. I hope he's really suffering. Is that wrong of me?"

"No," Mark said, "I'd say it's the most natural thing in the world." He looked at her—the way she was staring off into the middle distance, her chin resting on a fist. She looked young and vulnerable and very, very pretty. Something in him shifted.

She finally caught herself and shook her head a little, throwing off her musings. "Sorry," she said.

After dinner, they left and crossed the dusty parking lot toward their rooms, ducking against the knife-edge of the wind.

They had two rooms next to each other, an adjoining door between them. Mark felt awkward when he suggested they leave the door open.

But Anna said, "Hey, there're hundreds of guys around here. Half of them probably drinking tonight. I'll be very happy to leave the door open."

"Good," he said.

"Well." She stood in the doorway. "I guess I'll shower and turn in. Maybe tonight I'll sleep like a log."

He turned on the TV and stretched out on the lumpy double bed. In the background he could hear water running and he tried to concentrate on the news. Still, he could imagine exactly what she'd look like. The image was strong. He fought hard to bury it.

She appeared about ten minutes later at the door. She knocked lightly. "Mark?"

"Uh-huh," he said, one arm behind his head on the pillow.

"Can I, ah, talk to you a minute?"

Damn. "Sure."

"I'm not bothering you? You weren't asleep?"

"No, Anna." He looked across the room at her. She was in her nightgown but had put a sweater over it—he guessed she hadn't brought along a robe. Her hair was combed straight to her shoulders, her bangs slick and spiky, a shiny dark bronze color because they were wet. Her legs were bare from just above the knee. They gleamed as if she'd rubbed lotion into them.

She nodded toward the chair by the cheap round table.

"Sure, sit down," he said. He wished to hell she'd go to bed.

She sat, tucking her bare feet up beneath her legs. He looked away. "Mark," she said, "what happens now?"

"How's that?"

"Well, can you trace him? I mean, if he's the one?"

"Yes. We can trace him. It may take some time. But we'll get him."

"And you are *sure* it's him."

"Uh-huh." He stared at the TV screen.

"You still think he's connected to me somehow?"

"Uh-huh."

"Maybe through my work," she reflected. "Or Scott."

"It's a safe bet."

"Do you think he's using his real name?"

"Could be. I'd say our boy is pretty confident."

"Mark," she said in a small voice, "he's killed. He's killed people. That young woman . . ."

He shifted his gaze to her reluctantly. "Don't think about it."

"I can't help it." She wrapped her arms around her knees. "I keep thinking—"

"Don't," he said more harshly than he'd intended.

"But I can't help—"

Suddenly he sat up. "Look," he said, "I need a shower, myself, Anna. Go to bed. We both need some sleep. In the morning, I'll call Hoagie, get him rolling on this Larkin character."

She unfolded herself and stood. "Okay." Her voice was uncertain.

"Good night," he said. "Get some rest." And he turned away until he heard her pad off to the other room. *Jesus*, he thought.

It was 3:08 when Anna awakened with a start. For a moment, she had to orient herself. Motel room. Baggs, Wyoming. Then she realized someone— Mark—was groaning in his sleep. He was dreaming again. A nightmare. Was it the same one?

She reached out and turned on the bedside lamp. Light flooded her eyes. He was still groaning and maybe thrashing. She swung her legs to the floor, slowly, hesitating, remembering his reaction when she'd gone to him before. But she couldn't stand to listen to him.

Anna went to the adjoining door and carefully pushed it open. The light from her room spilled in, chasing away the total darkness. Mark was asleep but still mumbling. She stood there motionless and stared at him in the semidarkness. He seemed okay—caught up in that dream, but okay.

She started to back through the door when he groaned again, and the anguish in his voice was more than she could bear.

She'd wake him, she decided. She couldn't just stand there.

She stepped closer, put her hand out to touch him, then withdrew it. She stood there watching him sleep. She felt as if she were cheating in some strange way, watching him like that, spying. His skin was dark against the white sheets, and one leg lay flexed, uncovered. Her gaze flicked along its length—muscular, black-haired, the arch of his foot a strong curve. His tousled hair, so black in the dim room, his eyelashes lying against his cheek, the artful curve of his nose, the strong black strokes of his eyebrows and mustache.

She drew in her breath slowly, and watched, feeling as though she knew Mark Righter. She'd lied to Lydia when she'd said she didn't know him. She knew him through and through, the way a woman knows a man she's slept with.

One of his hands made a clutching motion, an expression flitted across his face, and she saw him go tense all over. She couldn't watch anymore.

When she neared the bed, she could make out his shoulder holster strapped over the headboard, within his reach. She pulled her gaze away and leaned over to touch his shoulder. "Mark?" she said softly. "Mark, wake up."

"No!" he groaned loudly. Suddenly he flung an arm out and his eyes flew open.

"It's just me," she said. "It's okay. You were dreaming."

Mark sat up and put his face in his hands. He was breathing hard, and she could even feel the heat emanating from his body. "Goddamn," he swore in a gravelly voice, his chest heaving.

"It's all right now," she said again, and without considering the consequences she stroked his shoulder and neck, the way she would a frightened animal.

He finally raised his head. "It's only a bad dream."

"I know. It's the same one you had before. Tell me."

"Anna . . ."

"Tell me, Mark."

It was like dragging the truth from a reluctant child. He sat next to her on the bed, the sheet covering his lower body, while she kept her hand on his arm. He told her he'd had the dream many times.

"It's the Orchid Rapist," he said.

"Jarrett Colby."

"Right. There's all this other garbage going on in the dream, but basically he gets out of prison. I'm there, watching him leave. He gets on a bus and I follow. I'm in a car. Not the Jag. Anyway, I follow him and he gets off the bus in front of a gun store. He goes in, I follow.

But instead of buying a gun, he starts looking at knives. Big suckers. I tell him he can't own a knife . . ."

"Oh, God, those girls," Anna breathed. "He used a knife on them."

"Yeah," Mark said, "he did that." He let out a breath. "Anyway, Colby buys this knife and then he laughs at me, says there's nothing I can do about it now. And in my dream I know he's right."

"You're not a cop anymore," she said quietly.

"That's about it."

"Oh, Mark," she said, "you're torturing yourself. You could go back to the police department. You're the one who quit."

But he only laughed without humor.

"You *could*," she repeated.

He turned his head and looked at her in the semi-darkness, his gaze trailing from her face down to where her hand lay on his arm. "We all have pasts, Anna," he said. "We all have stuff we just don't want to deal with."

She lowered her eyes and felt goose bumps raise on her skin. "I know what everyone thinks," she said.

"Do you."

"Oh, yes. They think because I lost someone that I'm a chicken. But I'm not. Not really. I just haven't found anyone worth going through that pain over." She looked up. "It's not like I've been in a nunnery. I just don't go out searching for Mr. Perfect. If it happens, it happens. I'll know it."

"Uh-huh," he said. She carefully withdrew her touch, but their eyes still met.

Something between them altered. Anna could feel it, intensely, as if a barrier they had carefully erected had suddenly been withdrawn. She felt a quickening of her body and senses, and a sweeping confusion.

Neither said anything for a long time. Anna felt as if all the air had been sucked out of the room, and she was acutely aware of every detail of him—the uncombed hair, the dark, whisker shadow on his face, the long corded muscles in his shoulders and arms. She grew very warm.

"Go back to bed, Anna, please," Mark said in a hoarse whisper. But she shook her head, knowing what she wanted, knowing that she didn't want to leave him.

"Anna," he said again, "you don't get it. If you stay here . . ."

"Be quiet," she whispered, and it was she who leaned close, who took his hands in hers and lightly pressed her lips to his.

At first he didn't respond, then abruptly his arms went around her and his mouth moved against hers. She could feel his naked skin on her, hot to the touch, and the heat fused them together. She thought, This is how he feels.

"Goddamn it, Anna," he said against her mouth, and she smiled.

He was quick and a little rough with pent-up passion, but she liked it like that. His mouth found places on her that made her curl her fingers in his hair and cry out, and when he did finally raise his hips above hers and they joined, Anna was just as quick, digging her fingers into his back.

Mark was full of surprises. After she'd reached her climax, she'd naturally expected that he would, too, and they'd lay in each other's arms, enjoying the closeness, the newness, the wonder. But instead, he began to make love to her all over again, waiting for her, teasing her until the age-old rhythm and need began to build anew deep inside her. When it was finally over, and at last they lay side by side, she had to tell him that she'd never done that before.

"What?" he whispered into her hair.

"You know. Twice like that."

"Twice what?"

"Stop it," she said, laughing softly.

"No, seriously," he said. "Twice what?"

"You're embarrassing me," she said, and his mouth covered hers gently.

She slept through the dawn, and when she opened her eyes, sunlight was stealing in through the crack in the curtains. Mark was not there, but she could hear the shower. She pictured him and smiled unbidden, then did something she'd never dared before. She got out of bed and, naked and blushing, went into his bathroom and joined him. They were quick and awkward and both laughed until he pressed her against the tiles and eased her legs up around his hips. Water steamed on them as she clung to him, her head buried in his shoulder, her climax long and powerful. Later, in her room, her body tender, pink and whisker-chafed, she knew something both wonderful and frightening had happened to her. And suddenly, desolate Baggs, Wyoming, population 272, was the most beautiful place in the world.

NINETEEN

Mark called Hoagie before they left the motel. When he hung up, he turned to Anna. "Well, sounds like we got Larkin's ass. Hoagie's running his name right now. Hopefully, we'll have something by the time we get back to Denver."

Anna felt great just knowing it was all going to come to an end soon. No more fear every time she heard a phone ringing or she picked up her mail. No more dreading the sunset. And she'd sleep again—for ten or twelve undisturbed hours if she wanted.

She imagined she'd share that bed with Mark. It had been so long, so many long years of wondering if she was ever going to meet another man she'd love with the intensity she'd known with Kurt. It was true that Mark Righter might not be the one, not forever, but what she was feeling as they drove across the Wyoming state line and back into Colorado was unfettered joy. Her body tingled with the pleasure of it, and she couldn't stop smiling. My God, she thought, she was falling madly, hopelessly in love.

It was snowing almost the whole way home—an early winter in the mountains. The radio station out of Vail announced that Arapahoe Basin and Loveland ski areas were planning to open the coming weekend if it kept snowing.

"You ski, don't you?" Anna asked Mark as they drove toward the summit of Vail Pass.

"Some. I used to take the kids."

"I'm fairly decent. Advanced intermediate, I guess."

"In that light, I'm pretty crappy."

There were dozens of things she was dying to ask him. Would he move into her place? She didn't even know if he liked it. And what about the conversation she'd had with Lydia, about his job? But she'd promised to say nothing until her sister-in-law had decided what to do. Surely Mark would go back to the force. It was his life. If someone had told Anna she'd fall in love with a cop, a homicide detective, she would have said they were crazy. She would have, at least, thought she'd do anything to dissuade him from returning to that kind of work. But now, well, now she knew that all that gruffness of his, that tough, streetwise manner was precisely what she'd fallen in love with. To Anna, his hardness, the things he'd seen and done, only made him that much more vulnerable, easier to love.

Anna glanced at him surreptitiously, knowingly, and felt warm and safe. He'd turned off the radio, and the only sound she heard was the swish of the wipers. It was snug in the car and hushed, the sound of the storm outside muffled.

She looked out the passenger window at the big snowflakes whipping by and felt as if she were inside one of those glass globes you shook. A winter wonderland. She was inside the globe, cozy and secure.

The outside world seemed unreal. There were only the two of them now.

It really *is* love, she thought.

They ate a late lunch in Georgetown, an old silver-mining town less than an hour west of Denver. The snow continued to fall heavily in the narrow valley that the interstate followed. No one seemed to mind the in-convenience of the storm, though, because Colorado was famous for its long winter season. The joke in the mountains had always been that Colorado had two seasons: winter and the Fourth of July.

Anna ate soup and a salad and watched Mark down a cheeseburger. She smiled to herself—there wasn't a thing she'd change about him, not even his bad eating habits. She'd take him and love him exactly as he was.

Maybe it was because Anna was so lost in her mus-ings that she didn't notice how quiet he became once they were back on the road. Maybe it was because she just didn't want to see the truth. She only knew that one minute she was on Cloud Nine, and the next she was crashing to earth.

"Maybe over Thanksgiving we could take Mark Jr. and Kelly skiing," Anna suggested.

Mark gave her a sidelong glance, his face impas-sive.

"What do you think?" she pressed.

He cleared his throat and checked the rearview mir-ror. "Look," he began, "it's sort of hard for me to make plans right now."

"Of course," she said. "It's weeks off. I just thought . . ."

"Anna," he said, and she heard a tightness in his voice. "It wouldn't matter if it was this afternoon."

"I don't—"

"I know you don't," he cut in. Then he gave her a swift look. "What happened...let's just say what happened between us last night was...a real bad idea. Please don't take this wrong, but..."

"Wrong?" she said.

"It's a job, Anna. I've got a job to do and I can't get things confused."

For a long, terrible moment she couldn't seem to fit her mind around what he'd said. "What do you mean?" She sat up straight in the passenger seat.

"Exactly what I told you. What we did together... What *I* did was a bad idea. I take all the blame."

"Oh, how gallant."

"Anna..."

"I can't believe this," she said. "You...you coward." She saw the hard line of his mouth. "You just needed an excuse, didn't you? It must have been driving you nuts since this morning. 'What can I tell Anna to get her off my back?' Your *job*," she said hotly. "Couldn't you come up with something more original?"

"Anna," he tried, "I really—"

"Don't. Don't make it worse. I've known plenty of guys like you before, Mark Righter. *Plenty*. But usually, I'm not fool enough to hop into bed with them." She looked over at him with tears burning behind her eyes. Then she couldn't help saying, "But sometimes I do, Mark, you bet. If I feel like having sex, I do. So let's write it off to that. We both needed a good—"

"Goddamn it," he said. "Don't you goddamn say it."

"Oh? It's okay for *you* to say it whenever you want? But not me? Then *screw* you, Mark. How's that?" She folded her arms tightly across her chest and stared out the passenger window. Everything was a blur.

* * *

The Hunter was ready. Winter was fast taking hold of the land and he'd prepared himself, emptying his refrigerator of perishables, paying two months' rent in advance to his landlady—the old-bitch. Earl was not around much anymore. He wasn't really needed now that work was finished—though Earl had quit a few weeks earlier than planned. But the Hunter had told him to, told him to get that last cash from his boss. Earl worked for cash whenever possible, because the Hunter needed to remain anonymous: he preferred no paycheck records, no bank accounts, no way to trace him.

Robert Larkin did not exist except as a name on a tax roll, an outdated Wyoming driver's license, a social security number, a birth certificate, or as a memory perhaps, in Baggs, Wyoming. He had no permanent address except a box number in Wyoming, and the old ranch. Few paths led to him; little paperwork contained his name. It was almost as if he'd disappeared off the face of the earth, which in reality he had. The Hunter had killed him off when Robert had become too dysfunctional to manage everyday life.

Now there was only Earl, the gardener, sweet kind Kate and, of course, the Hunter, who was in his most powerful cycle right now. It would soon be full-blown winter, after all.

He planned carefully, putting from his mind the knowledge that Anna was not in town. She would return. She had to. All he had to focus on was that one day—maybe today—he'd see her car round the corner and turn into her parking spot in the alley. He was a patient man. He'd wait.

As it turned out, the Hunter did not have to wait nearly as long as he'd imagined. He was sitting in his truck—where he'd spent most of the day—parked around the corner from the alley. The truck would be very difficult to spot, even for that arrogant cop. And the Hunter was prepared. He'd rehearsed the scene dozens of times, both in his mind and physically. Next to him on the truck seat was a tire iron. That was for the cop. In his hunting-jacket pocket was the little surprise for Anna: an ether-soaked rag rolled up in a carefully sealed Ziploc bag. Oh, he was ready, he thought, when suddenly her Camry appeared down the darkened street. Like magic.

For a moment, the Hunter froze in his seat. He'd expected to have to wait much longer for her return. This was too good to be true. Then he felt a pressure building inside him and a jagged-edge pain slice across his forehead. Reacting to the tensing of his muscles, he threw open the truck door just as her car pulled into the alley.

Stick to the plan, he reminded himself, and he began to breathe raggedly. Adrenaline pumped through his veins as he moved with the shadows along the brick wall of the building, watching her headlights swing when she pulled into her parking spot.

But it wasn't Anna driving, he registered instantly when the passenger door opened. The cop was at the wheel.

Stick to your plan.

He'd have to hit the cop first. Anna would, of course, try to run, maybe scream, but by the time anyone could react, she'd be subdued and in his truck.

The Hunter moved quickly, his eyes trained on the cop, who started climbing out of the car.

Slowly, carefully, don't give away your position.

Then something wonderful and wholly unexpected happened. Anna stalked away from the car, leaving the fool cop fumbling with the lock, yelling to her, "Goddamn it, wait up, Anna!"

The Hunter moved with the grace of a sleek cat, slipping through the darkness, his gut twisting with hate, the tire iron ready.

The cop spotted him a heartbeat too late. The Hunter swung the tire iron, catching the man behind his right ear with a blow that rattled the Hunter's teeth. The sound of iron connecting with flesh and bone was like the dull whomp of a watermelon hitting pavement.

The Hunter never stopped to watch the bigger man fall. He moved toward Anna, who was almost at the end of the alley. She must have heard something, because she stopped and turned. *Too late.*

The Hunter had the ether-soaked rag in his hand now, the chemical cold on his skin, the odor strong and nauseating.

He came up on her hard and quick, jamming the rag against her face, smothering a scream. She was strong, though, stronger than he'd dreamed, and he had a tough time fighting her flailing arms. But within seconds she sagged against him, her dark gold hair falling in a silky veil over his hand. His joy, his sense of absolute victory, made him weak for a moment before he collected himself and bent to drape her over his shoulder.

Anna, Anna, oh, what a wonderful time we'll have.

He moved back into the shadows, Anna heavy and warm over his shoulder. Behind him, a few feet from the Dumpster where he'd subdued her, was the Ziploc bag and the rag. He wouldn't remember it till he was in his truck, and then it would be too late.

Mark awakened in a haze of crimson pain. For a long time, there was only that pain and the sense of lying on something hard and cold.

Then he heard voices coming through the murk, as if people were trying to communicate with him underwater. He tried for a minute to swim up, but it was too difficult.

He must have sunk back down into that black abyss, because the next time he was aware of anything, the pain was not quite as ferocious. Bad, but somewhat subdued.

The voices were clearer. "Hey, come on, Mark, come on, partner," and he felt someone shaking his shoulder. Then, abruptly, came a searing white light in one of his eyes and he realized someone was holding his eyelid open.

"Can you hear me, Mr. Righter?"

Mark tried. But the pain. . . .

"Hey, partner, it's Hoagie. You're in the ER, pal, and right now you're scaring the shit out of all of us."

Mark groaned, and someone—a doctor?—shone that blinding light into his other eye.

Reality seeped back into his brain in slow, painful stages. He became aware of other people in the partitioned-off hospital alcove. He was on a gurney, in a helluva lot of pain, a bandage stuck to his head behind his right ear.

"Don't touch that yet," a young male doctor said to him when he reached up to feel the bandage.

Then Hoagie's voice again, "Careful, partner, you got some fancy needlework there."

Mark tried his own voice. "What . . . ?" but he had to lick his dry lips. He tried again. "What happened? How did I get . . . ?"

"Shh," came a woman's voice from somewhere above him.

Then Hoagie spoke. "Your doctor here recognized you, partner, and gave the station a call. They phoned me."

Suddenly, the whole thing came crashing back into Mark's brain—Anna upset with him, getting out of her car in a huff, walking away. He was looking up, mad at her, mad at himself, and then . . . blackness. And Anna . . .

He sat bolt upright. "Anna? Goddamn it, where is she?" But he knew.

Hoagie met his pained gaze. He nodded. "We checked her loft, the streets, everywhere we could think of. They're still searching the area, pal, but . . ."

Mark groaned and pushed the doctor's steadying hand off his shoulder. "You won't find her," he said. "Larkin's got her." He swore a string of oaths. "The son of a bitch got her, Hoagie."

Just then, Dunning and his wife arrived, Hoagie having called them. It was obvious they'd been at a dinner party or something, because Dunning was decked out in a tux and his wife was in silver and blue sequins, something long and nonrevealing. But what stuck in Mark's brain was that Lydia was crying.

"Can you tell us what happened?" Dunning was saying, his handsome face lined and drawn.

Mark fought down the pain and nausea and the mounting rage in his gut. He told them everything he could remember about the abduction, carefully leaving out the fight he and Anna had had. He told them about Robert Larkin up in Wyoming, and there, too, he left out vital information—that Larkin had undoubtedly killed both Valerie Duchesne and his own mother. The Dunnings were apt to learn that soon enough.

"But you've got his name now," Scott said. "Can't he be traced?"

Mark looked at Hoagie for help.

"Well," Hoagie said, "it's like this. I ran a bunch of computer searches on him today, and so far, zip."

"How the hell is that possible?" Dunning demanded.

Mark answered. "He's most likely been using an alias. Either that, or he works for cash, doesn't keep a bank account, stuff like that."

Lydia held on to her husband's arm and sniffed. "What about that truck? Anna said you saw some of the plate numbers . . ."

"We did," Mark said, a bolt of pain sliding through his head. "That is, *I* saw it. But the plate was stolen in Wyoming."

"He has to register the damn thing," Dunning put in.

"You know how easy it is to steal a current registration sticker off a car?" Hoagie asked.

"Of course," Lydia breathed. "No one gets new plates anymore, only those stickers."

"Exactly," Mark said.

Dunning looked up sharply. "We'll call in the FBI. This is a kidnapping."

"We can't call them in for twenty-four hours," Hoagie said. "That's the deal. Besides, no one knows where to look yet. We have to do some research. Then, *if* it's over twenty-four hours, we'll alert them." He grimaced. "They never do a goddamn thing right anyway, probably get your sister . . . Sorry."

"Look," Mark said, climbing painfully down off the gurney, ignoring the doctor's warning, "I'm going to get Anna back for you. For me, damn it, for her. I'll get her." He met Dunning's and Lydia's eyes. "It's my job. She was in my trust." He felt a sick, oily fear churn in his stomach.

"Oh, God," Lydia said, burying her face in her husband's chest. "What if she's . . . What if he . . ."

"He hasn't," Mark said in a deadly cold voice.

"But how do you know?" Dunning asked quietly.

"I just know," was all Mark would say. What could he tell them? That Larkin would keep her alive, rape and beat her over and over until she begged for death?

He staggered toward the curtain, pushing it aside. Oh, God, he thought, don't let me fall apart now.

TWENTY

$$\approx\!\!\diamond\!\!\approx$$

Anna woke up with a headache, a foul taste in her mouth and a heaving stomach. She lay where she was for a time, stunned and lost, trying to remember something. Confusion gripped her, and she couldn't make her mind work properly. She heard herself groan, and bile came up in her throat. Swallowing, she opened her eyes and it was like a dream—nothing was real, nothing was familiar.

The smell hit her senses first: wood smoke. Then sound: the crackling of a fire. She was warm, and when she tried to move, she was constricted.

Finally, her mind concentrated on something firm and real. *Mark*. Where was Mark?

She groggily pushed herself up on her elbow and tried to call him, but her mouth was dry, her tongue thick.

She was in a strange place, a room made of logs, with a fire in a square, black wood stove, a bed, a counter and buckets of water.

She looked down and saw an olive-drab sleeping bag pulled up around her. A small panic budded in her chest. Then she heard the sound, a rhythmic pounding. Someone outside was chopping wood.

She was so thirsty.

Standing up shakily, Anna walked to the bucket, cupped a hand and drank. Her stomach contracted violently, and suddenly it all came rushing back. Mark calling her, but she was too hurt and angry to stop, then a sound, a scuffle and an awful thud, then a shadow on her, the rag across her nose, the awful smell . . . She gagged and collapsed where she was on the wood-plank floor.

He had her.

Mark? What had happened to him? She'd seen him, hadn't she, on the ground? Oh, my God, she thought, was Mark dead?

Panic clawed at her. She had to think, but her head swam. He'd made her breathe something that knocked her out. The smell, yes, she remembered a sickening smell.

Think, think. Where was she? She stood and made her way to one of the small windows. What she saw took her breath away: a blinding white curtain of snow. Nothing else.

Where was she? She looked at her watch. Eight-thirty. In the morning. Over twelve hours had passed. She could be anywhere within a five-hundred-mile radius. No, not in this storm. She had to be in the mountains for it to be snowing like this. And not that far.

She walked unsteadily to the door and tried the latch. It wouldn't move.

She had to escape. But first she had to find out where she was and get together some winter clothes. She'd have to bide her time. He hadn't killed her right away, so that meant he wanted something from her.

Sex? Mark had said stalkers were often impotent. What else had he told her? She couldn't think, couldn't remember. Obsessed. Hated women. Delusional.

Mark. She stifled a sob. It was her fault. And now no one knew where she was, they wouldn't even know she'd been gone for all this time. Please, she prayed, let Mark be all right. But even if he was, he didn't know where she'd been taken. No one knew.

There was a sound at the door, and Anna stared at it in horror. The latch—an old-fashioned wooden latch—lifted and the heavy door creaked inward. She backed up until she felt the rough wall behind her. The door opened all the way, the whirling snow ushered in an apparition. The first thing she saw was a gun in the crook of his elbow, then an armful of wood.

She drew in her breath in a quick rasp and held it. White balaclava, an insulated winter camouflage suit, white Sorel boots and mittens. No face, only pale eyes in the opening of the balaclava. She knew those eyes.

He dumped the wood by the stove, brushed sawdust off himself, removed the balaclava and set the gun down. He smiled at her, a triumphant, smug rictus.

She watched him, horrified and fascinated. An ordinary young man about her own age: a narrow face, a long, pointed nose and blond buzz-cut hair. Pale eyes that were like empty holes through which the sky showed. He was of medium height, medium build. Where had she seen him before? Had she ever noticed him at all?

"Good morning," he said in a normal voice. It wasn't that awful whisper.

"Where are we?" Anna dared to ask.

"In my cabin."

"Where is your cabin?"

"I could tell you, but it wouldn't mean much to you. We're in the mountains."

"In Colorado?"

He looked at her shrewdly. "Yes, but that won't help you."

"Why have you been after me like this? What did I ever do to you?"

"Why, Anna, you exist, that's all. That's enough, isn't it? I wanted you. I have you."

"What are you going to do with me?"

"Lots of things. I'm going to enjoy you."

He sounded sane, though she knew he wasn't. How did you manipulate someone like this?

"How did we get here?" she asked.

"I drove, then we took my snowmobile. It's the only way in a storm like this."

She was silent for a time, and he just stood there looking at her, smiling.

"I know who you are," she finally said. "You're Robert Larkin."

He shook his head. "No, you're wrong. Robert Larkin is dead. I killed him."

She shivered. "The police know who you are. Mark told them. They're after you right now."

He laughed. "There is no Robert Larkin. They can't find him. I've made sure of that."

"Then who *are* you?"

"I'm the Hunter."

"Don't you have a name?"

"I'm the Hunter. That's who I am."

She tried to keep her wits about her. He was stark raving mad, but he wasn't stupid.

"What did you give me to make me so sick?"

"Ether."

"And Mark . . . what did you do to him?"

"Your precious Mark," he said with the first emotion she'd seen in him. "That disgusting hairy policeman. Stupid, crude. I hit him as hard as I could. I hope I killed him. Or maybe he'll just be real dumb the rest of his life."

She slid down the wall, knelt on the floor and put her face in her hands. *Mark.* But she was jerked upright. He stuck his face in hers. "Don't you cry for him. I'll see to it you don't, you slut. I'll make you cry, but it won't be for him!"

She pulled away, but his grip was like iron. Then abruptly he dropped her arm, turned his back on her and unzipped his suit. He stepped out of it and hung it on a peg. He wore jeans and a hunter's red-and-black plaid wool shirt, long underwear showing at the neck. A wicked-looking hunting knife hung from his belt in a sheath, and he wore a handgun in a leather holster. He knelt on one knee, opened the stove door and jammed some wood in.

"I have to go to the bathroom," she finally said to his back. "Do you have someplace . . ."

He turned on her, angry again. "Of course, I do. You think I'm a pig? It's outside."

"Oh."

"I'll take you."

She recoiled. "I can do it myself."

He pointed derisively. "Look at what you're wearing. You wouldn't even make it to the outhouse in those shoes."

"I wasn't planning on coming here," she said quietly.

"But *I* planned on bringing you here." The evil grin again. "I've been planning it for months. I had to wait for winter, though. So I have things for you." He puffed out his chest, proud. "And they'll fit. I know everything about you."

He went to a chest and pulled out Sorel boots, a knit cap, mittens and a one-piece insulated orange snowmobile suit. "Put them on. You'll be warm. Then I'll take you out there."

Don't argue, she told herself, don't rile him. Play along. Don't make him angry. She put on the clothes and pulled on the boots. Everything fit.

He suited himself up, grabbed the gun and opened the door, gesturing her out ahead of him. "Follow the path," he said.

Anna stepped into the storm. Snow was coming down in big, heavy flakes. There wasn't much wind, and it fell straight down; she could see it piling up. It wasn't very cold—but in the Rockies, she knew, the warm storms held the most moisture. She followed a footpath, keeping her head down. She almost bumped into the outhouse.

"Go on," he said, pointing with the gun barrel.

She opened the door and closed it in his face. It had no latch. At least he wasn't insisting on being in there with her. The outhouse was cold and her flesh rose in goose bumps, but at least it was new and clean and smelled of pine.

After she was done, she pulled the suit and mittens back on and opened the door. He was waiting in the snow, his balaclava pulled down over his face. He motioned with his gun, and she went ahead of him back to the cabin. She could see nothing around her; the snow was coming down too thickly. There was a snowmobile parked near the front door, and she could see a rapidly disappearing track that led away from the cabin.

An image flashed in her head—the snowmobile, noisy and snarling. She couldn't wake up, and he was dragging her, lifting her, then that awful smell again.

Inside, they stripped off the suits, hung them on pegs to drip, and he stuffed more wood into the fire. She watched him carefully, searching for any weakness in him, or any sudden danger. He moved well, easily and smoothly, without wasted motion. His cabin was snug and neat: a locked gun rack filled with various rifles, a handmade bed with a military sleeping bag laid on it, the big wood stove with buckets of water on top, open shelves with cans and bags of flour and sugar and coffee, and kerosene lamps. No radio or telephone, no electricity or running water. Just the heavy door and three sturdy, small-paned windows.

Escape would be very hard. She'd have to wait for the storm to end, in any case. A blizzard in the mountains was a deadly phenomenon—she knew enough not to fool around with it. Even if the Hunter weren't there, she wouldn't be able to get out until the storm was over.

She'd have to try a new tack. "You have a nice place here."

"Yes, I know. It suits me. I stay here for months in the winter."

"Don't you have to work?"

"Not in the winter. And *I* don't work. Earl does."

"Who's Earl?"

"A friend. You'd like him."

"Where is he?"

"I left him in Denver."

She prodded a little. "And the lady, the pretty blond lady."

"That's Kate."

"She followed me," Anna said.

"I made her. She was very clever."

"She was in that deli, wasn't she?"

"And lots of other places. You never noticed."

Kate. Earl. The Hunter. Were there others? "Do you have any other friends?" she asked.

"No, I don't need any others."

"But you're really Robert Larkin, aren't you?"

He laughed. "I told you, he's dead. Dead as a doornail. Dead and buried. He was a real loser."

"Robert was from Baggs, Wyoming, wasn't he?"

The pale empty eyes swung on her.

"I was there," she said. "Mark and I were there. We talked to your brother...I mean Robert's brother, John."

"John."

"Robert's brother, John Larkin. He lives on his mother's ranch. He has a wife and two little children."

"John Larkin."

"Yes." She watched him carefully. He seemed unmoved, but a little puzzled. Remembering something long forgotten.

"He looks a little like you, only shorter and broader. He was very nice. His wife was nice, too. They'd like to see you again," she lied. "They'd like you to see your nephews."

"I don't have any nephews."

She didn't press him, but she could see behind his pale gaze to the emptiness shot with a new uncertainty.

"I'm going now," he said abruptly.

"Going where?"

"To check my trap line. Snowshoe hares. I cook a real good rabbit stew."

"In this storm?" she asked.

"I like snow. I'm trained. I'm prepared. Winter is my time." He grinned at her. "I'll lock the door from the outside. And none of those guns are loaded, even if you could get them out of the rack."

"I'll wait here then," she said.

"Feed the fire. Don't let it go out or you'll freeze."

He dressed himself again, putting on a pair of big snowshoes. He took his gun and stepped outside. She could hear him locking the door—it sounded like a padlock. Then there was only silence, the pop of a burning log in the stove and her own heart pounding heavily, sluggishly, in her chest.

Maybe, Anna thought in that first blessed instance of being alone, he'd die out there in the storm and never come back.

The Hunter moved easily on his snowshoes, at one with the storm. He was dry and warm, everything he wore was waterproof, weatherproof, quick-drying, tear-resistant and the right color for this environment.

He carried his Remington .410 semiautomatic shotgun easily in the crook of his arm, as much a part of him as his arms and legs. He loved to be out in the weather. He'd often thought about moving to Alaska, but it seemed too much trouble. He could, though, if he wanted. He could do anything he wanted. He had the power.

He walked, sure of his direction despite the whiteout, and he thought about Anna Dunning. She was his at last. He thought about what he'd do to her, and he pictured her face changing, screaming, the fear in her eyes, the pain, the pleading. She was very brave, and she'd last a long time.

He hadn't had a woman for quite a while, not since the one on East Colfax last year, and she didn't count, not really. She'd just been for physical release; there'd been nothing spiritual about her death. He'd watched the papers for days, but there'd been no mention of the woman's disappearance. She must have been completely alone, that prostitute. How fortunate.

Anna's death would be a real celebration, a profoundly moving event. He wished he could share it, but Earl and Kate got upset. Only *he* knew the beauty of their deaths. And no one would ever find this one. The Hunter's victims always disappeared without a trace.

All except one. That one had been different. He'd left her lying there, all slashed and bloody, for the world to see. She had been pure evil.

The Hunter came upon his first trap—empty. He reset it and carefully brushed snow over its steel jaws. It'd be covered by new snow in a few minutes, anyway.

He went on, tireless, into the dim white curtain of endlessly falling snow. He thought about Margaret Larkin. She'd been Robert's mother, and of all creatures on earth the most hateful, cruel, unnatural mother that had ever existed.

Robert hadn't had the balls to raise a hand to her, not once in his miserable life. But the Hunter had.

She'd terrorized both her sons, though Robert more than John. She'd chased away their father years before, the ugly witch. A stump of a woman, short and thick, with stringy gray hair and pale eyelashes. She'd screamed at them, but she'd been more dangerous when she was quiet. She pinched and slapped and kicked, and she had more tricks up her sleeve than physical punishment. It was her faith that was the worst. Everything was a sin. What did little boys know about sin? She'd taught them.

She'd locked them in dark places, alone—closets, the root cellar. She'd set one brother against the other. Guilt tortured them both, guilt about everything and nothing.

She caught them once, the two brothers seeing who could pee the farthest, out by the barn. She'd backhanded one then the other, and dragged them into the house where she poured boiling water onto their crotches. He still felt the burning water, still had the scars.

No, that was Robert. The Hunter had no scars.

Screaming—he could still hear her voice ringing in his head—"Dirty filthy foul disgusting *boys!* I'll burn them off!"

He'd been ten or so, he guessed. No, *Robert* had been ten. Ashamed, scared, his skin blistering. It hurt when he peed but he was afraid to tell anyone. At school, he used the bathroom only when he was alone.

So, she'd deserved to die, and when the Hunter had become strong enough, he'd done it.

The second trap had been sprung, but coyotes had eaten whatever it had held. Only a few tattered skin flaps and some pink snow packed down around the trap remained. He reset it.

That was fair. If he came across a coyote kill and could take it away, that'd be fair, too. The coyotes and foxes and cougars were predators like him, and he respected them.

Two more traps on his line. He trudged on, shaking snow off his head and shoulders, liking the soft taps of the flakes on his waterproof suit. He smiled under the white balaclava.

Margaret Larkin. Robert had called her Mother. Both brothers had worked so hard on that dirt-poor ranch, busted their butts. She'd never even noticed when the Hunter moved in. But he'd studied her and waited. He'd practiced on another girl first, so the power could grow in him.

In the winter, always in the cold and snow.

No one could find the Hunter—not that anyone even knew enough to look for him, because he'd gone up into the hills after that girl and lived there for a year, growing smarter and stronger. He'd trapped and hunted and fished, eating berries and wild mushrooms. No one knew where he was.

Then, the next winter, in a big storm, with the wind howling down from the Medicine Bow Mountains, the Hunter came out of the hills to the Larkin ranch to take care of business. He was whipcord strong by then, lean and quick and sure, an avenging angel. Neither of the brothers were home, and he caught her alone watching television. He killed her with his hunting knife, brutally, without finesse, and left her there bleeding on the floor of the foul little house. And before he left, taking all her money and the keys to her truck, he kicked her dead body once, hard.

Then he'd had freedom. He'd found Earl, who was strong and could do hard physical labor all day without complaining—although nothing was as rough as working on the ranch. Earl found plenty of jobs, for cash, moving around. He saved just about every penny. Not in a bank, either.

Last year, the Hunter had been able to buy the cabin and fix it up and stock it. It made him happy—a warm, secure place he could always return to. No one knew where it was. He'd paid for it with cash and kept the deed in his strongbox. The only thing that had bothered him a little was the legal papers. It was easy enough to pay the taxes in person, but the deed and taxes had to be in someone's name, someone who had a real social security number. He'd had to give Robert's name. The address was fake, but he still didn't like it. It was, however, the price he'd had to pay.

The third trap held nothing and hadn't even been sprung. He moved on, thinking about Anna again. She was back there waiting, scared, though she tried to cover it up. He recalled the feel of her warm, unconscious body, and he shivered with delight. He'd do better than that, though. He had some creative ideas.

The fourth trap held a large snowshoe hare. It stared up at him with stupid, silent fear. He cut its throat cleanly, and watched the life fade out of its eyes. The difference between life and death, he knew, was one heartbeat, one drop of blood, one moment. He skinned and gutted it deftly, wiping his bloody knife off with snow.

Then he reset the trap and started back to the cabin, thinking of rabbit stew and Anna.

He felt renewed, the scent of fresh blood in his nostrils. He'd always loved to kill animals, even as a kid.

Or had that been Robert?

Twenty-One

Lil sat in a chair next to Mark's bed and watched him like a hawk. Twenty-four hours, Hoagie had said when he'd brought Mark home last night. The doctor had told Hoagie a concussion victim had to be watched for twenty-four hours because he could fall asleep and not wake up. And the only way anyone would let Mark go home was if someone was there to watch him.

She was tired, but it didn't matter; she just might be saving Mark's life. She could sit there all night and watch him, feast her eyes on him and spin crazy fantasies in her head. Dreaming about Mark was one of the few luxuries Lil allowed herself.

She watched him sleep, his chest rising and falling rhythmically. Once, during the night, she'd put her hand on his shoulder, his warm, smooth skin, just for a little while. He'd never know.

She could pretend, just for this one night, couldn't she? And then she'd be his old pal Lil again.

Mark wasn't even fully awake when the nausea hit him with the force of a hammer. He flew out of bed naked and hit the bathroom, not bothering to close the door.

"You damn fool," Lil said, standing helplessly in the bathroom door. "The doctor told you to stay in the hospital overnight. So did Hoagie. But not you, not Mr. Tough Guy."

Mark retched into the toilet. "Just shut up, Lil," he managed to utter between heaves. "And get me my goddamn robe."

He felt better in the shower; he realized he might live, after all. It was time to pull himself together, to forget the nausea and the headache and get to work. He figured he had three, four days tops, to locate Anna. Then that sicko Larkin would hit one of his violent spells and she'd be history.

He was getting out of the shower when Lil dragged the telephone in to him. "It's Hoagie," she said, giving Mark a once-over and smiling.

Mark took the phone while he wrapped a towel one-handed around his torso.

"Hey, partner," Hoagie said. "I take it you're alive."

"Barely."

"I've got some news. Remember the letter you left with me?"

"Sure."

"We got a partial thumbprint. But better yet, buddy, that Ziploc bag we picked up in the alley last night has a dozen good prints on it. They're a match to the partial."

"Where does that get us?"

"Not real far, because this dude isn't on any of our databases. No license, no income tax, no registration for the truck, no credit cards. I was hoping for an alias or something. But the good news is that the ether on the rag is relatively fresh."

"So?"

"So, our boy got it sometime in the last twelve, eighteen months. Probably at a med-supply house. Maybe here in Denver."

"What about hospitals?"

"I've got someone checking, but hospitals don't wash real good. Access problem. Our boy would have to be a nurse, at least, and you know the psychological profile—blue-collar."

"Uh-huh."

"Same deal with a pharmacy or dentist's office. Statistics say he pilfered it from a med-supply house."

"Makes sense." Mark ran a hand through his wet hair. "The only way we'll get a lead on our man through that source is if he used his real name."

"I know."

"And even if he did, that's not going to tell us where he's got Anna. Not unless he gave a legit home address, and not unless he's keeping her there."

"Remember Jeffrey Dahmer?" Hoagie said. "He kept 'em at home."

"Hell, don't remind me," Mark muttered, a stab of fear knifing through his gut, making him feel sick all over again. Anna . . .

"I can start at the med supplies," Hoagie suggested.

But Mark knew it wasn't going to work. Not this way. "Is Franklin there?" he asked suddenly.

"Yeah, sure. Why?"

"Because I need my badge and gun, Hoagie."

"Whoa, there. Thought you'd never, and I quote, not in a million years, come back to the department."

"Yeah, well," Mark said grimly, "that was before Anna."

Against Lil's—and everyone's—advice, Mark got out of bed and went to work. He marched into his old Denver Police Department headquarters forty minutes later and went straight to Franklin's office.

"I've been expecting you," Franklin said from behind his desk.

Mark held his gaze coldly. "I need my badge and my gun," he stated flatly. "I'm on this case, Franklin. It's kidnapping now."

Franklin stared straight back at him. "I guess you know I got a call from the police commissioner. *He* got a call from the mayor, it seems."

Mark was bewildered.

"Seems your new best friends the Dunnings talked to the mayor last night. I won't go into details, but the mayor wants you reinstated. Needless to say, Righter, I'm the one on the hot seat."

Mark didn't understand. The Dunnings called the mayor—and Franklin was on the hot seat?

"Puzzled?" Franklin asked, sneering.

"I'm trying to put two and two together," Mark allowed.

"I never liked you, Righter," the captain said. He reached into a desk drawer and pulled out a badge and .38 police special—Mark's old equipment.

Mark grinned.

"You're a maverick, Righter, and you've never learned how to follow orders." Franklin eyed him contemptuously as Mark picked up his badge and gun from the top of the desk.

"I'd stay and chat," Mark said, "but I've got work to do."

"Yeah," Franklin said. "You've got to find that Dunning broad you're screwing."

Mark was at the door. Slowly he turned back. "When this is over," he said, "I'm going to make you eat those words, Franklin. Count on it." And with that he left, heading toward Hoagie's desk.

They drove to every medical-supply house in Denver before noon, flashing their badges and asking to see personnel records for the last two years. Because the ether was fresh, the odds were that Larkin had gotten it in Denver, most likely stolen it as an employee. Still, Mark knew the odds didn't always pay off. And Larkin could have been using an alias, though these kind of businesses tended to hire legitimate workers who could produce proof of citizenship and social security numbers. So maybe this one time Larkin had used his real name. The question remained: What was the connection between Anna and her abductor? There always was one. And all Mark kept seeing through a haze of fear was that damn pickup truck. The Wyoming plates. If he could just remember. If the pain in his head would only subside for a few minutes.

The record keepers at the medical-supply houses were very cooperative for the most part. Still, Mark and Hoagie were batting zero, and it was beginning to look as if Hoagie's nose was wrong; Larkin had not gotten the ether from a supplier.

That left the hospitals and clinics. Hundreds of them. *If* Larkin even got the stuff in Denver.

They drove to the last address at twelve, just as everyone in the office was on the way out to lunch. It took all of Mark's finesse to persuade a Mrs. Anthos to check her personnel records before she left.

"I'm supposed to meet my husband in ten minutes," she said, her lips compressed.

"Please," Mark said. "I know this is a cliché, but it's a matter of life and death."

"No shit," Hoagie added undiplomatically.

The woman shot Hoagie a look.

"So what's this guy's name?" Mrs. Anthos asked, pulling open a file drawer.

"Larkin, Robert Larkin," Mark said.

"Oh, *him*," she said, and it was a full second before her words hit home. She pulled out a folder. Mark's heart was thumping. "Here he is. I remember him because he gave me a lot of grief over having to pay taxes. And when he left, because he sure didn't stay long, I found out he gave me a fake social security number. All my paperwork came back, all the government stuff. You can imagine what a mess—"

"Yeah, yeah, I'm sure," Hoagie interrupted. "But do you have anything else on him?"

"A picture. All our staff wear ID tags," she went on. "Strange guy. He didn't have a phone. And I had a real hard time getting his address. He wanted to give me a box number." She handed Mark the folder.

Mark opened it, and there was his picture in black and white, big as life. Certainly not Rod Miller or Kenneth Carter, but Mr. Robert Larkin of Baggs, Wyoming.

He was a pleasant-looking man, nondescript, really, so ordinary it was eerie. But then, Ted Bundy had been, too.

Mark scanned the pages and saw an address. His heart knocked against his ribs. "Write down 2603 Paramount Road, Lakewood," he told Hoagie. "Got it?"

"Uh-huh," Hoagie said.

Ten minutes later they were speeding out to Lakewood, west of Denver. As they neared foothill country, a light snow began to drift out of a gray sky. "God, I hate winter," Hoagie said. "Depresses me."

Mark said nothing.

Mark did the navigating while Hoagie drove, and they found Paramount quickly. "Turn left here," Mark said as he began scanning house numbers. He could feel his blood pressure rising as the numbers climbed, nearing the right one. Please, God, he thought, let her be here, let her be alive. He never even prayed that she'd be okay. He knew better. Larkin had had her for almost twenty hours now.

The house was a modest split-level brick job with a tidy yard and mature landscaping. It didn't seem quite right until Mark spotted an addition that ran perpendicular to it into the backyard. A rental unit.

Hoagie saw it, too. "Uh-huh," he said.

They went to the front door and Mark knocked, fairly certain no one in the rental could spot either them or the car out front. A woman, probably in her early seventies, answered the door. She was in a housedress, slippers and a hairnet. A soap opera played on a television set in the background.

Yes, the man in the photograph rented from her, but he called himself Earl, not Robert Larkin. And yes, he drove an older blue pickup, Wyoming plates.

By now Mark's heart was pumping furiously as he fought rage and the constant fear that he'd be too late to save her.

"You got a key, lady?" Hoagie asked.

"Well, I don't—"

"Don't make us get a warrant," Mark said in a deadly cold voice. "This tenant of yours is wanted for a federal offense, kidnapping."

She eyed him, disappeared for a minute and came back with a key. Then she dropped a bomb. "He won't be liking you looking around like this," she said.

"How's that?" Hoagie asked.

"Well, he's gone, you know. Left yesterday."

"Gone?" Mark demanded.

"Sure. Paid his rent for two months and took off. Hunting, you know."

"Where?" Mark and Hoagie asked in chorus.

"I wouldn't know." She began to close the door. "You bring my key back, hear?"

They were careful entering Larkin's tiny apartment and had their guns ready. Mark went first, praying the landlady was wrong, knowing in his gut she wasn't. It all fit, the hunting clothes, everything. He'd gone hunting, all right.

They searched the place in under a minute, found the Soloflex and the women's clothes—Mark recognized the ladies' coat. Then he saw something that rang a bell in his brain, a canvas bag in a corner with gardening tools stuck in it.

"Holy God in heaven," Mark breathed. "Dunning's."

"What?" Hoagie said from the kitchen area where he was opening drawers, searching for something, anything.

"The truck." Mark could hardly get the words out. "I saw that pickup the first day I drove over to Dunning's! Parked around the back." He sank onto the edge of the bed, head in his palms. He remembered the guy pruning rosebushes or something, real friendly.

His eyes snapped up to meet Hoagie's. "*Larkin*. I saw him the first goddamn day!"

They reached Dunning at his downtown sky-scraper on Hoagie's cell phone and met him on the street half an hour later. The traffic had been heavy, and Hoagie had used the flashing red light on the roof of his unmarked car to get them there quickly. They were lucky they'd reached him; Dunning told them he'd spent most of the night and day by Lydia's side, not taking calls, except from the police.

Mark filled Dunning in as fast as possible.

"Sunshine Landscaping," he told them. "But I only knew the workman as Earl, or something like that. I assumed the owner of the service paid them all cash. I mean that's typical, but I never dreamed... I never thought this...this *jerk* was a criminal. Oh, God." His eyes grew moist and distant. "Anna. The man worked for me!"

"Hey," Hoagie said, "you aren't to blame here, Mr. Dunning. That creep is."

"How the hell do you think *I* feel?" Mark muttered. "She was in my care."

Dunning searched his face. "Will she be all right?" he whispered.

"Yes," Mark lied. "This guy's not going to . . . hurt her. He took her because he's infatuated and sick."

"But when he's done with my sister," Dunning said brokenly, "then what?"

Mark couldn't answer.

They found the owner of Sunshine Landscaping working not far from the Dunning home in Cherry Creek. The guy, Larry, was as helpful as possible.

"Sure, Earl," he said. "He quit, though. Something about hunting season." He leaned on a shovel. "He do something wrong?"

Mark evaded the question. "You paid him in cash."

The man hesitated. "Ah, yeah, I did. Is that what this is about?"

"No," Hoagie said. "What we need is info on where this guy, Earl, hangs out."

Larry shrugged. "Nowhere that I know. He was nice enough, a good worker and all, but didn't really make friends."

"Where does he hunt?" Mark asked.

"Well, the mountains, you know. Deer, elk. He talked a little about that."

"Any favorite spot?" Mark asked, not expecting an answer.

"Oh, yeah, I do recall that he bought a cabin or something. Sure. He mentioned it."

Mark met Hoagie's eyes. "A cabin?" he asked Larry.

"Western Slope, I think. Yeah. He said he got it cheap and could live there for practically nothing. He said he could spend a whole winter there. I remember thinking I'd go out of my mind if I spent a winter in some mountain cabin. Me, I'm a summer type, you know."

"Uh-huh," Mark said.

Hoagie put his hand on Mark's arm. "If he bought this place, pal, the county where it's located recorded the sale. It'll have him on file. He's got to pay real estate taxes. Even if it's only a few bucks a year."

"Let's go," Mark said, "time for some of your computer magic." He was in the biggest hurry he'd ever been in in his life. Still, when he got to Hoagie's car, he paused, his hand on the roof, his gaze lifting to the

mountains. She was up there somewhere. Up there
with that goddamn sicko. Scared, alone, hurt—God
only knew *how* hurt. And what had Mark said to her?
Oh, Jeez, Anna, thanks for the roll in the hay, but I've
got to keep my mind on the job.

She'd called him a coward. And she was right. He'd
never been so afraid in his life.

Mark took off out of Denver that evening. The U.S.
Forest Service map of the High Tower Wilderness south
of Rifle, Colorado, lay on the seat next to him, the
route marked, the tiny spot circled: Robert Larkin's
cabin on the mining claim he'd bought for a thousand
dollars in 1995. It had taken Hoagie a couple of hours,
and some fancy footwork, but he'd finally found the
listing in the Garfield County clerk's records.

Mark drove Anna's car—it was better in the snow
than his, and the weather reports in the mountains
were for heavy snow on and off for the next few days.
He drove like a madman, planning to follow the same
route through the mountains that he and Anna had just
returned on. He bent over the wheel like a wild beast,
gripping it, white-knuckled. He had his winter gear in
the back seat: long underwear, flashlight, hunting
boots, insulated pants, parka, hat, gloves, sleeping
bag. He'd hated wasting the time it took to drag the
stuff out of the closet, but Lil had helped him. Then
she'd hugged him and wished him luck. She'd had tears
in her eyes.

Hoagie had begged him to wait until the mountain
storm stopped so that he could go in with proper
backup—the Garfield County Sheriff's Office, even
the FBI. A helicopter was standing by, but it couldn't
fly in the storm.

"Wait," he'd pleaded. "Don't pull your usual stunt and go alone. Righter, listen to me."

"I can't wait," he'd said. "It's my fault she's in danger."

"I goddamn give up on you," Hoagie had said. "*Cowboy.*"

He had his gun with him and an arrest warrant for Robert Larkin. He also had the cellular phone he'd made Anna carry, for all the good it had done *her*. But he had no idea how long the battery would last without being recharged. Less than a full day, he suspected.

It got dark as he hit Golden, just west of Denver, and it started spitting snow in Idaho Springs. Inside the tunnel was the only clear spot after that, and when he emerged from it, a white wall rose in front of his headlights. Traffic was slow, the interstate covered in slush and the snow as thick as he'd ever seen it.

Damn, he raged inwardly. He pounded the steering wheel in frustration, then swore at the pain in his hand. He tried to pull out around a huge semi, but only got a windshield of slush for his efforts and had to drop back, blind for a moment.

Off to the sides of the highway the dim lights of Frisco and Silverthorne swept past. He made the slow climb up Vail Pass—endless dark, slippery—then wound his way back down. Cars were off the road everywhere; Mark saw one spin out just ahead, its lights scoring circles in the darkness.

Hang in there, Anna, he thought a hundred times. Don't push the guy, play along. Let him...Mark ground his teeth and swallowed his bile...let him touch you, if he has to. You can do it, Anna. If anyone can do it, you can.

His head still hurt, but it was a small thing. He hadn't eaten all day. Lil had stuck a bag of cookies in the car, saying it was all she had, but he wasn't hungry, anyway.

Past Vail. Oh, wouldn't the skiing in the back bowls be great in the morning, he thought, fleetingly. Yeah, sure, if that's all you had to think about—fresh powder snow.

Through Minturn, Eagle, and finally into Glenwood Springs. He didn't stop, but he did call the Garfield County Sheriff's Office in Glenwood, explaining the situation. A state snowplow went past as he was on the phone, spraying his car with dirty slush, drowning out the deputy he was talking to.

"Robert Larkin," he repeated. "Thirty-one years old, a hundred and seventy pounds, five-ten, blond, blue eyes. Armed and dangerous. Vehicle is a dark blue pickup, Chevy, around a '73, plate number 43-4951 Wyoming. He's got a female hostage."

"You know he's in Garfield County?"

"Ninety-nine percent sure," Mark said. "You'll be hearing from my captain. We'll set up an operation with you. May even have to call in the fibbies."

"And you're from where?" the deputy asked.

"Denver PD, Detective Righter, main office. You can check with them. Captain Franklin or Detective Billings. I'm driving by you right now on my way to where he's holding her. Take this down."

"Go ahead."

"It's a cabin on a consolidated mining claim in the High Tower Mountain area of the White River National Forest."

"I know the area. Hunted there."

"You know an area called Mud Hill? Grid twenty on the map?"

"Sure do. And it ain't called mud for nothing. You'll never make it up there. Not in this weather."

"I realize that."

"Well, we can't help you out, Detective. We're pinned down by the storm, already got six camps full of hunters stranded all over the place. You might want to wait until the snow stops."

"I can't," Mark said.

"Call the Rifle police department," the deputy suggested. "They'll know the area even better than us."

"Will do. And will you put out that bulletin on Larkin? Armed and dangerous. I believe he's holed up, but in case he isn't, his hostage is a white female, five-seven, one-thirty, brown hair, brown eyes. Anna Dunning."

"Got it." A pause. "Good luck, Detective."

"Thanks." I'll need it, he thought as he hung up.

He drove out of Glenwood, past Storm King Mountain. He had only twenty miles to where he had to turn off, but the going was slow, his windshield wipers swiping at the snow hypnotically, back and forth, the tires hissing in the slush.

He called the Rifle police as soon as he was within range and spoke to a female dispatcher. He told her the story all over again.

"I'll phone the chief," she said. "This is too much for me to handle."

"Just give me his number," Mark said.

Police Chief Daniel Mundy was home. He listened and grunted a few times. "This is a real small force we got here, Detective," he said finally. "None of your big-city stuff. I can't say I have much to offer in the way of help. My men are pretty much tied up by the foul weather."

"I'm going in after this guy," Mark said. "The sheriff in Glenwood knows about it. He's got descriptions of the people and the cabin's location." He gave the same map coordinates to Chief Mundy. Grid, minutes and degrees.

"Yeah, I know it. Rough area. Gotta be crotch-deep in snow up there by now."

"There's a bulletin out on this Robert Larkin. Federal. Kidnapping."

"Okay."

"I should be out by dark tomorrow," Mark told him. "If you don't hear from me by then, you might alert Captain Franklin at Denver PD."

"Don't go messing around out in the storm tonight, young fella. You won't get far."

"I'll take that into consideration, Chief."

Mark turned off the interstate a few miles east of Rifle near a tiny place called Silt. He took Dry Hollow Creek Road south into the mountains, leaving the Colorado River valley behind. As he climbed, the snow only got worse. It was now nine-fifteen and pitch-black. At least in the city, during a storm, there was still some light. But up here in God's country there was only him and the vast wilderness.

He drove the rapidly disappearing dirt road until he found Alkali Creek Road—which was even narrower and more rutted than the last dirt track—and turned west. He went a couple of miles, real slow-going, and began to search for West Muddy Creek Road, which would lead him to Mud Hill. Mark couldn't even begin to imagine how bad the route was going to be. This

was back country *and* high country and, as the saying
went, it wasn't fit out for man nor beast.

The falling snow reflected back from his headlights,
creating a milky wall that was ever-shifting, ever-
changing, but perversely solid. Every few minutes he
had to blink away the mesmerizing effect of all those
millions of tiny, implacable snowflakes coming at him
from the dark.

He finally found Muddy Creek Road and made it
about a mile before the Camry drove into a drift, got
high-centered and spun its wheels uselessly.

"Shit," Mark muttered.

He checked the map by the dome light and figured
roughly where he was. It was about three miles to the
cabin, he guessed, four at the most. An easy walk, even
if it was uphill. But not in this weather. He peered out
of the car to where his headlights diffused into whirling white flakes. You couldn't see a damn thing out
there—for all he knew he wasn't even on the road. He
could be in the middle of a goddamn meadow.

It was almost ten. He wanted to go charging off up
into the mountains to find Larkin's cabin. He wanted
to be there *now*. He wanted to see that Anna was all
right, still alive and warm and beautiful and safe. He
couldn't even let his mind touch the thought of *him*
doing anything to her. It was like an electric shock
every time his thoughts strayed and got a split second
image of Larkin with her, his hands . . . *No*.

There wasn't one second to waste. He had to get
there. There was only one problem—he couldn't see a
thing. He didn't know where he was and it was snowing like hell.

If he tried to get up there now, he'd very likely get lost, freeze and die—and end up being not one bit of help to Anna.

But he couldn't sit *here* all night! She was up there scared to death, suffering, undergoing the most god-awful . . . *No*.

Emotion sat on one shoulder, whispering into his ear to get out of the car, go to her, find her, rescue her, *now*. Coward, it hissed, sniveling wimp, useless. Go get her!

Common sense sat on the other, cautioning him not to risk his own life, to be prudent and not go off unprepared, half-cocked. Experience admonished him not to be a maverick this time, not to bust down the door and go in, guns blazing. They could both end up dead.

He was so torn up inside he felt nauseated again. Anna's life was at stake and he was dithering around like a frigging rookie.

He wished he could talk to Hoagie—he knew what Hoagie would say, though. *Wait*. He'd say wait for backup, for the FBI chopper, for help. But Mark couldn't wait, not that long.

He could wait for morning, though. Till it was light. Okay, a compromise, he snarled mentally at his emotions. Shut up and I'll go at first light.

Crashing his fist into the dashboard, he cursed out loud. He'd have to wait, he'd have to goddamn wait!

He struggled into his winter gear in the cramped front seat, shivering as he stripped and pulled on long underwear. The car had been running all this time with the heater going, but he'd have to turn it off pretty soon, because the tailpipe would get blocked by snow and he'd suffocate from carbon monoxide. He reclined the seat as far back as it would go, set his flashlight and gun on the passenger seat and got into his sleeping bag.

He cracked open one of the windows, killed the lights and turned off the ignition. Utter silence enfolded him in total blackness. Snow began instantly piling up on the windshield.

Mark settled himself to wait for dawn, maybe six-thirty this time of year. He lay there and closed his eyes, willing himself to sleep. He was desperate for time to pass. He finally dozed off sometime past midnight, but woke not long afterward in the thrall of a nightmare. Not the same one this time, though. Not the one about the Orchid Rapist.

This time, the nightmare was about Anna.

Twenty-Two

The Hunter treated Anna fairly the first twenty-four hours he held her captive. He fed her and never laid a hand on her, except to take her arm and lead her outside when she had to use the outhouse. He touched her hair and stroked it several times, closing his eyes, drawing in her scent. But that was it.

A kind of dull acceptance came over her, and she began to believe that all his previous threats, the sick sexual fantasies, were merely that—fantasies. That first night, he slept right next to her, but he never touched her, only pinned her against the log wall to keep her from trying to move. She lay there still and trembling, waiting, waiting for the feel of his hot breath on her neck, but it never came. She almost wished it had; anything to end the terrible anticipation.

The first weak light of dawn oozed through the small-paned windows and Anna stared at it, praying the blizzard had subsided, praying someone had launched a rescue. She'd had all night to think about it, to wonder and agonize—surely there was a way to trace Larkin to this spot. Wherever *that* was. There had to be some trail he'd left. Mark had told her dozens of times that these creeps always slipped up. They *had* to be coming for her. She clung to the thought, clenched it to her as she would a lifeline in a storm.

Mark was never out of her thoughts. She worried herself into a near frenzy that Larkin had killed him. Then she convinced herself he was alive—Mark was as tough as they came. And he was a survivor. Once before, someone she loved had died. It couldn't happen again. Life threw you curves, but not *that* many. Now all *she* had to do was live.

As dawn broke over the Rockies, the storm finally let up. Thick gray clouds clung to the mountainsides, but she could tell visibility had improved in the valleys. Of course, the snow often let up at dawn, teasing, but Anna prayed for a break in her luck as she lay there staring at the window. *Someone find me.*

The Hunter awakened at six-thirty. He rolled off the bed and out of his sleeping bag and padded over to the wood stove, stoking it. Anna watched him surreptitiously, afraid to move, wishing she could vanish into thin air. It was inconceivable that he was going to leave her alone forever.

She was more right than she knew.

He shook her awake—or thought he did—and told her to get dressed and use the outhouse. She did. Carefully, she did everything he commanded, instinctively knowing it would be bad, really bad, to push his buttons. She had to buy all the time she could.

It was still trying to clear when she trudged through the drifts of snow to the outhouse. She could even make out a line of distant mountains, their peaks obscured by thick clouds, but not the formations she was used to seeing on the eastern slopes. These were barren flattops, cut by rivers of time, more desertlike. She was positive she was on the western slope somewhere, and for a moment that knowledge fortified her—until she thought of the immensity of the mountains, the thousands upon thousands of square miles she was lost in. No one was going to find her. *Never.* Mark, she thought, oh, God, where was he?

When they got back inside the cabin, the Hunter handed her a cup of coffee and glared at her. Yesterday his expression had seemed mild, deceptively pleasant. But today there was a change, as if he'd amassed strength during the night.

She put down the coffee cup and began to remove the snowsuit.

"You still don't remember, do you?" he asked.

In a small, neutral voice, Anna asked what he meant.

"Where you met Earl, that's what. You don't even remember meeting him."

"I don't understand," Anna began, but before she could react, he struck her and sent her reeling into the door, blood trickling from her lip.

"Slut," he said, moving toward her.

During the next hour, she lost track of how many times he hit her, calculatingly, never knocking her unconscious, just hurting her, bruising her, making her beg him to stop.

He took her clothes off and shoved her onto the bed. He began to touch her everywhere, making her sob in fear and shame. She fought him with everything she had left in her, but fighting him only made it worse. He kept striking her until she lay there, trembling but obedient.

"Is that all you've got in you, bitch?" he whispered in that horrible voice. "Giving up?"

Anna stared up at him through her tears. She could live through this, she had to. Did he want her to fight? Is that how he took control? Or maybe if she just lay there and let him do what he wanted ... Women had been raped and beaten before. They survived. She'd survive. But what did this maniac want?

Anna forced herself to lie there, her chest heaving, her limbs quaking. Even when he struck her across the face again, she refused to move or cry out. He swore at her, grabbed her hair, even lay on top of her in his clothes—and that was when she realized he wasn't aroused, not that way.

"You whore," he hissed into her ear. "Cheap slut! Fight me!"

She took her mind away, dragging it to another place, and looked past his shoulder to the window, to the white winter wonderland beyond, to freedom. Don't think, she thought. Don't feel. And she stayed there beneath his weight, his curses barely touching her consciousness. If you fight him, he'll think he's won. And then he'll kill you.

Anna suddenly became aware of a change in him. She noticed he was easing his weight off her, that the tension in his muscles was relaxing. She let herself come back to the cabin, cautiously, feeling the bruises and cuts on her lips, fear gripping her anew.

He sat on the edge of the bed, so still now and silent. For a moment, she thought all the air had been sucked from the cabin, and she couldn't get her breath. Oh, God, she thought, he was going to do it. He was going to kill her.

"My goodness," Anna heard him say, and his head swiveled toward her. "He's such a mean man sometimes. Are you all right?"

Anna had never known horror until that instant when she looked into the eyes of the Hunter and recognized the metamorphosis. No longer was *he* staring at her; instead, sickeningly, it was her, the woman at lunch that day, the one at the hockey game. Anna could barely swallow past the lump of shock in her throat.

"Let me get you a washrag or something," the woman said, "and wipe that blood off. Oh, my, but you are going to have a few black-and-blue marks."

Anna lay unmoving while that . . . *thing* went to get a rag. She came back and sat on the bed, carefully dabbing cold water on Anna's lips and on the knot rising beneath her eye. The whole time she spoke. "I want to apologize for him. He just loses control at times. But you know, it's not his fault. He had the most horrible mother." She shuddered delicately. "Oh, she was awful. She hurt him so much. She did bad things. But she's gone now."

Anna stared up into her face—the soft blue eyes, the grotesque parody of a Mona Lisa smile. She was gripped by that horror again, by the uncertainty— when would *he* be back?

After a time Anna dared to ask if she could put her clothes on.

"Sure you can," she said. "You must be freezing. As soon as the Hunter gets back, he'll rebuild the fire. I'd do it, you know, but he gets mad at me over the dumbest things. We better let him do it."

Anna hooked her bra up and nodded, afraid to speak again. God only knew what other *people* existed inside this creature.

The woman finally rose from the bed and put the washrag near the stove to dry. Then she tidied up the cabin, humming, her movements incongruously feminine in those hunting clothes. Anna couldn't tear her eyes away; even the pain of her bruised body seemed dull and remote in the face of her horrified fascination.

Anna was still watching, clothed and wondering if she dared make a dash for it, when the Hunter returned. The changes were subtle, but unmistakable. First the squaring of muscles beneath his shirt. Then the tension returned to his face. But the eyes were the strangest. The soft blue seemed to cool and become hard—glacial and distant. And all the time he was shaking out the sleeping bags, neatly folding them.

Finally, he turned to Anna, and his lips tightened into a thin line. "She was here, wasn't she?" he said. "That stupid bitch came here."

Anna kept deathly quiet, her heart pumping furiously.

"What did the bitch tell you? *What?*" he demanded.

Anna licked her dry, swollen lips.

"Answer me or I'll kill you right now. I'll cut you to shreds."

"She...she said you had a...a terrible mother. She said—"

The Hunter exploded. "That was Robert! He's dead! She wasn't *my* mother! Kate was lying!"

"I...I'm sorry. I didn't know."

"You still don't remember Earl, do you? He wanted to come here, but I wouldn't let him. He's such a wimp."

"Maybe you should let Earl come visit me," she tried. "Then I'd remember him."

"You'd like that, wouldn't you?" He was growing angry again. "You think I'm stupid. Let Earl come! You're *mine*, not Earl's!"

She shrank back against the wall. "I'm sorry. If you tell me where Earl saw me, I'll remember, I'm sure I will."

"You never even saw him. It was like he wasn't there."

She stared wide-eyed and tense, waiting for another onslaught. She could taste blood in her mouth.

"And then," he went on, "you and that man, that cop. It was disgusting. Don't you have any decency? You betrayed me. I had to watch. Everywhere you went, *he* was there."

"I was afraid. He was working for me, that's all," she said. "I . . . I didn't know it was you."

"You were screwing him!" he screamed. "And I had to watch!"

"No, no," she breathed.

"Lying bitch!" He began to tear the cabin up—the very same chair he'd just dusted off, the neatly stacked tin plates and cups on the shelf all went flying in his rage. Anna cowered against the wall, wishing it would swallow her. During his tirade, she saw the gun tucked in the waistband of his pants drop to the floor. Her eyes fixed on it. If she could somehow get to it . . .

But despite his rage, he retrieved the gun and stuck it back in his waistband. He seemed wholly unaware of her now, still kicking at everything, swearing, his chest heaving. She watched from her corner as he snatched up his snow gear and angrily climbed into it, then grabbed the wood ax next to the cabin door. His face was red-splotched, his blue eyes wild and opaque when he finally trained them on her. "I'll be back," he breathed hoarsely. "I'll be back, you slut. And when I do, you're going to die." He tore open the door, letting in a shock of cold air, then slammed it. She heard the bolt shoot into place. She stared at the door. He meant it. He was going to do it, she thought frantically, and that was when her vision focused magically on the shotgun. In his rage, he'd left it by the door.

Mark felt his long underwear sticking to his skin as he knelt in the woods less than fifty yards from the cabin. He had caught his breath, but the cold was finally seeping into him, made all the worse by his soaked underclothes. He'd have to move soon. If he didn't, they'd find him frozen in this spot—and that probably wouldn't be till spring.

He stared at the cabin door, feeling his muscles tense. His breath formed frozen white plumes in the frigid morning air. No better time than the present, he thought, when abruptly the door swung open and Robert Larkin came striding out, ax in hand.

Instantly, Mark fell back into the cover of the trees. Hell, he thought. This changed everything. He'd been planning to storm the place, take that sicko by surprise, but now there was no way Mark could stick to his plan.

He could try to take a shot from where he was, but his .38 was for close-range, not this. His odds of making the shot were less than ten to one. He wouldn't risk it. If he missed, Larkin would run inside and Anna would die. If she was still alive. She was. She *had* to be.

Larkin began dusting the snow off a pile of wood just to the left side of the cabin. He set a log on end and split it with his ax. He seemed to be working in a jerky fashion, as if he was angry, and all Mark could think was that maybe Anna really was alive in there. Maybe she'd ticked him off. Good for you, Mark thought as he watched Larkin and tried to form a new plan.

Anna saw the latch on the cabin door lift. She drew in a ragged breath and raised the shotgun. Oh, God, she thought. Once, almost twenty years ago, Scott had taken her skeet shooting. She'd hated it, knowing she could never raise a weapon to any creature.

The Hunter stopped dead in his tracks when his eyes adjusted to the dim light inside the cabin. He glared at Anna, then slid his eyes to the empty spot on the wall where the shotgun should have been.

"I'll do it," Anna started to say, pointing the gun. "I swear, I'll—" But she never finished.

Suddenly, the door behind Larkin crashed open, knocking Larkin toward Anna. She leaped out of the way, trying to make sense out of what had just happened, when Mark, crouched, gun in both hands, cried, "Get the hell down, Anna!" and she realized she was in the line of fire.

Catlike, the Hunter rolled over. In his hand was his pistol, and before Anna could move or Mark could take a shot, Larkin aimed and fired.

The report crashed in her ears, filling the space around her with a terrible noise and the acrid stink of gunpowder. She saw Mark jerk back as if flung by an unseen hand. Then Larkin was aiming again, and she was right behind him, thunder still reverberating in her ears. She closed her eyes and pulled the trigger. The gun smashed back into her, the sound buffeting her anew. When she opened her eyes, Mark was lying by the door, blood staining his parka. Robert Larkin, the Hunter, was facedown near her feet, and on the stark white of his suit a crimson flower was blossoming.

Anna couldn't think. She'd never be able to recall those moments when she stood staring at Larkin's bloody, inert form, the gun slipping from her hand, tumbling as if in slow motion to the floor. The only thing she'd ever remember was kneeling by Mark's side, saying his name over and over, crying, tears falling onto his face.

"Don't die," she cried brokenly. "Mark, don't you dare die on me!"

It was as if her will pulled him back from the brink of death—she'd always believe that. His eyes opened, a deep blue gleam between black lashes.

"Anna," he croaked. "Are you okay?"

"*Me*? Am I okay? Mark, oh, my God, he shot you. He . . ."

She felt him tense as he tried to raise himself. "Where is he? Where . . . ?"

"He's dead."

He looked at her, asking wordlessly.

"I . . . I shot him. He's over there, on the floor."

Mark closed his eyes, and she thought for a moment he'd left her, but he said something she had to strain to hear. "I'm sorry you had to do that."

"Mark, it doesn't matter. Not now. *You* matter." She touched his face and smiled through her tears. "You found me. I thought, I was afraid . . . what he did to you. Back in Denver. I was so afraid."

"I've got a hard head," he said.

She touched his head where the stitches were. "He did this? And now . . . oh, God, and now you're shot, and it's all my fault."

"That's a real unproductive line of thought, Anna." He grimaced. "Jesus, I hurt. Help me get this off, take a look." He was struggling with the zipper of his parka, but he fell back, his face parchment white.

"Let me do it."

"You shouldn't have to do this," he muttered.

"Shut up and let me do it." She unzipped his parka, gently sliding it off one arm, then the other. He clenched his teeth, but a groan escaped his lips. "Sorry," she said.

"Go on, do it."

She unbuttoned his shirt and pulled it away from his side. There was blood on it, above his waist on the right side, and a hole in his long underwear with more blood. She pulled the underwear top up and drew in her breath.

"Bad?" he asked.

"I don't know what bad is," she got out.

He raised his head, trying to look, then let himself fall back. "Tell me what it looks like."

"There's a hole. It's bleeding. I can't tell. Mark . . ."

"Feel around back, if it came out."

She slid her hand under him, feeling. Warm skin, muscles; she heard his indrawn breath. "I don't feel anything."

"Shit, it's still in there."

"Is that bad?"

"Sure, it's bad. 'Course, if it'd come out, coulda blasted a chunk of me away. I'd bleed to death then."

"Don't," she whispered.

"Anna, God, I hate to do this to you." He closed his eyes and swore. "The phone," he said. "Use the phone. In my pocket."

Her heart leaped in hope. "You have a phone?" She felt in his parka pocket, and pulled it out. Kneeling there on the floor, she pressed 911. There was only static, buzzing and echoing voices. Her heart fell like a stone to her belly. "It's dead. The battery's dead."

"Yeah, I kinda figured that might happen." He tried to grin.

"I have to stop your bleeding," she said. "Can you get to the bed if I help you? It'll be more comfortable."

"Maybe later," he said, closing his eyes. Pain etched harsh lines in his face. "Put something on the entry wound. Direct pressure."

She looked around. Still hanging neatly on a peg was a towel. It looked clean. The Hunter had been very methodical, even maniacal, about neatness. She stepped over the corpse's splayed legs without a downward glance and grabbed the towel, folding it and laying it on Mark's bare skin. His body jerked spasmodically.

"Oh, God . . ."

"No, press harder," he gasped. "Gotta stop the bleeding. The bullet's in there, can't do any harm now, not for a while. Didn't hit anything vital or I'd be coughing up blood."

"Mark!"

"That'd be messy," he said.

"Stop it." She pressed, watching the towel turn pink around the edges.

"Cop's humor," he said.

She watched the towel and prayed, afraid she was pressing too hard or not hard enough. She didn't know.

"Is it stopping?" he asked.

"I don't know. Yes," she lied.

"Don't lie, Anna."

"It's going to stop. Now be quiet."

"You gotta get out of here," he said.

"I don't know where we are. I have no idea . . ."

"This place is outside of Rifle. South. The High Tower Wilderness. The cabin, it's his . . . Robert Larkin. Hoagie found it."

"They know where you are then, don't they? Won't someone come?"

"Storm's too bad."

"But it stopped this morning," she said, feeling the hot blood under her hand.

"Still socked in. No one's gonna come right away."

"I won't go without you," she said, "if that's what you're getting at."

"Anna—" he reached up and grabbed her wrist in a surprisingly strong grip "—you may have to."

"No."

"You'll do what I say," he said through clenched teeth.

"I won't leave you."

His hand fell way, and he closed his eyes. "Always arguing," he said hoarsely.

"We'll get you fixed up. Stop the bleeding. Wrap you up. We'll get out of here on his snowmobile."

"Snow's too deep. Those things are a joke in this kinda snow."

"It'll work," she said, still watching the towel. "Don't talk."

"I gotta talk now, while I can. Listen, Anna. You can follow my trail out as long as it doesn't snow real bad again. It's downhill. You can make it."

"Shh," she said. "I'm not going anywhere right now."

"*Listen.*" He took a deep, slow breath. "Ah, God, that hurts."

"Mark, please . . ." She pushed back the hair from his forehead with her free hand. His skin was cool and oily with sweat.

"His truck's down below, parked. It's a four-wheel drive, maybe it can get out to the road. His key's gotta be around here somewhere."

"Don't worry about it now," she said. "Okay? Just concentrate on getting your strength up. We'll both drive out of here together. Or the snow'll stop and they'll come find us. With a helicopter."

"I don't fly," he said faintly.

"What?"

"Scared to fly," he whispered.

She wanted to laugh. Hysterically. He was afraid to fly. "I'll hold your hand," she said.

"Deal." He closed his eyes.

She leaned over and gently kissed his lips. "You're going to be fine, Mark."

His eyes opened and held her gaze. "You're one helluva lady, Anna."

She shook her head, at a loss for words. Tears brimmed in her eyes, and she blinked them away.

The towel was red right under her hand and pink around the edges, but the bleeding seemed to be slowing. She searched the room from where she knelt. Surely there was a first-aid kit or more towels—something she could use. And water. Hot water. The stove.

She had to keep feeding it wood; Mark had to be kept warm. She worried about him going into shock. That's what happened if you lost too much blood, wasn't it? A person could die of shock even if the wound didn't kill him. Keep him warm, she told herself.

She had so much to do.

Her eyes touched the facedown corpse, and she shuddered. She had to get rid of *that*.

After a few minutes, she dared to take her hand off the towel, and she lifted it carefully. Dark blood welled thickly out of the small round hole. But the flow had slowed.

"Can you hold this?" she asked. "I want to get some things." She lifted his hand and laid it on the towel, pressing on his big square hand.

"Sure, go on."

She got up, knees stiff. She opened the stove door and put in some wood, as she'd seen the Hunter do. There was a heavy cast-iron kettle, which she put over a burner. The bucket of melted snow sat on the floor. She took some out in a cup and put that on a burner, too. Then she searched the shelves, pushing things off in her hurry. Gauze, first-aid ointment, peroxide. The Hunter was prepared.

She went back to Mark. His hand had fallen away from the bandage, and he looked as if he was asleep. It scared her and she shook him, then replaced the towel with a thick pad of gauze. The wound seeped slowly. Mark shifted and muttered something, and she knelt there, holding the gauze to his side, and thought, he won't die, he won't die, he'll be fine, he won't die. It became a fierce mantra.

It never occurred to Anna, as she knelt on the floor of the Hunter's cabin holding gauze against a bullet wound, to wonder how she'd arrived at this place and time, to wonder, or rail at fate or feel sorry for herself. She had room in her mind for only one thought, to save Mark's life and to get them both back to civilization. So she just did her best, dabbing the wound with peroxide, covering it with clean gauze smeared with the first-aid cream and taping it in place. She sat back on her heels and pushed her bangs off her forehead with the back of a wrist.

It was warm in the cabin, almost too warm with the wood stove roaring. Mark was pale and sweating. He mumbled in a half sleep, wincing when she touched the wound. She wanted badly to get him into the bed, to change his clothes and dry out his sweat-soaked long underwear, but it seemed to hurt him so much when he moved. He needed fluids, and he was falling asleep, or sliding into unconsciousness, and she was afraid he'd go into shock.

"Mark," she said. "Wake up, Mark."

He opened his eyes groggily.

"Don't go to sleep. Stay with me, Mark, do you hear?"

She wiped his skin with a warm damp cloth, washing away the caked blood until the water in the bowl was tinged pink. He'd lost so much blood.

She covered him with his parka and laid a damp rag on his forehead. And she sat there, cross-legged, holding his hand, willing him to be all right.

He opened his eyes some time later. "Anna?"

"Yes, I'm here." She squeezed his hand.

"Thirsty."

She held his head while he drank. Water ran down his chin, across the black stubble and into the creases of his neck. She dabbed at the moisture.

"You're doing good," he said. He looked up at her and frowned. "He hit you."

Inadvertently, she put her hand up to the knot under her eye. "It's nothing."

"What else did he do?"

"Nothing much."

"Don't play me for a goddamn fool," he said harshly.

She put a finger on his lips. "He didn't do much of anything, slapped me around a little. Honestly. You came before he could . . . do that to me."

He turned his face away and closed his eyes, and she saw a tear leak from under his lid and roll down his temple.

"Mark," she said, her heart breaking for him, "don't, please. It was okay. Mostly I was just scared." She touched his cheek and stroked his hair back from his forehead. "Please, don't torture yourself."

"I want you to get out of here. Now, before it starts snowing again," he said.

"No," she whispered.

"Stubborn . . ."

"Don't say it. I won't leave you. Save your breath." She laid a hand on his shoulder. "Do you think you can get to the bed now?"

He grunted, then raised himself on one elbow. She helped him, straining to hold him up. He was heavy, and he leaned on her, teeth clenched against the pain. Finally, he sat on the edge of the bed, head hanging, hands on his knees. He swore softly.

"Lie back now. There, easy," she said, bracing herself against his weight until he'd slid onto the mattress. He was pale, and a small red spot showed on the gauze.

She found a knife and slit both sides of his long-underwear top, easing the garment off, and loosened the waist of his insulated pants. His long-underwear bottoms were soaked with blood, but it would be hard to get them off. She unlaced his boots and pulled them off, eliciting a painful grunt from Mark. She laid the Hunter's sleeping bag over him. He seemed exhausted, lying there, his eyes sunken. She felt a moment of panic—she shouldn't have made him move.

"Okay?" she asked.

"Yeah, top-notch," he said dryly.

She put wood on the fire. She knew there was plenty more outside. And there was food. They could stay there for days, if necessary. *She* could. Mark couldn't.

Outside, the sky stayed uniformly gray, heavy and low over the mountaintops, pregnant with moisture. It wasn't snowing, but she knew it could start any time. She wished there were a radio to listen to—snow reports, news, anything. Scott and Lydia must be so upset. And Monica. But it was almost as if the outside world didn't exist. Only she and Mark in this small cabin existed. That was her only reality.

Except for the dead body on the floor. Yes, she thought, she had to get rid of it.

Mark was resting, his eyes closed. She walked over to the body and stood at its feet. *God.* She shut her mind and pulled off its boots for an easier grasp, then put a hand on each ankle and began to tug. It slid across the floor. She backed up, one step at a time. It was heavy and slid reluctantly, catching on every little projection. She got it near the front of the cabin, finally, and stepped around it to open the door. The cold air felt good, but Mark must have felt it, because she heard him say, "What in hell are you doing, Anna?"

"Nothing," she said. "Go to sleep."

Getting it over the doorjamb was hard, but it slid more easily on the snow. She left it just off to the side of the door and scooped snow on it. She couldn't believe she'd managed this feat, closing her mind to the horror of it, but you did what you had to do, she told herself over and over. You did what was necessary and cried about it later.

Inside, she opened a can of soup, heated it up and forced herself to eat. She looked at her watch and was shocked to see that it was almost four-thirty in the afternoon.

It would be dark soon.

She took a bowl of soup and a spoon, and sat on the edge of the bed. "Mark?"

He opened his eyes. They were clouded with pain.

"Dinnertime."

"I'm not hungry."

"Eat a little."

"What time is it?"

"Four-thirty. Will you . . . ?"

"Is it snowing again?"

"No. Still gray, though."

"I want you to leave before it snows again. You could get out right now."

"Stop being silly. Here, eat this."

"Goddamn it, Anna."

"You say that a lot. Your daughter said you weren't supposed to swear."

"My daughter . . ."

"You'll see her again, don't worry."

"Jenn and the kids, they'll get the pension, anyway. Good thing I went to Franklin."

"What?"

"I asked for my job back. Had to. I needed it to find you. So, see, they'll get the money."

"You're going to get out of here and be fine."

"Yeah, that's right, I forgot for a minute there."

"Eat this."

She helped him sit up and spooned soup into his mouth. He ate half the bowl, then pushed her hand away. He drank some more water and looked around the room.

"Where is he?" he asked in a deadly quiet voice.

"Outside."

He looked at her. "For God's sake, Anna."

"I couldn't look at it anymore."

He eyed her and shook his head wonderingly.

"Who was he?" she asked. "I mean, where did he know me from?"

"He was one of the landscape men working at your brother's."

She thought back but all that came to mind were men with rakes and lawn mowers. Not one face. "I don't remember him."

"No, you wouldn't."

"*Why* did he do it?"

He shrugged. "We'll never know for sure."

She put more wood in the fire. "Maybe it'll clear up and they'll get us in the morning."

"Maybe." He looked at her across the room. "Come here."

She went to him and sat carefully on the edge of the bed. He reached out and put his hand on her cheek, holding it there, and she closed her eyes and leaned into his palm. "Mark," she whispered, "don't you die on me, damn it. I had that happen to me once, and I didn't like it. Don't you dare."

"I wouldn't dream of crossing you, lady. You're too scary." He slid his fingers around the back of her head and tugged gently. She moved closer until their lips touched, lightly, a feather-light caress. His mustache was bristly against her skin.

"Mark, I . . ." she said against his mouth, but he stopped her.

"Don't say it. Not now. There's too much going on."

"Okay, later," she said. "Deal?"

"Yeah, deal."

She crept up onto the bed as darkness fell and curled up under the sleeping bag against his side. She slept on and off, her ear alert to every sound he made, every twitch and groan and breath he took. She got up a few times to put wood on the fire. She woke before dawn and lay there in the silence, feeling his heart beat against her, strong and steady, and she could only thank God that he was still alive.

Twenty-Three

It was snowing lightly and much colder in the morning when Anna went to the outhouse. No helicopter, she thought. Maybe someone would try to reach them on snowmobiles. Maybe they were already on their way. At least people knew where they were—that was the important thing.

She went back inside, carefully avoiding the snow-covered mound by the door.

Mark was awake and sitting up in bed, his back propped against the wall, the sleeping bag fallen down across his stomach. The white of the bandage was startling against his skin.

"'Morning," she said, smiling. "You look better."

"I'll dance *Swan Lake* if you whistle the tune," he said. "More to the point, I really need to get, uh, outside."

"Think you can walk, or do you want . . . ?"

"I'll walk," he said quickly. "Just help me get my boots on."

She knelt at his feet, pulling on his boots and tying them. She felt his hand on her bent head and looked up.

"You're something," he said quietly, his fingers in her hair.

"I don't have much choice," she replied.

"People always have choices, Anna." He leaned on her heavily as he stood, hand against his wound, but he made it outside.

"You want to try to get to the outhouse?" she asked.

"No, this'll be fine. Go inside, leave me alone for a minute."

He came in by himself and sank heavily onto the bed, grunting with pain.

"I made some coffee. There's even sugar."

"Let me catch my breath."

"You're better, I can tell," she said.

"Better is a relative term."

"Did you sleep all night?" she asked.

"Yeah. I had dreams. Weird ones. Not the usual one."

She poured coffee into two mugs, spooned in lots of sugar and took one to him. "Drink this, then we'll decide what to do."

"I've already decided," he said.

"You *are* better," she noted.

"We're leaving, now, before it starts to snow harder. I don't want to chance my tracks being covered up and us getting lost."

"You can make it?"

"Oh, I'll make it, all right, only because I have to and you're too goddamn stubborn to go without me."

"Okay, good."

"We'll try the snowmobile, but like I said..." He took a sip of coffee. "If it doesn't work, we'll walk. It's not that far. Took me a couple of hours on foot yesterday. A couple of *hard* hours. We'll take the sleeping bag. If I can't make it, you leave me with the bag and come back with help."

"No," she began.

"Just a contingency plan," he said. "You always have to have a contingency plan."

"I won't leave you, Mark."

His expression silenced her. "Look, Anna, I'm not kidding around here. We'll probably both get out, but I'll be damned if I'll be the cause of any more harm to you than I already have been. Better one of us makes it out than neither."

She said nothing, but her eyes searched his face. Then, slowly, she asked, "Would you leave me, Mark? If things were reversed, and I was hurt, tell me the truth, would you leave me?"

He was quiet for a long time. "Yes, I'd leave you if I had to."

"You're a terrible liar," she whispered.

"Hoagie told me that once. He asked me if I thought he was handsome. I said no."

"Mark," she pleaded.

"We'll go, okay? I'll make it, don't worry." He looked around. "We need to find his keys, the ones to his snowmobile and the truck."

"He was a very well organized monster," Anna said calmly. "Two sets of keys are hanging on those hooks by the door. I already looked."

"Good girl."

"First you're going to eat something."

"Got any cheese Danish, the ones with the shiny tops?"

"Let me look," she said. "Gosh, I'm sorry, you'll have to make do with soup or canned beans."

"Soup." He shrugged, then winced in pain.

They ate, both trying very hard to choke down as much as they could. Anna managed a whole can, but Mark put his bowl aside with half of it left.

"Maybe they found the car," he said. "Your car. That's what I drove. But the deputy said there were six camps of hunters stranded, and they couldn't reach them, so they've got their hands full."

"How did you find this place?" Anna asked. "How did you ever find it?"

"It's a long story. Hoagie's computer, some luck. I'll tell you one day."

"You're a very good detective," she said solemnly.

"A lousy bodyguard, though."

They got dressed. Anna put on her jeans and sweater over the long underwear the Hunter had provided for her, plus boots, a hat and mittens. Mark made her wrap tape tightly around his torso over a new gauze pad. She loved touching his skin, even now, even in these circumstances. Mark's underwear top was useless and his shirt was bloody and torn. She found some of the Hunter's clothes in a military footlocker. His things were smaller than Mark needed, but they'd do: thermal top, fatigue sweater, a heavy camouflage hunting parka, Mark's own hat and gloves and boots. Anna rolled up a sleeping bag and tied it, put some beef jerky in her pocket, and took the keys off the hook. Mark put his gun and flashlight in the parka's pockets. Anna carefully closed the door of the wood stove and took the kettle off the burner. She stopped and looked around.

"Maybe we should stay," she said, suddenly unsure.

"No," Mark said, "not a chance."

It was cold out, with a gray glare of low clouds and snow. The land swept away from them in all directions, immense and white and empty. Anna could see the dimples in the snow that were Mark's footprints. They led into a stand of aspen trees.

She walked awkwardly in the deep snow to the snowmobile and brushed off the two feet of snow piled on it. Mark waited, leaning against the cabin, saving his strength.

"You ever drive one of those?" he called to her.

"No."

"Great. You know how to start it?"

"No."

"I'll talk you through it."

He told her what to do and it started right up, the roar filling her ears with a kind of joy. They'd drive out, no problem, she thought, and get to the road and flag someone down. Mark would be in a hospital by noon. She'd call Scott, he'd call Hoagie. It was practically over.

Slowly, painfully, Mark made his way to the machine. He was bent over, hand pressed to his side. He swung a leg over the seat and settled behind her, arms around her waist.

"Take it easy," he said into her ear. "No speed bumps."

She used the throttle, like on a motorcycle she'd once ridden. She jockeyed it out of the hole it was in, and it rode up on the snow, the machine snarling, whining, struggling for purchase in the deep snow. They made slow headway, becoming bogged down and having to rock the machine to free it. They followed Mark's footsteps, the faint indentation that had been a foot trail before the storm. Wind moved the tree branches above them, dropping streamers of snow on their heads. The handlebars yanked at Anna's arms, making them ache.

"Stop," she heard in her ear, and she pulled up, leaving the engine idling, and turned to Mark.

He was grimacing, holding his side. "Just give me a minute," he said. "Shit, that hurts."

"I'm sorry. It's so deep."

"Frankly, I'm surprised we got this far."

They started again, lurching forward, almost flipping over once. Anna couldn't bear to think what it was doing to Mark. She just kept going. She started revising her estimate of when Mark would get to a hospital.

They came out of the trees onto a downhill slope. Here, where the hillside was exposed, the snow was deeper, too deep for the machine. It ran into a drift halfway down the hill, heeled over and wouldn't budge.

Anna tried again and again. She revved the engine until it screamed. She jockeyed it back and forth—she even tried digging away snow with her hands. Finally, Mark reached out and turned the key. Silence fell on them like a curtain going down.

"I'll try again," Anna said. "Let me just try to—"

"It's stuck, Anna. I told you. These things aren't meant for deep snow."

She felt like crying. "Damn it!" she yelled, kicking at the snowmobile. She lost her balance and sat down in the trampled snow.

"Okay, we'll walk," Mark said. "It can't be more than a mile."

"How can you be so calm?" she cried.

"Don't have the energy to throw a hissy-fit. Come on, give me a hand. We're outta here."

She carried the sleeping bag slung over one shoulder while Mark leaned on the other. She was thankful she could still see his footprints from yesterday, because the entire world was a white wasteland, with the wind moaning through the trees and blowing snow spouts across the high, barren meadows. An occasional chickadee chirped from a bare black branch.

Anna took one step at a time, sweating inside her heavy orange suit, her face cold. Mark leaned against her, silent, his face pinched and old-looking. She was afraid, but there was no time to be afraid. They floundered through sometimes crotch-deep snow, and it seemed to suck every ounce of energy from her. What must Mark be going through?

They stopped once and ate cold snow; she was surprised at what little water content it had.

"You okay?" she asked.

"Good enough." He was breathing shallowly, carefully. In obvious pain.

"It can't be far," she said.

"Let's go. It looks like it's going to snow. I don't want to be caught out here," he said grimly.

They continued, one foot, then the other. It was such an effort. She was hot and cold at the same time, sweating and freezing.

"Do you want to rest?" she asked Mark a little later.

"No," he lied.

The world was closing in on them, the clouds lowering, so that nothing at all could be seen of the surrounding mountains. Wind scoured the surface of the snow, wiping out the footprints they were following. High in the sky, a pale sun glared through a thin spot in the clouds, then it disappeared.

"It's gonna snow," Mark said.

"We'll get there," she said, breathing hard. One step, then another.

She squinted, trying to see ahead; there seemed to be a strange dark spot, neither aspen trees nor buck brush. Something incongruous out here in the middle of all the white.

"What's that?" she asked.

Mark stopped and hung on her, head lowered, gasping, his mustache caked with snow. Finally, he looked up. "It's his truck," he said. "It's his truck, Anna."

The hardest part was getting the door open; snow had blown against it, and she had to dig it away by hand. When she had it uncovered, she climbed in, took off her mitten and dug in her pocket for the keys.

She thrust the keys into the ignition. The engine started, chugging, spitting then dying on her, but finally it was running. She got out and Mark climbed in, then she got in again, feeling the heat begin to fill the cab.

Mark's head was back against the seat, his eyes closed, his throat a strong curve.

"How far is it to the road?" she asked.

"You mean, to where they've plowed," he said. "I don't know. I left your car a quarter mile or so down the road."

It had begun to snow harder, so Anna turned on the windshield wipers.

"Is it in four-wheel drive?" he asked.

She looked at the shift lever. "Yes."

"Try to get as far as you can," he said tiredly.

She put her hand on his arm. "Hang in there, Mark. We'll get there soon."

"At least it's warm. How much gas is in the tank?"

"It's half-full."

She grasped the big wheel, shifted into first, let up the clutch and gave it gas. The wheels spun, half buried in the snow. She backed up, put it in forward then back again, rocking the big old truck. It lurched ahead, rode up on the snow, skewed sideways, then at last the wheels gripped and drew it forward. She shifted up, and it half slid, half crawled downhill through the snow, following a rapidly disappearing trail.

"Good girl," Mark said.

"How far?" she asked again.

"I don't know. It was dark, snowing hard. Slow-going. A few miles, maybe five or six to the interstate."

"We're so close," she said.

She drove slowly, getting stuck once, and rocking it out. Mark seemed to doze, exhausted.

It began to snow harder. She squinted through the cracked windshield, trying to stay on the road—or what had once been a road.

They passed a mound of snow: her car, buried almost to the roof. She steered carefully around it and went on. It became more and more difficult to see, and she steered the truck where she thought the road was. But suddenly they were in a deep ditch filled with snow. The truck lurched, tires spinning, and the vehicle slid sideways and settled.

"God, no!" she cried.

"You did real good, Anna," Mark said. "I couldn't have done any better."

"We're stuck."

"Yeah, we are. What time is it?"

"Almost three. How could it have taken so long?" She couldn't stand being so close, so very close, and then going into a stupid ditch!

"We could stay in the truck, wait till tomorrow," Mark said. "Or I could stay in the truck. You can make it out."

"No!"

"I don't know how much farther I can go," he said. "I'm bleeding again."

She swiveled to face him. "Why didn't you tell me?" He shrugged.

"Let me see." She reached for his parka zipper.

He put a hand on top of hers. "What're you gonna do, Anna, suture me up?"

The truck engine purred, the heat blew into the cab, the windshield wipers swished back and forth. It seemed too easy to stay there, and how far could Mark go? He'd be better off in the truck than collapsed out in the snow.

"You go," he said. "It can't be far now. I'll wait here."

"I told you I won't."

"I hate stubborn women," he said. "You're being illogical."

"I couldn't live with myself. What if I went, and something happened to you before help got to you? How could I live with that?"

"You'd do just fine. You'd know you did your best."

She shook her head. "We have to stick together, Mark. I know that."

"What am I gonna do with you, Anna?"

"Come with me. Now. I'll help you. I'll carry you. I'll drag you." She turned the engine off, leaving the key in the ignition. "Please, Mark."

"Why in hell do you care so much about me?" he asked angrily. "You don't need me."

"I do. I need you. I can't go without you." She wanted to say more, knowing it was not the time or place. She grasped his hand and held it in both of hers. "I've never known a braver, stronger, better person, and I'm not going to lose you."

In answer, Mark opened the door on his side. "Well, for God's sake, then, get over here and help me down."

The snow dragged at her legs and hit her in the eyes, but the road was easier to follow down here. They staggered on drunkenly, Mark's breathing labored, Anna bent under his weight. Their progress was agonizingly slow. She felt light-headed. Hungry, thirsty, bone-weary. Aching all over. How must Mark feel? They trudged along for an hour maybe more. It seemed to be getting darker out, but Anna reasoned it couldn't be that late.

"I gotta rest," Mark said.

"Five minutes."

He sank onto the snow, head bowed, his breath coming painfully. She was scared. They couldn't stay here.

"Mark," she said, "get up . . ."

"Shh."

The hopelessness of their situation closed in on her, suffocating, cloying. They were lost in the immensity of the wilderness in a snowstorm, infinitesimal specks of nothing on the face of the frozen, corrugated land. They had no food or water or anything to keep them warm. Mark was hurt and bleeding. And the way out was too hard, the snow too deep, the highway too far.

She swallowed at the bubble of panic that rose and choked her, but it wouldn't go down. It was over. There was no place to go. They hadn't made it. Night was coming, and they'd be dead by morning.

She looked over at Mark. He seemed frozen, a crouched, unmoving statue with snow collecting on his shoulders and head. She tried again to swallow her fear. "Mark," she said, "we have to . . ."

"Shh," he said again.

"*Mark.*"

"I think I hear something."

She listened. There was a distant grinding sound. An engine. Suddenly, over the next hill, a light flickered, reflecting off the clouds.

"They're coming," she breathed. "Mark, they're coming for us!"

"It's a goddamn good thing, too." He reached inside a pocket and pulled out his .38. "Here, shoot this up in the air. Make sure they don't miss us."

She stood there in the midst of the rapidly gathering dusk, pointed his pistol up into the sky and pulled the trigger once, twice. Deafening echoes reverberated off the heavy sky itself. She sank onto the snow beside Mark and began to cry, her body racked with sobs. She felt his arms go around her and he said something, but she couldn't hear it because she was crying so hard. She was all used up, every bit of her.

And that's how the Garfield County rescue team in the big red Snow-Cat found them—huddled together in the snow, Anna crying as if she'd lost everything, as if she and Mark were doomed to perish in the snow. As if they hadn't cheated death.

Twenty-Four

The ambulance took Mark to Valley View Hospital in Glenwood Springs, where he was stabilized, x-rayed, and stuck with IVs full of painkillers and antibiotics. The doctors decided not to operate there. The facilities were better in Denver, and a Flight for Life helicopter was standing by, ready to take him the minute the storm lifted.

Anna held his hand all the way in the ambulance, saw him into the emergency room, then waited impatiently while he was examined. A young doctor tried to convince her she, also, needed attention, but she shook him off as if he were a pesky mosquito.

It seemed like eternity before the doctor came out to see her. She popped out of the chair and practically ran to meet him.

"Miss Dunning?" he said.

"How is he?"

"He's lost a lot of blood, and the bullet is still in there. But he's pretty lucky. It broke two ribs, missed almost everything, nicked his liver, then lodged against his ribs in back."

"He'll be okay?"

"The bullet will have to be removed, but, barring something unforeseen, the prognosis is good. He'll be pretty sore for a while."

"He won't die then?"

"No, he won't die. He's tough, walking out like that. He'll make it, no problem."

She felt her knees go weak as relief flooded her like a warm bath. Tears sprang to her eyes. "Thank God," she whispered. "Can I see him?"

"I'd like you to be examined first. You've been through quite an ordeal yourself."

"I'm fine. I need to eat, that's all. Where is he? Can I go see him now?"

"He's pretty fuzzy from the morphine. They're taking him to intensive care now."

She walked down the hospital corridor, vaguely aware of how she looked—the orange suit pulled half off, dangling down around her hips, her skin bruised, her hair tangled around her face.

When she got to his room, they were just moving him onto a bed, and she waited. After the nurses left, she went to his side and bent over, whispering his name.

"Yeah?" he said, opening his eyes, blue sapphire glinting between half-closed lids.

"You're going to be fine," she said.

"Uh-huh."

"They'll move you tomorrow. The helicopter's waiting, but if it's still snowing, you'll go by ambulance. Then they're going to take the bullet out."

"I can hardly wait."

"Everything's going to be all right, Mark."

"That's good. Anna . . ."

"Yes, what?"

"Take care of yourself. Let them check you out, okay? You had a rough time."

"I will. But I'm fine, Mark."

"And, hey, will you call Hoagie? And Jennifer? And Lil?"

"Of course. And I'll call Scott and Lydia and Monica. And my parents. Don't worry. I'll take care of it."

"I hope it keeps snowing," he said.

"Why? The helicopter will be so much faster . . ."

"I don't like to fly. I told you. Scares the bejesus out of me. This bullet doesn't kill me, the flight might."

"Remember, I'm going to hold your hand? I promised."

"Yeah, I remember."

"You rest now," she said.

"God, I'm sleepy. Can't think so good."

"It's the morphine."

"Yeah, I'm really zonked."

"Go to sleep, Mark."

He stirred restlessly. "Hey, one thing. Anna, listen. God, I wish I could think better. Don't say anything about what happened up there, not yet. Don't talk about it."

"Why not?"

"Don't argue. Trust me. For once, will you just do what I say?"

"Yes, yes, I will. Just rest. Don't worry about anything."

She sat by his bed, watching him and listening to the clicks and buzzes of the machines that were checking his heartbeat and controlling the drip of the IV into his arm. He lay there so quietly, breathing evenly, his bare chest rising and falling under the sheet, finally asleep.

Stiffly, Anna stood up. She was bone-tired. She had to go to the bathroom, and she was hungry and thirsty. She'd leave him for just a little while; after all, he was in a glass cage with nurses outside, watching him.

She leaned over and kissed him on the lips and, knowing he was asleep, she whispered against his mouth, "I love you, Mark Righter." Then she went out to the nurses' station and asked where there was a phone she could use.

After taking a shower, Anna fell asleep in an empty room. She rose once in the middle of the night, walked barefoot down the corridor in her borrowed hospital gown to ICU and asked how he was.

"Sleeping like a baby," the nurse said.

"You'll call me if there's any change?"

"Of course. Now, why don't you get some sleep."

When she woke again, the sun was shining through the window. It was absolutely clear out, the sky washed a clean, bright blue. The temperature had dropped to five below zero.

Anna dressed and trotted down the hall to ICU. "How is he?" she asked, looking in the window to his room.

"Fine. The helicopter's on its way."

"Oh, wonderful." Anna smiled.

"We had some calls already this morning," the nurse said.

Anna looked at her questioningly.

"Channel Four, the *Denver Post*, *Rocky Mountain News*, and the sheriff's been asking if you're up to making a statement now."

The hungry media was easy to handle: Anna simply refused to speak to any of them. But the Garfield County sheriff was a little more difficult. She didn't exactly lie about what had happened up at the cabin; she merely said there was a lot she was still fuzzy about and, thankfully, the sheriff looked at the bruises on her face and didn't press her.

She held Mark's hand all the way to Denver in the helicopter, as she'd promised. He was white-faced and tense as a coiled spring, even with the morphine. "Goddamn, Anna, I hate these things. It's unnatural."

"It's fine. We'll be there soon."

"You called Hoagie and Jenn?"

"Yes."

"What'd Hoagie say?"

"That you were a stupid cowboy, and he told you not to go."

Mark managed a smile. "Yeah, he did tell me."

They landed at St. Anthony's helipad, and Mark was whisked off by an awaiting team. Anna was left standing there, still in her orange suit and the wool hat. But the minute she walked into the hospital, she was besieged.

Monica, Scott and Lydia were all there. And Hoagie. Monica and Lydia threw their arms around Anna and cried. Scott hugged her wordlessly. Hoagie pumped her hand. "I told him not to go off halfcocked," Hoagie said. "Good thing you were there to save his ass."

"It was one of the landscape men," Scott said. "One of Larry's crew. He called himself Earl around us. My

God, we even let him into our home, and that's where
he got your unlisted number. Did Mark tell you?"

"Yes, he told me."

"And you're okay? Really?"

"Yes, I'm okay."

"You've got a nasty bruise under your eye there."

"It's nothing."

"Honey, we were so worried," Lydia said. "Mark
almost went out of his mind. He wouldn't stay in the
hospital, you know. He had a concussion, but he left,
anyway."

"He saved my life," Anna said. "He found me."

"More likely, you saved his, like I said," Hoagie put
in.

"I'm waiting here until they operate," Anna said,
"but you don't have to."

But none of them wanted to leave. They waited with
her and Lydia held Anna's hand. At one point, she told
her, "Scott called your mom and dad. They were going to fly back, but by the time they got a flight, you
were already out. They're frantic. You've got to call
them."

"I will." It was so wonderful to have her family and
friends around her, but it was a little jarring being
thrown from a life-and-death crisis to the antiseptic
halls of a Denver hospital. Her mind couldn't quite fit
around it. She decided to not think about it for the time
being. It was Mark who mattered.

"You'll tell him now, won't you?" Anna asked Lydia. "About his captain and the evidence."

"Yes, I'll tell him," Lydia said. "I owe him that. We
all do."

"He already got his job back, though. Did you know that?"

Scott and Lydia exchanged glances. "I made a phone call," Lydia admitted.

"You did?"

"It was the least I could do."

Anna smiled. "Does he know?"

"He might. If he went to Franklin to get his badge back, he might very well have found out."

"You do good work, Lydia," Anna said.

The doctor came to talk to them in the waiting area, his greens still on, his mask hanging from its ties. "He's fine. It went well. We got the bullet out, no trouble. He's going to be in pain for a few days, though."

"Where is he?" Anna asked. "Can I see him?"

"He's in recovery. It'll be a couple of hours before they take him to his room. Then you can see him."

"Thank you," Scott said, shaking the doctor's hand. "We appreciate it."

"The press has been calling. Do you want me to make a statement?" the doctor asked.

"The press. Good Lord," Anna said.

"I'll take care of it," Scott said, unflappable. "You don't need to be bothered by it."

Anna was on pins and needles, so Monica insisted on driving her home to change her clothes.

"Hurry," Anna kept saying. "What if he wakes up and I'm not there?"

"We've got plenty of time."

She changed quickly, wadding up the orange suit and tossing it in the bottom of her closet with a shudder. They raced back to the hospital. "Hurry," Anna said.

"Boy, you better get your car back," Monica told her. "This is too dangerous."

"God, my car." Anna supposed someone would tow it out sooner or later. She couldn't worry about it now. It seemed so terribly far away.

She raced through the halls and up to his room. He was there already, still asleep, a clean, new bandage on his side. She stood over him and laid her hand on the warm skin of his chest, feeling his heart beat. She closed her eyes and whispered a prayer of thanksgiving.

"Anna."

Her eyes switched to his face.

"Anna," he said again.

"You're awake," she breathed.

"Sort of."

She bent over him, smiling. "You're all fixed up."

He looked up at her. "Then why do I feel like something the cat dragged in?"

"You'll be better soon."

He felt his side with his hand and winced. "When can I get the hell out of here?"

"*Mark.*"

"I hate hospitals."

"A few days. The doctor said you'd hurt."

"That's a fair statement," Mark said. "For once, a doctor's right on."

"Everyone sends their best."

"Thanks."

"The, um, papers and TV stations are bothering the hospital," she said.

"Aw, hell, not that again."

"This time, you're a hero."

"Spare me."

She smiled and patted his arm.

By the next day he was shaved, sitting up and walking to the bathroom. Anna came into his room in the morning to find Hoagie there.

"So I ask the guy, does he have any defense," Hoagie was saying. "Yeah, he says, the two-dude defense. What's that? I ask. Some other dude did it, he tells me."

Mark laughed, then held his side in pain, grimacing. "Oh, God, don't do that," he said.

Anna wanted to go to him and kiss him, but she didn't dare with Hoagie there. And she wasn't at all sure how Mark felt. Now that the crisis was over and everything was different, she wondered how it would be between them. She couldn't assume too much.

She opted for a neutral subject and no kiss.

"There are TV cameras outside," she said. "My God, they're all over the place."

"Keep them away from me," Mark said. "I swear..."

"Don't worry," Hoagie said. "Scott made a statement. So did Franklin. It was on all the news channels last night—CNN picked it up this morning."

Mark groaned.

"Well," Hoagie said, "I'm gonna go back to work. The guys are putting together a collection, getting you something."

"Tell them thanks," Mark said. "I'll be back soon. And tell that Wu character to clear his stuff outta my desk, will you?"

Hoagie left and they were alone. She felt suddenly very unsure, very anxious. Mark was getting better, and he had his friends, his kids, his job back. He had Lil. He didn't need her anymore. Maybe he was sick and tired of her hanging around, and was too polite to tell her. She felt suddenly very cold. She stood halfway between the door and his bed, clutching her backpack. Nervously, she brushed back her bangs and forced a smile. "You look a lot better," she said.

"I'm getting there." He patted the bed. "Come here."

She sat carefully, so as not to hurt him.

"I've been thinking," he said. He took her hand in his, playing with her fingers. "I don't work for you or your brother anymore."

"No." Her heart squeezed.

"So what I said that day we were coming back from Wyoming . . ."

"Uh-huh." She looked down at his hand on hers.

"Well, it was pretty mean of me, and I want to apologize."

"Okay." She couldn't meet his eyes.

"I did . . . do . . . care about you." He shifted uncomfortably in the bed. "I didn't want you to think . . ."

"I did think . . ."

"Don't," he said. "I mean, don't think I didn't care."

"Okay," she said softly.

"God, this is hard," he said. "Worse than getting shot."

She finally got up the courage to look at him. "When you're out of the hospital, what will you do?"

"Go home, I guess."

"You're going to need some help for a while."

"I'll manage. Maybe Lil can—"

"Would you consider staying with me?" There, she'd said it.

His eyes came up to meet hers, and there was a long pause. The moment stretched out, as though fate required extra time to make a decision. A momentous decision.

"You've thought about this?" he finally asked, his tone carefully neutral.

She nodded.

"I can manage on my own, you know." He searched her face.

She held her breath.

"You really want this?" he asked.

"I'd like to try," she breathed. "Would you?"

His gaze switched away, and he frowned. Anna's heart fell. "Mark . . ."

"Are you sure it's a good idea?" he asked.

"No, I'm not sure, but I thought . . . I thought there was something between us, and I didn't want to lose it." She pulled her hand gently from his grasp. "Maybe I was wrong, and it was just the . . . oh, you know, the situation."

"You weren't wrong."

"I'm pushing you," she whispered.

"No, no. I'm just a coward, remember?"

"You're the bravest man I've ever known."

"Not about this."

She managed a tiny smile.

"You really want me messing up your life?" he asked.

"Sure I do."

"We could give it a try," he said.

"We, um, well, we seem to make a good team," she said, afraid and thrilled and full of hope all at once.

"And you're even prettier than Hoagie," he said.

Jennifer called him later that day, and he spoke with Kelly and Mark Jr. Anna took the opportunity to leave his room and go down the hall to get some coffee. A man approached her at the machine.

"Are you Anna Dunning?" he asked, pulling out a notebook.

"Yes . . ."

"I represent the *National Enquirer*. I'm authorized to pay you for an exclusive story, Miss Dunning. I'd like to . . ."

"Go away," she said.

"But we pay very well. Photographs. The works."

"Leave me alone. I'll call the guards. How did you get in here?"

An orderly came by, wheeling a gurney. She called to him. "Please, could you get this man out of here?"

But the reporter was already hurrying down the corridor, pants flapping around his skinny legs.

She decided not to tell Mark about it when she went back to his room. "Are your kids okay?"

"Yeah, they're fine. Thrilled to death I've been on TV. Kelly has a soccer match next weekend, and she wants me to come."

"Think you'll be able to?"

"Gotta die trying," he said. "It's important. Normal stuff like that."

"Yes, it is."

"I want you to start getting back to normal, Anna. You can quit hanging around here . . ."

"You don't want me here?" she asked quickly.

"I want you to get your life back. That life you wanted so much when you couldn't have it."

"It doesn't seem so important now," she said slowly.

"Anna, listen, I'm okay. I'll be in your place in a couple of days. I just hate to see you running back and forth to this damn hospital."

"I don't mind."

"Goddamn it, Anna."

She grinned, ignoring his temper. "Did you know they're putting a policeman on your door?"

"What for?"

"To keep the press away."

"Bloodsuckers," he muttered.

That afternoon, Lydia and Scott came to visit. Anna discreetly left the room, saying she was going to look for a milk shake for Mark. She was gone for quite a while, and when she got back Mark looked very satisfied. Lydia had told him.

Lil came that evening. She brought a huge box of fudge and a *Playboy* magazine. She kissed Mark and cried a little. "Now it's my turn to visit *you* in the hospital," she said, sniffing.

"We're even," he said..

"And I just bet I'm going to have to get a new renter," she said, looking from Anna to Mark.

"Whoa, don't give my place away just yet," he said.

"I'll miss you," Lil said.

"Hey, I'm not leaving town."

"I'm real happy for you, Mark."

"*Lil.*"

"Don't try to kid a kidder," Lil said.

"Hey, you're my *friend*. I never forget a friend."

"Promise?"

"Yeah, I promise."

Anna watched, feeling her heart swell. She wondered if she would be as magnanimous if she were Lil.

She met Lil's eyes over the hospital bed and saw the pain in them despite the brave smile on the woman's lips. An unspoken message passed between them, and Anna hoped Lil was assured that she would never give away her secret. Anna knew Mark meant what he'd said; he'd never forget a friend. Never.

That night when Anna left, she kissed Mark lightly on the cheek. "I won't come tomorrow, okay? I'll call. Monica's been after me to do some work."

"That's good," he said, nodding.

"I need to give you some space," she said. "Right?"

He eyed her, head cocked. "Yeah, some space. Smart girl. Come here."

He caught the back of her neck with his hand, pulling her close, and kissed her hard. "There," he said. "Now you can give me some space."

She drew in her breath, dizzy.

That night, she lay alone in her bed thinking about Mark. Her body ached and yearned for him, but she would force herself to stay away—a small test for them both. She didn't want to smother him; she was going to have him here, in her loft. Until he was completely recovered, anyway, and then . . . She'd let the future take care of itself.

She watched the news the next morning. There was Captain Franklin, looking very official, making a statement. When she heard what he was saying, she froze.

"Yes, Detective Righter was forced to shoot the man to save Miss Dunning. There will be an internal investigation, but there seems to be no question that it was an unavoidable shooting. Detective Righter is on sick leave right now, and we all look forward to his return to duty. He is an exemplary officer. Denver is fortunate to have him."

What? She sat down on her couch and listened to the rest of the interview, but her mind whirled. Mark was taking the blame, leaving her out of it. She didn't know whether to laugh or cry or be angry or love him even more. He was protecting her, still—even after the nightmare was all over, he was protecting her.

She brought it up when she phoned him that day. "So, I guess I have you to thank for, um, shooting him."

"Yeah, I guess so."

"You didn't have to do that," she said.

"Sure I did. And don't you dare contradict me, Anna. It'd be real embarrassing." He paused. "They took out my IVs. I can leave tomorrow."

"I'll pick you up."

"Hey, what're you driving? Did you get your car back?"

"No, the Garfield County sheriff has it. I'll pick it up one day. I've got one of Scott's cars to use for now."

"You could use the Jag."

She laughed. "I can hear the agony in your voice as you say that."

"Hey, Anna, I mean it, you can use it. Anytime."

"You're still a bad liar, Mark."

"Can you bring me some clothes?" he asked. "Would you mind? They threw all my stuff out."

"Of course, I will."

"Lil can let you in."

The next day, Anna went to pick him up. Predictably, Mark refused to be wheeled out in a wheelchair. He walked, painfully slow, but under his own steam.

He climbed into the car beside Anna, while photographers snapped pictures and cameramen took video footage for that evening's news. Mark smiled and waved to the cameras out the window, then rolled it up. Turning to Anna, he said under his breath, "Sharks."

It took him a long time to climb the stairs to her loft, and he was pale and drained by the time she got him inside.

"Damn," he said, "I'm a mess."

"You're wonderful," she said. "You look terrific."

He pulled at the waist of his trousers. "I've lost weight."

"I'll fatten you up."

"With your great cooking?"

"Well . . ."

Anna was in luck—Scott and Lydia came over, bringing one of Lydia's gourmet concoctions. Then Monica arrived with a big casserole. Even Lil showed up with a bag of bagels from Barry's.

Kelly and Mark Jr. called, and Mark promised to make Kelly's game Saturday. "Mind if I bring a friend along?" Mark asked his daughter, and Anna waited for the response. "It's okay then? Good. See you then, sweetheart." He hung up and smiled at Anna. "It's okay. You're cool, she says."

"I was worried there for a minute."

When they were finally left alone, Anna could see how tired Mark was, even though he wouldn't admit it.

"You're going to bed right now," she said.

"I'd pull out the couch, but it'll hurt. Do you think you could . . . ?"

She looked at him. "My bed's more comfortable."

He scanned her face. "Is that what you want, Anna?"

"Yes."

"I'm not much good right now," he said.

"I just want you to hold me."

"I think I can manage that."

She lay in bed with the lights turned off and the familiar yet unfamiliar feel of Mark's big body next to her. She was nervous, until she felt his arm reach out for her, drawing her against his side. Everything was all right.

"Are you okay with the shooting?" he finally asked. "I've been worried about that."

"As much as I can be. I'm glad he can't hurt anyone ever again."

"It gets to you, killing a human being," he said carefully. "I know all about that. Some people can't take it, they freak out. It can be bad, so if you feel that, you have to tell me."

She clung to him, her face against his chest. "I'll be okay, I think."

He stroked her hair gently, and she breathed in his scent. God, how she loved this man.

"I'm going back to work pretty soon," he said. "I'm going to be a cop again. Will that bother you? A lot of women can't handle it. Jenn couldn't. I want you to think about it, Anna, because it's what I am."

"I know." She put a hand flat on his chest, feeling the coarse hairs, the warmth, the beat of his heart. "I have to ask you something," she said carefully. "Something really personal."

"So ask away. I'm an open book."

"Sure you are," Anna said, smiling against him. "It's just that, well, how do you really feel about Franklin, about having to live with people thinking it was you who planted that evidence? I mean, the truth can't ever be made public."

Mark was silent for a long time. Finally, he sighed. "We don't know the whole truth. Lydia's probably right, but we'll never know for sure. It's not going to change my opinion of Franklin, anyway. We've always rubbed each other wrong."

"Yes," Anna said. "But doesn't it hurt to know you *could* be exonerated?"

"Not as much as it would hurt to see the Orchid Rapist freed. Hell, he'd kill again, Anna. He honest to God would. No," Mark said pensively, "I'll live with the smear on my name if it keeps that murderer behind bars. The people who matter will all know the truth."

"That's very... good of you. Very moral."

"Hey, I'm a regular martyr."

"Will you tell your children the whole truth someday?"

"Sure. Someday. When they're grown."

"Good," Anna said.

"But back to the point," Mark said quietly. "*Can* you live with me being a cop? It won't be easy sometimes."

"I know what you are, Mark."

"Women say that, but then they can't deal with it. I don't want to hurt you, but I'm not going to change."

She rubbed her face against him, feeling the stubble on his cheeks. "Then you must think I'll be around for a while."

"Did I forget to ask you?"

"Uh-huh."

"And now I suppose you'll want me to say all that icky stuff."

Anna felt his arm tighten around her. "Uh-huh," she said.

If you enjoyed this suspenseful tale
by bestselling author

LYNN ERICKSON

Don't miss the opportunity to order
her previous title by MIRA Books:

| #66054 | ASPEN | $4.99 U.S. ☐ |
| | | $5.50 CAN. ☐ |

(limited quantities available)

TOTAL AMOUNT	$
POSTAGE & HANDLING	$
($1.00 for one book, 50¢ for each additional)	
APPLICABLE TAXES*	$ _____
TOTAL PAYABLE	$ _____
(check or money order—please do not send cash)	

To order, complete this form and send it, along with a check or money
order for the total above, payable to MIRA Books, to: **In the U.S.:** 3010
Walden Avenue, P.O. Box 9077, Buffalo, NY 14269-9077; **In Canada:**
P.O. Box 636, Fort Erie, Ontario, L2A 5X3.

Name: _____

Address: _____ City: _____

State/Prov.: _____ Zip/Postal Code: _____

*New York residents remit applicable sales taxes.
 Canadian residents remit applicable GST and provincial taxes.   MLEBL1

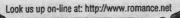
Look us up on-line at: http://www.romance.net

Take 3 of "The Best of the Best™" Novels FREE

Plus get a FREE surprise gift!

Special Limited-time Offer

Mail to The Best of the Best™

P. O. Box 609
Fort Erie, Ontario
L2A 5X3

YES! Please send me 3 free novels and my free surprise gift. Then send me 3 of "The Best of the Best™" novels each month. I'll receive the best books by the world's hottest romance authors. Bill me at the low price of $4.49 each—plus 25¢ delivery per book and GST*. That's the complete price and a savings of over 20% off the cover prices—quite a bargain! I understand that accepting the books and gift places me under no obligation ever to buy any books. I can always return a shipment and cancel at any time. Even if I never buy another book, the 3 free books and the surprise gift are mine to keep forever.

383 BPA AZ7L

Name	(PLEASE PRINT)	
Address	Apt. No.	
City	Province	Postal Code

This offer is limited to one order per household and not valid to current subscribers.
*Terms and prices are subject to change without notice. All orders subject to approval.
Canadian residents will be charged applicable provincial taxes and GST.

CB03-197 ©1996 MIRA BOOKS

"Jayne Ann Krentz entertains to the hilt..."
—Catherine Coulter

JAYNE ANN KRENTZ

There is no getting around it once you realize it *is* the

LADY'S CHOICE

After sharing the passion and soft intimacy of his embrace, Juliana Grant decides that Travis Sawyer is Mr. Right. And Travis realizes that his desire for revenge has gone way too far—but he can't pull back. As Juliana gets caught in the cross fire, she discovers that she can also play the game. Travis owes her—and she intends to see that he pays his debts...in full.

Available in March at your favorite retail outlet.

MIRA The brightest star in women's fiction

MJAK

Jake wasn't sure why he'd agreed to take the place
of his twin brother, nor why he'd agreed to commit
Nathan's crime. Maybe it was misplaced loyalty.

DANGEROUS
Temptation

by *New York Times* bestselling author

Anne MATHER

After surviving a plane crash, Jake wakes up in a hospital
room and can't remember anything—or anyone...
including one very beautiful woman who comes to see
him. His wife. Caitlin. Who watches him so guardedly.

Her husband seems like a stranger to Caitlin—he's full of
warmth and passion. Just like the man she thought she'd
married. Until his memory returns. And with it, a danger
that threatens them all.

Available in February 1997 at your favorite retail outlet.

MIRA The brightest star in women's fiction   MAMDT

Look us up on-line at: http://www.romance.net

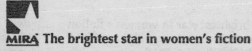